Zeno served with the British 1 ⟨...⟩ Africa, the central Mediterrane⟨...⟩ commissioned in the field. In more ⟨...⟩ won the Arthur Koestler Award ⟨...⟩ imprisonment, once in 1963 for a collection of short stories, and in 1965 for this grippingly realistic novel set during the tragic fiasco of Arnhem.

'This impressive novel, written by a man who fought there with the 4th Parachute Brigade, is a memorial of which his comrades would be proud'
Daily Mail

'A book written by a hero about heroes . . . It conveys the smell of battle, the pain of doomed men as few other books have ever done . . . a stirringly painful, true account of how a band of men behaved fighting against overwhelming odds'
News of the World

THE CAULDRON

ZENO

PENGUIN BOOKS

TRANSWORLD PUBLISHERS
Penguin Random House, One Embassy Gardens,
8 Viaduct Gardens, London SW11 7BW
www.penguin.co.uk

Transworld is part of the Penguin Random House group of companies
whose addresses can be found at global.penguinrandomhouse.com

Penguin
Random House
UK

First published in Great Britain in 1966 by Macmillan and Company Ltd
Pan Books Ltd edition published 1968
This edition published in Great Britain in 2024 by Penguin Books
an imprint of Transworld Publishers

A CIP catalogue record for this book
is available from the British Library.

ISBN
9781804996621

Typeset in 12/14.75pt Van Dijck MT Pro by Falcon Oast Graphic Art Ltd.
Printed and bound in Great Britain by Clays Ltd, Elcograf S.p.A.

The authorized representative in the EEA is Penguin Random House Ireland,
Morrison Chambers, 32 Nassau Street, Dublin D02 YH68.

To Major John Lander, TD, who raised the Independent Company, and who was killed in action in Sicily in July 1943. And to Colonel B. A. Wilson, DSO, MC, who continued in command of the company until the end of the war in Europe. And to all officers and men, living or dead, who served under either commander in a unit which in the words of the late General Sir Frederick Browning, ground commander of the Allied Airborne Army, was 'unsurpassed in the world'.

AUTHOR'S NOTE

This is a novel, although the battle and many of the incidents described in the book are true. All the central characters, with the exception of Tim Jordan, are imaginary, and their behaviour reflects only what experience has taught me to expect of men of the same calibre in similar circumstances. I found it quite impossible to conceal behind the character Tim Jordan the identity of Colonel B. A. 'Boy' Wilson, DSO, MC, who commanded the Independent Company in the Battle of Arnhem.

I have referred to some commanding officers by their correct names, among them Major-General R. E. Urquhart, CB, DSO, of the British 1st Airborne Division, Major General Sosabowski of the Polish Parachute Brigade (under General Urquhart's command during the Arnhem operation), Brigadier, now, General, Sir Gerald Lathbury, DSO, MBE (now Governor of Gibraltar), of the 1st Parachute Brigade, Brigadier, now Lt-General, 'Shan' Hackett, DSO, MC, MBE, of the 4th Parachute Brigade, and Brigadier 'Pip' Hicks, DSO, who commanded the glider-borne troops of the 1st Airlanding Brigade.

A reference is also made to Lt-Colonel Johnny Frost, DSO,

MC, who commanded the 2nd Parachute Battalion and other elements of the division round the north end of the road bridge at the height of the battle. And another to Major Dickie Lonsdale, DSO, MC, who commanded the 'Lonsdale Force' which held the final positions from the Neder Rhine up past the Oosterbeek church.

But if any ex-member of the Independent Company or the division seeks to discover the identity of Sergeant Murray or Corporal McEwan he will be disappointed. There were no such characters or their equivalents. There were no headquarter sections in the Independent Company, and therefore no headquarter section-sergeants or corporals.

This is essentially a story of one platoon in the Battle, and although references are made from time to time about the general dispositions of other units in the division, no attempt has been made to describe the battle as a whole. This has already been done by the one man in a position to do so. General Urquhart, in his book *Arnhem*, has given us the definitive account of his division's battle north of the Neder Rhine.

The characters in this book are at times bitterly critical of 2nd Army, 30 Corps, the RAF, and everybody else concerned with the operation, and so were those who fought at Arnhem twenty-two years ago. Whether or not their criticism was justified is not a matter upon which I am prepared to commit myself.

ZENO
March 1966

INTRODUCTION

> 'The Independent Company clung to its houses in Oosterbeek, the approach roads into its positions cluttered with burned-out tanks and half-tracks.'

The Battle of Arnhem sits at the centre of modern imagination around the Second World War as one of the headline events that jostles for commemoration alongside D-Day, Dunkirk and the Battle of Britain. The epic story of 1st Airborne Division's stand at Arnhem, sixty miles behind enemy lines, holding on for longer than they were expected to, has everything. It offers a British Alamo, a last stand: bumbling generals, hubris, overreach, staggering bravery from the British, stoic endurance and generosity of spirit from the Dutch civilians pitched into disaster by the arrival of British airborne soldiers in Arnhem, and even a morsel of gallantry from the Germans in their treatment of the wounded. It brims with what-ifs and if-onlys; armchair generals will doubtless opine for another eighty years.

The battle's endurance in public memory since the war owes much to the artistic representations of it, which began almost immediately with the film *Theirs Is the Glory*, directed by Brian Desmond Hurst and shot on the battlefield itself, among the burned-out tanks and shattered buildings, by survivors from 1st Airborne Division. Intercut with the footage shot by the Army Film and Photographic Unit, this black-and-white oddity was a huge hit at the time of its release in 1946. One of the cast, Lieutenant Hugh Ashmore, later said that the film's problem was that no one in it was frightened enough, the special-effects explosions were nothing like the real thing, and that '[the battle] was very hectic from time to time.'

In the 1970s came *A Bridge Too Far*, Sir Richard Attenborough's star-studded story of the whole of Operation Market Garden, of which the Arnhem battle was only a part. In search of verisimilitude, Attenborough took advice from the men who had been there: Lieutenant Colonel John Frost offered Anthony Hopkins – who was playing him – advice on keeping his composure under fire; and Sean Connery spent time with Major General Roy Urquhart, whose family had had to explain to him who Connery was. A sprawling Bank Holiday Monday war movie, it was my introduction to the Battle of Arnhem, as I am sure it was for countless people. The scenes of British and American airborne soldiers parachuting into Holland are breathtaking and convey the confidence and might that the Allies thought would force a decision from the war in September 1944.

Just as these two films sought to depict the battle as truthfully as they could, the limitations of film, of time and of characterization inevitably hinder the viewer's understanding of the ultimate question: what was it like to be there? For the cognoscenti, there was only ever one answer: Zeno. Apollo 12 astronaut Alan Bean retrained as an impressionist painter after he left NASA, reasoning that had the missions to the moon continued, eventually they would have sent a poet or a painter; so Gerald Lamarque, aka Kenneth Allerton, aka Zeno, is the soldier who became a novelist.

Fighting in the 21st Independent Parachute Company – alongside, among others, Lieutenant Hugh Ashmore – Zeno experienced the entire nine-day battle. The Independent Company's role as pathfinders meant that they arrived first in Arnhem, setting up beacons to guide in the rest of 1st Airborne Division on 17 September and the lifts that came on the days that followed, as the operation unravelled around them.

Eventually receiving a battlefield commission, Zeno fought to the last and escaped in the evacuation across the Rhine at the end of the battle. *The Cauldron* tells this story in intimate, thrilling detail. Zeno spares the reader nothing, working his way through the men who live and die in the random deadly maelstrom of modern combat. Characters are introduced in great detail, their innermost thoughts related and then, as often as not, they are dispatched in an instant. The bitter business of fighting, and the internal struggle of the men to keep their spirits up as hope of relief fades around them and their friends are killed, wounded or simply disappear, is at the heart of *The Cauldron*. The novel is a vivid depiction of their terror, their stoicism and their endurance in the face of almost certain defeat. Set free from simple memoir or reminiscence, the story of Zeno's fictionalized Independent Company depicts what it was like to fight at Arnhem rather than what happened, though he does let the reader know more than perhaps the soldier on the ground would have done, outlining the progress of the battle as

1st Airborne Division's plans to seize and hold the bridge at Arnhem unravel and metastasize.

His central characters, Captain Alan Bridgman – Zeno is at times not necessarily a subtle author – and Private Adams, offer the key perspectives through which we view the fighting. Bridgman, experienced, cynical, paternal, and seemingly indestructible; Adams, green, naive, fighting his first engagement and learning the hard way about combat, men and indeed himself in the furnace of Arnhem. Zeno ruthlessly performs the cruel trick of introducing us to a cast of characters, the men of Bridgman's fictionalized platoon, offering us their inner lives, their thoughts, memories, hopes and fears, and then, almost without warning, killing them. It is this, the random, arbitrary nature of combat, the lottery of infantry fighting, that Zeno captures better than any. Life is nasty, brutish and cut short. Sergeant Leyland, thinking of Sicily, Muldoon, the English-loathing hard-fighting Irishman, Cassidy, the German Jew, Hardy, the self-confessed 'bastard' who refused to do officer training – the men on the list that Bridgman carries with him, keeping tabs and crossing out the names of the fallen as they are killed.

To have this novel, written twenty years after the battle, republished to allow new eyes the chance to read Zeno's dark, hard-bitten prose about the Battle of Arnhem, is remarkable.

Zeno's life was in itself another equally extraordinary story. The author came to writing in Wormwood Scrubs prison when he was serving a sentence for murder. Zeno went on to win the Koestler Award, which had been created by the author and journalist Arthur Koestler, to recognize prisoners' literary efforts. One of his close friends in prison was the traitor George Blake, who later escaped from the Scrubs.

At the time, Zeno was suspected of helping him. Zeno had escaped the noose for the murder he had committed in 1958 because it was a 'crime of passion' – he had stabbed the man his ex-girlfriend was seeing. It was the full-stop to what had been a career of crime, theft, embezzlement, dodgy dealings, arson and black-marketeering.

Prison and his subsequent literary success made Zeno obsessed with covering his tracks even further. The men he had fought alongside in Arnhem in 1944 knew him as Kenneth Allerton, a name he had taken from a school friend, but his real name was Gerald Lamarque – and though his literary work offered Lamarque some kind of respectability, he still made sure that until his death his identity remained secret. Even his obituary in the airborne forces magazine *Pegasus* was under the name Allerton, rather than Lamarque. His comrades remembered him as a peerless soldier, indefatigable, resourceful – his obituary said: 'He will always be remembered with pride for the standard of his leadership in battle, his fearlessness and his cool assessments of situations under extremes of pressure.'

The Cauldron offers us a glimpse of the world that this man, brought down by crime, and then reborn in prison as a writer, knew best – battle – a man who knew and understood men whose 'dedication is to death'.

Al Murray
London
June 2024

CHAPTER ONE

The twelve Stirling bombers stood ugly and unwieldy on the runway; each in its isolation creating the image of a pterodactyl surviving in an age other than its own. The air-crews stood in two large groups watching the men of the Independent Parachute Company, pathfinder parachute troops, de-bus from the TCVs which had brought them to the edge of the runway. The members of the two services had something in common. The airmen were themselves pathfinders: their present task was to drop the parachute troops accurately on three dropping-zones where they would set up the ground-to-air aids which were to ensure the accurate delivery of the first half of the airborne division half an hour later.

The company formed up: each man looking grotesque and huge under his excess of arms and equipment. They waddled away to draw their parachutes, and a New Zealand navigator who watched with the remainder of his crew felt his stomach tighten at the thought of what they would be facing within a few hours. As his aircraft turned for home, its mission over, a little under two hundred men, split into three groups, none near enough to support or be supported by the others, would be marking out the landing and dropping-zones for their division. If they were attacked, they would have to hold the area secure, sixty miles behind the German lines, less than two hundred men, alone during half an hour of feverish activity. They would not have the protection of darkness, but were to land at noon on a summer's day, the farthest fringe of a carpet of airborne troops stretching over sixty miles and three great rivers, from the Maas to the Neder Rhine, from Grave to Arnhem.

They had drawn their 'chutes, and now they stood about, sixteen men round each Stirling bomber. Sixteen human projectiles waiting for the moment when they would float down from the aircraft's belly to land beyond the last river obstacle between the Allied armies and the great German plain stretching out to Berlin.

Sergeant Eric Leyland reached down and pulled the two webbing straps up between his legs and clipped them into the box about his middle. He straightened up, feeling the straps tighten against his thighs. He would not be free of their grip again until he stood on the soil of Holland.

He called his section together, and forming them up checked their equipment and the fitting of their parachutes. He did not expect to find anything wrong, but he did the job carefully, for if there were a fault to be found, the platoon commander would find it when he carried out his own inspection.

Leyland could never quite make up his mind whether or not he liked Alan Bridgman, and if he did, exactly how much. It was difficult to know with any certainty how the platoon commander's mind worked. He seemed always to view situations, military situations, in a different light from anyone else. In the field, there was something a little inhuman about him, something completely divorced from the drinking companion of a thousand bars in half a dozen different countries, from the husband, and the father of two children.

Bridgman watched Leyland check his section, but most of his attention was directed to where Corporal McEwan busied himself with the half section which, together with Bridgman and his batman-runner, Bilting, made up the plane's complement. McEwan was new to the company, having joined after the unit's return from Italy. He was a tall man, heavy-boned, with a rough, craggy head, high cheekbones, and deep-sunk eyes. He was fond of his beer and ready to fight at the drop of a hat but he was inclined to overlook detail.

The New Zealand navigator approached the lieutenant. They had met at the briefing, and shook hands now as they recognized each other. The New Zealander unrolled an aerial photograph of the dropping-zone.

'Would you like to show me where you intend to rendezvous on the ground?'

Bridgman squinted down at the photograph. It was an exact replica of the one he had spent so much time studying.

'There,' he said, jabbing with his finger, 'the southeast corner of that wood.'

'What number are you jumping?'

'I shall be jumping No. 1. Why, does it matter much?'

'It doesn't matter to me, but I thought that if I knew, I could try to put you down as near your rendezvous as possible.'

Bridgman smiled a little cynically. There had been occasions when he had missed the dropping-zone by miles. He would be thankful if he came down within a thousand yards of his RV.

'Thank you,' he said, 'the nearer you can get me to the corner of that wood, the happier I shall be.'

The navigator held out his hand again. 'Well, the best of luck to you, old son. Sooner you than me. Perhaps when it's all over we'll be able to have a drink together.'

They shook hands briefly, and Bridgman smiled his acknowledgement. The airman rejoined his crew and the lieutenant turned back to his men.

After checking equipment, he called the NCOs and signallers together. Apart from the 38 sets, the walkie-talkies, and the bigger, inter-unit 42 sets, they carried another and very special piece of radio equipment. It was a Eureka, a portable homing-device weighing under fifty pounds. It could transmit signals which would be picked up by any of the Allied aircraft tuned into the right frequency within a radius of fifty to sixty miles. The main drops and the future supply drops depended to a great extent on these sets being in the right place and on the correct frequency at the precise time a drop was due.

He checked with the NCOs and the signallers as a group, and then called each one apart and checked with him separately. With the exception of McEwan, they accepted this double check with a stoical resignation. It was a bore, but they knew it was necessary. McEwan did not say anything, but his eyes and lips sneered at the over-caution and double insurance of the platoon commander. Bridgman saw the sneer, but ignored it.

Bilting nudged the officer's arm.

'Major Jordan on his way over, sir.'

Alan looked up, then walked towards the CO and his second-in-command as they approached on the grass verge. He saluted.

'No. 2 Platoon ready to emplane, sir.'

Tim Jordan waved his stick in reply.

'Right, Alan. Just call your platoon together, will you. I'd like a word with them before take-off.'

Bridgman nodded at Bilting. The batman broke into a lumbering run, towards the remainder of the platoon waiting by the other two aircraft.

The three officers strolled slowly over to where Leyland had been joined by Jim Nash, the platoon sergeant, and the rest of the platoon. Major Jordan waved down the move they made to get to their feet, and they sank back. At this stage it was all part of a game everyone knew and understood. Still in England, and yet within hours to be behind the enemy lines, they made the show of peacetime soldiering. Jordan was an old soldier: he had fought as a cavalry officer in the First World War, and he was the oldest man parachuting in the division. He was a man's man, but above all he had the confidence of his company. They were not particularly interested in how brave he was, or how good a tactician he might be. They saw him as a crafty old fox, experienced in the ways of war; one would not shirk responsibilities, but would always accomplish what was required of him with the minimum cost to his command. Human lives, and the lives of his own men in particular, mattered very much to Jordan. He was cautious, but it was the caution of the skilled and experienced fighter who waits his opportunity to strike.

Alan Bridgman kept his place by the CO's side. Old Tim was going to give them a pep talk, and Alan always found this embarrassing, and he knew the men did as well. He wondered why Tim did it – he knew perfectly well how his men thought and reacted: most of them had been with him for a long time.

Perhaps to Tim it was just another ritual, like Church or Muster Parade, something which was done simply because it was expected of one, and had always been done before.

When it was over, the men got to their feet shuffling and grinning like Boy Scouts. Alan walked a few paces with Jordan and his second-in-command. When they parted, they did so hurriedly, with only a few brief words and a casual handshake. Sentiment hung in the air like treacle, and the three of them were glad to be free of it.

Inside the Stirlings, they cursed the discomfort of the British planes. The parachute brigades would be flown in American-crewed Dakotas, each man with his bucket-seat and room to move, but the pathfinder squadron was British, and so it had to be Stirlings or Albemarles: of the two the Stirling was the less uncomfortable.

Bridgman stirred on the deck of the plane and moved his head so that he could see the men about him and watch their faces. He had only one fear at this stage in an operation: one man, somewhere in the middle of the stick, might at the last moment lose his nerve and refuse to jump, and by his refusal hamper or prevent the men behind him from getting out. A number of reinforcements had joined the company since its return from Italy in January. Bridgman had got to know them as well as he could during the few months of training and rehearsals, but there were still a few he was uncertain about. Airborne operations did not allow the opportunity of breaking troops in gradually. Only a couple of hours lay between the calm of an English countryside and the whiplash reaction of a surprised enemy, an enemy who knew only too well that immediate and violent counter-attack with every available resource was the most effective method of dealing with airborne landings.

He looked at young Adams. When making out the jumping-order for the stick, he had given careful consideration to the exact placing of this twenty-year-old newcomer. He had even considered putting the boy first, with himself immediately behind him, but had realized that this departure from the normal would attract attention to Adams which might do him more harm than good. Instead, he had placed him No. 15 in the jumping-order, with Leyland following him as last man.

Adams turned his head and his eyes met those of the platoon commander. Bridgman smiled encouragement, and gave the boy an exaggerated wink. Adams grinned back weakly, and then turned away, afraid Bridgman would see the fear in his eyes. Over his head, Bridgman's and Leyland's glances met, and they nodded to each other. Bridgman turned away content. If Adams fainted, he would still leave the aircraft. Leyland's brief nod had been sufficient to convince Bridgman that if necessary the sergeant would pick Adams up bodily and throw him out through the aperture.

Adams leaned back against the fuselage. He closed his eyes and yawned prodigiously, then snapped his jaws together and looked about him from the corners of his eyes to see if the yawn had been noticed. He had just remembered the old soldier's saying that a frightened man always yawns. He had yawned, and he was frightened all right. He felt suddenly sick, and wanted more than anything in the world to be at home with his family in the small Midland town which had been all he knew until his age-group had been called up, and a romantic imagination coupled with an unthinking thirst for glory had made him volunteer for the Parachute Regiment.

What a fool he had been to think he was the equal of these other men! Of men like Sergeant Leyland, sitting beside him with his hands on his lap, and his untroubled eyes fixed to a spot on the fuselage in front of him.

Leyland thought that Adams would be all right. He supposed that Bridgman's concern about the individual links in the platoon chain was warranted, but not to the degree that Bridgman carried it. It was almost as if he considered that a momentary act of fear on the part of one of his men would be a personal affront, an unforgivable reflection on the efficiency of the unit he commanded.

The sergeant looked at his watch. There was still half an hour to go before the drop, perhaps the last drop he would make in this war. He might be killed or maimed: there had always been that chance, and it was no greater or less now. Certainly it could be the last airborne operation of the war: the Germans must be very near the end of their tether. This was a new thought, that the war might end. It had gone on for so long that it had become part of his life. His old life between Sally and the Board of Trade had a dreamlike quality about it, which made it difficult for him to accept that he would, if he survived, return to it. As proof that that life had ever existed, he forced himself to recall that the Ministry made up the difference between his Army pay and his Civil Service salary. This was all that enabled him to keep up the mortgage payments on the house that had at one time represented the sum of his and Sally's ambition. When he thought about the semi-detached house now, it was with a feeling of restriction: a self-imposed shackle which might tie him for ever to a suburbia he was beginning to hate more than he hated the war. He supposed he did hate the war. He was no longer very sure. It was difficult to imagine a life which did not contain Bridgman, Nash, Bob Blake, Frank Gorman, and John Murray. There was something closely knit and tribal about the entire company, with Tim Jordan as its paternal head, that had almost succeeded in ousting his family from the first place in his affections. Was this how homes were broken and marriages split? Was it that another and different kind of love, a deeper and more embracing loyalty, replaced the emotions felt for wife and family?

A movement in the front of the aircraft attracted his attention and he looked up. The navigator was signalling back that there were only twenty minutes to go before the drop. The sergeant looked at Adams. His eyes were closed and his face was white and wet; his lips were slightly apart and the lower one was trembling. Leyland swallowed quickly. For a second, Adams had looked exactly as his own five-year-old son had looked when he had been knocked down by a bicycle: not hurt, but terribly frightened by the suddenness with which the even tenor of his life had been interrupted. When he had climbed into the aircraft, the whole of Adams's life as he knew it ceased, exactly as if it had never existed. He would land in a foreign country for the first time; strive to continue living in the foreign antagonistic element of war; surrounded by men he had thought he knew, but who had become somehow different now that they were returning to conditions they had experienced before, but which he knew about only from hearsay.

Far out in the almost cloudless blue sky, under the bright September sun, Major Tim Jordan thought about his wife and two young sons, the boys who refused to believe that so old a man was really a parachutist. His unit looked upon his late forties with respectful awe: to his sons he must appear a Methuselah. His mind jerked back to his larger responsibility, to the two hundred men who from now on were the instruments with which he was to carry out the orders of higher command. He was a lucky man in more ways than one. The all-important role his unit played in divisional operations had enabled him to pick and choose his men with care. Any officer or man he considered unsuitable he was permitted to return to the man's former unit with no explanation as to why he was not retained. He had almost thirty European Jews among the men under his command, and apart from their usefulness as interpreters, the spur of hate made them some of the finest soldiers he had ever served with.

His was an independent command, answerable only to General Urquhart, the divisional commander. Much as he admired the young brigadiers and colonels of the division, he would have found it irksome to take orders from them. He had complete confidence in his company. His concern was not that his men would fail him in any way, but that in some way, at some critical moment, he might fail them. He felt suddenly very tired. The newspapers were right: it was a young man's war.

As the twelve Stirlings approached the Rhine, Tim Jordan closed his eyes and addressed a prayer to the God he knew so many of his men did not believe in, '. . . and please give me the strength not to let them down.'

'Prepare to jump!' Bridgman's voice cracked through his Stirling, bouncing back off the fuselage and reverberating through the length of the aircraft. The light had come on: there were five minutes to go before the drop. He stood up, and working together he and McEwan unbolted the folding doors which covered the six-foot aperture in the floor of the bomber. They booked the two leaves outwards against the fuselage. Bridgman crouched in a forward stoop at the edge of the gap, his hands outstretched, bracing his weight against the sides of the aircraft lest a sudden lurch should throw him out before his time. These five minutes were always the longest part of any flight.

A draughtboard of fields flashed past five hundred feet beneath him, a strip of silver divided it and they were over the Neder Rhine. Fields – a wood – his eyes went to the light and then back to the aperture – it was not his job to watch the light. Bilting's hand tapped his shoulder and he plunged down into the warm September air.

CHAPTER TWO

The impact of the slipstream forced Bridgman's eyelids together, but he opened them again at once for no better reason than that almost everyone admitted keeping them closed until their 'chutes opened. It was a vanity he was ashamed of, but it was part of his character.

The canopy cracked open above his head, and he reached up for the lift-webs to check the oscillation of his swinging body. As he steadied, he looked about him. He was facing the north, and could see the remainder of his stick stretching out in an ascending line in front of him. Looking up their line he saw the last two figures quit the aircraft very close together. Away to the east the remaining two sticks were dropping parallel with his own and only one or two hundred yards away. He had time to glimpse the wood on his left before the crack of single rifle shots attracted his attention, but before he could pinpoint the direction from which they came, the ground rushed up to meet him.

He tried for a stand-up landing, but the final oscillation and the weight of his equipment proved too much for him, and he rolled over in the dry, sandy earth. He had twisted and struck the release-box which held his harness together before he finished rolling, and within seconds he was on his feet, his Sten gun in his hands and the magazine fitted, although he could not remember fitting it. The New Zealand navigator had kept his word: the southeast corner of the wood lay under twenty-five yards from where he stood.

The fallen 'chutes and the running figures of his men seemed to fill the great open field of the landing-zone. It seemed too much to expect that in only half an hour from now he was to guide in nearly two hundred gliders, some of them bigger than the biggest aircraft, at fifteen-second intervals.

He stood quietly watching the apparent chaos of forty-seven men sorting themselves out, and soon had the satisfaction of seeing a correct, comprehensible pattern of movement.

He could hear firing away to the north, and knew that either Tim Jordan or Gordon Brown, who commanded No. 3 Platoon and was his own closest friend, was having to fight for possession of his dropping-zone. The rifle shots he had heard while still in the air he knew had come from his own area, but he had heard no more since landing.

McEwan and his three men passed Bridgman as they headed for the rendezvous at the corner of the wood. They carried the Eureka, the radar homing-device, and Bridgman resisted the temptation to accompany them and ensure that it was erected correctly and tuned into the right frequency. He could see Nash, his platoon sergeant, heading in the same direction, Murray and the remainder of headquarter section behind him. Nash had already thrown away his heavy steel helmet and replaced it with a camouflaged beret.

As he passed within ten yards of Bridgman, he shouted.

'The shots came from the big house . . . they probably got scared and buggered off.'

The big sergeant kept on running, a controlled trot which covered the ground but did not exhaust his men. Bridgman turned back to watch the rest of the platoon. The organization of platoon headquarters and the setting up of the radar set could be left safely to Nash.

Leyland's section had finished laying the giant twelve-foot recognition letter in the centre of the landing-zone, and two men were returning to the southern edge of the huge field. They dropped behind a fold in the ground and disappeared from sight. Bridgman watched the ditch long enough to see their hands appear and place coloured smoke canisters on its edge. When lighted, the drift of their smoke would indicate to the glider pilots the direction of the wind, enabling them to make the necessary turn so that they would land up-wind and not across it.

Gorman's section had disappeared into the wood, halfway up its hundred-yard length. Inside its cover they would be moving up to its northern tip to protect the landing-zone from any interference from that direction.

Blake's section was in position in a ditch on the eastern extremity of the area on which the gliders were due to land. They were only seventy yards short of the big house from which Nash had said the shots had come. He was probably right in his guess that whoever had fired them had been impressed by their numbers and had cleared off. They could be only line-of-communication troops so far from the front, and parachutists in the air always appeared far more numerous than they really were. But it was just possible that the Germans might be commanded by a determined man who had stopped the firing and was waiting for the main drop. Bridgman decided he could not afford to take that chance. He and Bilting were the only men left on the dropping-zone. He glanced at his watch; they had been on the ground for seven minutes. He had time enough; twenty-three minutes before the airborne division arrived. He walked the twenty-five yards which separated him from his rendezvous with platoon headquarters. His orders to the other sections would keep them away from the RV unless their landing had been so heavily opposed as to make their initial roles impossible to carry out.

He slipped into the wood and was greeted by Nash. The sergeant's face was wreathed in smiles, and the blue eyes on each side of his hooked nose shone with satisfaction.

'It's like a bloody exercise, sir. In fact, it's better. I've never known things go so smoothly. Dead on time; dead on the target; all landing aids out and not a casualty. He cocked his head and listened to the firing to the north of them. 'Either the old man or Mr Brown is not having it so easy – that was a Spandau.'

Bridgman looked quickly about him: headquarter section under Sgt Murray were lining the narrow southern edge of the wood, their weapons covering another thick wood running parallel to the Rhine. He had nothing to fear from the west, for on that side of the wood Phil Ramsden and No. 1 Platoon were carrying out a similar task to his own, except that instead of gliders they were to bring in a brigade of parachute troops – nearly two thousand men. He turned back to his sergeant.

'I think you were probably right about the Jerries who fired at us, but I shan't be completely happy till I've had a look. I don't want to break wireless silence, so send McEwan up to Gorman's section to check that he's all right. If I want any help I'll get through on a 38 set. I might need Leyland's section or a bit of mortar fire – you take over here.'

Nash shrugged his heavy shoulders. He was a good soldier, but he believed in taking things as they came. He disliked any movement he considered unnecessary, but Bridgman could be right.

Bridgman walked up the inside of the wood with his runner, Bilting, behind him, and found Leyland and his section relaxing along its eastern side. They were covered by Blake and his men, three hundred yards away on the opposite side of the landing-zone.

As Bridgman approached, the sergeant got to his feet.

'Quiet enough, sir. It seems almost too good to be true.'

'We're a long way behind the front. Intelligence said we should have no initial interference except from L of C troops, and apart from those first few shots they don't seem much in evidence down here, although they seem a bit busier up above.' He jerked his head to the north. 'Nash said he thought the shots came from the house over there – I'm going over to have a look. I'll use Blake's section – they're almost there already. Split your section up north and south of us so that we shan't mask your fire. If there's anyone there, you can cover us – if they break for it you can catch them on the flanks, and you can use your mortar on the dead ground behind the house.'

'Right, sir.'

Leyland turned at once and called to his section, and Bridgman and Bilting walked out into the hot midday sun and the open field.

Walking steadily across the soft, sandy soil, he reflected on the advantages of having hand-picked men under his command, even although it was not his hand which had picked them. They understood things at once, and never wasted time with idle or irrelevant questions.

Bilting walked in silence at his side, and a little behind him. His mind was busy behind his expressionless face. If there was anyone in that house, he and Bridgman were sitting ducks, but so they had been before they entered the wood. Anyone in the house would know there was a section in position only seventy yards from them – a section they had allowed to get into position without firing on it. Nash must be right, they had fired a few shots at the parachutists while they were in the air, and then bolted when they hit the ground.

Bridgman's gaze swung over and around the big house standing in its own grounds opposite him. He was walking easily, but was ready to drop at the first shot or sign of the enemy. One half of his mind was occupied with the overall plan. Fifteen minutes would have been enough for their job – half an hour was too long: it gave the enemy too much warning. Every German commander in the area must by now be working flat out to concentrate all available troops for a counter-attack, and to place as many men and as much armour as possible between the airborne men and the bridges over the Rhine. They were eight miles from their objective – it was too far. What happened at this stage was important, but what was of even more importance was how quickly the 1st Parachute Brigade could move into and through the town of Arnhem, on to the bridges. Allowing for time to regroup after landing, they could not start for another forty-five minutes.

In the circumstances it was too long but if things had not gone so well it might not have been long enough. Perhaps it would have been better to have landed a company north and south of the road bridge, in the streets of the town, and accepted the casualties that would have been incurred. Gliders might have crash-landed even better.

They dropped into a ditch beside Blake.

'Everything all right?'

'Yes, sir. I thought those rifle shots came from somewhere round here, but we haven't seen anything. I was going to take the section in and have a look but I saw you coming just as we were going to make a move. What do you think, are we going in?'

'Yes, give me half your section. You take the left – I'll take right. Take the bushes and the water tank as your two steps. I'll take the brick shed and the garden wall. We'll go in together from there. Take the mortar with you – the range is too short to use here.'

They split the section, and Blake's group crouched, ready to leap out and make the first run. Bridgman and Bilting, with the remaining five men, lined the ditch, their weapons trained on the most likely spots round the house.

Bridgman nodded to Blake craning his neck thirty yards up the ditch. In a second, the sergeant was out in the open followed by his men, their heavy run seeming incredibly slow to the watching officer. They covered the twenty yards and threw themselves down behind the bushes, but in the instant they dropped a Spandau opened up to the right.

The low garden wall prevented the German gunner from directing his fire at the base of the bushes where Blake lay with his half section. Leaves and twigs showered down on the sergeant and his men, and Blake grinned to himself and waited.

He heard three grenades explode in quick succession, and at once he was on his feet, calling to his men to follow him to the water tank. As he rose he heard the slower bursts of the Bren answering the quick snarl of the Spandau, and he guessed Bridgman and the remainder of the section were searching the area to the right of the building with their fire.

Blake didn't stop at the tank, but kept on round to the back of the house, his men extended and well spaced on each side of him.

Under the cover of its gable-end, he halted and gave his men fresh orders. Since he had got so far, he knew that the platoon commander would not stay where he was and attempt to keep the enemy gunner pinned. He could hear the far chatter of Leyland's Bren as it fired bursts into the upstairs windows of the house, unable to aim lower, for fear of hitting their own men.

The half-section pepper-potted out from the cover of the wall into the gardens at the rear of the house. They moved through the shrubbery in short, darting runs, each one of them covering another as he moved. By the time they reached the far end of the house the Spandau had stopped firing. They halted and waited: their eyes straining to cut through the mixture of cover in front of them.

Suddenly, two Germans broke from behind an old horse disc-roller, running to the rear, one throwing down his rifle as he ran. Blake swung his Sten gun up into his shoulder, but someone to the right of him was quicker off the mark. 9-mm bullets ripped into the running Germans. One of them dropped at once, the other continued for a few paces, running at an odd angle as if he were leaning away from the bullets, his head twisted to one side and his mouth open. Then he was ploughing forward into the ground and jerking over on to his back.

Blake kept his eyes on the big roller. With his Sten in his left hand, he waved his men down to the ground, with his right he took a 36 grenade from his pouch. The roller was only fifteen yards away, and the grenade had a four-second fuse. He drew the pin and released the striker, counting two before lobbing it gently into the air. He dropped to the ground, his gaze never leaving the twisting grenade. It disappeared behind the roller, and at once another German leaped to his feet and ran back, the Spandau in his right hand. Scruffy Butcher, the untidiest man in the platoon, dropped him with a rifle shot before he had covered three yards. He hit the ground in the instant the grenade exploded.

There were no more Germans in the area of the house. The first two were dead. The man who had handled the Spandau was not, but he was badly wounded, for apart from the bullet through his chest he had been hit in several places about the buttocks and legs by fragments from the bursting grenade. Bridgman and Sergeant Blake looked down at him as one of the men bandaged his ribs. He was a warrant officer in his late forties, wearing ribbons earned in the First World War.

Blake looked over his section and frowned.

'How many men did I leave with you in the ditch, sir?'

'Five. With Bilting and myself, we were seven. Why, what's up?'

'Matthews is missing.'

They found him in the bushes, back on the far side of the

house. He must have been a fraction of a second behind the others in dropping to cover, and a bullet from the Spandau had entered his head through the hollow behind his right eye. His dead face looked only mildly surprised.

Bridgman left Blake and his section in the area of the house, and he and Bilting made their way back to the main body of the platoon.

Nash had joined Leyland on the eastern edge of the wood, and they stood together watching the platoon commander and his runner walking back across the open ground towards them.

Nash was the older by seven or eight years, and he was the only regular soldier in the platoon. He was a big, solid man with a head of fair, wavy hair, and a strong, lined face; his cheeks were slightly hollowed, but his lips and eyes were ready enough to smile if given the chance. Had he been less relaxed, he would not have been well accepted in the unit, for at one time Major Jordan had wondered if such a typical regular NCO would feel too much out of place in a unit which contained more university graduates among its ranks than it did among its officers, but Nash had proved a good enough soldier to shed his parade-ground manner when in the field and yet still retain his grip on the men. He was unmarried and an orphan. Counting boy's service, he had been in the Army for eighteen years, and he knew no other life. To Nash, a barrack room, a billet, or a slit trench in the field were all the same.

He glanced down from his greater height at Leyland's keen intelligent face. He knew the section commander's mind worked much more quickly than his own, but he also thought that Leyland saw too much, and dwelt too long on what he saw. He over-complicated issues by giving too much consideration to the just possible but highly improbable.

Bridgman and Bilting had reached the recognition letter halfway across the field. A warm September breeze had sprung up and lifted one arm of its length. They stopped and gathered stones to weigh it down.

Leyland cursed softly under his breath.

Nash grinned. 'Never mind, Eric, you can't think of everything.'

Leyland looked up at the platoon sergeant, his dark, good-looking face troubled.

'Christ Almighty, we've had to weigh them down before. Just because there was no breeze when we set out was no guarantee it would stay calm for the rest of the day.'

He spoke quietly, for he was careful never to allow his men to become aware of his doubts, or that he was troubled by any deficiency in himself. To them he presented a controlled facade: it was important to him that they should never see it slip.

Bridgman and Bilting trudged the last few yards to the wood, ankle-deep in the soft, dry soil. They were coated with a fine dust, and where it had mixed with the sweat on their faces it showed black and channelled – they might have been in action for days.

Nash spoke as they entered the wood.

'I was expecting you to come through on the 38, sir. There wasn't much we could do – you were too close. What's the damage, sir?'

'Matthews and two Jerries dead, and an old Boche warrant officer who will be shortly. They were line-of-communication troops all right – the house is some sort of store. It's a good thing we found them – that WO was one of the right sort, he'd have taken on the whole of the Airlanding Brigade if we hadn't nailed him.'

Bren and rifle fire broke out to the north of them. They all froze and listened. There had been no firing from that direction for some time, and they tried to estimate the distance.

Bridgman spoke more to himself than to the others.

That's too near for the other LZs. It sounds as if Gorman might be in trouble.' He turned to Nash. 'You'd better get up there and see what the matter is. Take over if necessary, but don't break wireless silence unless you have to.'

Back at his headquarters, Bridgman looked at his watch. Ten minutes to H-hour. He hoped that the enemy who had been engaged by Gorman's section were in no position to damage the landing. He would have liked to slip through the wood and contact Phil Ramsden, just to find out how he was getting on, but there was too little time. He had heard no firing from the other side of the wood and that was good. He looked up into the clear sky to the south. All firing had now ceased and he might have been anywhere in a European countryside on a beautiful September day. He listened to the silence as his eyes searched the sky for the first sign of the airborne division's approach.

He saw the first dots high up and over to the east, and then there were more in front of him, and yet more to the west. A minute later the fighters roared overhead, banking away in every direction as they searched for German aircraft that might interfere with the landings.

When he turned back from watching them, he caught his breath. The advance guard of the greatest airborne armada the world had ever seen had appeared in the south while his eyes had been on the fighters. The whole sky below the Neder Rhine was filled with aircraft. The block farthest to the west, well over a hundred and thirty planes, was flying in tight formation, a great wedge-shaped phalanx of aircraft, their wing tips seeming almost to touch. Two thousand men of the 1st Parachute Brigade were arriving in their Dakotas.

From directly in front of where he stood, and slightly to the east, came the gliders preceded by their tug-aircraft, hundreds upon hundreds of planes filling the sky as far as he could see.

He found himself laughing with relief. At his side, Bilting was jumping up and down in his excitement, and once he slapped his platoon commander on the shoulder.

CHAPTER THREE

Alan Bridgman ran out on to the landing-zone, followed by Bilting. He fired a red over green recognition signal for the gliders, and glancing sharply to the southern edge of the field he was in time to see Corporal Marsden, the second-in-command of Leyland's section raise himself from the fold in the ground and strike the brassard on the first smoke canister. At once an oily, yellow cloud drifted heavily away in the light air.

As he ran back to the wood he looked up over the trees to where the Dakotas roared five hundred feet above Ramsden's dropping-zone. The first three men fell away from the leading plane, and at once, as if it were a signal for the remainder, the sky became suddenly filled with the falling bodies of nearly two thousand men. The 1st Parachute Brigade, who were to lead the assault on the Arnhem bridges, had arrived.

Back in the wood, Alan looked out on to his landing-zone: gliders were banking steeply and one had already landed. His pathfinding role for the first day was over: there was nothing further he could do to ensure the gliders landed in the correct place. In the moments before landing they reminded him of swans: beautiful in flight, but clumsy and awkward in the last seconds before a touch-down.

The air in front of him was thickening as the gliders swept in to land. Two nearly collided, and swinging away one of them failed to line up before touching down. It ploughed its way forward for twenty yards, one wheel still in the air the other almost buried in the soft soil, and then the under-carriage collapsed, pitching it over on to one wing. The wing held for a moment till the weight of the giant glider proved too much for it, and it disintegrated under the pressure.

The landing-zone was filling up fast and the crashes became more numerous. Alan watched each crash until the pilots jumped or crawled out and opened the nose of their gliders to release the men and heavier equipment inside.

He heard an increase in the movement behind him and looked round. The wood appeared to be full of parachute troops advancing towards him in their camouflage smocks. He recognized the leading figure and went to meet him. The last time he had seen Peter Ditch had been on Catania Plain in Sicily. Then the objective had been another bridge, one over the Simeto river which barred the way to the 8th Army's advance to Mt Etna and the north.

Major Peter Ditch was one of the best-known figures in a division plentifully supplied with striking characters. Although commanding a company, he always seemed to be carrying his battalion's reserve of grenades and small arms hung about his slight body. He stuttered, and as he gripped Bridgman's hand said, 'I k-k-keep exp-p-pecting to see b-b-bloody umpires. It's like a s-s-stuffing exercise. Or h-h-have you k-k-killed 'em all?'

Before Alan could reply, young Adams panted up. The excitement of carrying his first message in battle and the presence of the major from the 1st Brigade was too much for him. He attempted a salute with his rifle still held in his right hand, and realizing too late what he was doing, he froze with the rifle extended above his shoulder.

The officers laughed, and for the first time that day Adams's face showed some colour.

'Please, sir, one of the gliders is on fire. No one seems to have got out. Sergeant Leyland says may he take the section to help?'

Bridgman, Bilting, and Adams ran to where Leyland stood waiting at the edge of the wood, his men behind him. There was no need for him to point out the burning glider. Alan stopped, for a moment undecided. This was the only type of situation he had encountered in war in which he was unable to make an immediate decision. There was no doubt in his mind that, regardless of the limits of responsibility, he would and should give assistance to the men in the burning glider. Should he send it, or take it? His place was at his headquarters or with the bulk of his troops. Leyland was quite capable of dealing with a burning glider – but there might be a way out for the men inside that he wouldn't think of. Alan pushed his primary responsibility to the back of his mind, and calling to the section to follow him he ran out on to the landing-zone.

One man had been thrown half through the fuselage, midway down the length of the glider. The lower part of his body was out of sight. He hung outwards from the hips, his spine bowed back. One moment his arms were flung out as if he were crucified against the thickening air, the next they were plucking at his middle, while all the time he screamed over and over again, 'Oh, Christ, oh, Christ, my stuffing legs.'

They tore at the side of the glider with their bare hands,

but as pieces of the thin fuselage came away the flames leaped out through the enlarged hole, licking over the hanging man's stomach. Leyland seized Bridgman's arm and shouted in his ear.

'We've got one of the pilots out of the front. We can't find the other one. The inside's an inferno. From what I could see from the nose it looks as if a jeep trailer has turned over and trapped his legs.' Leyland paused and took a deep breath before shouting again, 'You're not going to get him out!'

Under the threat of the flames they had stopped trying to enlarge the hole, and instead, as many as could get near him had taken a grip on his arms and body and were heaving in an effort to break the grip of whatever held his legs trapped inside the glider.

Alan looked down at the soldier's face: he had fainted. He shouted to the men to let go their hold and stand back, and he fumbled in his smock where he had put the dead Matthews's identity disc and morphia hypodermic. As he broke the seal and screwed on the needle he called to Leyland to open the soldier's smock. The sergeant took one look at the needle in the lieutenant's hand, then swiftly unzipped the trapped man's smock. His battledress blouse was torn open and his shirt and vest ripped down even as Bridgman leaned forward, the needle in his hand. He paused for a moment, his head down: the round steel jumping-helmet protecting him a little from the heat. The fifth rib – and it wasn't on the left – it was nearly in the centre. He counted quickly with the fingers of his left hand. Five! He plunged the needle in as far as it would go and squeezed the tin tube dry, then jumping back, he beat at the camouflaged veil round his neck which had caught fire even as he had injected the morphia into the doomed soldier's heart. The man was still now, his arms flung right back and his fingers nearly touching the ground. Leyland was kneeling, his fingers on the man's pulse, and after a few seconds he looked up at the subaltern and nodded. Before rising and walking away from the burning glider, the sergeant undid the strap on the dead man's wrist and slipped his watch into a smock pocket, also cutting loose the identity disc that hung backwards against the inverted chin.

Bridgman moved round to the nose of the glider. In war the first loot usually comes from your own: it was better that Leyland should have the watch than it be destroyed in the fire or be taken by the Germans.

At the front of the glider three of his men were digging frantically in the loose earth. He found himself looking at Adams, an Adams who had moved beyond the stage of fear for his own personal safety. The slackness of terror had gone from his face, and now the skin was stretched tight against his cheek and jawbones. For him, the past few minutes had contained more horror than the whole of his previous life. It was a real man hanging dead from the burning glider, and he waited now with his mouth dry and his eyes fixed for what fresh horror the digging hands would uncover.

They had stopped digging and were struggling to get a grip on something solid. Bridgman could see a patch of khaki and a strip of camouflaged smock. They found their grip and heaved: for a moment nothing happened, and then the man's body came free of the earth like a cork from a bottle. Alan saw sergeant's chevrons on the man's arm and Glider Pilot's wings on his breast, and then the small group were struggling desperately in the loose dust, the pilot screaming through a mask of blood and dirt, sometimes pausing in the middle of a scream to gulp a lungful of air: his arms and legs thrashed about like those of an epileptic in a fit, and it took four men to pin him to the ground.

Brogan, the platoon medical orderly, came panting up. It was impossible to separate the dirt from the mess of raw flesh where the man's nose had been, and Brogan wrapped a big shell dressing over what had been a human face, a face to be caressed and loved by someone. Two men arrived from the Field Ambulance which had landed on the LZ, but they had to strap the pilot down before they could carry him away on the stretcher. The second pilot walked after them, a broken arm tucked into his open smock.

Leyland started to lead his section back to the wood, labouring through the loose earth of the Dutch field, which had started off as an ally that cushioned their landing, but which, as the afternoon wore on, now tired their legs and impeded their movement.

Adams was the last man, and Bridgman called him back, for he wanted a word with him out of earshot of the rest of the platoon.

The boy turned at Alan's call, and now stood with his legs apart staring back at his platoon commander, twenty yards away from him and making no effort to return. His mind worked sluggishly, stunned by what he had seen in the few minutes spent round the glider. He had the vivid imagination of a boy, but until now it had operated only in one direction: he could not reconcile his brief baptism of war with how he had imagined it would be. He had day-dreamed vaguely of gallant assaults on enemy positions, of assaults which were always successful, and in which he always played a promi- nent and heroic part. Since he joined the unit Lieutenant

Bridgman had become the centre-piece round which these dreams revolved. His mind's eye had developed clear pictures of the lieutenant leading the platoon into the attack. It had never occurred to Adams that in the first twenty minutes of action be would hear casually that Johnny Matthews had been shot through the head and killed; that he would stand dumbly by and watch his platoon commander kill one of their own men; and that Sergeant Leyland, Eric Leyland who watched over his section like a father, should help him to do it. He had not believed it possible that a man could scream as loudly as the glider pilot had screamed, and not in his wildest dreams had he imagined anything to compare with the bloody ruin of the pilot's face. And everyone was talking about how lucky they were, how successful the operation was turning out to be, and how good it was to have the platoon together, and almost intact, so soon after landing. What had they expected to happen? What lay ahead of them in the coming days and weeks?

He shook his head to clear it. Bridgman was shouting at him to join him. Adams stumbled over to where the lieutenant waited. When he arrived there he stood looking down at Bridgman's feet, his chest rising and falling as if he had just completed a forced march. His breath left his mouth in broken jerks like silent sobs, and without warning he began to cry. Shame became something he had forgotten or was completely irrelevant to the reality of dead and maimed men. His tears blinded him to his surroundings, but he could see clearly a picture that had been building up inside him of Johnny Matthews lying in the grounds of the big house, alone and already forgotten by the others. He did not need to look to his left to be reminded of the death of the man in the glider; of how he had screamed before he fainted; and of how, without hesitation or prayer, Bridgman had killed him. All the tears in the world could not wash the blood and dirt from the terrible face of the pilot they had dragged out from his premature grave.

'Adams,' Bridgman spoke quietly, 'look at me and listen to me for a moment.'

Adams did not want to look at Bridgman, but the discipline instilled in him during his two years in the Army made him look up, and as he did so he brushed the tears from his eyes with the cuff of his smock. The action opened the floodgates of his memory and he had to resist a temptation to throw his arms round the officer's waist and bury his head in the security of the older man's chest, as he had done as a child when only his father had stood between him and something unpleasant.

'Yes, sir.' His voice was almost a whisper. Looking down at the short, stocky figure holding his rifle in his left hand as if it were something he had been told to carry but had nothing to do with him personally, Bridgman felt a sudden wave of anger that this boy should be there at all, this boy who was all of five years younger than himself. He tried to rationalize his anger; to convince himself that it was wrong for one so young and immature to be thrown into battle with so little preparation, but he knew this was not the real reason for his anger. His chief concern was that the young soldier might crack badly at the wrong moment and endanger at least his section, if not the whole platoon. He felt guilty at this lack of humanity in himself, and forced a note of kindness into his voice when he spoke again.

'Look Adams, you're going to see some bloody awful

things during the next few weeks. Things a lot worse than that. He jerked his head towards the smouldering glider. 'In Sicily part of the dropping-zone was on fire as we landed. And hundreds of men were dropped miles from the objective, some of them the wrong side of Mt Etna. We've been very lucky today, and I hope it lasts, but even if it does, it won't be as easy as this all the time.'

He paused to see if he had made any impression on the young soldier, but although Adams had stopped crying it was difficult to tell from his face what he was thinking.

'Now come along with me and buck up. There's nothing glorious about war except the men in it. Try to see it as a dirty, rotten job that's got to be done, and the better we do our part of it the sooner it will be over.'

He patted Adams awkwardly on the shoulder, and turning away made for the wood, threading his way through the great mass of gliders. He looked back once, to see Adams following him and wiping his face with the yellow, triangular recognition signal that hung round his neck.

When he arrived back at his headquarters Sergeant Nash told him of Gorman's brief action against a small group of Germans who had not attacked him but were trying to get away. There was also a message from the CO who had wire-lessed through that, according to plan, glider-borne infantry of the Airlanding Brigade was moving into defensive positions round the dropping- and landing-zones to secure them for the second drop on the following day. Bridgman would be told when they were in position, but until then his platoon was to remain where it was.

Major Ditch's company had now moved out to join its battalion in the advance towards Arnhem and the bridges, and the wood was strangely quiet. Out on the landing-zones, parties of men from the Field Ambulance were at their work recovering the injured. Occasional firing came from the north-east: none of it lasted very long, and Alan guessed that the 1st Brigade was brushing aside light resistance on its three-axis advance. He strolled through the narrow wood and joined Philip Ramsden in the opposite corner.

As he left his own headquarters he had heard Nash issuing orders for a brew-up, but Ramsden's platoon was already drinking. Looking out on to Ramsden's dropping-zone, carpeted with two thousand collapsed parachutes, he realized even more fully than before just how successful the initial landings had been.

Ramsden's platoon sergeant passed him a mess tin of tea, and the three of them sat down on a fallen log. At first they joked a little, but then relapsed into silence. Then Ramsden said:

'I feel like Damocles, but I can't see the sword or the thread. Here we are, in the midst of prosperity, and all of us convinced there's something phoney about it. No operation goes as well as this.'

'Perhaps Intelligence are right for the first time in their lives.' The platoon sergeant was a cynic. 'After all, the astrologers do turn up trumps now and again. If you make enough prophecies you're bound to be right every once in a while.'

Alan sipped his tea. It was possible that the entire operation might go according to plan, that they would really encounter only line-of-communication troops in the early stages, that these would be swept aside, the bridges seized, and the town of Arnhem consolidated and held by their three brigades, plus the Polish Parachute Brigade under Major-General

Sosabowski which was to land as a third lift south of the river. There was even a plan for the 52nd Lowland Division to land at a later date in transport aircraft at Deelen airfield to the north. It all sounded very good, and had started very well. Alan drank the last of his tea and stood up.

'Well, they say General Horrocks will be here with 30 Corps within forty-eight hours. Let's hope he is.'

As he started to walk back to his own platoon the sergeant called after him.

'I shouldn't take too much notice of that guff, sir. Monty said he'd be at the Primosole by noon the following day, but don't remember seeing him, or the 8th Army, till the day after that. I'll be happy if 2nd Army's only one day late.'

Back in his headquarters, Alan decided that with 1st Brigade troops approaching the village of Oosterbeek, and glider-borne infantry east of the big house, it was no longer necessary for Blake's section to remain in its area. He sent Bilting to recall them.

When they arrived, Alan pulled them into the headquarter area while they made their own brew-up, and sent another man to collect Leyland. He now had three-quarters of his platoon under his hand, and Gorman's section lay directly on their route to the company RV: he could be picked up when they moved to the north.

With sentries well posted they relaxed for the first time since landing.

When Bob Blake had come into the wood, his step had been jaunty, and a grin which was as much part of him as his head had been spread across his face. His first remark had been typical.

'Just what I expected to find. The whole bloody platoon sitting on their arses swilling tea while poor old 5 section does the dirty work.'

Bridgman returned the sergeant's grin. He liked Blake. He thought he had a correct attitude to war: it was not the same as his own, but he thought that Blake had the best emotional balance in the company. He was never dismayed, never lost his temper, and carried out all orders with a cheerfulness that made others ashamed of their irritability. All Blake's actions were natural; what Leyland did consciously and conscientiously, Blake did as a matter of course. He performed nothing because it was a duty, but simply because to him it was the obvious and right thing to do. He had not Leyland's keen and far-reaching intelligence, but in a junior commander this could be an advantage.

Blake and Leyland were great friends, and yet they had hardly a thing in common. Leyland was short and dark, his face reserved and secretively handsome; he was always in control of himself, but Alan guessed at tenseness hidden under the section commander's calm surface. Beneath his almost paternal attitude to the men, Leyland was a worrier. Blake, on the other hand, jollied his men along, and was as near being their friend as his rank would allow. In civilian life he was a skilled artisan, and he tackled his job in the Army with the same casual mastery which he had shown in following his trade before the war. He was taller than Leyland, heavier built, and very fair of skin and hair. He had a broken nose, and this somehow combined with his permanent grin to make him immediately popular and accepted wherever he went.

Blake had occupied his time well while in the area of the house. He had buried Matthews and marked his grave; and he had brought back with him a pillowcase full of rye bread and fruit. The German WO had died soon after Alan and Bilting had left, and Blake had removed the corps flashes from the three Germans' tunics for identification by Intelligence.

Alan looked round at the familiar faces of his men. They seemed relaxed. They had been highly trained in specific roles, and now they unconsciously exuded the general satisfaction of those who know that no matter what might go wrong in the future, they at least had carried out to perfection the first part of their most important role.

The afternoon wore on, and shortly after 1700 hours Major Jordan issued orders over the 42 set for the company to close on its RV.

The platoon moved off, picking up Gorman and his section from where they lay facing the railway line connecting Arnhem and Amsterdam, and passing the enemy soldiers killed by the sergeant and his men. The Germans had not deliberately attacked the section concealed in the north of the wood, but had run into them as they sought an escape from the fire of Major Jordan's headquarters and Gordon Brown's No. 3 Platoon on the landing-zone north of the railway.

They crossed the railway line west of Wolfheze, and turning to the northeast, passed a company of the 2nd Battalion, the South Staffordshires. Coming into the company area they were greeted by Jordan, and Alan gave him brief résumé of his platoon's activities during the afternoon.

Jordan had not been inactive on his own landing-zone. There they had captured a number of L of C troops and brought in part of the 1st Airlanding Brigade successfully. Jordan's spoils of war included a German staff car and a Dutch horse and cart. He had magnanimously given the staff car to Div HQ. He explained: '. . . no bloody good to me at this stage, and anyway, I thought that if I gave them that they'd keep their covetous hands off the horse and cart. Just look what we can get on it.' He pointed to where the horse plodded its way towards the company's HQ. The broad flat bottom of the cart was covered with boxed ammunition, and at one end Alan spotted two German MG 42s. He knew Sergeant Blake had the Spandau captured at the big house but very little ammunition for it, and made a mental note to win one of the boxes he could see beside the German guns.

He sited his section positions; and then, leaving his men digging-in under Nash, made his way to Jordan's HQ to attend the O Group that had been called. But before joining the other officers, he whispered to Bilting, and even as he greeted Gordon Brown he saw his batman idling his way to where the horse was being unharnessed. A thousand rounds of German machine-gun ammunition were as good as in his hands.

Tim Jordan looked round at the faces of the five officers who had come together to form his Order Group. With the exception of Alan Bridgman they all seemed cheerful and on top of the world. They knew they had done a good job and they were justifiably pleased with themselves.

The CO gave them the situation as he knew it. 'The landings have gone off splendidly,' he said. 'The 1st Para Brigade are moving in to Arnhem on their prearranged routes, and the Airlanding Brigade is in position round the dropping- and landing-zones.'

He looked up from the map on which he had been pointing out the movements of the battalions, and watched the eager faces about him as he continued.

'Unfortunately there have been two rather serious snags. In the first place, most of the gliders carrying the vehicles for the Recce Squadron have not arrived, and this means that the expected lightning strike against the main bridge is out. The para battalions are going it alone. The second bugbear is that the long-range wireless sets beaming back to 2nd Army are not functioning properly, but what's far worse is that our internal communications appear to have gone to hell. The General doesn't seem to have been able to contact 1st Brigade HQ, or any of its battalions. He's on his way now to join them somewhere below Oosterbeek.'

The CO looked down at his map while his officers digested the first bad news they had heard since landing. He was thinking about the General's move up to the forward battalions. Jordan held strong views about the duties of commanders in the field, believing that their place was where they could exercise most control, and that place was not normally in the front line.

The conversation became general, and many of the suggestions and suppositions were humorous. Collectively, his officers did not appear unduly concerned by what they obviously considered to be minor mishaps. The CO dismissed them after giving them instructions for their night in laager, but as they moved away still talking among themselves he called Bridgman back.

The major wondered what was going on behind the earnest high-cheekboned face and wide brow. They could both hear firing down towards the river, in Oosterbeek, and farther up to the north of Johanna Hoeve, and west of Lichtenbeek.

'What is it, Alan, don't you feel happy about the operation?'

He waited while Bridgman marshalled his thoughts. Alan

always moved quickly, and the CO knew his mind worked as fast as his body, but he had grown used to the way in which the lieutenant considered his choice of words, and so was surprised at his vehemence when he replied:

'I think the whole operation, as it's been conducted, is wrong, sir. I've thought so since the very beginning. Somewhere between ourselves and the CIGS there's a victory-happy group who have succeeded in getting out of touch with reality. An airborne operation, in a European country, in which the attacking troops are dropped eight miles from their objectives, is farcical. It could only succeed if the ground troops were within easy striking distance, or if the German Army was so demoralized as to be no longer effective. 2nd Army is sixty miles away – and I don't believe the Jerries have cracked yet. And now that the Recce's vehicles aren't here, we've lost the element of surprise their speed would have given us. The whole division should be on the move – heading for the really vital objectives – the bridges. We should be advancing, not only down the main roads, but down every side road and track that leads to them. Of course there'd be some confusion. Of course some of our troops would be fired on by our own men. But by dawn tomorrow the bulk of the division would be where it's most needed – on and around the bridges, and not sitting on our arses west of Oosterbeek, waiting for the Germans to build up the striking forces they'll throw at us and between us, tomorrow.'

He paused for breath, and Jordan looked at him, surprised.

'But Alan, haven't you forgotten that nearly half the division isn't here yet, and can't arrive until tomorrow?'

'That's one of the things I had in mind when I said the operation was all wrong, sir. If enough aircraft were not available to land the division in one go, then that's all the more reason why we should have accepted the casualties to be expected in a landing closer to the objective, and thrown everything we had at the bridges at once. I believe we shall have far more casualties getting to the objective than we should ever had if we'd landed on it.'

Bridgman stopped speaking, his face faintly flushed under suddenly revealed emotion.

Tim Jordan made no reply for a long minute, and when he did speak his voice was quiet.

'Alan, you may be right. I'm an old soldier, and although I've felt no happier than you about this operation, I've been cheerful and optimistic about it from the beginning, because I'd see no point in being otherwise. There's nothing that I, let alone you, could have said that would have altered the plan in any way. Once it was made I could secure only those alterations which affected our unit directly. Try to look on it as I do. No matter what may happen from now on, we have so far done our job according to the book, and we can't be criticized in any way. We'll go on doing that, tomorrow and the day after, and the day after that, until it's all over. No man's shoulders are wide enough to carry the burden of everyone else's responsibility. My intention is that this company shall carry out to the best of its very high ability every task it is given. Just that and nothing more. Let your only concern be that your platoon does the same.

The CO's lined face broke into a grin.

'Well, we are a gloomy pair for a couple of men who have so far done a first-rate job and know it. I think we deserve a drink.'

He produced a bottle of whisky, and they toasted future

successes with smiles on their faces and their doubts hidden again, even from each other.

Bridgman rejoined his platoon. Nash had made all arrangements for the night. Alan approved them, then visited his sections and had a word with their commanders. Then he dropped into the shallow slit trench that Bilting had prepared for him, and with his hands supporting the back of his head listened to the crunch of falling mortar bombs and the intermittent bursts of machine-gun fire which came to him from the east. Once or twice he heard the sound of a bursting 88-mm shell.

CHAPTER FOUR

Bridgman ordered a stand-to an hour before dawn on the second day, and moving about in the dim half light he felt the pleasant contact of clammy dew-laden air brushing his face and hands. Isolated shots and short bursts of machine-gun fire broke the silence at intervals, and the sound came from every direction except the south. The still open hand of the German Army was closing round the division as it lay in its temporary perimeter awaiting the arrival of the 4th Parachute Brigade and the remainder of the glider element. He found himself hoping that the grip would not become unbreakable by the time they were ready to move into Arnhem. The pathfinder company was inside the perimeter, for it had still to bring in the second lift, and until that was done it could play no part in defence or attack.

Bridgman took out his platoon-roll and laid it on the rough parapet in front of him. The names set out in their solid squares inspired him with a feeling of confidence.

> Lt Bridgman
> Sgt Nash
> Pte Bilting

Pte Dwyer
Pte Brogan

No. 4 Section	*No. 5 Section*
Sgt Leyland	Sgt Blake
Cpl Marsden	Cpl Heibling
L/Cpl Hudson	L/Cpl Cobbald
Pte Laverty	Pte Hardy
Pte Wilcox	Pte Ewing
Pte Cowper	Pte Matthews
Pte Gregory	Pte Jennings
Pte McGrath	Pte Butcher
Pte Keeley	Pte Stewart
Pte Adams	Pte Taylor
Pte Chambers	Pte Bignall
Pte Wallace	Pte Sadler

No. 6 Section	*Headquarter Section*
Sgt Gorman	Sgt Murray
Cpl Armstrong	Cpl McEwan
L/Cpl Summers	L/Cpl Manning
Pte Woodley	Pte Warke
Pte Storrs	Pte Bobrow
Pte Cummings	Pte Muldoon
Pte Liddon	Pte O'Neill
Pte Fraser	Pte Edwards
Pte Jarvis	Pte Banham
Pte Mocock	Pte Waterson
Pte Chamberlain	Pte Black
Pte Norfolk	Pte Cassidy

He drew a line through Matthews's name, and wrote 'Killed' alongside it. He looked at the other names on the roll, wondering how many would be scored through before the action was over. At present the roll looked good: the proof that he had over fifty first-class troops under his command.

An hour after dawn he stood the men down, and posting sentries he went to company headquarters while his men ate from their forty-eight-hour packs, and cleaned their weapons against what the day might bring. There were no fresh orders. So far as the pathfinders were concerned everything was still going according to plan. At 0800 hours he moved his platoon out of the company area and retraced his footsteps of the night before.

The company of South Staffs were no longer in the position they had been occupying. The second break from the original plan had been made. The Midland battalion was fighting its way into Arnhem to reinforce those parachute battalions which were still held up far from their objectives by the tanks and Grenadiers of the 9th and 10th SS Panzer Divisions, of whose presence Allied Intelligence had not known.

As his platoon crossed the railway line and moved down to the wood, Alan pieced together the scrappy information and the more probable bits of rumour he had picked up.

In the area of the landing and dropping-zones all was going according to plan. With the exception of the South Staffs, the glider troops were in their prearranged positions; the second lift would not be opposed at close quarters, but in the town of Arnhem things were not going well. The German prisoners now being filtered back to the divisional area were strange line of-communication troops: for they included elements of the crack Waffen SS commanded by General Willi

Bittrich, and highly trained NCOs from the SS school for junior leaders.

Alan turned to his platoon sergeant as they entered the north end of the long wood they had quit the previous evening.

'It's almost like coming home,' he said, 'but I think we'd better put out a line of beaters – snipers could have infiltrated during the night.'

Nash called up the rear section and ordered its riflemen out in front, and the platoon advanced more slowly behind the extended screen. The platoon sergeant was unusually quiet, and Alan asked him why.

Nash hesitated for a few moments as if reluctant to put his thoughts in words, and when he did Alan detected a sharp and puzzled note in his voice. It was as if the sergeant had suddenly become aware of something he felt he should have known all the time, and was wondering why he had not seen it before. Words came from him, at first slowly, then in a flood.

'I've been thinking, sir,' he said, turning and looking at Bridgman, his brow puckered by a rare frown. 'I hope to Christ I'm wrong, but I reckon this operation is all to cock. Whoever dreamed it up must have been bomb-happy. It seems funny to be saying this now when everything seems to be going so well, but I can almost see the reaper reaching out to gather in the Div. I never thought of it back in England, during the briefings or while we were waiting on the airfields – it all seemed so pat. But I've got a feeling in my water that somewhere along the line someone very inconveniently forgot about the Germans. I was looking at the map at stand-to this morning – Arnhem is such an obvious place for regrouping. Nijmegen, Eindhoven, and Grave are too near the front. I'd bet a month's leave that by the time the second drop is ready to move there'll be so much stuff between us and 1st Para that we'll never link up.'

Bridgman was surprised to find Nash thinking along the same lines as himself. His view had been arrived at in England as a result of what he hoped was logical thinking, but he realized that Nash had the old soldier's instinct for a phoney situation, not felt until actually in battle.

They had nearly reached the southern edge of the wood, and Alan spoke quickly while he still had time.

'Have you said anything of this to the others?'

'No, sir. To tell you the truth I wasn't sure what I thought myself till I heard myself saying it, but now that I have, I think I'm right.'

'If it's any consolation, I think you're right too. I wish to God I didn't. But for Christ's sake don't mention your opinion to anyone else – we don't want any of them looking over their shoulders.'

Alan halted the platoon, and from the cover of the wood he, Nash, and the section commanders looked out on to the dropping-zone on which the 1st Parachute Brigade had landed the day before. For the second lift another two hundred gliders were to land on the discarded 'chutes which carpeted the vast field.

They saw no sign of movement. Bridgman was reluctant to send the signallers out into the exposed field to set up their Eureka, but he wanted it clear of the wood so that its beam would not be screened by the trees, and he spent a long time searching the ground. He spotted what he wanted, and sent for the two men who were to operate the set. A long and apparently thick wood lay some two hundred yards to the south of where he stood; all the ground between was open field, but halfway across and under a hundred yards to their right lay a mound of dung, about four feet high and seven or eight feet square. He pointed it out to the signallers, and told them they were to erect their set on the near side, keeping the heap between themselves and the far wood.

He checked the frequency on the Eureka, and when he was satisfied he turned to his section commanders and ordered up all Bren groups and two-inch mortars. He personally laid down a field of fire for each group, and ordered that should the signallers be fired on as they crossed the open ground, the gunners were to concentrate their own fire in slow bursts at ground level along the edge of the wood opposite. He brigaded the mortars in a small clearing, and instructed them to lay smoke between the wood and the platoon, but only on his order. He called up two more signallers and had them lie down under cover to his right. When he was satisfied, he sent the section commanders back to their sections with orders to give more covering fire if it became necessary.

Nash looked from Bridgman's face, set and tense, to the faces of the two signallers who were waiting for the order to make their hundred-yard dash to the pile of dung. It was probable that the wood opposite was unoccupied, and Nash had to suppress a wave of impatience at the meticulous care with which Bridgman went about the job of placing his covering parties. He was honest enough to realize that most of his irritation was caused by the natural resentment felt by a professional who sees an amateur doing a better job than he would have done himself. He knew that had he been in command he would have placed the Eureka just clear of the wood's edge, and that even if he had decided on the dung-heap as shelter, the signallers would have been already on their way, covered by a Bren group: from there on he would have acted off the cuff; dealing with each situation as it arose. He knew that Bridgman had decided that the Eureka should be in the centre of the field, where it would be most effective and suffer the least interference from the surrounding woods, that he was making every possible preparation to get it there, and if necessary, was literally going to 'shoot' the signallers into position. It was this foresight, this preparedness for every eventuality, that compensated for what Nash considered a dangerous tendency on Bridgman's part to undertake tasks other than those specifically ordered.

Watching the elaborate preparations being made to cover their run to the dung-heap, one of the first two signallers turned to the lance-corporal who was to accompany him and laughed, 'How does it feel to be a VIP?'

The lance-corporal looked at the dung-heap quizzically.

'I don't know about VIPs,' he said, 'I think we're just going to be dropped in the shit.'

Bridgman grinned and glanced quickly round to ensure that everyone was in his right place. He spoke quietly, and at once the two men were out of the wood, running steadily towards the isolated pile of manure. They had covered about twenty yards when the Germans opened fire.

Edwards dropped at once, and Lance-Corporal Manning checked in his stride, and turned as if to assist him.

The platoon's Brens had opened up simultaneously – barely a second after the Germans had opened fire. Bridgman and Nash had dropped to cover at the first shot, but now Alan was on his feet again, shouting to the lance-corporal.

'Keep going, damn you – keep going!'

Manning hung for what seemed an eternity, half-stooping over Edwards's body. Then he turned and sprinted for the dung-heap. He was fifteen yards short of it when the Spandau burst hit him. His legs sprawled out like a horse landing heavily in the Grand National; he sank on his wide-apart knees, and Alan could see him fumbling blindly at the Eureka set as he tried to get the telescopic aerial out, but he died before his fingers found it.

Bullets were cutting the branches and twigs on each side of Alan, and he dropped back into his place alongside Nash. The big sergeant was firing carefully aimed rifle shots at the eastern end of the thick wood where he thought he had spotted the muzzle-flash of a German gun. Alan waited as Nash fired another shot, then grabbed him by the arm.

'Go back and take charge of the mortar group. Get three of them laying smoke. The fourth can drop some HE in the wood. When it's thick enough I'll send the other two.'

As Nash slipped back through the undergrowth, Alan jumped up and doubled to where he had left his headquarter group. He grabbed the 42 set and called up the CO. By the time Jordan came on the air Alan had his map out and had worked out the map reference of the German-occupied wood. He explained the situation briefly, and asked for instructions about clearing the wood before the gliders came in. He switched to receive and waited for Jordan to speak. There was a pause, then the CO's voice came over clearly.

'When your Eureka is in position, you will take no further action except in defence of the set and your own immediate area. The map reference you have given me has been reported clear. The enemy must have infiltrated back. I'll get someone on to it right away. I'll contact you as soon as I know something for sure.' Jordan paused again, then continued. 'Remember, Alan, no further action from your platoon other than returning fire. There is two hundred yards of open ground between yourself and whatever force is in that wood. If there's no one else available you may have to clear it, but you'll do nothing till you hear from me.'

Alan got to his feet. The section commanders had ordered a cease-fire the moment Manning had been hit. With nothing specific to aim at, they were disinclined to waste ammunition. Alan stopped at each section and gave them fresh orders as he made his way back to where he had left the second pair of signallers. As he sank down beside them, the first mortar bombs landed fifty yards short of the far wood. The gaps thickened up so quickly that he decided Nash was firing one of them himself.

He spoke to the two signallers.

'Leave your haversacks here, but take your water bottles with you. Go flat out till you reach Manning. Decide now which one is going to pick up the Eureka, and whoever it is must keep in front so that if he's hit or fails to grab it the other one will know. You've got a 38 set with you, but don't use it unless you have to. Any questions?'

They had none. They slipped their haversacks off and raised themselves on one knee. Alan gave the word and they started to run, their weapons on their left shoulders and their heads up and back, one of them a pace or two in front of the other. The Germans were firing random shots and the occasional burst through the smoke, but it was unaimed fire, and as the signallers broke of from cover the platoon's Brens had again opened up on the wood opposite them. Alan

watched the leading man snatch up the Eureka set, hardly
checking in his stride as he reached down and grabbed it,
and then the two men had flung themselves down behind
the dung-heap.

Bridgman continued to watch them. They lay still for
some moments, recovering their breath, and then first one of
them and then the other sat up. He saw the tripod and aerial
erected, and one of the signallers gave him the thumbs-up
sign to indicate that the set was operating and in good order.
The two men were sitting with their backs to the heap, confident that seven or eight feet of wet dung would stop any
small-arms fire.

A movement to Alan's right attracted his attention, and
he saw that Leyland and one of his men had taken advantage
of the smoke to get to Edwards. Now they were staggering
back, supporting his weight between them.

Nash rejoined him, and looked with satisfaction to where
the two signallers sat, for all the world like sunbathers on a
beach. Turning to Bridgman, he saw a frown on his platoon
commander's face.

'What's up,' he asked, 'we got 'em there all right, didn't we?'

Alan gave a wry grin. 'Yes, they're there all right. But we
forgot to tell them to dig in – it'll never even occur to them –
have you ever known a British soldier dig in unless he was
given a direct order?'

Nash grimaced. He thought Bridgman was carrying anxiety a bit too far.

'No, sir, I don't suppose they will, but is it really necessary?' He looked at his watch. 'It's 9.30 now – the second
drop is due in an hour. I should think that dung-heap would
stop anything.'

'It'll stop anything that's fired at it, but that's not the point. In the first place the Jerries may have spotted them getting there. In the second, their aerial is sticking up above the heap. I can see it though my glasses, and the Germans are no further away from them than we are. If they decide to mortar them, all the dung in the world won't stop mortar bombs from landing this side of them. Get back and try to raise them on the 38 set. Tell them they've got to dig in — if only deep enough to get themselves below ground level.'

Now he reorganized his platoon positions, and made sure the men were digging shallow trenches, deep enough to protect them from ground bursts and small-arms fire. He returned to his headquarters to find that Nash had raised the signallers on the 38 set, but had not yet heard from the CO. He joined the medical orderly, Brogan, who was attending to Edwards. The wounded man was very white and his eyes were closed. 'How is he?' Brogan shook his head and turned his mouth down at the corners.

'He's got two bullets through the belly, sir. The lower one came out but not the top one. He may have a kidney wound, but I can't be sure. We've contacted Company HQ, and with any luck there'll be someone down from 181 Field Ambulance to pick him up. If not, we can grab someone from 133 Para Field Ambulance when they arrive. They're coming down on this LZ, aren't they, sir?'

Alan nodded. 'Yes, they are. But you'll have to move him back a hundred yards or so, past the bend in the ride. If a jeep ambulance comes blinding down from 181, Jerry'll knock seven kinds of hell out of them, and they won't be in such a hurry to come the next time we're in trouble. Get him round the comer of the ride so you can stop anyone before they come into the open. Leave a man with him, and then come back here.'

Dwyer, the signaller on the 42 set, called Bridgman over. Jordan was at the other end, his voice matter-of-fact as he asked for a situation report. Alan told him the Eureka was in position, and that they would be able to throw the smoke canisters far enough out on the LZ to give the pilots the wind direction. Then he switched to receive and waited for what the CO had to tell him. The signaller held the code-sheet in front of Alan as Jordan spoke; it covered only place names and units.

'A company of the Border Regiment are already moving from northwest of Heelsum to clear up your little spot of trouble. I imagine you'll hear them pretty soon. The moment they report it clear I'll let you know. Don't worry too much about recognition signals – if the pilots can't see two thousand chutes on the ground, nothing much you can do will help them. Just make sure the Eureka's working.'

Bridgman went along his section positions, chivvying his men to dig harder. He knew exactly how they felt; it was possible that within an hour or so they would be moving out, and digging trenches with small entrenching tools while encumbered by their excessive equipment was enough to make the most even-tempered man irritable.

He moved to the southwest corner of the wood, where he had drunk tea with Phil Ramsden and his sergeant yesterday. From the cover of a thick bush, he studied the wood opposite him through his glasses. He could see no movement, but that meant nothing – the Germans might have moved out, or they might still be there. He would know shortly when the company from the Border Regiment arrived. He looked at the dung heap. The two signallers were digging steadily, for feeling more exposed than the rest of the platoon they were not so reluctant to get below ground.

A sudden burst of firing to the west made him swing his glasses in that direction. He could see nothing. The firing was coming from inside the wood, and he lay with his head cocked, picking out the different weapons in action. There were scattered shots from British and German rifles, sharp bursts from Schmeissers and Stens, and then a Spandau opened up, its terrific rate of fire making each shot barely distinguishable from the one that followed it. A Bren answered it, and the other weapons ceased their orchestration as if a conductor had suddenly silenced them with his baton. For what seemed a long time, he listened to the quick brrr-brrr of the Spandau, and the steady rat-tat-tat of the Bren as it replied. And then there was a silence, a silence which hung in the air like a pause before the finale. There was a sudden rush of new fire, and faint shouts reached the ears of the listening men.

Nash dropped down alongside Bridgman, who asked, as if the question were purely academic, 'Which was the last to fire? I'm damned if I can be sure.'

Nash frowned as he looked through his glasses.

'I'm not sure either. It's funny how you can be listening for just that thing, and yet when it happens you're never absolutely certain which it was.'

Whichever gun had fired the last burst had won the machine-gun duel. If it had been the Bren, then they might well expect the clearing of the wood to be proceeding at some speed, but if the Spandau had been the winner they could anticipate a short hold-up while the enemy gunner was winkled out of his position or killed in it.

Alan spotted a slight movement on the fringe of the wood, about a quarter of the way up from the far end. He steadied his glasses on the place, and was able to pick out the barrel of a rifle extended outside the screening of the trees: from its foresight hung a camouflage veil. The Bren had won. The men from the Border Regiment were carrying out meticulously the drill for wood-clearing. Somewhere to the rear, whoever was directing the operation would see the signal and know how far up the wood the leading beaters had reached.

Alan left Nash watching the wood, and under cover of the trees strolled back parallel with the ride. Round the bend and hidden from view, Edwards lay on a patch of dark grass. Squatting by his side was the Dubliner, Muldoon, who had deserted from the Free State Army to enlist in the British. Privately, Alan was of the opinion that Muldoon would have enlisted as quickly in the German Army if it had been in any way possible. Unlike the European Jews in the company, Muldoon was not fighting for a cause. He was not, in fact, overfond of the English, and he had never given serious consideration to what the war was being fought about. He was where he was because he hated the thought of there being a fight and he not in it.

Alan could now see clear to the top of the wood, but there was no sign of any vehicle from the Field Ambulance. He spoke to Muldoon.

'Has he regained consciousness at all?'

'He has not, sir, and I'm thinking he never will. At least not in this world.'

'Well, if he does, you're not to give him any morphia. He's had one injection already.'

'I will not, sir. The idea of sticking a needle in anyone

turns my stomach as sour as a flat Guinness in the heat of summer.'

Alan looked his surprise. Muldoon had always been a particularly bloodthirsty soldier.

'I hope you don't feel the same way about a bayonet.'

'Not at all, sir. A bayonet's an entirely different kettle of fish. It's the sort of tool a man can handle. It's the wee things which throw a man sideways.'

Alan grinned down at the big Irishman. 'A bullet's "wee" enough, isn't it?'

'That's true, sir, but sure that doesn't matter at all, for you never see them coming, and you never know which one's for you till it hits you – and then it's too late altogether.'

Alan was still smiling when he got back to the platoon. Men like Muldoon did him good. He rejoined Nash and asked him how the wood-clearing was going.

'I think Jerry must have scampered after the first brush, sir. The Borders had cleared up to that wide track over there just before you came.' He pointed to a gap in the trees only two hundred yards short of the eastern edge of the wood.

Alan looked at his watch. It was 1015. The second lift was due to arrive in fifteen minutes. He crawled back a few yards, then getting to his feet walked over to his headquarter group. Dwyer had his earphones on, and neither saw nor heard Bridgman coming. He looked up sharply when Alan touched his shoulder and waved his hand for silence. He switched to transmit and spoke into the set. After a pause he switched again, and pulling his earphones back till they dropped round his neck he looked up at the platoon commander.

'Major Jordan is not at his headquarters, sir, but the message is from him. The wood has been reported cleared by the Border Regiment.' He handed Bridgman a sheet from his message pad.

Calling Bilting, Bridgman rejoined Nash. Lying at the sergeant's side he made a careful appraisal of the situation as he knew it.

The wood behind them, and all to the north of them for a distance of about four miles, was reasonably secure. There might have been some infiltration by snipers and small groups of Germans but he thought it unlikely that any considerable body of the enemy had made its way into the area held by the Airlanding Brigade and divisional troops. To the east, towards Oosterbeek and Arnhem, the Germans would be more than occupied in their battle with 1st Parachute Brigade and the 2nd South Staffs. Three companies of the Border Regiment were in position to the west on a line running south from the railway to the village of Renkum resting on the north bank of the Neder Rhine, and their remaining company had cleared the wood two hundred yards to the south of him, from which he had been fired on earlier in the morning. He wondered where this company was now, and wished he knew for sure.

Nash rolled over on to his side and looked at his watch.

'Seven minutes to go, sir – I'll get the smoke party ready. Do you think it will be all right to send a couple of men out on to the LZ when we spot the lift?'

Alan thought for a moment. 'I'll fire the recognition. Very Lights when I see the fighter escort. If there's no reaction to that send two of them out. If there is – throw the canisters from the wood.'

Nash slid back, and picking up two men from Blake's section, he made his way to the western edge of the long, narrow plantation. Standing in the cover of the trees, he looked out on the broad expanse in front of him, at the two thousand 'chutes: the odd coloured ones making him think of the pieces of some giant jigsaw puzzle waiting to be put together.

Bridgman trained his glasses on the sky to the south. The last minutes before a parachute drop or glider landing were always a great strain on the pathfinders. There was the possibility that something might go wrong with the Eureka, that an operator had by accident changed the frequency, or that a freak twist in the terrain would in some way mask the beam.

He looked at his watch again. It was 1035 – the second lift was already five minutes late. Bilting nudged him. 'There, sir, I can see aircraft straight ahead.'

Alan swung his glasses up to his eyes, adjusting them hastily to focus the faint dots pointed out by Bilting. He counted them quickly. There were between twenty and thirty, and none were line astern: they were not tug-aircraft and gliders, and there were too few to be the Dakotas carrying the 4th Parachute Brigade.

He jumped to his feet. 'It's the fighter escort. Here,' he fumbled in his pouch, 'take the second cartridge. Hand it to me as soon as I've fired the first one – come on.'

With Bilting at his heels, Alan trotted out into the open. They ran for a hundred yards, until they were midway between the two woods, taking a quick look at Manning. He was dead. They halted parallel with the dung-heap and only about thirty yards to the east of it. The fighters were much nearer now, and Alan raised the Very Light pistol and fired the first shot. He snatched the second cartridge from Bilting's hand and inserted it, fired again and watched the lights burst red over green against the sky. Bilting was tugging at his arm and shouting something about the signallers. Alan tore his eyes away from the approaching fighters and looked towards the dung-heap. One of the signallers was standing up, only his legs out of sight in the foxhole.

'There's no triggering, sir – they can't have picked us up yet – the set's working all right.'

Alan stood staring back at the signallers, his brain racing as he calculated distance and time. The Eureka could pick up their planes at a distance of fifty to sixty miles, and would receive a reception signal from the Rebecca equipment in the aircraft – the triggering referred to by the signaller. The planes must still be at least ten minutes' flying time away. He had started to move over to the Eureka operators when Bilting grabbed his arm and shouted.

'Jesus Christ! They're not ours! They're Messerschmitts!'

Alan swung round. The fighters had wheeled to the west, preparatory to strafing the landing-zones. He could see the black crosses marked clearly on the fuselage. The hundred yards back to the wood might have been a hundred miles.

CHAPTER FIVE

Alan felt Bilting jerk away from him as if to start running back to the wood. He must have realized the futility of his intention almost at once, for he stopped in his tracks, and throwing himself on the ground, rolled over, his rifle springing to his shoulder. He saw no sense in being fired at without hitting back.

Alan's knees bent to join his batman on the ground, but even as he did so his mind suddenly became occupied with the theory of small-arms fire. Horizontal planes, quadrant angles, the axis of barrels, the culminating point of trajectories, and danger zones flew disconnectedly through his brain. He realized that, when fired at from the air, many of these were no longer applicable, or if they were, their application would be relevant in a different way. He decided he would be a smaller target standing up. He straightened his legs and looked up at the diving Messerschmitts. Their menacing shapes, the roar of their engines, and the chatter of their guns filled his visual world and deafened his ears, so that he missed the sight of the hundreds of puffs of dust that their bullets kicked up down the length of the long narrow field in which he stood. And then they were past him, and turning, they swung up the previous day's LZ, their guns blazing at the empty gliders.

Alan shouted to Bilting, and the pair of them ran for cover. As he ran, Alan threw a quick glance at the dung-heap, and in time to see the head of one of the signallers emerge from the foxhole, and hear the beginning of a remark flung at his back. 'Stone the stuffing crows, you might as well have sent an invite to the bleeders, you'd think . . .' The rest of the man's words were lost under the pounding of Alan's boots and the throbbing of his pumping heart.

They reached the sanctuary of the wood and flung themselves under the protection of the trees, achieving cover from view if nothing else. He heard the growing volume of the engines as the Messerschmitts came back for their second run, but this time they swung wider, leaving the long field on their left and concentrating their fire on the gliders. And then they were gone, the sound of their engines dying away as they headed east for the Reich.

Alan sat up and wiped the sweat from his face. It had been a close thing, and ruefully he acknowledged the justice of the signaller's sarcastic comment shouted at his running back. Aircraft recognition had never been one of his strong points. In addition, he had felt confident that the fighters were their own because he had expected them, and now he became worried. The timing of the attack, just five minutes after the second lift was due to start landing, was rather more than he could swallow as coincidence, and he felt thankful about what was obviously a postponement. The Messerschmitts would have played havoc with the defenceless transport aircraft had they been able to attack in the first minutes of a landing.

He could obtain no information from Company HQ about

the probable time of arrival of the second lift. With the wood below him clear of Germans, he posted sentries and allowed the remainder of the platoon to relax while remaining in their positions. Muldoon returned with the information that Edwards had been picked up by a recovery party from 181 Field Ambulance. Corporal McEwan brought in a straggler from the 1st Para Battalion who had become cut off from his company and had made his way back south of Oosterbeek; he confirmed some of the rumours about which Alan had been uncertain.

The 2nd Parachute Battalion had definitely reached the area of the bridge the night before, and had captured and was holding the north end of it; some, but not many, of the 3rd Battalion had managed to link up with them; the 1st Battalion, two companies of the South Staffs, and the bulk of the 3rd Battalion were still fighting their way towards the centre of Arnhem. The man had seen General Urquhart and Brigadier Lathbury the night before, but he knew nothing about what had happened to them since then. The man was very shaken, and it was clear that he had been involved in some bloody fighting. The Germans had been using self-propelled guns and half-tracks; the 1st Para Brigade had only one battery of anti-tank guns under command, and these had been too few to deal with the armour thrown at them by the Germans; the airborne soldiers had been driven off the streets into the houses, and from their cover were attacking the German tanks with Gammon bombs and Piats, but they were making very little progress towards the bridge.

Alan felt suddenly very angry. He had no idea why the second lift had not yet arrived, but he sensed that somewhere away from the battlefield there was a lack of urgency. The delay meant that not only had the 4th Parachute Brigade and the remaining two companies of the South Staffs still to land but that the Airlanding Brigade and the bulk of Div troops had to be withheld from the vital battle for the bridge and the town of Arnhem until they were joined by the delayed contingents. He walked deeper into the shade of the trees to cool off.

Leyland watched Bridgman's back as the platoon commander strolled away from the platoon. The sergeant could sense Bridgman's anger, but he was not sure what had caused it. He did not think it likely that the subaltern was angry with himself about the loss of Manning and Edwards: the necessity of placing the Eureka in the best possible position for its signals to reach the aircraft of the second lift would outweigh the responsibility Bridgman would feel for the lives of two of his men. Leyland knew that his platoon commander believed wounding and death to be the occupational hazards of soldiering: hazards to be avoided so far as possible, but not to the extent that success of overall operations would be endangered by too nice a consideration for the lives of men. Bridgman looked always to the ultimate end; he had a flair for detail, and although his decisions were arrived at quickly, he displayed a careful and efficient approach to every task, while at the same time keeping his eye on the main picture; it was this ability to see the whole of an operation in perspective which enabled him to look on the lives of soldiers, including his own, as expendable. Leyland could understand this as a natural viewpoint of senior commanders and staff officers: they were concerned with strategy and the constantly altering lines on the war maps; by the very nature of the job they did, the individual soldier became an incidental, and Leyland did not see how this could be otherwise. But what never ceased to surprise him was that a subaltern of twenty-five, a regimental officer who was only a wartime soldier, an amateur, could reconcile his daily contact with men he knew well and liked with an unhesitating preparedness to sacrifice their lives in order to gain an end not immediately related to the unit he commanded.

He transferred his gaze to the wood opposite him, half of him listening to the firing in the town to the east and far to the north, where he imagined it was the KOSBs' Brens he could hear defending the 4th Brigade's dropping-zone from attack. The other half of his mind ranged between his wife and son at home and his section here. The newspapers would have carried the story of the landing north of the Rhine, and now Sally would know why she had not received a letter from him during the ten days the division had spent in the wired camps before the operation. He had been able to write during that time, but he had known the letters would not be posted until after the division had gone into action. He looked to either side of him, where his section lay in line, their bodies pressed into the shallow grooves they had made in the ground. When the Messerschmitts had fired he had seen Adams and two of the other new men tremble against the earth in anticipation of a bullet's strike. He wondered if Adams remembered how his arms had frozen against the sides of the Stirling, and how he had been unceremoniously bundled out with Leyland nearly on top of him. It was easy afterwards to rationalize the panic of a moment into simply the slight hesitation while the body braced for an effort. Leyland knew this to be true, for something similar had once happened to him in Italy. It was a secret he had shared with no one else, for the only person who had known of his single moment of blind panic was dead. Leyland and Tait had been on a daylight reconnaissance patrol west of Bari, and they had both been confident that there were no Germans in the area. They had entered the village slackly, side by side and unprepared for anything but the riotous welcome offered by the Italian villagers. They had been so unalert that they had not even been alarmed by the absence of the very people they expected. They had turned a corner, and there had been the three German soldiers, standing in the middle of the road, their Schmeissers and rifles over their shoulders. Leyland remembered the frozen moment of flat-footed shock, Tait struggling to get his Sten off his shoulder and himself running back round the corner and towards a side street. He remembered the burst of German fire which followed the rattle of Tait's Sten gun, and his own slithering horrified halt as he realized that he had left Tait facing the Germans alone. He had found the courage to return, and peering round the last corner he had seen two dead Germans and the crumpled body of his companion. The third German had disappeared. Leyland had forced himself out into the open, and over to Tait's body. He had been dead.

His report had been factually accurate, and only false by omission. They had entered the village, been engaged by the enemy, and Tait had been killed.

At the time, he had rationalized his action nearly to his own satisfaction. It had been a reconnaissance patrol, its object to find out if the village was occupied or being patrolled by the enemy. Their orders were to avoid conflict, and to get back with the information: he had done that. He had succeeded pushing the incident to the back of his mind for months, but it had nagged and torn at his conscience until he had dragged the memory back from where it skulked in the recesses of his mind, and re-examined it. It came always to the same thing: as the NCO in charge of the two-man patrol he had been entitled to avoid an action and to get back with the information, but all the rationalizing in the world could not make his desertion of Tait anything but what it was – an effort to save his own skin without having given a thought for the man left behind.

Leyland had learned to live with what he had done, simply because he had examined his conscience and admitted to himself that he had been guilty of a momentary act of cowardice. His intelligence told him that nearly any man might under similar circumstances act as he had done. But not Bridgman. Leyland was honest enough to admit that the resentment that prevented him from warming to his platoon commander was made up of two things: a sense of inferiority when he compared himself with the officer as a soldier and a sense of superiority when he compared himself as an individual, away from the battlefield. He knew of the completely amoral streak in Bridgman, and while it shocked the puritan side of his own character he was forced to admit that this amorality may have extended to but did not adversely affect Bridgman's qualities as a soldier.

Nash came over and squatted on his haunches by Leyland's side. 'Check your section's ammunition, Eric. And while things are quiet we'll clean weapons, one section at a time. Yours first.' The platoon sergeant looked round. 'Christ knows how long we're going to be here. Perhaps we ought to make a better job of those slit trenches. Get 'em cracking when they've cleaned their weapons.'

Nash got up and moved on to the next section.

Leyland pulled his men thirty or forty yards back into the wood and set them to work. The section was very quiet; first doubts were making each man consider seriously the consequences of the delay in the arrival of the second lift. Corporal Marsden looked at the clear sky through the trees over his head. When he spoke, it was to no one in particular.

'Whatever is holding them up, it can't be the weather. What the hell can it be?' He turned to Leyland. 'Do you think there's been a change of plan? Are they going to drop them somewhere else, perhaps near the bridge? 2nd Battalion must be having a hell of a time there on its own.'

Leyland shook his head slowly. 'God knows,' he said, 'it's probably something quite temporary that we know nothing about. I expect they'll be here before long.'

Marsden looked across to where the platoon commander was berating the men of Gorman's section for not having made a better job of their positions. 'Bridgy doesn't seem too happy. He's behaving as if we're going to be here for ever. He loves this digging lark – you'd think his father was a navvy.'

Leyland smiled. 'He doesn't like it any more than we do, but like us, he's no idea how long we're going to be here, and it would be bloody silly to be caught by a mortar stonk with no holes to hop into: no matter what they sling at us, we're stuck here till the gliders come in. If you can't take evasive action, there's only one thing you can do – dig a hole and get into it.'

Marsden shrugged. Leyland was right and Bridgman was right. But it was difficult to make men dig when they were not under fire, and when moreover, they might be leaving the positions within minutes of completing them.

★

When the second lift appeared, the firing to the north and the west of Wolfheze increased to a crescendo of sound and, as he walked out on to the narrow field for the second time that day, Alan realized that the KOSBs were having to fight hard to retain their grip on the heather-covered dropping-zone north of the Arnhem–Ede road. His own platoon might well be fortunate: he wondered how Gordon Brown was getting on, for he had the task of bringing in the 4th Para Brigade, and at this very moment he must be lying somewhere in the centre of the battle raging between the Germans and the KOSBs and Border Regiment.

He fired his Very Lights and walked back to the wood, glancing at the grinning, relieved faces of the signallers, and then at the landing-zone where Nash had seen to the lighting of the yellow smoke canisters. It was almost a repetition of the previous day.

Back in the wood he looked quickly round at his sections. They were all in position, but the tenseness of expectation had gone from them. He moved to the western edge of the wood, and the smoke party passed him as they came back to rejoin the platoon. He stood watching the great Horsas as they swept in to land, each one to its own accompaniment of sound, like the hiss of compressed air escaping through a narrow valve. He saw the incredible precision with which the pilots put down their unpowered craft, and the short distance in which they pulled them up, often only a few feet short of another glider. He watched the landing-zone filling with moving men and vehicles. He tried to distinguish the different units, and at first this seemed impossible, for all the airborne soldiers looked alike in their camouflaged smocks. He looked instead for the weapons and vehicles which would identify them: the guns of the Light Regiment and the anti-tank batteries and the vehicles of the Field Ambulance. He spotted the typical infantry movements of the two companies of South Staffs as they formed up to move off, and he remembered they were yet to discover the change of plan – that the remainder of their battalion had been detached from its brigade and was even now fighting its way into Arnhem. It had taken forty Horsas and one giant Hamilcar to bring in the second half of that battalion, and Alan knew that by the time the last glider touched down, over six hundred and fifty of them would have landed north of the Neder Rhine in two days.

The German Spandaus opened up without warning, and as Alan spun round he saw the first mortar-bombs explode on the landing-zone. The machine-gun fire came from the wood reported clear by the Border Company earlier in the morning, and Alan cursed them as he ran back to his platoon. He arrived to find the sections already in action, their fire disciplined and controlled, and as he threw himself down in the gap between Leyland's and Blake's men he heard the captured machine-gun add the vicious crackle of its fire to their own guns' slower bursts. Searching the wood with his glasses, he managed to pinpoint the muzzle-flash of a German gun. He shouted to the sections to cease fire, and then directed all guns on to the German automatic. Five LMGs opened up on the single target he had indicated, and the Spandau stopped firing abruptly.

Their own firing had attracted the attention of the Germans, and some of the guns which had been directed at the glider element now switched to the pathfinder platoon. Alan heard the startled cry of a wounded man in the wood behind him where he had left headquarter section and the brigaded mortars. He quickly saw that their own tongue of wood screened most of the landing-zone from the eastern tip of the German-held wood, and it was from this end that the enemy fire was coming. The Germans could direct machine-gun fire only on the western quarter of the LZ, although their mortars could reach any part of it. Bridgman realized that the curses he had called down on the Border Company were probably unwarranted. It was likely that they had cleared the wood completely, and that a German detachment had slipped back into its far edge when the Borders had returned to the position they were responsible for in the west. The glider men would be getting off the landing-zone as fast as possible, and with any luck they should not have suffered many casualties.

Alan shouted to the men in Blake's section who were handling the captured German LMG to cease firing, so that he could more easily assess the volume of the enemy's fire. He strained his ears, but he had to order the whole platoon to stop before he could be certain that there were no more shots coming from the far wood.

Down to the left he could see Brogan crawling up to a wounded man in Gorman's section, and on the ground in front of him the last of the gliders were coming in to land. There were four of them and, as if acting on a common thought, the pilots of all of them swung their machines to the east, and making a one hundred and eighty degree turn sank towards the deadly strip of open ground between the Germans and Bridgman's platoon. The overcrowded landing-zone had put them off, and they were taking advantage of what must have appeared to them a better and safer place to bring in their gliders. The platoon watched helplessly as they came in to land.

Just before they touched down, almost in line astern, the German guns opened up again. The platoon withheld its own fire till the gliders came to rest and they could safely open up without the certainty of hitting their great bulk.

Two of the gliders caught fire at once; there was no movement from the third, but from the nose of the fourth two glider pilots jumped down. They came under fire at once, and making a lightning and accurate decision they dropped on the safe side of one of the glider's giant wheels.

Alan shouted to Nash to lay smoke between the gliders and the far wood, and within thirty seconds the bombs were dropping. He kept his eyes on the four gliders as the smoke thickened up, watching for any sign of movement. There was one: even the two pilots lay motionless, as if dead, and Alan wondered if perhaps they were. He stood up and fired a yellow flare to attract their attention. He thought it likely that they were uncertain if the area behind them was safe.

Bullets whistled into the trees around him, and as he dropped to the ground he cursed himself for a fool: he could have fired the flare just as easily lying down. He decided there was no future in wasting his smoke bombs to cover the movement of men who were dead, but as he was opening his mouth to shout to Nash to cease fire he saw one of the glider pilots stand up and bend over his companion. He appeared to be urging him to get up: the second pilot lay still, and the standing-man turned and ran unsteadily towards the platoon. They put scattered shots and a burst or two into the smoke to keep the enemy ducking, and he had almost reached their positions when a chance shot from the Germans brought him down: but he was on his feet again almost at once, hopping the last few yards into the wood.

Alan looked across to where the heads of his two signallers showed above their slit trench. One of them seemed to be fanning himself with his beret, and as Alan fired a flare over them to attract their attention, he wondered what the man could be at. Their faces turned in his direction, showing white against the dark heap behind them. He waved to them to take advantage of the smoke and rejoin the platoon, and as soon as he saw them on their feet and running towards him, he called to Nash to cease fire.

The smoke cleared slowly, hanging for a long time in the still air. Alan moved over to where he could see out on to the landing-zone. The last vehicles and men were disappearing from sight as they made their way to the divisional area to the north.

Running out at a right-angle from the southwest corner of the wood they were in was a sparse avenue of trees which had to some extent screened the gliders coming in above them, and at its point of juncture with the wood he spotted what seemed to be an abandoned jeep.

Nash joined him, looking hot and tired. The mortars had kept him busy. They grinned at each other, and then both looked at the jeep.

'That,' said Nash, 'is a turn-up for the book. I wonder if we're the first platoon in the company to win its own transport.'

'I'm wondering if we shall be allowed to keep it. Slip over to HQ and stay by the 42 set in case the old man comes through. I'm going to have a look.'

Low-hanging branches from a tree had screened the Bren

fixed to its Motley-mounting in the rear of the jeep, and as he got closer Alan saw two sprawled figures. Bilting pulled at the shoulders of the one crouched over the wheel, and the man rolled out through the open side of the jeep on to the ground. He was dead, and so was the lieutenant who had been firing the gun. Alan seized him under the armpits and dragged him out, laying him alongside his driver. The dead officer's face showed him to have been in his forties – an unusual age for a lieutenant. Alan decided he must be a Lieutenant-Quarter-master, and turned eagerly to find what the jeep contained.

There were three boxes of .303 each containing twelve hundred rounds. Bridgman had been concerned about the amount of ammunition expended in getting the signallers into position, and in covering the landing of the gliders. He could now replace it all and start building up some sort of platoon reserve. Tim Jordan kept a tight hand on the company's reserve of ammunition, but Bridgman never allowed this to worry him: he was a great believer in self-reliance, and the amorality in his temperament acted as a buffer between an inflexible will to maintain his platoon at a peak of effi-ciency, and the whispering of a conscience which might remind him that this was occasionally done at the expense of other units. This worried him not at all: and now he was quite confident that the ammunition would be put to better use by his platoon than by any other formation.

He pushed the starter, ran the engine, and switched off. He removed the dead men's rations, personal weapons, and the ammunition they were carrying on their bodies, putting it all in the jeep. Then he searched the bottom of their vehicle for mortar bombs which by now were running short; he had started the operation with only forty-eight. He found none.

Corporal Marsden came through the trees towards him. He was wanted by the CO on the 42 set.

'You will disengage and proceed north to rejoin the company. There will be a guide to meet you south of the railway line and west of Wolfheze. What casualties have you?'

Jordan's voice lacked its usual warmth, his words carrying an air of detachment, as though he were thinking of other things as he issued his orders. Alan sensed that the division's position had not improved. He kept his reply as brief as possible, for he would learn any bad news as soon as he reached the lodgement area.

'Two walking wounded, sir. I shall be moving in five minutes.'

He called his section commanders together.

'We're to disengage and join the Company. We're to be met by a guide south of the railway. We have good cover behind us, but I have no intention of getting up and walking away from the enemy. They are not L of C troops: if they were they wouldn't have come back after being driven out by the Borders. Sergeant Blake's section will remain here for fifteen minutes after we move. If the enemy guess we're pulling out, they'll be after us like a dose of salts, and if it can be avoided I have no intention of fighting a running battle as we fall back.' He turned to Blake. 'After we RV with the guide, I shall give you twenty minutes and then try to contact you by 38. In the event I don't succeed, I shall leave a guide with the map reference of the company area, but he will wait only a further half an hour. Any questions?'

The five sergeants sat in silence on the soft leaf-mould of the Dutch wood, the quiet of their immediate surroundings seeming a thing apart from the noise of the battles to the east and north of them. Nash made a suggestion.

'Why not take the whole platoon, sir, and leave a man with me? We can use the Bren on the jeep if we're engaged, and we can drive in it when your time limit expires. Like that you'll keep the platoon together, and we'll be able to rejoin you much quicker than a section on foot.'

Alan considered the suggestion. He had intended ferrying most of the platoon in relays in the jeep while they were still in the cover of the ride, but the platoon sergeant's suggestion was better.

'Good idea, sergeant. We'll do just that. Break open two of the boxes of .303, and distribute the bandoliers among the sections. Keep the other box with you in case you need it.' He turned to his section commanders. 'Prepare your men to move, and when Sergeant Nash is in position, form up under cover on this side of the ride. Order of march, Blake – Leyland – Platoon HQ – Gorman.'

Nash called to Muldoon, and together they walked over to where the jeep stood under the cover of the trees. They broke open the ammunition boxes, and as the sections filed past they handed out the cloth bandoliers. One or two of the men muttered about the extra weight, and wondered why it could not stay in the jeep till it joined them in the company area. Nash did not bother to reply. He had thought of the same thing himself, and he knew Bridgman must have done, but he also knew the platoon commander had a 'thing' about ammunition and hated it to be in one place and his platoon in another, no matter for how short a period.

Bridgman and Nash synchronized their watches, and the lieutenant looked out at the open field. 'Well, if they do take a crack at you, you've a bloody fine killing ground.' With a wave of his hand, he started to move away, telling Bilting to go over and pick up the personal weapons, ammunition, and rations belonging to the dead men.

Muldoon was in the back of the jeep, and as Bilting left them and followed Bridgman up to the waiting platoon he asked:

'Shall I get the Bren off the mounting, sergeant? It'll be better on the ground. We should be a hell of a target up here if they spotted us.'

Nash shook his head. 'No,' he said, 'the ground rises very slightly in the centre, and then falls away again. That's the main reason why we only had two men hit. Black was firing over a log, and Jarvis was kneeling. If they can't hit us from ground level, we can't hit them. We'll keep it on the mounting. It's easier to traverse anyway.'

Nash climbed up into the jeep and got behind the gun, while Muldoon stacked Bren gun magazines ready to hand. He looked at the glider behind which the two pilots had sheltered and wondered if the second pilot were still alive. The man who had hopped into their positions had had a slight flesh wound in the calf of his leg which he had received just before he reached the wood, and another, slightly worse one in his upper arm which he had collected while hiding behind the glider wheel. Before limping off to the north, he had told them that the other pilot was not badly wounded, but was not prepared to leave the cover of the glider.

Nash grunted to himself. The pilot was no concern of his. The man had had his opportunity and had declined to take it – you seldom had a second chance in war.

A movement to the southeast attracted his attention, and he moved his head to see better through the leaves. A section of Germans had left their cover and were running towards the shelter of the gliders which the platoon had brought in on the previous day. Nash swung the gun round on to its mounting and waited.

The Germans had dropped out of sight behind the glider nearest to their corner of the wood. They were three hundred or three hundred and fifty yards away, and Nash realized that if they were allowed to cover another fifty yards they would be hidden from him by the width of the wood in which he and Muldoon were concealed: they could enter it at any point above the previous day's platoon RV. Nash raised his sights and looked through the aperture.

When the Germans reappeared they were running hard, their weapons at the trail, and as Nash aimed off in front of the running figures he was reminded of some tin soldiers he had had as a boy. He emptied his magazine in one long burst, swinging the gun slowly in towards the running Germans as he fired. With the exception of one man, they hit the ground, kicking up little puffs of dust from the dry earth as they landed: the dead, the wounded, and the unharmed impossible to distinguish from where the sergeant crouched behind his gun. He swung after the one man who had not dropped with the others, but who had turned in his panic and run back towards the cover of the wood. Nash took his time. The enemy soldier was within ten yards of safety, and must have felt already the first upsurge of hope when Nash shot him.

The sergeant had just time to look back at the figures of the German section scattered on the ground, and to notice movement from two of them, when the Spandau opened up to his right, from inside the opposite wood. They had pinpointed his locality fairly accurately, and bullets hit the trees and tore through the bushes around him. A few hit the jeep below him, and he felt a sharp tug at his left leg. He looked down to see if Muldoon was trying to attract his attention, but Muldoon was crouching on his left, a third magazine in his hand, and Nash realized that he had been hit, and also that the first magazine change had been so fast and so efficiently effected that he could barely recall it.

There was another burst from the Spandau, followed by the explosion of one of the jeep's tyres, and the little vehicle sagged over to the left. As it settled, Nash picked out the muzzle-flash of the German gun. He lowered his sights and emptied the remainder of the magazine in its direction. He shouted to Muldoon to get out with the rest of the magazines for the gun, and unfixing the Bren from the Motley mounting he followed him. They threw themselves down ten yards inside the wood. At once Nash started crawling to the southern edge of the wood, fifteen yards east of where they had abandoned the jeep: he could hear Muldoon grunting along behind him. He stopped a few feet short of the open ground and raised his glasses. With his body propped up on his elbows he looked at the spot where he had picked up the Spandau fire, and was in time to see its flash again. He heard the bullets cut into the cover they had just left, and some of them hit the jeep again. They had got out just in time: the Spandau gunner was well zeroed on his target.

Nash thought quickly. If his theory about the rising ground was correct, it meant that if he fired the Bren from ground level he would either hit the centre of the field at its highest point, or his shots would go over the enemy gunner's head. He thrust his arm out at full length in front of him, and measured off on his knuckles the distance from a large bush to the spot where the Spandau was concealed.

Then he looked round at Muldoon and grinned. 'Paddy,' he said, 'I never thought I'd find a use for you, but I have.' He explained quickly what he wanted and watched Muldoon's face change as he spoke. The big Irishman appeared to be disgusted; but there was a faint twinkle in his eyes.

'Isn't that just what you'd be expecting from a stuffing Englishman,' he jerked out. 'Who else would think of using the body of an Irish peasant as a parapet to protect him from the return fire of the poor devils he's been trying to kill for the past ten minutes.'

Muldoon pulled himself up till he was level with Nash and then crawled round to the front of him. As his face came opposite the sergeant's, he turned it so that their eyes were only inches apart, and his breath, and the strong sweet smell of his sweat, struck human and warm against Nash's cheeks.

'I wouldn't have missed this for a barrel of Guinness,' he muttered. 'What a story to tell in the pubs of Dublin about the ruthlessness of the English.'

He stopped and lay still when the haversack on his back was level with Nash's head. The sergeant folded the bipod of the Bren, and slid the gun forward on the Irishman's pack. He remeasured the distance from the tree, and when the Spandau fired again the Bren was high enough to clear the centre of the field. Nash's reply cut the German gun off in mid-burst. He lowered the butt and waited.

For minutes nothing happened, and Muldoon began to stir restlessly under him. Nash looked at his watch. Twelve minutes had passed since the platoon had left for the company area. He wondered what damage had been done to the jeep. The flat tyre did not worry him overmuch; it was the near-side rear one which had been hit by the Spandau fire, and would not affect the steering to any extent, but he knew the jeep had been hit many times, and anything might have happened to it. He checked the time again. 'Right, Paddy, let's get moving.' He slid the Bren off Muldoon's haversack, and followed by the Irishman, he crawled back deeper into the cover of the wood.

They had just got to their feet and were moving to their left, towards the edge of the ride, when the Germans opened up with a combination of multiple-mortar and Spandau fire.

Nash had hit the ground as the first bullets spattered like the rain of a summer storm against the trees and branches, and before the rattle of the machine-guns' fire and the high-pitched moan of the falling mortar bombs had reached their ears. While falling he had looked towards Muldoon, and had seen the Irishman stagger as if thrust against by a body heavier than his own. Muldoon went down slowly, his big face expressionless, but his eyes shocked and a little bewildered by the suddenness of his wounding. He hit the earth on his right side, his face turned toward the platoon sergeant, and he opened his mouth as if to speak, but a froth of bright-red blood from his lungs dribbled out from his lips instead of the words he intended.

Nash crawled back to the edge of the wood, dragging his Bren behind him. He slid in to one of the shallow section weapon pits and pushed the gun out in front of him. The mortar bombs were bursting on the ground to his rear and high up in the trees, scattering their fragmented death in every direction. He doubted if he could break back through the curtain of flying metal behind him and get Muldoon to the jeep. He waited for the mortaring to die down, and while he waited he watched the German-occupied wood for any sign of movement.

The first smoke bomb landed directly in front of him, completely blanketing his view. He watched its drift to his right, and jumping up he hobbled on his stiffening leg downwind to the left from where he would be able to see if the Germans broke cover. He had reached out to break the fall of his body when the Spandau burst hit him, low down in the stomach. He fell forward on his knees and left hand; his right released its grip on the carrying-handle of the Bren; he sat back on his haunches, his mouth open and both hands clutching at his belly; the second burst took him squarely across the chest and he toppled over. He was dead before his shoulder struck the ground.

Muldoon was sitting back-propped against a tree, nine-tenths of his mind empty and the pain in his chest forgotten. The blood tasted strange and unclean in his mouth, and he spat out a clot of it in disgust. He watched the sergeant's still body for what seemed a long time. One part of him was convinced that Jim Nash was dead, another and smaller part, the same part which enabled him to have faith in a God he had never seen and whose works were beyond his understanding, believed the platoon sergeant would get to his feet at any moment and help him back to the company. Through a gap in the smoke he caught a glimpse of the advancing German infantry. He picked up his rifle in his left hand and held it across his lap at the point of balance. His right unzipped the front of his smock and groped till it found his rosary. 'Holy Mary Mother of God . . .' he had liked Jim Nash . . . and half the stories they told at home about the English were untrue . . . 'pray for us sinners, now, and in the hour of our death. Amen.' The Germans were through the smoke and almost at the edge of the wood. Muldoon let go his rosary and gripped his rifle round the small of the butt. It was as silly as drinking flat porter, for his eyes wouldn't focus properly, and the German soldiers seemed to dance to the left and right as they came into the wood.

The company had a new area, two miles to the southeast of the position they had held on the previous night, and south of the railway line below Johanna Hoeve farm. The KOSBs were now brigaded with the 4th Para Brigade. They had replaced the 11th Para Bn who were driving into Arnhem on the lower road to reinforce the three battalions held up in its centre. The glider men from the Scottish regiment were all north of the railway line: two companies on the main Utrecht–Arnhem road and to the west of Johanna Hoeve, the remaining two companies above the embankment and south of the farm. The following morning was to see a brigade drive for the high ground to the north of Arnhem.

The Independent Company dug in in the grounds of a large house. Alan Bridgman's platoon faced the north, Phil Ramsden's the open ground to the west, and Gordon Brown's men looked east to Arnhem.

Alan sited his two forward sections ten yards short of the secondary road running across his front. He put Blake's section on the left, in the sharp elbow where the road broke back at right angles and ran nearly straight to the Heveadorp ferry west of Oosterbeek; Leyland's section he put on the right where his field of fire was limited to some thirty yards. They looked down ten feet of sloping ground to where a four-foot wire-mesh cattle fence enclosed the grounds they were in. Across the road there was another cattle fence round an even bigger house and grounds, and beyond it the shrubbery and growth of an extensive garden. Fifty yards inside the garden a tall, four-storey house looked menacingly down on the company positions.

Bridgman asked permission to occupy the house with a standing patrol. Jordan gave his assent and before returning to his Company HQ added, with a perfectly straight face, 'The Boche has cut off all water supplies, and I'm worried about our horse. See if you can rake some up.' Then he walked away, leaving his casual words hanging in the air – an implicit order that the horse was to be watered. In his youth he had ridden in the Grand National and in consequence his concern for the welfare of the horse was rather more than that of the remainder of the company, who were already referring to the heavy, hollow-backed animal as 'Tim's hunter'.

Alan made up a composite section under Sgt Murray, and handing the platoon over to Leyland, he made his way cautiously into the grounds on the far side of the road. The KOSB battalion lay to the north of him, covering his front, but the Germans had already started a determined infiltration through the many gaps in the divisional perimeter. An elderly Dutch woman met them as they entered the house. Her English was imperfect but she spoke German, and O'Neill interpreted for Alan. O'Neill was one of the many European Jews in the company, and when given the opportunity of choosing a new name, in common with some of the others, he had selected an Irish one. 'She says, sir, that she is an old woman and had better go for she would be in our way. She says we must do what we must do, but please not to damage her furniture too much.'

Before the old woman had got clear of the grounds of her house, the section were preparing it for siege. They methodically smashed the glass in every window; they made their way into the attics and broke through the tiled roof to gain vantage points from which they could observe and fire; they stacked Bren-gun magazines on her upholstered chairs and on the big polished table they mounted a machine-gun so that they could fire from the centre of the room, away from the windows, and the blankets they tore from her bed to lay over the table were not to protect its surface, but to prevent the legs of the gun from slipping. Her furniture became breastworks to protect the parachutists from German fire. Within fifteen minutes the old woman would have found the interior of her home unrecognizable.

Alan returned to the platoon's main positions, he and Bilting carrying between them a huge crock of water they had taken from the woman's half-filled bath. 'Tim's hunter' would not die of thirst during the next twenty-four hours.

The men were digging in with a better will than they had shown earlier in the day, and Alan realized that, despite his short field of fire, the position was a good one; Murray's advanced section would serve to break up the first wave of an attack and give some degree of warning to the entrenched company.

He had sited a command post between the two forward sections, and when he got back he helped Bilting to complete the digging of it. They would certainly be in position for some time the following day, while the brigade attack to take the high ground and northern suburbs of Arnhem was launched across their front, above, and a mile to the north of them.

He visited his sections for the last time after stand-down, and went back to his command post without having nominated a successor for Jim Nash. Despite the heavy firing they had heard as they moved to the Company RV, it was just possible that the platoon sergeant might yet make his way back to rejoin them. Leyland was the next senior sergeant, and after him, Bob Blake. But they were both too valuable as section commanders to be taken away from their men. He decided that if Nash did not return he would not replace him.

CHAPTER SIX

Bob Blake awakened under a gentle tugging at his smock sleeve, and looking up in the light of the false dawn he saw a head hanging suspended over his own. He stirred slowly, cramped muscles wakening more sharply than his mind and it was the nagging complaint of his body which brought him to a more general awareness rather than the trunkless head whispering incomprehensible words above him. He eased his shoulders away from the clay and sat up. The movement unblocked his sleep-plugged ears, and the thrice-mouthed 'stand-to' registered as the head disappeared and Bilting slid away to the next section.

Blake got cautiously to his feet and looked out from his slit trench, first to the two men manning the Bren, and then to where Corporal Heibling's shoulders showed, hunched and still. Apart from the one he was in, there were five more slit trenches in the section position, three of them facing the north and two the open ground to the west: the last two served as his link with Lt Ramsden's platoon.

He started to crawl over to Heibling, and at the sound of his movement the corporal swung round, his Sten half-raised. Blake called his name softly, realizing that Bilting had got to

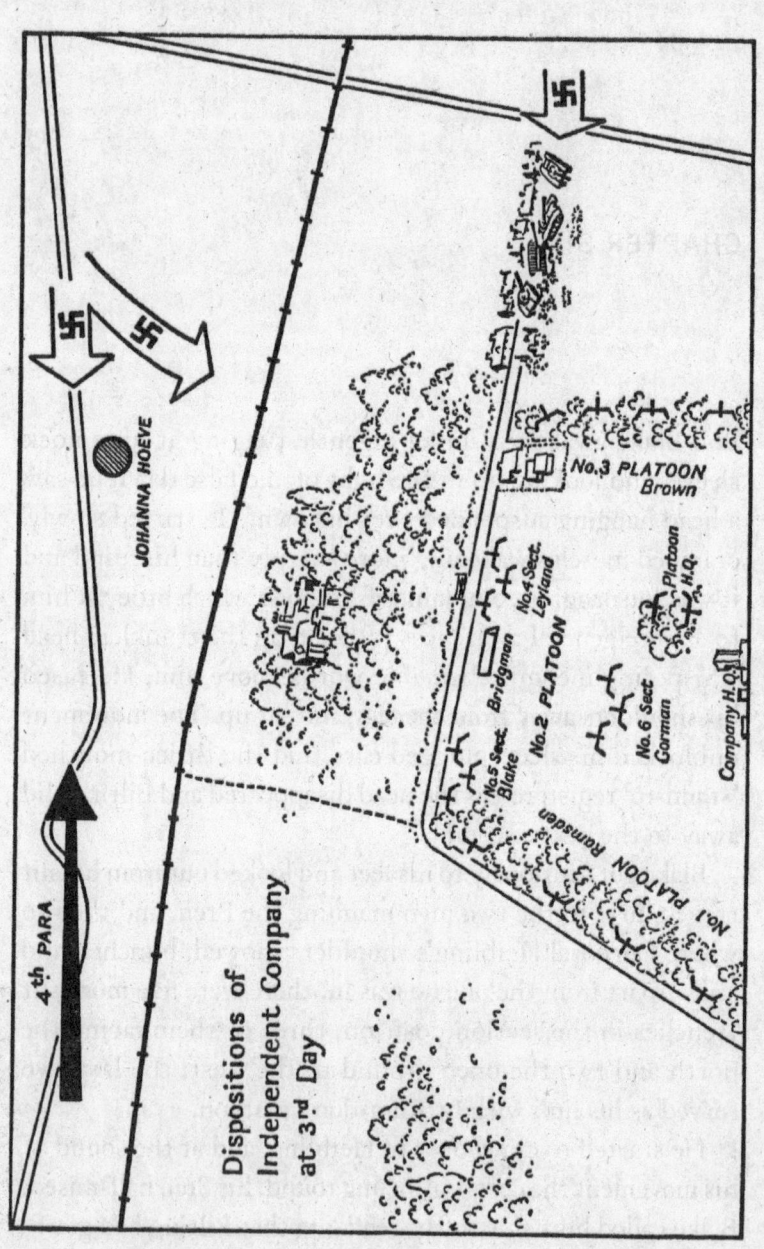

Dispositions of Independent Company at 3rd Day

4th PARA

JOHANNA HOEVE

No.3 PLATOON
Brown

No.2 PLATOON

No.5 Sect.
Bridgman

No.4 Sect.
Leyland

No.5 Sect.
Blake

No. 6 Sect
Gorman

Platoon
H.Q.

Company H.Q.

No.1 PLATOON Ramsden

him and awakened him without Heibling or the two sentries being aware that he had come and gone again. He got close enough to his corporal to speak quietly and be heard.

'Who's on stag?'

'Jennings and Ewing.'

'Change them with the regular Bren group – I'll wake the others.'

The section post became alive with the rustling of moving bodies, the whispering of subdued voices, and once, the startled, immediately muffled curse of a man too rudely awakened.

The Bren gun was tucked into the sharp angle of the road. It could fire into the grounds of the house opposite them, and down the road to the right, enfilading any attack on Leyland's section; it covered the track to the north which ran away directly above the sharp bend in the road which carried it to the south, and it could be swung round to cover the open ground in front of Lt Ramsden's platoon. Most of the men in the slit trenches facing the dense cover to the north were armed with Sten guns: it was in this direction that their short range and rapid rate of fire would be most effective. The two weapon pits covering the open ground contained his riflemen: on the parapet of his own foxhole lay the captured MG 42.

Blake slid back into his own weapon pit. Ramsden's men had the happier position, with a two-hundred-yard field of fire: they were more likely to attract mortar and artillery fire, but the company area was so confined that they would get no greater share of it than anyone else.

Blake opened the straps of his haversack and took out his forty-eight-hour pack. Selecting the solid square lump of dehydrated oatmeal, and resting comfortably behind the

German gun, he nibbled at one corner. It was hard work, and he ended by rubbing it against the biting edge of his upper teeth, using them as one would a nutmeg grater. His shoulders shook suddenly in silent laughter. The British pack was said to be better than the American by those who had eaten both, but this was his first experience of British dehydrated food, and now the Germans had cut off all the water supplies, perhaps he would never know what it was meant to taste like when prepared properly. They had been warned that if they ate too much of the dehydrated food in its dry state and then drank a quantity of water, the whole thing would swell up inside them and might burst their gut. Blake decided that long before a sufficient quantity of the food could be consumed, the consumer's teeth would have been worn down to the gums. He put the oatmeal away and unwrapped a boiled sweet.

It had got darker, the hushed darkness that comes before the rising sun. Blake wondered what the day would bring. Perhaps a divisional advance into the town, and the securing of all their objectives: the relief of the 2nd Para Bn on the bridge and the landing of General Sosabowski and his Polish Brigade south of the river. Perhaps 2nd Army, spearheaded by 30 Corps, would keep their word and link up with the division. At midday their forty-eight hours would be up. Perhaps the 1st Allied Airborne under the command of General 'Boy' Browning would really turn left and face the German garrisons in the 'box' formed by Utrecht, Rotterdam, and Amsterdam, while the 2nd Army, reinforced by American divisions, poured across the North German Plain to Berlin. Perhaps all or some of these things would happen. Perhaps none of them. Perhaps the wedges driven by the Germans between the force on the bridge and the battalions in the town and the remainder of the division would prove unbreakable, and the 1st Airborne Division would fight its last fight in three separate pockets and be defeated in detail.

Looking out at the damp dew-encrusted trees in front of him and at the silvered grass in the open field to his left, Jake became aware that all firing had ceased and that an atmosphere of expectancy hung over the battlefields. Suddenly and with certainty, he was convinced that this day, the third day, would decide the success or failure of the whole operation. They would break into the town in force or they would not. And if they failed – what then?

The click of metal on metal away to his right brought the section sergeant's head round, and he saw that he could now make out the figures of Leyland's men as they strained their eyes into the lightening mist of the early morning. He wondered what Eric Leyland was thinking about. Had it been two years ago he would have known for sure that his friend's thoughts would be concentrated on Sally and their boy. Now he was not so sure. The Company, the war, and the Army – in that order – had succeeded in creeping into the marrow of so many of their unit that earlier loyalties had become displaced or of no consequence. Training and preparation; operations; the killing of Germans and the taking of objectives had become the be-all and end-all of their lives. They talked among themselves of 'after the war', but their voices lacked conviction. It was not so much that they believed the war would never end as an uncertainty as to whether they wanted it to – whether they would know what to do when it did. Wounding and death, burning towns and rotting bodies, the stench, the carnage and horror of war: all these could become as habitual and acceptable as commuting on the eight-fifteen. It was a life they now knew better, were more familiar with, than the earlier one.

The Polish glider contingents would be landing later in the day, and Blake wondered if their landing-zone would still be in the division's hands by the time they were due to arrive. It would not affect his own platoon: the Poles were to be brought in by Lt Brown and his men.

It became lighter. The rim of the sun would be above the horizon that was hidden from him by the houses of Oosterbeek and Arnhem. Away to the north the machine-guns opened up, and the burst of shells sounded like maroons heralding the third day – and on the third day he rose again from the dead. Their dead would not rise – how many dead had they? He had not had time to think about the casualties. Johnny Matthews and Lance-Corporal Manning were dead. Edwards was certain to die if he were not dead already. Black and Jarvis were wounded, and Jim Nash and Muldoon were missing. Seven casualties within the platoon. It didn't sound so many, and yet they had occurred in two days without the platoon being in any real action. The platoon was much stronger than an ordinary infantry platoon because of its specialist role. It totalled over fifty men, a few of whom had had to land from Company HQ aircraft, as the three Stirlings allotted them could carry only sixteen men apiece. But even so they had had one-sixth of their force put out of action within a little over forty-eight hours, and unless 2nd Army broke through and linked up quickly the casualty rate must go up as the Germans brought reinforcements into action.

Two figures darted across the road from Leyland's position, and Blake watched Lt Bridgman and Bilting clamber over the fence ten yards to the left of the gate and head for the tall house. Within seconds they were out of sight in the shrubbery.

Bridgman and Bilting climbed through an open window into an empty room. They moved to the back of the house without meeting or being challenged by any of Sergeant Murray's section. They found two men armed with Stens in the kitchen, and the Bren group in the dining-room. Bridgman met Murray coming down the wide staircase. He had been visiting the two snipers he had positioned in the roof, and he was unprepared when Bridgman tore a strip off him for leaving the front of the house unguarded.

Blake saw Bridgman return and stop where Leyland's men were dug in. It was light enough now for the watching section commander to see that Leyland's face, as he looked up and answered Bridgman, had taken on the strained expressionless look it always wore when he was talking to the platoon commander. It was not mistrust, nor was it apprehension and yet somehow it conveyed a little of both. Blake liked Bridgman, and Leyland was the closest friend he had made in the Army: he found it difficult to understand why Eric, who got on so well with all ranks, seemed permanently to be on his guard when talking to this officer. Blake found it impossible to believe that Bridgman was unaware of Leyland's feelings towards him. Apart from his abilities as a soldier, Bridgman was no fool, and he judged character accurately and well; he could not help but notice Leyland's attitude. But he had never for one moment betrayed any resentment of it, and he had always shown a greater trust in Leyland's assessment of a situation than in that of anyone else.

After stand-down, Bridgman went to Company HQ, and when he returned called his own Order-Group into the shelter of some trees behind the forward sections.

'I'll give you the good news first. There's not much of it. Just as we were leaving the CO, news came through that General Urquhart had got back to Div HQ.' Alan looked round at the brightening faces. It was extraordinary how the absence of a commander created a feeling of insecurity, and just as extraordinary was the way in which the mere knowledge of his return brought about a new cohesion, a feeling that once again the reins had been taken up, and that the division was now going somewhere. '2nd Para are still holding out at the bridge, although they only have the north end. The 1st and 3rd Battalions, the South Staffs, and the 11th Para are still fighting their way through the town, but they've met a lot of armour and suffered a lot of casualties. Brigadier Hackett is launching a brigade attack along the axis of the railway to secure the high ground at Koepel and from there break into the northern outskirts of Arnhem. During the day Mr Brown's platoon will be bringing in the Polish gliders, and Mr Ramsden's platoon a supply drop. Our platoon will be holding the whole company area. Each section will be holding a platoon front: Sgt Murray will have to be withdrawn from the big house to act as the only reserve we have outside Company HQ. I shall allocate your new positions as the other platoons move out.'

The section commanders went back to their positions, and as he dropped into his slit trench again Blake wondered why Bridgman had changed the normal routine of issuing orders. It was usual to give information about enemy strength and dispositions before proceeding to the intentions and objectives of their own troops – but Bridgman had omitted to mention the enemy at all.

CHAPTER SEVEN

For Bridgman's platoon the morning of the third day was a morning of waiting, an interminable morning in which its sections were shuffled around the company's perimeter. They became an isolated pocket of men. To the north of them the 4th Parachute Brigade launched its expected attack along the axis of the railway to secure the northern arc of the bridgehead; to the south, the Borders and divisional troops held out against attacks from the west, and to the southeast the battered remnants of four battalions fought on in a last desperate bid to reach and relieve the 2nd Parachute Battalion, cut off and surrounded at the northern end of the road bridge in Arnhem.

Early in the afternoon, Tim Jordan and Alan looked at their hastily constructed battle map. Immediately to the east and west of the company position the map showed ominously empty areas: a drive by the Germans from the east along the road from Arnhem to the ferry would slice across the front held by the platoon, and completely cut off the 4th Parachute Brigade from the remainder of the division. Jordan and Alan exchanged glances. Something would have to go by the board: it was impossible to hold the company area secure and at the same time be in any position to deny the Heveadorp–Arnhem road to a determined enemy. Alan handed over the western sector, previously held by Ramsden and his platoon, to the sergeant-major and a scratch group from company headquarters, and moved his own platoon forward and to the east, astride the middle road to Arnhem.

Blake and his section were now north of the road, and as they prepared to defend the house they had taken over they listened to the battle raging beyond the railway line. The firing seemed to be remaining static; it did not, as they had anticipated, diminish and then restart farther to the east as 4th Brigade advanced along their northern route.

Blake looked across the road to where he could see Gorman's men at work in the house opposite. Both sections had their Bren groups in the front gardens of the houses they were holding and their riflemen and Sten gunners in the upstairs rooms and in the roof.

Bridgman joined Blake as the sergeant linked six Hawkins anti-tank mines to a clothes line, and satisfied by the progress being made by the two forward sections, he moved down the road to where Leyland was preparing the drop-end of the tank trap. He watched young Adams as Leyland explained the tactics his section was to use should enemy armour pass the first two sections. The young soldier had lost some of his earlier apprehension, and as Leyland positioned the men and gave them their instructions he showed an interest quite different from the stunned apathy he had exhibited since the shock of his first brief action.

Alan crossed the road and looked in on his headquarter section as it prepared for the part it was to play in conjunction with Leyland and his men. They were as well advanced as the remainder of the platoon, and after a few quick words with Murray he went back to where he had left Blake.

The platoon now occupied four houses; two, those held by Blake and Gorman, were opposite each other and thirty yards short of the crossroads formed by the road they were on, which ran across the north of Oosterbeek, and another which ran south from the Arnhem–Amsterdam road. Seventy-five yards farther back Leyland and Murray occupied two more houses, also on opposite sides of the road. In the event of a German attack from the east, the area between the two pairs of houses was to be the platoon's killing ground.

Back with Blake, Alan listened to the sounds of battle to the north, the German fire coming from a little to the west of where he guessed the brigade to be.

'It sounds as if 4th Para have been taken on from behind.' He spoke without surprise, as if it were something he had expected to happen. 'If they're too tightly squeezed they'll have to get back into the divisional area before taking a new line.'

Blake shut his eyes and tried to visualize the battle scene. He could imagine the brigade held up on their axis and being harassed from the rear. They would not dare take the risk of disengaging to the north and putting an even greater distance between themselves and the division – they would have to come south.

'That means they'll come down through the company position, doesn't it, sir?'

'Some of them might, but if the whole brigade comes due south they'll lose their transport. They can't get it over the railway embankment, and the nearest crossing is back at Wolfheze. If we're not still holding it, it'll have to be retaken.'

I don't think Div can help them – judging by the firing to the south, the Borders have troubles of their own, and there's no other infantry unit not already committed. They may use the Glider Pilots, there must be a thousand or so of them some-where. I should think . . .' He broke off and listened.

The slow clank of a creeping tank took the two men to the side of the window in the bedroom where they were talking. The angle of the wall prevented them from seeing more than thirty yards up the road towards Arnhem. They slipped out of the room and ran down the stairs, their boots breaking the close silence of the house. The front door was wedged back on its hinges, and dropping to the ground they joined the Bren group whose members were staring through the privet over the low garden wall.

Bridgman spotted a slight movement at the crossroads, and was able to make out a German helmet and half a face a few inches above the pavement. The man was peering round the corner from the road leading up from Oosterbeek, and Alan wondered if the armour they had heard was on the same road, and if so, how it had got there. Somehow the Germans must have got behind the parachute battalions and the South Staffs in the centre of the town.

The head disappeared, but almost at once the man himself ran out from his cover and crossed the road. He was followed by four others, and the five of them entered the front garden of a house on Bridgman's side of the street. They were out of his sight almost at once, but he knew Gorman's men would know where they were and would be able to neutralize them at the right time. Another half-section of Germans scram-bled over the garden wall round which the first soldier had peered. Alan turned to Blake.

'Where's the MG 42?'

Blake jerked his head backwards. 'Up there in a bedroom.'

'Get back in the house and tell them that last lot are their first target when the firing starts.'

Blake crawled away and into the house.

Alan continued to watch the crossroads. He guessed that after a period of observation by their infantry section, the German armour would start up again and come out from behind its cover. He had no idea whether it would turn left and come through his platoon position, or whether it would continue up the road it was on and cross the railway embankment, reinforcing those enemy elements which were holding up 4th Brigade.

He could hear the noise of more than one engine running, but it was difficult to decide exactly how many German vehicles were concealed behind the houses and how many of them were armoured. Blake rejoined him, and Alan looked round at the sergeant's grinning face.

'Spot on, sir. The MG 42 crew can actually see three of them. They won't give us much trouble.'

The sudden revving of engines gave the impression of an armoured division starting up, and the first tank, an old Mk IV, lurched into sight. The watching men held their breath as it crawled forward. It seemed to hesitate in the centre of the crossroads. And then it locked one track and swung round towards them. Bridgman slid backwards to the front door of the house, and once inside he pounded upstairs to the bedroom. He crossed it quickly and stood behind the crew of the captured German machine-gun. A second tank had followed the first, and both were clanking warily down the road towards the platoon. Alan wondered what they would do when they spotted the clothes line across the road. It had been laid as carelessly as possible; it wound slackly across the tarmac surface, and on the far side it stopped short of the garden gate by a good eighteen inches. He hoped that a free end of rope might allay any suspicion. A self-propelled gun and two infantry carrying half-tracks had followed the two leading tanks, and the Mk IV had got to within ten yards of the clothes line. Alan pulled the Very Light pistol from the inside of his smock and waited. The leading tank ground to a standstill, and its gun traversed slowly from side to side like a solitary antenna on a blind crab. Without warning, the top half of a German officer emerged from the turret. Alan stepped back farther into the room, pressing down with his right hand on the head of the man behind the machine-gun.

The German's eyes followed the clothes line to where its unattached end showed on the pavement. He glanced sharply at the houses on each side of the road, and Alan hoped the man waiting out of sight behind the far garden wall would not show himself in his anxiety to be ready to snatch at the end of the rope and pull it in.

The Panzer officer had started to sink back into the tank when he seemed to change his mind, and stood up again. He half turned, his mouth opening as if to shout back to his infantry, but again he had second thoughts, and dropped out of sight into the tank. The Mk IV lurched forward with the other armour following it.

Alan ducked and crossed to the other side of the room where he could look back towards his two rear sections and at the same time follow the movement of the German tanks.

They picked up speed a little, and Alan just had time to thrust his hand out of the window and fire his flare over the leading tank, and to watch the second clothes line come to life as it was dragged across the road with its attached cargo of anti-tank mines. The leading tank ran on to one of the mines, and it seemed to him that it skipped sideways like a girl playing hopscotch before it came to rest, one track severed and trailing. The platoon's Piats opened up. Gammon bombs and grenades rained down from the windows above, and Sten-gun fire was poured into the open-topped troop-carrying half-tracks. The captured Spandau belched German bullets into the German half-section back at the crossroads.

The two rear vehicles had started to turn round before Alan realized that at his end of the trap the road was still clear of mines. The line had been caught up by one of the German tracks and dragged several yards along the road. Its loose end now lay ten feet from where the dismayed face of one of Alan's men looked out from the gate opposite.

Bridgman ran from the bedroom and down the stairs. He reached the front door in time to see Blake dart out of the garden gate, his Sten gun in his right hand and his left dragging the rope-linked mines behind him. The last German vehicle was the self-propelled gun and it completed its turn as Blake ran across its front. It started back in the direction from which it had come, and crushed one of the mines as Blake leaped for the pavement on the far side of the road. Alan had time to see the sergeant blown through the open gate opposite him before he himself was thrown off his feet. He scrambled up and put a burst of Sten-gun fire into the backs of two Germans attempting to clamber over a wall into a garden. One of the half-tracks had run up on to the pavement; it had come to rest with its front end half through a garden wall; its occupants had been thrown about by the violence of its sudden turn and sharply arrested movement; some had been jerked clean out of the vehicle as they stumbled to their feet; some were struggling to rise from where they had been hurled on the deck; some would never move again, and as the survivors looked desperately about them, death singled them out from the windows above.

The firing had almost stopped, and Alan shouted across to Gorman to keep his Bren aimed back at the road intersection. He could see Blake still lying on his face in the open doorway opposite, so he turned to where Corporal Heibling was looking down from an open window above him.

'Keep the two MGs trained on the crossroads. I'll take the rest of the section. Send them down now.'

The men joined him in the garden, and with their fingers hooked expectantly round the triggers of their weapons they made their way to where the German armour lay like stranded ships on the road and pavements.

The surviving occupants stood about in small groups, their hands resting on their steel helmets, and with shocked, apprehensive expressions on their faces. Blake's section rounded them up quickly, and Alan sent two men back with them to Company HQ, ordering the rest of the section back to the house. He shouted to Leyland to salvage anything of value from the enemy vehicles, and then made his way to the gateway of Gorman's house. Blake no longer lay where Alan had seen him, and when he went through the open doorway he found Blake sitting in an armchair, smoking a cigarette. He looked white and shaken, but his eyes showed their usual steadiness.

'What happened to you? I thought you'd bought it.'

'I wasn't scratched. Just knocked out by the blast. I landed on my Sten mags, and they knocked all the wind out of me. I thought I was never going to start breathing again.'

Alan called to Gorman.

'We needn't worry about any more armour coming down this road – they've made their own tank obstacles. Leave your Bren group where it is and get most of your section to the back of the house. The Jerries may try to push their infantry behind you.'

He went back to the open doorway and looked towards where Leyland and his men were at work salvaging ammunition and arms. Alan spotted Leyland on the far side of the road, halfway up the staggered line of wrecked vehicles. He called to attract the sergeant's attention.

Leyland turned, his thickset body looking square and resolute under the bulking smock and equipment. The sling of his Sten was over his left shoulder, adjusted so that the gun fitted comfortably into his hands at waist height. His face bore the calm determined look of a man busy with a task well within his competence. He raised his chin slightly in recognition of Bridgman's shout.

'Clear up as quickly as you can and get back under cover. Watch the back of your house – I don't think they'll come down our side, they won't know where 4th Brigade extends to, but they might just chance it.'

Leyland waved and shouted to his section to get back into the house with all they had collected. He moved to the open doorway and watched them come past him laden with captured arms and ammunition. Adams was staggering towards the building under a load of seven or eight German rifles. Leyland was about to call to him when Corporal Marsden shouted to the sweating youngster, his voice irritable:

'You can sling that stuffing lot away. We're not starting a museum. There's a Schmeisser and two boxes of ammo in that half-track – get those.' He pointed to where the vehicle stood, exactly in the centre of the road where it had been halted. It appeared completely undamaged and looked as if it might drive off at any moment.

Adams stood flat-heeled and irresolute, the rifles bundled in front of him, his mouth open and his face pink and sweating. He looked at the other men as they made their way past him. They carried Spandaus, Schmeissers, and ammunition, but no rifles. He had thought he was doing well, and had been so busy grabbing the rifles and propping them against the side of a tank so that he could pick them up in one go that he hadn't had time to see what the rest of the section were doing. His lips turned down in disappointment. He looked at the rifles in his crooked arms as if he hoped they would disappear. He raised his head and saw Eric Leyland smiling at him from the open doorway. He grinned back, a sickly grin which betrayed his embarrassment, and unconsciously lowered his arms so that the rifles cascaded on to the road. The sudden clatter made him jump, and at once he started to move quickly. He ran back to the half-track and clambered up its side. He threw the two boxes of ammunition out on to the road, and he took the Schmeisser from a dead German's hand, looking away from the vacant drained face of the man they had killed because he happened to have been born in a country where in their despair the people had permitted, and even encouraged, the rise and rule of a megalomaniac. Adams climbed down, and holding the Schmeisser in his left hand he looked at the two boxes. If he carried both he couldn't carry the Schmeisser. He tried to come to a decision – he did not want to make a fool of himself again. He looked at the gateway but Leyland had gone back to the house. Adams suddenly realized that he was the only living man left in the road. And with that realization came the smell of burnt cordite and hot engines. He looked about him as a man might who was lost in a forest and hoped to see something which would help to orientate himself. For the first time he saw the dead Germans as fellow human beings. He had never really thought about the enemy as being like himself and his new recognition of the obvious filled him with a compassion which made him imagine himself in any one of the dusty, blood-bespattered grey uniforms.

He grabbed one of the boxes and, dragging it behind him, set out for the gate. The German soldier must have fired in the instant that Adams moved. He heard the whine of the bullet as it passed behind him. He broke into a run, the ammunition-box suddenly increasing its weight till he imagined he was being dragged back to be displayed like a target in the butts. He started to release his grip on the handle of the box, but remembered Leyland and Bridgman and the other men in the platoon, and the way they might look away from him, ashamed of his failure. He tripped on the kerb and fell sprawling on the pavement as another bullet cut the air where he had been a second before. He scrambled to his knees, and as he half turned to seize the box which had broken from his grasp he heard Corporal Marsden's voice screaming at him, 'Leave the stuffing thing! Get in here, you bloody fool!' But Adams had obtained a fresh grip, and he was through the gate and into the hallway of the house before the meaning of Marsden's words had registered in his brain.

He stood facing the corporal in the hall, his chest rising and falling with a combination of exertion and relief, his face happy and shining with success so that Marsden's words came through to him in disjointed lengths, like snippets from a sound-track. '. . . ing idiot . . . bloody ammunition . . . Bridgman's a raving lunatic about . . . 'd think we were a bloody salvage squad not . . . 'll sit up all night counting the rounds like a stuffing miser.'

Corporal Marsden's voice became lower and lower as he blew off steam, and eventually he ground to an unintelligible mutter. Adams shuffled his feet and looked away. It was impossible to be sure what these people expected of him. Back in England Lt Bridgman had always been emphasizing the unreliability of resupply drops, the necessity of conserving ammunition, and how important it was to take advantage of every opportunity of capturing the enemy's, and neither Corporal Marsden nor any of the others had disagreed with the platoon commander then; but now Tom Marsden seemed really angry because Adams had not dropped the box and run for cover at once. Adams had vaguely imagined that he would be praised for what he had done; instead he was being slated for an idiot. Corporal Marsden was talking to him again in a voice that was normal and could be understood.

'You're meant to be a sniper. At least you've got telescopic sights on your rifle. Get up into the roof and see if you can get the bastard who fired at you.'

Adams climbed wearily up the stairs. He was suddenly very tired – almost exhausted. As he got to the top and stood still holding the banister rail, Leyland came out of a front bedroom. The section commander glanced at Adams's face.

'Come in here a moment.' Leyland spoke quietly, and

without waiting for a reply he walked back into the bedroom, Adams following him.

The sergeant moved over to the position he had left at the window. He didn't look at Adams but kept his eyes fixed on the farthest point he could see on the road into Arnhem.

'Sit down a minute,' he waved towards the bed. Adams seated himself, and then had to fight to keep upright. He was filled with an almost uncontrollable desire to lie back and sleep, to sink into the oblivion of unconsciousness, and only to awaken when it was all over, or perhaps to discover that the whole thing was an unpleasant dream and that he wasn't in Holland surrounded by German soldiers and tanks who wanted nothing else but to kill him and all the others who were with him.

'Don't take too much notice of Tom Marsden.' Leyland threw Adams a quick smile. 'He was only angry because he thought you might have been killed or wounded unnecessarily. Try to get some sense of proportion in your head about the things we have to do. The ammunition and arms were objectives that were desirable but not essential. If we're thrown into a defensive role of course we shall want every automatic weapon and all the ammunition we can lay our hands on. But you don't have to risk your life at this stage for a thousand rounds of ammo. There may come a time when ammunition may be of more value than men, but that time isn't yet. When you have to do a job out in the open, try to be as quick as you can. Do it properly but get it over with and get under cover again as soon as possible. Now get up in the roof and remember, you don't have anything to prove.'

The firing started as Adams was climbing the attic steps. He made his way gingerly to the front of the house, stepping carefully on the spaced rafters. Close to the eaves was the mattress he had placed there earlier on, and he knelt on it now and looked through the gap where the tiles had been torn away. He could see one house beyond the one held by Sgt Gorman and his section, and he thought the firing was coming from behind it, and farther to the east, towards Arnhem. He could hear other members of his section moving about below and behind him at the back of the house, and to the north the distance-dulled, incessant fire of 4th Brigade as it tried for the high ground from which it could sweep down and form the northern arc on the edge of the town.

The detached houses on the far side of the street stood bright and clean in their red-bricked isolation. They looked very like the houses on the new estate in the Midland town which was his home, but despite the noise of battle they seemed quieter houses than the ones he remembered. They were better cared for, but in a cold remote way that he did not understand. He found it hard to believe that real people lived in them, and he wondered where their owners were. He realized how few Dutch people he had seen since they landed: there had been quite a lot of them in the divisional area on the first night; young and middle-aged men wearing orange armbands, some with weapons and some unarmed. He had been told that they were members of the Dutch underground, and he wondered where they were now. They had seemed very calm and confident, almost as if the descent of an airborne division on their doorstep was an everyday occurrence.

The firing round Gorman's house hotted up, and Adams moved his head a few inches at a time in an attempt to spot some sign of movement, but he could see nothing.

He wanted to go into the bedroom below him where he could hear the voices of the men watching the gardens leading up to the railway embankment. He did not want to stay with them, but only to fortify himself, to draw encouragement from the warmth of their presence.

There was a sudden and prolonged burst of Bren fire from the direction of Gorman's house, and as if it were a signal that both sides waited for, small arms of every calibre opened up, the fierce staccato crack of the individual explosions blending into one long cacophony of sound that rose and fell in successive waves, beating against Adams's head and making him wince as each screaming crest broke over him. Enemy mortar bombs landed on the roofs opposite him and in the road among the German armour.

Adams shifted his position continually but he could see no movement at all. It was like being struck blind at a Cup-tie, and only being able to guess what was happening from the unintelligible roar of the crowd.

He could hear Leyland shouting in the house below him and a few seconds later he saw Corporal Marsden and Wilcox run across the street carrying a German MG 42. They entered the gate of the house above the one held by headquarter section. Marsden smashed a downstairs window with the butt of his Sten and clambered through the gap in the broken pane. He turned at once and took the light machine gun from Wilcox's extended hand. Adams saw the second man start to climb into the house, and then sensed rather than saw a movement up the road to his left. He turned his head and was in time to see Bridgman and Bilting bolt through the gate of Gorman's house, Bilting carrying another MG 42. Adams looked back and saw that Wilcox had not yet disappeared from sight. His arms were through the window and his boots were scrabbling at the wall. Then his legs were still and he hung like a man who has slipped on the high wire: his body strangely conveying catastrophe by its stillness. Marsden reappeared at the window and seized the sagging man by his shoulders. He was pulling him in when the mortar bomb landed in the next garden. The explosion threw up a great cloud of soft earth, and Adams ducked as stones and fragments of metal showered on the tiles about his head. When he looked again there was no one at the window opposite him, but he could see a barely distinguishable movement in the room beyond it. He was wondering if Wilcox had made it after all when Marsden looked out and down into the garden. One side of his face was red and dripping and only partly concealed by the handkerchief he held to it. He seemed to stare for a long time at what lay out of Adams's sight three feet or so below the window ledge, and then he turned away and disappeared towards the back of the building. Wilcox was dead. Adams was quite sure about this. He could not imagine Marsden leaving him if he were only wounded.

He looked back up the road, at the front doors and windows of the houses that hid from him the battle being fought in the garden to their rear, and he felt terribly alone. For the first time since landing he actually wished himself in the battle. There he would be among his friends, and their shouted defiance and hot curses, and the tingling excitement of their aroused emotions; he would have felt Bridgman's grip on the battle, and would himself have been part of the team working together to deny the Germans' advance into the almost defenceless company area where the CO and the sergeant-major held the position with under thirty men.

A German machine-gun opened up due south from where he knelt, and as his head snapped round he realized that he could now spot the difference between the enemy's guns and their own. He decided that the gun was the one taken across by Wilcox and Marsden, and was pleased that the sounds of battle were no longer as meaningless to him as a page in a foreign newspaper. With this knowledge he was born a new confidence. If he could now read the writing of war, it was possible he might write a few lines himself before the end.

The firing quietened to a series of intermittent exchanges, and he could again pick out the more distant sounds of the other, bigger battle being fought by 4th Brigade. Some freak atmospheric condition made the sound of the firing to the north vary in intensity; sometimes it sounded very far away, at others, as if it were just outside in the back garden of the house he was in. He remembered this sort of thing happening before.

In the bed he shared with his elder brother, he had lain listening to the sounds of the fairground on the outskirts of the town, to which he had been forbidden to go on that particular evening because of his failure to do his share of the family chores in the morning. The street outside was quiet with everyone away at the fair, and the summer evening held a dusty closeness. He lay thinking of the happy noise and the laughter, and the whirling of the giant machines, the raucous calls of the barkers and the excited, exciting screams of the girls as they were swung high on the swings by their chaps. And the sound of it all had alternated between the very loud and the barely heard. Lying alone, his tears finished and his throat sore from the self-pitying sobs he had strangled, he had day-dreamed the evening away: the immeasurable span of his unlived life reaching out, a golden carpet stretching on to the infinity of a romantic child's dreams. Curled up in the loneliness of the big bed, holding his body close in his crossed forearms, he had cradled his secret thoughts of the future to his innermost self. He would forgive them in the hour of his triumph, but they must know that he remembered, and recognize that it was their stupidity he forgave. They would be proud of him when he returned from wherever it was he would have gone to. That was the part which was never quite clear, either now, in the quiet of the deserted evening with the music of the fair as a backcloth to his thoughts, or at those other times when he had dreamed of the green path his growing youth would cut through the world, leading always away from the sordid ordinariness of his native town.

The glamour which surrounded the Parachute Regiment, and the promise of glory which it held out, had fixed in his impressionable mind the certainty that it was by far the most romantic and exciting regiment in the Army, and it had been a 'must' long before his call-up. When he had been accepted, it had been as if a half-doubted password had been given and opened the door to a way of living he had known existed outside the dream-world in which he had spent so much time.

The sound of the 4th Brigade's firing rose and fell, rose to a frantic pitch and died again. There was something desperate about the sound, like a dying man fighting for each succeeding, hard-won breath.

Adams heard increased movement below him and towards the back of the house. He stood up, straightening his aching

body, but as he started to move over to the trapdoor, he heard
the sound of boots on the road outside and turning back he
crouched again and looked down. He had only time to see
the top of a steel helmet and the smock below it before a
figure of one of their own men disappeared from his sight as
it entered the house.

He moved over to where the steps led down from the attic
and listened. He could hear Leyland's voice, and Marsden
answering him – it must have been the section corporal whom
he had seen crossing the pavement and entering the house.

'. . . happened to your face?'

'Nothing much, but the bastards got Wilcox before we'd
got into Murray's position. I reckon there are some Jerries
in a house on this side of the road. Gorman couldn't have
knocked out all the ones who came over to cover the armour.'

'How are things going over there? It sounds as if you've
got it under control.'

'It's all right now, but it was touch and go for a bit. They
must have used the best part of a company against us, but
this cattle wire the Dutch use between their gardens really
buggered them up. It kept checking them every few yards,
and I've had enough automatics over there to knock seven
kinds of shit out of 'em. I don't think they'll come back in a
hurry. How have you had it?'

'It's been quiet enough here, but I should think 4th Brigade
have had it on their present line. Carter came in a few minutes ago from 3 Platoon. They've landed the Polish gliders,
but it sounds as if it was a proper cock-up. The LZ was bang
between the 10th Para and the Germans. 3 Platoon has been
shot to hell and they'll be coming back into the company
area any time now.'

'What about the Poles? They were bringing in anti-tank guns, weren't they?'

'Yes they were, but I don't know what the exact position is. The chap from 3 Platoon says they got some of them unloaded and away, but it seems the Poles decided that everyone was an enemy, and opened up on the KOSBs, 10th Para, and 3 Platoon as well as the Germans. Can't say I blame 'em. An opposed landing's a bastard. You've no idea where the firing is coming from. Anyhow, you'd better take over here and keep your eyes skinned for 3 Platoon – I'm going to see Bridgman and find out what the next move is.'

Adams crept back to his place in the eaves. How bad was 'shot to hell'? And what exactly did '4th Brigade have had it on their present line' mean? He crouched for a long time on the mattress in the roof without seeing any of the enemy. There seemed to be an incessant coming and going below stairs, and every now and again a familiar figure would dart quickly across the road. He heard 3 Platoon arrive in the houses to the west of where he knelt, and he heard them move out again through the gardens south of the railway embankment. He guessed they were returning to the company positions, and wondered how many of them had failed to come back, but instead lay somewhere to the north, on or near the Polish landing-zone, their dead faces pressed into the Dutch soil or staring with unseeing eyes at the Dutch sky.

For Adams, the afternoon drew to its close amid bewildering and unexplained movement which he could hear but only rarely see. Halfway through the short evening he was called down from his post, and joined the remainder of his section as they came together in the hall. Leyland gave them their orders.

'The other two platoons are back in the company area, and in their original positions. We are to join them and take over the sector we held before. The 4th Brigade, including the KOSBs, are coming down inside the Div perimeter. God knows how or when they'll arrive, so for Christ's sake make certain that you don't fire on them in mistake for the Boche. The 4th have had a hell of a pasting and they're having trouble in disengaging. We can look for them at any time from now. We're going back by sections. Sgt Blake's first, then Sgt Gorman's, then ourselves and Platoon HQ last.'

From the door and lower windows they watched the advanced two sections fall back, covered by headquarter section from the far side of the road. Their own house was of no use to cover the others: the sniper who had shot Wilcox was on the same side of the road as themselves and so could not be seen by Leyland's men.

Leyland moved down to the garden gate and looked west to where the two sections were disappearing out of sight as they fell back into their old positions. Across the road at the open doorway opposite, Bridgman was standing just inside its frame, peering after the last man in Gorman's section. He turned his head and his eyes met Leyland's. He nodded and waved his hand from right to left, and the section sergeant spoke quickly to Marsden.

'Right, off you go, Tom. Remember, this side of the road for thirty or forty yards, then all over together to cover headquarters as they come out.'

Listening, Adams felt his back grow cold. As they crossed the road the German sniper would be taking aim at them from less than a hundred yards' range. The section quit the house and moved to the gate. Adams found his mind frantically tumbling in an effort to decide whether it was safer to be among the first or the last to leave cover. Before he could make up his mind, Marsden was out and sidling down the right-hand side of the pavement, the section behind him. Adams followed. The decision had been made for him. With the exception of Leyland and the Bren gunner, who were remaining to cover the crossroads at the southern intersection, he was the last man, and as such, he decided at the last moment, the most vulnerable.

They halted forty yards down the road and lined up with their backs to the garden wall, facing the opposite side of the road. And then at a word from Marsden they were pounding across the open sixty feet, the sound of their ammunition boots ringing in their ears. Adams ran with his head up and his mouth open, as if ready to cry out before he was hurt. He heard the two shots, but he did not look to see if they had taken effect. He had already seen the body of Jimmy Storrs from Gorman's section lying sprawled with his shoulders on the pavement and his hips and legs twisted so that they followed the line of the gutter.

The gateway seemed filled with men, so without checking in his stride Adams kept straight on, and at the last moment thrust his stocky body upwards, his weight propelled by muscles grown stronger through his wish to survive at any cost. He cleared the privet head first, his rifle extended and held away from his falling body. He felt his boots catch for a second in the tight-trimmed wood of the hedge, and then he landed on his hands and knees in the Dutch garden. He stayed for a moment with his chest heaving and his head hanging down between his braced arms. He looked up only when he heard Marsden's voice urging three men into the house. He started to follow them but the section corporal called him back.

'No, not you. Get in the corner there.' He pointed to where the dividing fence joined the low wall and privet of the front garden. 'The bastard's in that last house, just this side of the crossroads. Gorman's lot must have missed him when the kerfuffle started. The sod's done two already. You see the stuffer doesn't get any more.'

Adams knelt at the spot pointed out by Marsden and looked at the house on the far side of the street before the crossroads. It looked exactly the same as any of the others, except that all of its windows were smashed and the red gashes of bullet-scarred brickwork showed in greater abundance than on the other houses. The German armour obscured much of his view and he could see only one of the downstairs windows. The broken windows gave the upstairs rooms an impression of being gutted but in one of them, or perhaps in the roof, the sniper waited.

Adams eased his rifle forward and looked through the telescopic sights. The house jumped towards him, and he began a slow search of the windows and tiled roof. In the lower right-hand corner of the farthest window he thought he spotted a movement, but he could not be sure. He was trying to make up his mind whether to put a shot in when Leyland broke cover, followed by Ted Wallace carrying the Bren gun. Adams watched them as they made their way along the far side of the road as he had done minutes earlier with the rest of the section. They halted for a moment opposite him – and then they were running across the road.

Adams heard the thud of the bullet which hit Wallace, and watched him stumble for a few more paces before going down. Leyland ran on to the gate, then stopped and looked back as if he had been called and was trying to place the direction of the cry. He turned, very slowly, and looked towards where Wallace lay in the middle of the road. Adams stared at the section sergeant, his eyes wide and a look of incredulity on his face. Time seemed to stand still. Leyland was frowning a little, the slight frown of one who struggles to recall something, and his eyes had the far-away unseeing look of a man who sees an internal picture, and one so vivid that it obscures the reality of his surroundings. Leyland was no longer in Holland, and the road before him was not in Oosterbeek. He saw a market square in Casamassima, and instead of the crumpled form of Wallace he saw the figure of Tait struggling to get his Sten gun off his shoulder.

He started back across the pavement. Not with the hurried, furtive action of a man under fire, but firmly, as if bent on an inevitable course which brooked neither deviation nor retreat. He neither ran nor slunk, but walked with a sure step as a brave man might to the scaffold and the first bullet barely checked his stride. His knees bent slightly, and then straightened. He had taken three more steps when the sniper fired again. He stopped, both legs apart and one hand raised to his chest: his head swung slowly to the right, towards Bridgman and platoon headquarters, and smiling quietly he fell forward over the body of Wallace, one leg staying cocked in the air as it lay across the barrel of the Bren.

Adams heard his own breath, a harsh grating sound which seemed to originate high in his head, and his tongue had become a dry, swollen foreignness which threatened to choke him. He jerked his eyes from the two still bodies and looked back at the house by the crossroads.

He sensed rather than saw Bridgman and headquarter section as they raced down the pavement towards where he crouched, but he did see the raised rifle, the head, and one shoulder of the German sniper as he took aim. The sweat dried on his hands; the rifle leaped to his shoulder, and the crossed hairlines of the telescope settled where the German's head joined his body. He squeezed slowly on the trigger and the rifle jerked in his hands. He watched the German's rifle fall forward into the garden, and he waited expectantly as if prepared for the sniper's body to follow his weapon. He stared through the telescope, but for long seconds he saw nothing, and then a white hand showed for a moment on the bottom of the empty window pane: the fingers groped and crawled like blind, pink-white slugs; they straightened at last, stiffening and reaching upwards towards the sky, but they closed on nothing as they disappeared, pulled from sight by the weight of a body sagging in death.

With the sniper gone, the platoon moved quickly back to the company area. They improved the positions they had already dug, but they did their work for the most part in silence. Used to death, they were all stunned by the manner and pointlessness of Leyland's dying.

Bridgman called his order group half an hour before stand-to, and his section commanders came together in the cover of the trees which separated their platoon from Gordon Brown's. Bridgman tried to be brief.

'I can't give you much of a picture of the German's dispo-sitions. The whole battle is still too bloody fluid, reckon it's grinding to a standstill, and by this time tomorrow we shall know exactly where we stand.' He paused for moment before adding, 'or fall. What's left of the KOSBs will be coming back at any time now and will be taking up a position to our right, in the houses along the road we've just left. The 10th and 156th Para Battalions will be coming into the divisional area at first light tomorrow morning or at least they will if the Germans allow them to disengage. I can't be sure, but I imagine the General will give them a fresh line and orders to get to the bridge at all cost. I believe the whole three battalions are down to about half strength.'

Blake broke in, his voice a little higher than usual, carrying a note that one who was ignorant of the sergeant's qualities might have thought slightly hysterical. Bridgman knew the higher pitch denoted only urgency.

'If they're rejoining Div, why the hell don't they come on during the night? They haven't far to come, and they'll stand a much better chance of making it under cover of darkness.' The sergeant spoke half in anger, half in bewilderment. 'Christ Almighty, if they'd give us their map references we could send a couple of sections to guide them in. There can't be any considerable force between them and us. I reckon it would be a doddle.'

Alan Bridgman turned till he looked squarely at Blake. 'You're so damned right that it makes me sick to think of them attempting it in daylight. For all the cock they talk about the confusion of night attacks, I'd sooner tackle nearly anything during the night. The other side is always in a worse position because they haven't a clue as to what's happening. My own view is that a commander who's not prepared to commit his troops to movement by night hasn't much confidence in them or himself. Either that or there's a big gap in their training somewhere.'

Bridgman stopped abruptly as if he felt he had said more

than he should have done. He swallowed once or twice before continuing, and his section commanders knew that it was rage he was forcing down and no other emotion.

'What is left of 2nd Battalion and one company of 3rd Battalion are still holding out at the bridge, but the four battalions in the town have had it, and are being withdrawn to the southeast corner of the Div perimeter. There's a resupply drop tomorrow afternoon and our platoon is bringing it in.'

Frank Gorman looked up from his map, his thin face concerned. He stretched his long legs out in front of him before he spoke.

'But we're a long way from the DZ,' he said jerkily. Gorman did nearly everything in jerks. He was very tall, over six foot two in height, and when he moved he appeared to be all elbows and knees. He had small, darting eyes, and to those who met him for the first time seemed always to be nervous and flurried. In fact he was a very good section commander, and the last man to be panicked or hurried into a hasty or wrong decision. 'Do we have to take it?'

'There's not a chance in hell of it being taken by us or anyone else. We're to use a new area on the western edge of the perimeter, and I don't think there will be anything between us and the Boche either. I'll give you more dope on that in the morning, but you,' he nodded to Gorman, 'will operate the signals. The remainder of the platoon will cover you.'

They sat in silence for a few minutes, each thinking his own thoughts. Marsden was the first to voice what was uppermost in all their minds.

'What about 2nd Army? What the bloody hell has happened to them? They're twenty-four hours late already.'

Marsden's temper was as quick and as well directed as the movements of his dapper body. Even in the midst of battle he somehow managed to give the impression that he thought nothing was half so difficult as those in authority tried to make out, and to prove it he managed to shave and appear well groomed under conditions which everybody else went along with.

When Alan answered there was a slight edge to his voice. He liked Marsden well enough, but was impatient with the corporal's preoccupation with matters beyond their control.

'I don't know, and from what I can gather, no one else does either. It's no use speculating about it. We've our own job to do, and after the resupply tomorrow that means any job they give us. No matter what the final outcome is, let those who survive be able to live with the knowledge that we didn't fall down on any of our tasks.' Bridgman paused for a moment. He was not quite certain whether he ought to continue, but did. 'I'd like to think that those who have fallen down on their jobs, whether through lack of guts or because they're too bloody dilatory and "victory-happy" to feel any sense of urgency, I'd like to think that they will find it difficult to live with themselves. But they won't. They never do. They'll be able to rationalize anything, even their own gutless incompetence.'

He stood up. 'Right, now get back and tell the men the essentials. I don't think tonight is going to be as quiet or as easy as last night. Make sure all the men are on their toes.'

They got to their feet and started to move off, all except Blake. He squatted back on his heels and waited for the others to get out of earshot. Alan stood in silence looking down at the sergeant's face, that seemed, without its usual grin, almost that of a stranger. He felt sure that Blake wanted to speak to him about Leyland's death, and he was right.

'Why did he do it, sir? I saw the whole thing from down the road. It wasn't even as if he was trying to save Wallace, or help him, or . . . or anything. He didn't take cover or hurry. He just walked out and waited to be killed. I can't start to understand it. There was nothing wrong between him and Sally; if there had been I should have known. What could have made him do that, quite suddenly – what can have been in his mind?'

CHAPTER EIGHT

Gorman was not certain that waking up was worse than the illusory suspension of danger granted by sleep. The platoon had stood to four times during the night, and had twice opened fire on probing enemy patrols. Now he wondered what time it was, but made no move to look at his watch. To move would be to disturb and disperse the small pockets of warm air which had built up between his clothing and his skin. The inside of his mouth felt unclean, and he was tired. It was a tiredness he recognized, and he knew he would have to fight against continually from now on. It was a mixture of many things apart from weariness of the body: the sense of physical ill-being suffered more by junior commanders than by anyone else.

Company commanders and higher ranks had a buffer between themselves and immediate events. They might switch units or commit reserves, but apart from these actions they were debarred, by their position, from sharing the strains and pressures which were continually at work upon the platoon and section commanders who controlled the men actually in contact with the enemy.

The private soldier shared the tiredness brought on by

prolonged physical exertion and the constant pressures of fear and uncertainty, but when the firing stopped and the front was quiet, when someone else was the sentry, he could find time to relax and recuperate: he could abandon himself to rest, and recover to some degree the strength which had been drained away from him. When the need for his presence and action arose, there would be someone else – his platoon or section commander – to tell him so, and to decide what was required of him.

Gorman moved, arching his back against the sudden chilling round his shoulders and knees which had been in contact with the clay of his weapon-pit. If the enemy attacked now, one or other or perhaps both of the forward sections would be immediately in action without warning or time to prepare. Bridgman would be waiting in the darkness, or crawling towards those under fire so as to know at once if either post was too badly endangered to hold out on its own. He would be holding himself ready to call Gorman's section or platoon headquarters into a counter-attack if one of the vital forward positions was overrun. Every junior commander was permanently on the alert, and would have to remain so for the indefinite period during which they were in direct contact with the enemy. For days they would only cat-nap: section commanders sliding from weapon-pit to weapon-pit, platoon commanders from section to section. For them, no opportunity would come to sit back, if not content, at least satisfied that the best dispositions had been made, knowing that from now on they could do nothing but wait on events.

Gorman moved his right forefinger slightly until it touched metal not warmed by his hand, moved the upper part of his body, feeling it slide easily inside his clothes. He turned his head, grimacing to ease the stiffness in his neck; he brought his bent knees together and hunched himself forward till his shoulders were clear of the earth behind him, and he looked at his watch. Twenty minutes past three. He had dozed for fifteen minutes since changing the last sentry and handing over to Stan Summers, his lance-corporal.

He sat for what seemed a long time, his Sten gun resting in the V formed by his hunched body and the thin thighs which ran up to the bony knees he held together with his hand. He heard a muffled movement, a faint click, and a smothered sneeze from where the sentries, Summers and Woodley, strained their eyes into the night. He cocked his head and listened intently, his eyelids closed, screwed together by the intensity of his effort to hear. He could pick out nothing unusual, nothing that could not be explained. Not even the odd shot from a nervous sentry. Silence reigned over the entire battlefield – even the firing from the bridge had ceased. He wondered if they had at last been overrun, and the Germans now held the really vital objective. If they did, the whole operation was a failure and thousands of men would have been killed and wounded to no purpose.

He heard a sound behind him and looked up. Bridgman spoke in a clear whisper.

'How's it going, Frank?'

'All right, sir.' Gorman got to his feet and leaned over the back of his trench so that his head was only inches from Bridgman's.

'What's the general position, sir? You know, casualties in other units and that sort of thing.'

'I can't be very sure, Frank. You know what rumours are as well as I do, but compared to most of the division we've been bloody lucky. When the KOSBs came through a few hours ago and took up their new positions to the east of us, they were down to under two hundred men. They lost two companies in the last scrap when they were trying to disengage. I hear that 10th Para are down to two hundred and fifty, all ranks, and 156th to two hundred and seventy – and of course, they're still cut off from the division.'

'But what's happening in the town? Christ! There's five battalions there somewhere.'

Alan didn't answer at once. He was thinking about the men in the town. The 1st, 2nd and 3rd Battalions – the famous 1st Parachute Brigade who had taken the Bône airfields in North Africa, and had then fought as infantry with 1st Army until the German surrender. The same men who had taken the bridge over the Simeto in Sicily, and had been with the division at the naval landings in Taranto harbour. Two thousand strong, they had landed at Arnhem to take this other bridge and open the gate for the Allied victory march to Berlin. He was thinking of the names which were now more familiar to him than the names of his boyhood friends. Of Johnny Frost, the commanding officer of 2nd Battalion, or what was left of it, still clinging to the northern end of the bridge. Of Gerald Lathbury, the brigade commander, cut off somewhere in the centre of the town with the remnants of his other two battalions; the 11th Parachute Battalion, and the 2nd South Staffs, all of them cut to ribbons by the tanks of the two German Panzer divisions, and all still striving desperately to get to the bridge to reinforce Frost and his depleted handful of men.

'There's not much left of any of them, Frank. By tommorow, there'll be nothing, or what is left of them will be back with us trying to hold a small bridgehead this side of the Rhine, while 2nd Army ambles along, held up by the odd German company or a single field gun that has survived from the '14–'18 war.'

Gorman tried to see Bridgman's face, but it was too dark, and he could only guess at its bitter expression.

'Surely they can't all be as bad as that, sir? It's like saying that none of them have any guts at all.'

'Oh, there's individual guts there all right. But it's the guts of a whole unit that really counts. They'd probably dig in and fight a defensive battle well enough – at least, most of them would. It's in the attack, when they're advancing, that the trouble lies. They go to ground as soon as they're fired at, and wait for the guns and the armour to sort it out. And when they've hung around for half a day, they find an eight-hundred-strong battalion has been held up by a mediocre section of ten men commanded by a man with a bit more determination than average. This war was won on the day that Monty broke out at Falaise, but they'll fiddle and fart-arse about until this time next year before they're finished with it. And in an effort to avoid casualties they'll finish up with twice as many as they would have had if they'd really pulled their finger out.'

Bridgman's sibilant whispering ceased. Both men listened to a sudden burst of firing that came to them faintly from the direction of the bridge. It stopped as abruptly as it had started, and Bridgman spoke again.

'Sorry, Frank. I got carried away. I don't suppose they're half so lackadaisical as I pretend. Perhaps they'll be here tomorrow – or the day after.'

Bridgman turned and crawled away into the darkness,

heading for the road and track junction where Blake and his section were dug in.

Gorman went over and checked with Summers and Woodley, then made his way to the right of the section post. He found Corporal Armstrong awake, or so shallowly asleep that he was awake in an instant.

'It's nearly four o'clock, Ted. If you come with me now it'll save Summers coming over for you. Don't relieve Woodley – he was only posted at three o'clock. It's the chap in the next trench – Fraser, I think.'

The two NCOs crawled back, and when the relief had been posted Gorman sank down in the bottom of his own weapon-pit again. He wondered how long they could go on posting two sentries and an NCO throughout the nights. So far, this section had come out of it better than any in the company. He had had only one man killed and one wounded. Including Armstrong and Summers he still had nine men, ten counting himself. Even now, his was stronger than the average infantry section. He hoped their luck would last. He wriggled his shoulders and tried to settle back, but he had to turn and remove a stone from the dry clay before he could relax and snatch a few more minutes' sleep.

The company stood down an hour after dawn, and Bridgman went back to the house in the rear where Major Jordan had his headquarters. He was the first of the platoon commanders to arrive, and he looked into the room on the ground floor that was being used as a forward dressing station. The unique composition of the Independent Company granted it a section of Royal Corps signallers, the same complement as for a brigade, but its establishment did not include a medical officer. Each platoon had a man from the RAMC attached to it, and at company headquarters Sgt 'Doc' Barber bandaged, cleaned, and dispatched the casualties; the not too bad back to the line, the more severe to the casualty clearing-stations set up by the Field Ambulances.

Doc Barber looked very spruce in the fresh light of the morning, in contrast to the verandah Alan had crossed to enter the house, which was littered with bloodstained clothing and the weapons of the wounded. On the evening before, when he had looked in for a moment, he had seen Barber at work, stripped to the waist and with a rubber apron about him. The room had reeked of blood, and in the shaded light behind the blacked-out windows Alan had thought the scene might have been a ship's surgery in the days of Trafalgar.

He stepped across to the room on the other side of the hall where the CO was holding his order group. Ramsden and Brown had come in, and they exchanged nods.

Jordan had not shaved yet, and Alan was struck by the way in which the stubble on the CO's cheeks revealed his age as nothing else had ever done. He looked an old man; his face lined and haggard, his eyes dark and sunk far back in his head. He was a small man of quick decisive movements, but now his body seemed frail and shrunken under his camouflaged smock; his rough beard showed iron-grey and white in patches, and yet the dark, sunken eyes gleamed, and there was a quick smile on his face as, looking up, he offered a packet of cigarettes to his young subalterns.

'Well, what started as a copybook operation now seems to have gone slightly adrift.' Jordan's face made a good attempt at showing only wry humour, but Alan could glimpse the cynicism lurking deep in his eyes, and wondered what Jordan really thought about the chances of the division surviving, let alone securing and holding any more of its primary objectives. They would not be told now: they would hear nothing from the old man that might smack of defeatism; bad news would come from him quietly in a series of half-humorous understatements; his orders would be directed towards the next action of their unit as if the fate of the ten thousand men who had landed north of the Neder Rhine was a thing apart from the tight life of the Independent Company he commanded.

The KOSBs had taken up positions to their right, '. . . rather knocked about, I'm afraid, and without much transport.' The 10th and 156th Battalions of the 4th Brigade would be entering the divisional area when opportunity allowed, and would probably take a fresh line on the centre of the town. '. . . it may be a little difficult for them, as Brigadier Hackett's command has now been reduced to about five hundred all ranks. However, that's for the future.' Frost was still holding out at the bridge, but his casualties had been very high; Jordan did not elaborate about these forces at the bridge, or their chances of survival. The battalions in the centre of the town had been badly cut up by the tanks of the Panzer SS, but reinforced by 4th Brigade they might be able to reach 2nd Battalion. The Borders and some divisional troops still held the western flank.

The CO looked at each of his platoon commanders in turn and smiled tightly.

'We're going to stay here – I should imagine for today at least, and I should think we could expect a visit from the north, from the Teutonic gentlemen who have kept 4th Brigade so busy.' He turned to Alan. 'For you, nothing has changed since last night. You will fetch in the resupply at the map reference I gave you. The drop is due at 1400 hours. I'll see you again at midday in case there are any fresh developments by then.' He sat back in his chair and addressed the rest of his remarks to all of them.

'There's nothing really specific I can tell you. I know the question you all want to ask – what has happened to 2nd Army? I'm damned if I know. I suppose they've hit far more trouble than they expected. We can only hope for the best, and try to hang on to at least some sort of bridgehead till they arrive.'

Dismissed, the officers made their way back to their platoons, Ramsden going to the west of the house, to where his platoon lay along the edge of the grounds facing the open fields and the threat of rolling armour. Alan and Gordon Brown went the opposite way, and under the trees to the east where Gordon's platoon was dug in, they stopped and talked for a few minutes.

Gordon spoke, his eyes fixed on the single house held by part of his platoon, which lay in the northeast corner of the company position where their two sectors joined.

'Well, what do you think, Alan?'

'I think the same as you think. The division . . .' He paused for a moment and then went on. 'I was going to say that the division is going to be cut to pieces, but it already has been cut to pieces. I did a little sum last night. I reckon we've had at least five thousand casualties to date. The only battalion left with anything like operational strength is the Border Regiment, and they're all that stands between what's left of the division and whatever Jerry decides to throw against us from the Utrecht–Rotterdam–Amsterdam "box".'

Brown looked at Alan, his huge black handlebar moustache seeming to bristle with a sudden indignation which wiped away the rather stoical, resigned look his face had worn while he had stared at the house.

'Christ! I hadn't thought about the casualties cumulatively. I've simply taken them in a bit at a time as I heard them. Five thousand! Stuff me! That takes some thinking about. How long do you think we'll be able to hold on?'

'Till we fall below brigade strength, I should think. Alan looked at the backs of the men in the trenches on the slope. 'Longer perhaps – they're good troops. With most divisions, I should say it was all over now: we've read so many times about garrisons digging in to hold out to the last man and the last round, and the next thing you hear is that three-quarters to seven-eighths of them have been put in the bag.'

'There must come a time though, surely, when no useful purpose can be served by continuing to have men killed?'

Alan looked at Brown's set face, conscious of his friend's concern for the lives of those who were still fighting, and yet not feeling it himself in the same way.

'War *is* killing – if it's nothing else, it's that. I suppose a case can be made out for laying down arms if they can no longer be used to effect, but—'

Brown looked about the company position at the heads and shoulders of digging men; at the upthrown earth and the cut branches of trees and bushes which camouflaged the slit trenches. When he spoke he spoke more to himself than to Alan.

'No longer effective? But who can decide that? Who draws the line? No man is God, Alan. I don't think you appreciate the position that commanders sometimes find themselves in – to sit alone and weigh up all the possibilities, and to decide when men shall continue to be killed, and when the time has come to put a stop to it. At what stage do you think this should be stopped? Don't get me wrong – I'm not suggesting that the time is now, or even fairly soon – but at what point in a battle like this do you stop the killing because nothing can be gained by continuing it?'

'I can't answer that because I can't think about it.' Bridgman took a deep breath. 'I don't have that sort of strength. Once you start drawing fresh lines, there's no end to it, and they always creep nearer and nearer the easy way out. I find it simpler to consider that all aspects of soldiering, of fighting, are incidental to the main purpose – killing the enemy. Other things may go by the board, but all the time any opportunity remains to do that there should be no thought of surrender.'

'Is there any point in having hundreds of men killed for the problematical satisfaction of killing a few more of the enemy with the last rounds that are left?'

'It isn't a question of satisfaction. It's a question of continuing to do the only job you're still able to do.' Bridgman smiled suddenly, and for a moment his eyes showed an unusual warmth. 'The trouble with you is that you're a historian, Gordon. You spend too much time thinking of the individual. It's strange that you and I should each hold our particular viewpoints. As a Socialist, you should consider that the end justifies the means: as a Tory, I should be prepared to compromise.'

They both laughed, suddenly and together, and each moved as if to grip the other's arm.

Alan watched Brown as he stomped off, his powerful,

rugby-player's body looking enormous under his smock and equipment, his pleasantly ugly face scowling and frowning as he made his way down to the house. Alan realized with a sudden pang that it would matter very much to him if his friend were killed. He turned and made his way back to his command post between the two forward sections.

Going down the gentle slope, he passed through Gorman's section, twenty-five yards to the rear and midway between the two forward positions. The section-sergeant looked up. 'Any change of plan, sir?' he asked.

'No, nothing new, Frank, except that the CO seems to think that with 4th Brigade withdrawing through Woltheze, the Jerries are likely to come down at us from over the railway line – and he might very well be right. Keep your eyes skinned and cut all movement down to a minimum.'

Bridgman joined Bilting in the slit trench overlooking the road and the gardens of the big house which Murray and his composite section had occupied on the second night. The CO now considered it too far from the support of the company to be held.

Bilting was busy with a Tommy-cooker, and within a few minutes they were drinking weak tea from unwashed messtins. Bilting was a silent man, and difficult to know. Apart from the fact that he was a Londoner and came from south of the river, Alan knew very little about him. It was not lack of interest on his part, but rather because Bilting was not forthcoming about himself or his family, or what he had done before he joined the Army. His letters home, which Alan had to censor, were of the type common to most soldiers – dull, limited in scope, and short.

'Things are a bit dicey, aren't they, sir?'

Alan was surprised. If there had been any doubt in his mind about events, it was removed, for if things appeared sufficiently bad for Bilting to comment, the situation must have got beyond the point where only one's instinct knew that something was very wrong.

The man's broad, rather pale face was turned towards Alan, and Alan could not help but notice its complete lack of expression. He wondered what could have moved Bilting to join the Parachute Regiment. He smiled.

'Yes, Bilting. As you say, things are a bit dicey. But still, 2nd Army should be here any time now, and then with any luck most of our troubles should be over.'

Bilting took his eyes from Bridgman's face and looked towards the north. He drank the last of his tea and wiped his mouth with the cuff of his smock. He rubbed the inside of his mess-tin with a handful of earth and polished it with a piece of flannelette, his mouth pursed and his tongue sucking at his teeth.

'I don't reckon 2nd Army will make it, sir. And if they do, there won't be many of the Div to welcome them. Someone's stuffed the show up somewhere.'

He put the two parts of his mess-tin together and fitted them back into his haversack.

There was not much Alan could say, and while he was thinking of reassuring words, his runner spoke again, his voice as level and flat as ever.

'It doesn't matter what goes wrong now – they can't blame us for it, can they, sir?'

Bilting was looking at his platoon commander again, and Alan saw on the man's face the first expression of concern he had ever seen there. He cursed Gordon Brown. Any conversation with Gordon always left him with a stronger feeling of how much the individual mattered than he was happy with. He would miss Bilting if anything happened to him.

Alan was happy with men like his batman. Men whose uncomplicated loyalty to their unit was stronger than the fear of death, stronger than the always present urge to avoid the drudgery that is so much of a soldier's life; men whose pride was impersonal, embracing the group and not the individual. Perhaps few of them would have admitted it, but most of the company felt the ties of the tribe that lives a self-contained life of its own. They felt themselves as part of, and yet separate from, the rest of the division.

Alan felt a sudden lift, as if he had downed a large whisky.

'No, it won't be our fault, Bilting. Come along, we'll get some bandoliers of ammo from HQ and take them round to the sections.'

They walked together up the rise to do the job that would have been done by Jim Nash had he been there; and both wondered what had happened to the big sergeant, and whether or not he was still alive.

CHAPTER NINE

Bridgman and Bilting had left the platoon headquarters, to the rear and to the right of Gorman's section, and dropping off two hundred rounds of .303 with the sergeant, they slipped into the cover of the trees which shielded Ramsden's platoon. From there they made their way down the slope to the road and track junction at the bottom where Blake's men were dug in, watching the track to the north and the grounds of the house opposite them. Bilting distributed the ammunition while Bridgman and Blake talked together.

'What's the ammunition position like generally?' the sergeant asked.

'Murray checked at first light, and at that time we were fifty rounds up on what we started with. On top of that, we have eleven thousand rounds of MG 42 ammo, and eight of their guns to fire it through. We've nine or ten Schmeissers as well, but not much fodder for 'em.'

'And the rest of the company?'

Not as well off as we are, but at least they're living off the country. I don't think the old man has had to part with any yet – and I expect there'll be an inquest before he does.'

Alan looked round the position. It was well dug, and

the weapon-pits well sited. It was camouflaged, and from somewhere had come old doors and baulks of timber which, propped back over the trenches, would give some protection from air burst. Leaving Blake, he and Bilting walked across the ground with its sparse cover which separated them from Marsden and his men, waiting at the northeast corner with their right flank just short of the house which marked the beginning of Brown's position.

Bilting was a few paces in front of Bridgman, walking with his head down, bent under the weight of the full bandoliers which hung from his shoulders.

They had passed behind their own slit-trench when Bridgman spotted the German soldier standing on the far edge of the road by the gate to the grounds of the big house. He froze, flat-footed, his hands linked in front of his belt and the bandoliers dragging, a dead weight, on his arms. It seemed impossible that the German had seen none of the men in position twenty yards in front of him and, on the rising slope, only just above the level of his eyes.

Alan glanced down to his right where Marsden's Bren group were dug in. He saw Lance-Corporal Hudson and the Belfast gunner, Laverty, their heads turned to each other, and he caught the faint murmur of their voices. He felt his nostrils dilate under the pressure of the anger which surged up inside him. He threw a quick look towards Bilting. His runner had halted, the heel of one foot still off the ground, his head thrust forward like a pointer and his eyes fixed on the German. Time stood still as the solitary figure looked casually about him, and Bridgman's mind raced.

Blake's men might have the German covered from the road junction. Brown's men might have spotted him, and be waiting for the remainder of his patrol, which must be in the bushes of the big garden. It might be a reconnaissance patrol of only a few men: it might be a strong fighting patrol. He and Bilting had been caught with their trousers down – with their arms full, they could not get at their weapons quickly.

The German turned his head and spoke over his shoulder. Two more figures rose from the cover of the garden and joined him at the gate. One was an NCO.

Bridgman swore under his breath and his eyes stole again to the Bren group. Laverty was grinning – and then, as if under the compulsion of the platoon commander's will, he glanced in Alan's direction. Their eyes locked. Alan jerked his head a fraction towards the road. He saw Laverty's ears move back as the skin tightened on his face, and the quick, darting search of his eyes as they swung from Alan to Bilting, and onward. He saw him turn his head and shoulders – gently – his right hand drifting towards the Bren, his left closing on Hudson's arm. Bridgman looked up at the Germans.

The NCO spotted him. For that millionth of a second that can last an eternity they stared into each other's eyes.

Alan dropped flat on the earth, his arms swinging free of the bandoliers, his head still raised and his gaze still on the enemy: his Sten was off his shoulder and moving in front of his body. The German NCO's arms swung out to attract the attention of the men on each side of him, and he opened his mouth to shout.

The butt of Alan's Sten was still inches from his shoulder when Laverty fired. The NCO and one of the German soldiers went down where they stood. Bridgman shot the other as he passed through the gate.

The man's back arched, and he stepped backwards slowly,

groping with his feet like a man in pitch darkness. He half turned, and one hand reached out for the gatepost. Inches short of its support the fingers closed and his body lurched sideways, twisting as it fell. His face thudded against the post and dragged down its length to the ground. Bridgman found himself thinking of the splinters.

Laverty was firing bursts into the bushes and trees, and one of Brown's sections opened up from the house. During a pause in the firing, Alan heard his friend's voice bellowing to his gunners to raise their fire so that it searched the ground running back to the railway embankment. Alan looked to his right. Bilting was spreadeagled on the earth, his rifle in his shoulder, firing deliberate, well-spaced shots at the densest patches of cover.

Alan thought quickly. There might be any number of Germans still in the grounds, there might be none except the casualties. The whole situation was much too close. He would have to find out. The CO might oppose an immediate reconnaissance. Alan decided not to ask him.

He took two men from each of the sections and had a few quick words with Brown. Then they moved down the slope, across the road, and lay extended behind the wired edge which fronted the big garden. Bridgman signalled with his arm for covering fire, and he heard Gorman's section open up from high up on the slope, firing over his head to the bushes and foliage in front of him, while from the right, Brown's men were firing from their vantage-point in the house at the farther cover towards the railway.

He waved for the cease fire, and in the sudden silence after the shouted orders he called to the patrol. They were on their feet, over the wire, and through the hedge almost as one man, Murray racing for the cover of the house, three men leaping and darting round obstacles behind him. Alan moved to the right where trees interlarded the bushes. He had gone only ten yards when he saw Germans, and he just had time to stop two of his men from opening fire.

The Germans were crouched together as if to find comfort in numbers. There were five of them: two badly wounded, one slightly, and two unhurt. They surrendered with a relief that was pathetic.

Bridgman went back to the gate and waved to his platoon, and when he was sure of their attention he called the Germans forward. They came out, two of them carrying one, and the slightly wounded supporting another. He saw them start across the road before turning back to his men.

They had already started to search the bushes and close vegetation of the garden. He took them to the north, towards the railway, covered by Murray and his men from the house. They found no live enemy between the company position and the embankment.

Behind the cover of the high mound, Bridgman halted his men and sat down to think. To look over its edge was inviting trouble but he had to know what lay on the other side. He called to Bilting, and together they crawled up the steep, grass-covered earth-work. Just below the brink, Bridgman motioned to Bilting to wait, and crawling on a few more yards he raised his head cautiously, partially screened from sight by huge thistle. Open fields and woods stretched out in all directions in front of him. He looked through his glasses, but could see no sign of friend or enemy, although to the west, in or behind a thick wood, he could hear firing. He wondered what lay out of his sight in the foreground hidden by the embankment. He decided to find out.

He had got no farther than the first railway line, and had just started to ease his body across it, when he heard the whine of the bullet over his head. The report of the rifle which had fired it reached him just as another bullet hit a metal rail and ricocheted high in the air, its nasal scream filling his ears as he scrambled to his feet and turned back. He saw Bilting's anxious face raised above the level of the embankment, and then the third bullet caught him off balance before he was quite on his feet. He went down in a heap and at once started to roll towards the reverse slope. He saw Bilting clamber to the top of the embankment and start to run in his direction. He shouted to his batman to get back, but even as he shouted Bilting half-jumped in the air, and as he landed slipped on the grass rim. The two men rolled down the slope within inches of one another.

At the bottom, each sat up and looked at the other, and at the faces of the remaining four men.

'Well,' asked Bridgman, 'are you hit?'

Bilting didn't speak, but he nodded and looked up at the trees.

'Where?'

Bilting swallowed and then blushed. Bridgman's control slipped for a moment, and he gaped at Bilting – it was incredible to see a man blushing, in the middle of a war. He repeated his question.

'Where?'

Bilting continued to gaze at the treetops as he muttered an unintelligible reply.

Bridgman became angry. 'For Christ's sake, man – where have you been hit?'

'In the arse.'

Everyone laughed except Bilting. He turned to Bridgman. And where've you been hit, sir?'

Bridgman stopped laughing and tried to remember.

'I don't know. It must be somewhere in my shoulders or back. I can't feel anything now, but I felt a bloody great wrench at the time – it threw me over.'

In fact Alan was untouched. The bullet had entered his haversack and ploughed its way through his mess-tin and forty-eight-hour pack before coming out on the far side.

A protesting Bilting was laid face downwards on the ground and his trousers were taken down. One of the soldiers said with simulated concern, 'You really ought to take Yeast-Vite, mate, your blood's out of order – there's pimples all over your arse.'

Bilting swore, blushing angrily again when Bridgman laughed aloud.

'Bilting, you've set a record. You've got four holes from one bullet. It's gone in one cheek, out in the middle, into the next, and out on the far side.'

They bandaged him roughly and he limped back with them to the platoon position. The others rejoined their sections, and an embarrassed Bilting accompanied Bridgman to company headquarters.

Doc Barber took most wounds seriously, but he laughed when Bilting muttered out his story.

CHAPTER TEN

Bridgman realized that any number of Germans might be hidden behind the concealing bluff of the embankment. He sought out Gordon Brown, and together they made a complex and close-woven fire plan.

His own platoon was down from fifty-three to forty men: Brown's was in even worse shape after being caught on the Poles' LZ on the previous day.

The platoon had the four Brens they had started with, and another they had picked up on the previous evening; they had eight captured German Spandaus and about fifteen hundred rounds for each; nearly half of the men were armed with Sten guns, and the riflemen had captured Schmeissers as alternative weapons; the Piats were with Blake, for the only possible way open for tanks lay beyond his position.

Alan was certain that Tim Jordan was right and that, true to form, the Germans would exert immediate pressure, tightening their grip and launching probing attacks of company strength or more. The Germans would flow into the gap left by 4th Brigade as they fell back to join the division, and that gap was immediately in front of his platoon.

At 10.30 and without warning the Germans opened up

with a Spandau from high up in the big house. They hit two of Marsden's men to the right of his Bren group, and they laced the house held by one of Brown's sections.

Gorman acted in accordance with the prearranged fire plan, and his reply was instantaneous and devastating. Four machine guns opened fire on the tall building and every shot passed over the heads of Bridgman and Marsden's Bren group. The gun combed the tiled roof and searched the dark recesses of the rooms behind the paneless windows; they stabbed at the buildings round the house, their bullets piercing the wood and plasterboard of sheds like machine needles through cloth. The remainder of the platoon crouched in their weapon-pits, holding their fire.

Gorman's voice cracked an order, high and clear, the two syllables ringing like trumpet notes through the roar and chatter of the guns, and the whole position was suddenly still in the shock of silence: the men frozen in expectancy, their knuckles white on their guns, and the skin tight on their faces.

The German machine-gun did not fire again, and in his command-post Bridgman felt confident that the enemy would not attempt to reoccupy the house in the face of fire which by its very volume would neutralize any movement in the building.

From the corner of an eye, Alan glimpsed Brogan slip into the slit trench which held the two wounded men. And then the Germans were coming in darting rushes, only occasionally glimpsed through the trees clustered at the far end of the grounds close to the embankment. The platoon's riflemen took snap shots at the fast-moving grey targets, and Laverty fired slow bursts at where the enemy seemed to have congregated behind cover which protected them only from view. Alan looked to his right at Marsden's depleted section. He could see the butt of the Bren jammed in Laverty's shoulder, and the Belfast man's face gleaming with sweat and excitement.

A Bren fired from Gordon Brown's position, and spaced out in the bursts was the odd round of tracer. It showed Bridgman that the gun was being fired diagonally across his front, towards the back of the big house. Either the gunner or Brown was letting him know that the Germans were concentrating behind the protection of the house.

He could hear orders being shouted in German.

He waited for a lull in the fire and then called back to Murray to send down O'Neill and another man. While he waited for them to join him he tried to build up a picture of how the German attack might develop. He surmised there was something like a company in front of him, but it might only be a scratch one and not up to strength. This meant anything up to and possibly above a hundred and fifty men. The Spandau the Germans had put in the big house had been silenced, and he wondered what other plans the enemy had for covering fire. He could see very little movement now in the ground in front of him, but he imagined that a considerable body of men lay behind the building. He thought this force would probably break from cover to their right, hitting his left flank on the road and track junction. He was glad Blake's section was in that position.

He looked round as two men squeezed into the trench beside him. He spoke quickly: there might be very little time.

'O'Neill, try to pick up what you can. There's enough shouting going on. You might hear something useful.' He turned to the second man. 'Get back to Sergeant Murray and tell him to brigade mortars on the lawn behind Company HQ. He'll have to fire them bloody nearly vertically – the range can't be more than a hundred yards. Tell him to watch his ammo – there isn't much left.'

The man clambered out behind him, and Alan turned to O'Neill.

'Well, what do you make of it? Have you heard anything that means anything?'

The German Jew pursed his lips, and Alan knew he was going to be precise. He sometimes thought that O'Neill and his fellows were far more Teutonic than Semitic.

'It's hard to say, sir, but there are more than three platoons. More than a company, I would say. But I do not know how many men. One of them shouted something about mortars. If the next man who shouted was replying, then the first man was a company commander, and his unit is of the Waffen SS.'

Bridgman let out his breath in a long sigh. If what O'Neill guessed were true then the attack, when it came, would be pushed home with a desperate determination. He had met the Waffen SS before. He looked at O'Neill. The man's dark face was still, the lips turned down and the eyes slitted, and yet he radiated a suppressed delighted excitement. No matter what the outcome might be, O'Neill was looking forward to what was to come.

Both side's mortars opened fire within seconds of each other, and at first it was difficult to distinguish them, but Bridgman soon picked out the regular whine of the German multiple-mortars, the Moaning Minnies. The German bombs burst in the trees behind him and on the roof of company headquarters and he saw the billowing earth where their own HE was landing, too far back, behind where he thought the bulk of the Germans were concealed. Then the bursts were nearer, and he knew Murray had a good observation post and had shortened his range. The barrels of his mortars must be nearly upright.

The mortaring and counter-mortaring went on for some minutes. Murray's bombs were fired at intervals; the German fire was almost continuous and their aim improved until their bombs were bursting in the platoon position. Then the enemy fire stopped abruptly and Bridgman could see the heads of his men emerging at once from their slit trenches as they readied themselves to repulse the attack which must follow the last of the enemy bombs.

The Germans came within seconds of the last explosion. A single, sharp order rang out, and then the grounds of the house were alive with grey-uniformed figures advancing, and the air was filled with the screamed 'Sieg Heils' of the SS as they advanced against the equivalent of nearly forty machine-guns, for at that range the Stens and Schmeissers of the waiting men would be as deadly, if not more so, than the heavier, more difficult to handle Brens and Spandaus.

Alan waited until the SS were ten yards short of the farthest cattle-fence, and had begun firing from the hip as they came on.

He knew what to expect after his shouted order, yet no amount of anticipation could have prepared him for the shock, the incredible roar which burst about his head as every gun in the position opened up together.

The advancing Germans seemed to halt suddenly, as if they had come up against something solid, and then they were moving forward again, their 'Sieg Heils' sounding a different note, shriller and more disjointed.

Alan had to resist a temptation to fire himself; he knew that once committed as an individual the total absorption in conflict would cut him off from the battle as a whole.

One German section tried for the open gate in front of Laverty, and scattered like leaves in a sudden gust as the Bren gunner emptied a magazine into their bunched rush. All along the length of the cattle fence the German soldiers were struggling and clambering through to the road. Behind them, others were throwing stick grenades high in the air; one landed a few feet in front of Bridgman's trench, and he grabbed O'Neill and pulled him down below the rough parapet until it exploded and the hot blast of its eruption passed over their heads.

When he looked up again he saw that groups of the enemy had got on to the road, but even the Waffen SS could not face the terrible concentration of fire that was being poured at them and as they came on to the second fence Alan saw that the impetus had gone from the attack – they were perceptibly wavering.

A few managed to clamber over, and now Alan joined in the fight as the SS men got close enough for him to see the despair on their faces. And then the survivors were running back, and their follow-up force was melting into the cover of the trees and the sanctuary of the embankment.

O'Neill grabbed Alan's shoulder and pointed to the left. Following the direction of the extended arm what Alan saw brought him upright, the upper part of his body well above the top of the weapon-pit. Blake's position was a confused mass of struggling, leaping figures. The Germans had got through to him, and hand-to-hand fighting was going on in the slit-trenches and the bushes round them.

Alan leaped out of the weapon-pit and felt O'Neill follow him. He turned his head towards Gorman's section, and saw them already clambering out of their slit-trenches. The sergeant was on his feet and looking towards the platoon commander. Alan had started to move up to join them for the counter-attack when he spotted movement in the trees on the western edge of the company area, above and behind Blake. He shouted to Gorman to get his men back in their trenches, and then, with O'Neill at his heels he was running diagonally across the slope to join Phil Ramsden as he showed at the head of two of his sections in a flat run down the slope to Blake said. Then, in a rush, they were all in among the fighting men.

Alan had his Sten in his left hand but he made no attempt to use it: the confusion was too great for automatic fire. Instead he had drawn his pistol, and seeing a German climbing up from a slit-trench, his jackboots pressing down on the crumpled body of a parachutist, Alan jammed his automatic into the man's face and pulled the trigger. Turning away, he nearly fell into another trench, the one that held Blake's Bren group. He saw Corporal Heibling lying backwards over the parados, his arms flung out and his helmet half twisted off his head; his lids were still open but his eyeballs were already sunk in death. In front of his body the gunner crouched, still firing into the bushes. Alan could not tell who it was, for from the eyebrows down he could see nothing but blood, the man's open mouth showing like a dark pool in a red desert.

There were more besmocked figures than grey now, and the firing had nearly ceased. Alan saw that Ramsden was accepting the surrender of a small group of enemy, and he saw O'Neill standing in exactly the same position in which he had first halted on the outskirts of the fighting. His Sten was in his shoulder and he was taking carefully-aimed shots at any German sufficiently detached from the struggling mass. Alan had just decided that O'Neill's method was more constructive than his own when he saw the fair, unhelmeted head of a prostrate German soldier move slightly, and the man's two hands close more firmly round his Schmeisser. The soldier lay only a few feet from where Bridgman stood, but the SS man's head was turned away from him, and the sub-machine gun he was easing forward was intended for another target than the watching officer. Alan took two quick paces forward and shot the man in the back of the head, the muzzle of his automatic only an inch from the German's hair. It was the last shot of the brief action.

Alan found Blake, and together they had a word with Ramsden. Blake was down to four men and it was essential he should be relieved. Ramsden took over the post temporarily, and Bridgman and Blake moved back with the remnants of the section.

As they arrived at Frank Gorman's position, Alan looked beyond it to Company HQ. He saw Tim Jordan standing up against the front wall of the house with the sergeant-major at his elbow; lying extended on each side of them were the remainder of the men of company headquarters, their weapons in front of them and their bayonets fixed. Alan smiled as he called Gorman's men out and replaced them with Blake and his four unwounded men: Tim Jordan was taking no chances – he had been ready to take in an immediate counter-attack himself had the situation developed badly or got out of hand. Alan signalled a brief thumbs-up to the CO before leading the reserve sections down the slope to the crossroads.

When Gorman had taken over the position, Ramsden took one of his sections and rejoined the rest of his platoon. He left the other with Alan to move back the wounded.

Doc Barber came down himself to superintend the movement, and Alan followed him round as he sorted the living from the dead. Corporal Heibling and Stewart, a German Jew born in Berlin, had fought their last fight and were put on the same stretcher to be buried behind company headquarters. Tony Hardy, the Bren gunner, walked back on his own, the drying blood forming a corrugated mask on his face. Jennings they handled gently: he had been shot in the groin and the right thigh; his femur was shattered and the least movement had him screaming and sobbing with pain. They found Scruffy Butcher behind a bush, the contents of his haversack strewn round him; there was a cigarette between his lips, and he was trying rather ineffectively to strike a match with one hand. He held up the other as Bridgman and Doc Barber approached. The forefinger of his left hand was missing down to the second joint, and the top of the one next to it was hanging by a shred of skin. He looked pale under his dirt, but he managed to grin as they came up to him.

'I've got a blighty, sir, but you'll have to tell me 'ow to get there.'

Alan Bridgman smiled as he walked on, but Doc Barber wasn't amused. 'I can't tell you how to get to blighty,' he said, 'but Company HQ is in the house, and you can bloody well walk there.'

Unabashed, Butcher shambled off up the slope, his rifle and haversack trailing from his undamaged hand.

The German wounded were a bigger problem, for there were sixteen of them in the position and on the road in front of it. It took half an hour to get them back, and to carry the enemy dead across the road and dump them over the fence. Bridgman hoped that if the platoon were to stay any length of time in the position, the wind would blow continually from the south.

Tim Jordan sent a patrol under the sergeant-major into the grounds of the big house. They were gone for about twenty minutes, and during that time the waiting company heard five or six single shots at irregular intervals. When the patrol returned it brought more German wounded with it, and two boys who could have been no more than sixteen years old: these were physically unhurt, but the sergeant-major had found them cowering in the bushes, their faces twitching and their limbs jerking with shock. No one bothered to ask what the shots had been fired at.

Bridgman looked at his watch. The morning had gone and the main task of the day lay ahead of him.

CHAPTER ELEVEN

Bridgman stood on the top of a tower at the western edge of the allotments which were to be the new supply dropping-zone. Corporal Armstrong and Fraser crouched over the Eureka behind the protection of the three-foot-high brick and stone balustrade. O'Neill knelt at the top of the spiral staircase.

From where he stood, Alan could see the remainder of Gorman's section in position round the tower. Murray and headquarter section lined a wood to the northwest of the allotments, and Blake straddled the road with a force made up of the remnants of his own section and Marsden's. Farther away, on the other side of the allotments, he could see the men from the RASC Recovery Company waiting in readiness to carry out their task of retrieving the supplies and assembling them at the divisional dump.

He was worried about what might lie farther back in the wood beyond the point where Murray's men lay in the shallow, grave-like slits they had scratched for themselves with their short entrenching tools. He checked the Eureka and followed by O'Neill, went down the spiral staircase and along the western fringe of the allotments to the edge of the wood.

Fraser peered over the balustrade at the officer's retreating back. Armstrong called to him sharply.

'Get back here, you bloody idiot. Your head's stuck up there like a target at a shooting gallery.'

Fraser grunted and, squatting down, lit a cigarette. As an afterthought he offered one to the corporal and gave him a light from his own. He sat back against the outside wall of the tower and watched Armstrong as he raised the earpiece to his head. Armstrong's eyes were as red-rimmed as an albino's, his grubby cheeks were sunken, and the points of his shoulders were inclined inward by that extra fraction which to an observant eye denotes imminent physical exhaustion. Fraser wondered whether his own appearance was at all like that of the corporal.

Armstrong looked up at Fraser.

'I can't hear a thing,' he said, 'if they're going to be on time they should be triggering by now.'

Fraser shrugged and looked at the sky to the south.

'I don't think it matters very much,' he said. 'The whole show's cocked up anyhow. Everything depended on speed and surprise, and both have gone by the board. If 2nd Army does get here, and manages to bridge within our perimeter, they'll be in no better position, really. They'll be sealed off on this side of the river instead of on the other, that's all — there'll be no lightning armoured thrust across the great German plain.' Armstrong lowered the earpiece and looked at his companion. He didn't understand Fraser any more than he did the other men in the company who were of the same social background and upbringing. He knew Fraser had been at Cambridge, and had come down after his first year to join up. He had had the opportunity of going to an OCTU, but had refused, preferring to remain with the Independent Company as a private soldier. Roy Fraser, Tony Hardy, and the other public school and university men had all refused stripes at some stage in their soldiering, and yet any one of them could have become an officer if he had chosen to. They had an air of cynicism that was deceptive; at least, it had deceived Armstrong for a long time. He had discovered that beneath their cynical attitude and pretence that nothing was really worthwhile, they were good soldiers, and were to be relied upon in an emergency. He wondered why they considered the contrived artifice of their manner to be necessary.

Armstrong raised the earpiece again, but still hearing nothing he lowered it and looked back at Fraser. Fraser was reclining easily, managing somehow to look as relaxed as if he were on a lawn at his home, lightly dressed in flannels and an open-neck shirt instead of the levelling uniform and smock. Corporal Armstrong was proud of being in the Parachute Regiment, and even prouder of being in Major Jordan's company, and his greengrocer father was proud of him and for him, and so was his mother. He couldn't understand the attitude of these men who deprecated everything they or their unit did. He knew his own attitude was the more honest one, but he was not sure whether or not it made him a better man. He had been in action with Fraser, Hardy, and the others many times, and he knew he would have to be very good indeed to be better than they were.

Fraser was one of those who had thrown his steel helmet away on landing, and had replaced it with his red beret covered by a camouflaged veil. Now, as he took this off and ruffled his fair hair, his good-looking face untroubled and disdainful, Armstrong was filled suddenly with a love-hate emotion which disturbed him and sent him frowning and muttering back to the Eureka.

If only the triggering would start, he would get the exhilarating and omnipotent feeling he always experienced when bringing in aircraft or gliders. Perhaps the others felt the same way, felt the same power that he did when, with the aid of the small, compact box, he summoned the great planes and gliders out of the sky and on to their objective.

'I shouldn't worry too much about that little box of tricks, if I were you.' Fraser's voice carried the trace of half-contemptuous amusement which angered Armstrong more than anything else. 'If I'm not very much mistaken, here they come now.'

Armstrong pulled away from the obscuring brickwork of the tower's centrepiece and looked back over his shoulder. At first, he failed to pick out the aircraft and then he saw them as faint specks in the clear sky far to the south. He looked at his watch – the time was right – it was unlikely that they were enemy fighters. He knelt, his head pounding with apprehension. What had gone wrong? He checked and rechecked the erection and frequency settings of the Eureka and found no fault, but he had no way of being absolutely certain that his set was transmitting. The highly secret instruments were serviced and charged by the RAF; the job of the Independent Company was only to land and operate them.

Armstrong stood up and looked over the parapet towards the wood. He was looking for Bridgman although he knew it was too late for anything to be done: the aircraft would be overhead long before another set could be brought into operation. He failed to see his platoon commander and turned to join Fraser, now also on his feet, and together they watched the first planes cross the Rhine, growing bigger every second as they flew at between five and six hundred feet, straight through the flak which was beginning to burst about them.

And now the first planes were overhead, and Bridgman and O'Neill were pounding up the last stone steps of the staircase to join the watching pair.

'They didn't trigger.'

Armstrong jerked the words out defensively, as if it might be his fault that the aircraft were continuing on to the north, beyond the area still held by the division.

Bridgman glanced quickly at the set. So far as he was able to judge it was in order, and the frequency the right one. He swore aloud.

On the allotments, Gorman had lit smoke canisters, and other members of his section were waving the yellow recognition signals. Some of the men were on their feet, waving their weapons and steel helmets in an effort to attract the attention of the pilots. On the tower, the four men watched with sinking hearts as the planes flew straight and steady through the bursting flak which had increased till it seemed to the watchers that nothing could live through it. Plane after plane peeled off, one or two engines on fire, and crashed in the open fields to the north or, turning back, came down in or beyond the Rhine.

One pilot spotted the signals, although a little late. A few containers dropped from his aircraft and floated down towards the extreme edge of the dropping-zone, and the plane swung away before turning to make another run. As it turned, its starboard engine caught fire, and under the fascinated gaze of the men on the ground the aircraft completed a one hundred and eighty degree turn and came in again, much lower, no more than three hundred feet above the watchers' heads. This time the containers came out directly above the allotments, and the men on the tower could see clearly the strained faces of the men from the RASC Delivery Company as they pushed out the panniers of supplies. And then one wing was gone, and the plane crashed: a blazing wreck, far out of the sight of the spellbound watchers in the houses and trenches below.

'Stuff me,' Armstrong breathed, 'that took some guts.' He looked round him. The other three were all looking towards the trees behind which the plane had crashed. O'Neill's face was expressionless but his eyes shone with approbation. Bridgman was smiling quietly, his head nodding slowly up and down. Fraser had for a moment been shaken out of his affected composure: his face was white, his eyes wider than usual, and his lips were apart.

The last of the planes made its run, and dropped its supplies into the hands of the Germans in the north. Bridgman turned to Armstrong, his lips pulled back tight against his teeth.

'For all the good that supply-drop did, they might as well have stayed at home and saved some valuable lives. Whatever happens, we'll get that Eureka checked by the RAF when we get back. I shall be very interested to know where the fault lies. Get it packed up – I'll give you a shout when to come down.'

'When we get back!' Fraser looked at Armstrong as Bridgman and O'Neill disappeared down the stairs. 'That's what I call optimism. Do you think he really imagines we're going to get back?'

Before Armstrong had a chance to answer, a bullet struck

the brickwork between them, and they both ducked behind the cover of the balustrade.

Armstrong collapsed the telescopic aerial and grinned wryly to himself. The fascination of watching the supply drop had made them all oblivious to danger. Earlier, he had reproved Fraser for showing his head, and yet for long minutes the whole four of them had stood head and shoulders above the brickwork. He supposed that, like themselves, the Germans had had eyes only for the low-flying aircraft.

They completed the packing of the set, and had just lit cigarettes when they heard the whine of a shell as it passed to one side of the tower. Their eyes met, and then Fraser inhaled deeply and looked away as if uninterested in the decision Armstrong had to make. The corporal thought quickly. They had no duty to perform in the tower. Bridgman had left them there merely because they were under cover and out of the way, and because he had no need of them until the platoon moved back to the company area. The Germans had obviously spotted them, and probably thought the tower was being used as an artillery observation post. It might well become very unhealthy for them.

'Come on. Let's get out of here.'

Bridgman must have heard the whine of the first shell, but failed to register it as a threat to any particular part of his platoon. It was just one more sound to be added to the incessant crackle of small-arms' fire and the roar of bursting mortar bombs and shells that never quite stopped, but rose and fell around the fringes of the tightening divisional perimeter; sometimes holding out the promise that it would die out altogether, and at other times rising to a pitch of unbelievable intensity until it became necessary to shut off one part of the mind as a protection against the build-up of sound which attacked and made raw every nerve in the body.

He had collected headquarter section from the edge of the wood, and as he started to move back he signalled to Gorman to close his section behind Blake on the road. He was fifty yards short of the tower when the first 88-mm shell hit it, high up, just below the balustrade. Another blew a hole half-way down its sheer side.

Bridgman shouted a quick order to Murray to get his section to the RV. He called to Corporal McEwan and O'Neill and together they ran towards the tower. As it was hit for the third time, he saw a figure stagger out from the door at its base. He recognized Fraser, and saw blood on his face and on the back of his two hands where he held them high up by his shoulders, one grasping the sling of his rifle, the other a German Schmeisser.

While still ten yards short of where Fraser stood shaking his head, Alan heard a sudden burst of firing from beyond the RV where Blake and his men lay on each side of the road, denying German infiltration between two companies of the Border Regiment.

Alan slowed his stride. 'O'Neill,' he jerked over his shoulder, 'get Fraser back to the RV. McEwan, get there and see what's happened to Armstrong.' He broke into a run, again, and shouted back to the corporal. 'Whatever else you do, collect the Eureka.' McEwan raised his free hand in recognition and headed for the door of the tower. Alan kept on running to where he could hear Blake and his men engaging the enemy.

McEwan slid through the open door and looked quickly round. It was all right for Bridgman – he was heading away from the tower, and it was the tower that was being shelled. There was a pile of rubble just past the door, and the corporal climbed over it. He could see a gaping hole in the wall half-way up the stairs, and through it the blue sky and the tops of trees. That was life – this was death. It was like standing in an open tomb waiting for the lid to be sealed down. He could hear his own breathing sounding high above the settling brickwork on the stairs and the noise of firing muffled by the tower's walls. He could see one boot and part of a gaiter sticking out from the mound of bricks and plaster on the stairs and looking above it he could see a small patch of camouflage smock and then more bricks and part of a steel helmet.

He climbed up warily, one hand extended. He gripped the gaiter. It felt dead. He rested one hand on the rubble and reached out for the square of camouflaged cloth. The fourth shell hit the tower at its highest point, and clouds of dust and splinters of brick rained down on to his back. He snatched his hand away as if it had been burned.

At the open door he paused long enough to gulp great lungfuls of air which quietened the heaving of his chest and soothed the fluttering of his mind, and then he was running hard for the RV.

Bridgman threw himself down beside Blake. 'I'm not quite sure what the position is,' the sergeant said. 'It's either a small patrol, or just snipers infiltrating. I think we got a couple of them, but they nailed Bert Taylor before we spotted 'em. I reckon we can disengage all right, it's just a question of sliding back one at a time till we're round the bend. They're not going to follow up – there's not enough of them.'

'Right – then let's get moving. I'll take Marsden's chaps – you bring your own as soon as we're out of sight.'

Presently, while he waited for Blake to join him, Alan gave his orders for the march back to the company area. Then he called Corporal McEwan over.

'What happened to Armstrong?'

'He was dead, sir. There was nothing I could do.'

'And the Eureka?'

McEwan hesitated for a moment. 'I blew it, sir.'

'Why? I told you I wanted it. It wasn't just a matter of recovering the set. There was something wrong with it, and I wanted to find out what it was.'

McEwan's eyes slid from Bridgman's face. 'I didn't know that, sir. The set was smashed. There was a great chunk of brickwork on top of it. There seemed no point in carting it around.'

'All right – join your section.'

Alan looked back to where he could see the last of Blake's men slipping through the bushes. He was angry, but he was trying to be fair. There was no point in carrying unnecessary equipment and increasing the possibility of a secret Eureka being captured by the Germans; but the Independent Company had never lost a Eureka set yet. Still, perhaps McEwan's action had been the best one in the circumstances.

The march back across the divisional perimeter gave all of them an uncanny feeling that their platoon represented the only real life inside the German ring. The occasional head cautiously raised from a slit trench, or peering from the window of a house, to eye them curiously as they plodded by, seemed to have no substance.

They came into the company area from the south, and

were told that their positions were under fairly accurate fire from snipers, and that it was going to be difficult to relieve the sections from the other two platoons who were holding them. They accomplished the relief in short, half-section dashes, but not without having two men wounded, one from their own platoon as he went down the slope, and one from Ramsden's as he came up.

CHAPTER TWELVE

Ted Armstrong regained consciousness in fits and starts. First, half his mind awoke to a woolly world in which only one thing stood out clearly. A magazine or grenade, part of his equipment or perhaps his Sten, was digging into his shoulder. The pain was sharp and continuous, and when he tried to ease it he found himself trapped by unexplained pressures. He supposed he was jammed in the corner of his slit trench. His left arm and both his legs became focal points of pain, and yet remained in some way detached from him as if they were artificial extensions of his body: he suspected they had become cramped and gone to sleep. It was the sharp-angled, gritty pressure of the bricks against his face which brought the second half of his mind to life, and then, suddenly, he knew where he was and what had happened.

He opened his eyes: a fine dust ran into one of them and forced him to close it. The other one did not help him very much at first. He could see broken lines, and patches of darkness which varied from dove grey to the jet blackness of a closed cellar, and for a while he pondered the shades of sombre colouring: to his right there was light and the movement of air, and although he could see only from the corner of his eye, it seemed like the wind of promise blowing the light of hope into his darkness.

He knew now that what he had imagined was the side of a slit trench pressing against his back was in fact weight bearing down on him. A sense of claustrophobia for a moment fragmented his thoughts and sent them in scattered search for an immediate solution, but he realized the danger inherent in panic thinking; he must discipline the fear which had poured into him as an accompaniment to the knowledge that he might be trapped.

Concentrating on each limb in turn, he made cautious experiments. His two legs were either broken or badly injured in some other way; any attempt to move them built up pain in them which swept out in rolling waves up the length of his body. His left arm was pinned at the wrist, but he could move the elbow, although this hurt the shoulder which was throbbing continuously. It was damp, and when he raised the elbow as high as it would go he felt warm blood trickle under his armpit and down his ribs. But his right arm was comparatively free and apparently uninjured. Without moving any other part of his body, he started to wriggle it gently. From the elbow down it seemed completely free, but between the elbow and his shoulder was a weight of brick rubble which prevented him from raising it.

He twisted his arm till it lay outside, then bent it, reaching up and towards his body with his fingers. He touched bricks and began to pull at them; the smaller pieces came away at once and he jerked them away with short flicking movements of the wrist. Where two or three whole bricks were joined together he had to push and roll them to one side, and it was some time before his arm was free up to the shoulder. He tired quickly and rested often, but at last he was pulling at the rubble on his neck and shoulders. He pushed the loose plaster away from his face and turned his head to the right; he looked up the stairs to the gaping hole in the side of the tower through which an 88-mm shell had come. He could just see the tops of some trees and the fleece-flecked sky to the north where Dakotas and Stirlings had dropped their loads of ammunition and food into the waiting hands of the Germans, and made him think of the Eureka and then of Fraser. He tried to call out to his companion. The cracking noise which came from his mouth frightened him, and for a moment he felt his mind begin to break up again. He spat and rolled the dust from his mouth with his tongue. He chewed at his cheeks to make saliva, and he licked his lips. When he called again his voice was more like he remembered it, but it rang weakly in the tower, throwing faint despairing echoes back at him from the rounded walls, and there was no other reply.

He groped down the right side of his body, tugging and snatching at the broken bricks. Pressing down on his hip he could feel a mass much larger than the rest, and it was only with difficulty that he could work his hand and wrist under it. At first he could make no impression on it, and he had to steel himself to use the weight of his body despite the pain it would cause him. He heaved his trunk and thrust out with his arm at the same time, and the relief as the great hunk fell away from him and rolled heavily down the stairs was some compensation for the agony which in a single moment drenched his body in a sweat of pain, so that he called out against it in a thin plaintive voice.

He lay for a long time recovering from the shock brought

on by the pain. He trembled and the sweat grew cold on his skin: he mumbled to himself over and over again the same senseless words. 'Oh, Christ, why, why, why?'

When the answer became clear to him he stopped. He was where he was, and in the condition he was, largely because of a decision which had been entirely his own. He had not had to join the Parachute Regiment: it had been his own wish, although he was by no means certain what had prompted him to do so. Vanity had played a part; the adulation of his mother and Jean, his girl friend, the admiration of his father and his younger brothers had at the time seemed more than enough to outweigh the rather vague promises of increased danger that his action in volunteering had held out. The possibility of it ending in just such a way as this had never really occurred to him. Somewhere in the back of his mind had lain the thought that he might be killed, or more possibly wounded – but not that it should end like this: a mangled body in dirt and filth; a swollen tongue and a dry mouth; a body racked with pain, and a mind filled with the fear of death and the anticipation of more suffering before the death he feared came to relieve him of the pain which increased as more and more of his body came to life under its nagging urge.

He had no idea how long he had been unconscious, and with his watch on his trapped wrist he had no means of finding out. He looked at the hole in the wall. There was plenty of light still. Perhaps he had not been unconscious for very long: at any moment Lieutenant Bridgman or Sergeant Gorman might return for him. He felt suddenly a lot better.

He turned his head and looked at his left arm. His hand and part of his wrist were out of sight under a solid lump of brickwork; he could see a dark patch of blood on the white of his skin, and in one place it had stained the putty-coloured plaster. He brought his right arm across in front of him and attempted to lift the brickwork so that he could free his left hand. He could move the mass a little, but not enough to allow him to pull his hand clear. He thought for a moment and then hunched himself forward on his right forearm. He felt his legs pull clear of the loose bricks which had lain on top of them, and was surprised at how little his pain increased. He leaned to the left till his steel helmet rested against the brickwork, and with his right hand bearing down on a tread of the stairs he braced his neck and shoulder muscles. For a moment nothing happened, then he felt the brickwork lift and he snatched his left hand out from under it.

It looked quite foreign lying in the dust under his face. Not only did it not seem to have anything to do with him, it seemed unreal altogether – not human or even animal. It was a caricature of a hand: swollen, misshapen, some fingers huge like grey bananas, others unchanged in size but looking ludicrous, like rose-grafts on a fungus. Armstrong looked away, raising his eyes to the hole in the wall. He felt sick at the thought of what his legs might be like, and thinking of them he remembered his shoulder. He eased his right hand inside his smock and under his shirt. His exploring fingers felt drying blood and then the wet patch where blood still seeped. One of his fingers touched something jagged which moved under pressure. He guessed it was a shell splinter from the 88 mm.

It took him a long time to turn over on to his back and sit up. He made a sling for his left hand out of his camouflage veil, and he took his steel helmet off. He wriggled his shoulders free from his haversack straps and drank from his water bottle. He lit a cigarette and looked at his legs. The water and the tobacco improved his outlook to such an extent that he no longer thought about death as even a possibility.

He sat on one of the steps, his back resting against one of the risers, his legs hanging down over a succession of them, the tread cutting into his calves and thighs. Fraser might be lying dead out of his sight farther down the spiral staircase, but he thought this unlikely. He looked at his watch. It was nearly four o'clock and almost two hours since the start of the resupply drop. The platoon must have gone, but he could not understand how they would have done so without coming for him. It was possible they had been driven from the area by a German attack, but that was irrelevant at the moment. He was alone, unable to move, and badly hurt.

It would be very painful, but it was possible for him to get down the stairs somehow, and out into the open. North and south of him were two companies of the Border Regiment, but he did not know how far away they were, nor how far apart they were from each other. Still, he would have to try it, for there was nothing else to be done. He looked about him for his Sten. He saw it at last a few feet above him, and alongside it and half buried in a pile of rubble he could see the top of the Eureka.

He dragged himself up the stairs using his shoulder and forearm to obtain a purchase on the treads, his broken legs trailing soggily behind him. He reached the Sten and spent a couple of minutes freeing it of dirt and cleaning its action, and then he turned to the Eureka.

It lay on its side with the top exposed and facing him. It was firmly embedded, and a great chink of brickwork bore down on it. Armstrong was thankful that a particular piece had not landed on him. He tried hard but it was impossible to free the Eureka with one hand.

He wondered what he should do. If he left it it might be captured by the enemy, and if it was it would be the first time that had happened. He looked at the set again. To one side and away from the dials which set the frequency was a diamond-shaped shield held in place by a single screw in one corner. If he pushed this to one side a small brassard would be revealed, and running down from this was a short safety-fuse which led to a detonator and the explosive packed in the space round the working parts of the set. If he struck the brassard with the edge of a safety-matchbox, he would have four seconds to get his crippled body far enough down the circular stairs to be shielded by the inner wall before the set blew up. He knew he would never make it. He wished Bridgman or Gorman would come back. Or Fraser. What could have happened to Fraser? He could not have been wrong about him. Fraser would never simply have left him in order to save his own skin. Off-hand he could not think of a man in the platoon who would have done that. He could not go and leave the Eureka where it was, but neither could he see what was to be achieved by remaining. He could not defend the set on his own, or at least not beyond killing two or three Germans. At the most he could by his presence postpone the capture of the secret equipment by minutes. To stay was absurd: there was nothing to be gained by staying. He wondered what Bridgman, Blake, or Gorman would do if they were in his position. The possibility of what they might do made him think hastily of something else.

He drank from his water-bottle again, and wetting a

handkerchief he wiped his lips and eyes. He must look a terrible sight. His mother's face would crumple up if she could see him, collapse suddenly in the funny way it always did whenever any of her children were hurt, no matter how slightly. His father would look grave and suck his pipe, and would turn away as he always did from anything unpleasant. He would look very solemn, but he would wait for somebody else to do something, and he would have a good reason for his own inactivity: he always had. He would go to the big, shady living-room at the back of the shop and sit behind his paper pretending to think; but in reality avoiding the consideration of anything unpleasant. Real things, other than the everyday chores of his business, were something that Tom Armstrong never allowed himself to think about. And Jean, whom he was going to marry when the war was over. What would she do if she could see him now? It was silly to conjecture because he suddenly knew that her behaviour would depend upon the nature of her audience. It was strange seeing her for the first time as she really was, without any lengthy analysis of what he knew of her character. She was silly, vain, weak and shallow and if he lived he would no more marry her than he would go back and work in his father's business and listen all day to his stupid pretentious talk. If he lived he would do something real. Something which would ensure he spent his time with men like those in his platoon. Real men whose first thought was not always of their own immediate welfare. Men whom you first respected and then loved because you respected them. He did not want to live with people whom he had to love because of their relationship to him, and then have to spend half a lifetime excusing their behaviour because he loved them.

He lit another cigarette and thought about how he would get down the stairs. His hand was returning to life and beginning to throb painfully. His legs were not too bad provided he did not move them, but his shoulder felt hot and a bigger area round it was starting to burn in sympathy with the wound.

He heard the voices very faintly, so faintly that he was not sure whether he had imagined them or not. He stubbed out his cigarette and strained his ears. He could hear them distinctly now, and they were coming nearer, but he could make out no words. They might be either German or British. He felt his pulse-rate increase at the thought that they might be the enemy but when they got nearer to the tower and he knew that they were in fact Germans his pulse slowed again and he felt very calm.

Everything that mattered to him in his life came through to him as if uttered by someone else in clipped precise phrases. The Germans would come to the tower. He could surrender himself, blow the Eureka, or open fire on them. His earlier resolution was stupid and unreal. If he returned to England he would marry Jean and go to work for his father. His character would not allow him to hurt them, and it would upset his mother too much if he broke away from the family.

He laid the Sten down gently on the stairs by his side and took two grenades from his pouch. Turning to one side he swivelled the shield on the Eureka and groped in a smock pocket for a match-box. The German voices were lower now. He could hear them, almost whispering, at the entrance to the tower, and then jackboots on the rubble.

He struck the brassard quickly, and turning he seized each

grenade in turn, and pulling the pins with his teeth he lobbed them one after the other down the stairs.

He listened: one ear to the sudden scamper of German feet; the other to the faint hiss of the burning fuse in the Eureka. He hoped the grenades would catch some of the Germans, but he knew he would never hear them explode – the fuse in them was the same length as the one in the Eureka.

CHAPTER THIRTEEN

Lt Bridgman
~~Sgt Nash~~   Missing   2nd Day
~~Pte Bilting~~   Wounded   4th Day
Pte Dwyer
Pte Brogan

No. 4 Section			*No. 5 Section*		
~~Sgt Leyland~~	Killed	3rd Day	Sgt Blake		
Cpl Marsden			~~Cpl Heibling~~	Killed	4th Day
L/Cpl Hudson			L/Cpl Cobbald		
Pte Laverty			~~Pte Hardy~~	Wounded	4th Day
~~Pte Wilcox~~	Killed	3rd Day	Pte Ewing		
Pte Cowper			~~Pte Matthews~~	Killed	1st Day
~~Pte Gregory~~	Wounded	4th Day	~~Pte Jennings~~	Wounded	4th Day
Pte McGrath			~~Pte Butcher~~	Wounded	4th Day
~~Pte Keeley~~	Wounded	4th Day	~~Pte Stewart~~	Killed	4th Day
Pte Adams			~~Pte Taylor~~	Wounded	4th Day
Pte Chambers			Pte Bignall		
~~Pte Wallace~~	Killed	3rd Day	~~Pte Sadler~~	Wounded	4th Day

No. 6 Section			*Headquarter Section*		
Sgt Gorman			Sgt Murray		
~~Cpl Armstrong~~	Killed	4th Day	Cpl McEwan		
L/Cpl Summers			~~L/Cpl Manning~~	Killed	2nd Day
Pte Woodley			Pte Warke		
~~Pte Storrs~~	Killed	3rd Day	Pte Bobrow		
Pte Cummings			~~Pte Muldoon~~	Missing	2nd Day
Pte Liddon			Pte O'Neill		
~~Pte Fraser~~	Wounded	4th Day	~~Pte Edwards~~	Wounded	2nd Day
~~Pte Jarvis~~	Wounded	2nd Day	Pte Banham		
Pte Mocock			Pte Waterson		
~~Pte Chamberlain~~	Wounded	4th Day	~~Pte Black~~	Wounded	2nd Day
~~Pte Norfolk~~	Wounded	4th Day	Pte Cassidy		

Alan Bridgman looked up from the dirty half-sheet of paper in front of him and stared out at the mist-white lightening of the fifth day. He tried not to think about the dead men individually, but it was no use: nearly all of them he had known well, intimately. Their faces, their peculiarities, amusing incidents in which they had played more or less prominent parts, all these broke into and interrupted the constructive train of his thought. He felt sure that Jim Nash was dead. He could not imagine anything but death or a crippling wound preventing the big sergeant from rejoining his platoon. And wherever he was, there Muldoon would be and, if alive, the humour of this one-track mind directed against the iniquities of the English.

Eric Leyland.

Bridgman felt the salt of tears and a sudden drying in his throat. He shook his head in surprise at himself, and as a physical act to dismiss sentiment from his mind. But the image of Leyland could not easily be obliterated. As his lips tightened at the remembrance of the sergeant's death, Alan realized with something of relief that his threatened tears were more of anger than of grief. Anything more pointless than Leyland's death was hard to imagine. Alan felt sure that the incident had its root somewhere in Italy, for at some point in the campaign there he had noticed a more pronounced withdrawal on the part of the normally reticent section commander. But he could not fix the time and place when it had started. What it was didn't really matter. Leyland was dead, unnecessarily dead, and the platoon much the weaker as a consequence. A part of Bridgman accepted without question Leyland's disregard for his own life, but what he could not come to terms with was the futility of the sergeant's death – the profitless waste.

He made a conscious effort and organized his thoughts. His platoon was down to half-strength and he had to make a decision about what to do with Blake's and Marsden's sections. At the moment they were still combined and holding the position at the road and track junction. To separate them would mean reinforcing both with men from his remaining two sections. Murray's headquarter section was fairly strong, and Gorman's was not in too bad shape. Four weak or three reasonably strong units, that was the choice. Alan decided to leave things as they were for the present. If the situation altered or the platoon's position in the perimeter was changed he would have to think again.

Alan looked across to his right, to where Gorman's men held the position previously held by Leyland and, after his death, by Marsden. He could see the thin sergeant's face showing greyly above the parapet of his slit trench to the right of his Bren group. Gorman was a good man to have in a tight corner: perhaps as good as Blake – it was hard to tell. Bridgman preferred Blake as a person, and he wondered why. If he became a casualty, Blake would take over. This would be automatic; the Army had precise rules about the transfer of command to the next or most senior in rank, although in practice it did not always work out. One NCO might be a better section commander than another, but a less effective platoon commander, and this was true right up the ladder of command. Nearly every man had a ceiling above which his efficiency ceased to be one hundred per cent.

The ground mist had lifted completely, and Bridgman turned and looked at the company positions. As his eyes passed over the buildings to his rear they were arrested by a slight movement, and after a moment's concentration he was able to identify the figure of Tim Jordan standing alone against the wall of the house.

Alan felt a rare wave of compassion as he looked at his CO. At his worst, Jordan could be irritable and unfair over details, at his best it would be difficult to find his equal. Alan knew the older man felt a deeper and more sincere sense of personal loss for the dead men of the company than he did himself, and again he found himself wondering why this was so.

He turned back and looked out over the shrubberies towards the railway embankment. Self-analysis was something from which he had always refrained. He believed that it could only lead to disillusionment, disgust, and inadequacy and, if carried beyond the field of introspection into the realm of action, to suicide. He knew Jordan had the empathetic ability to project himself into, and understand, nearly every one of the diverse characters under his command. Alan felt it not impossible that he too might possess the same capacity, but he did not wish to exercise it. He saw very often the workings of other men's minds; he saw the motives which prompted them to certain courses of action; motives of marginal gain, of concern for their own safety, and the scores of other reasons of varying relevance which prompted the course of their actions. He saw, but he did not want to understand. By understanding he would associate himself with what he considered weakness. Understanding could be followed very easily by a sympathetic tolerance of cowardice, which he saw as an unforgivable vice, as a too ready acceptance of the frailty of human nature. Understanding affected both the weak and the strong. The weak might grow marginally stronger, but the strong must grow appreciably weaker. It was easier to destroy than to build.

He was an entity. Complete in himself. Inviolate for so long as he stood alone, his approach to friendship calculated, and to some degree academic. His close friendship with Gordon Brown was possible because Gordon made no demands upon his privacy. Gordon was prepared to accept him exactly as he was, suppressing the ebullient questing of a warm nature out of consideration for Alan's obvious desire to surrender very little of his private self.

Sudden firing from the southwest, from down near the north bank of the Neder Rhine, brought Alan out of his rare introspection. The Border Regiment was either under attack or had surprised an enemy patrol.

From every part of the company position he could detect the faint whispering of movement as heads were cocked and men listened, each man building up a personal picture of what might be happening below them and to their left.

The firing died as suddenly as it had started, and Alan's thoughts explored the divisional situation as he knew it. The fifth day might bring many things, but they would all be unpleasant. The previous day's action had demolished any possibility that the 1st Airborne Division could again adopt an aggressive line of action. As the platoon had returned to the company area on the previous afternoon, they had been in time to see Brigadier Hackett bring the last of 4th Brigade into the divisional perimeter. Sixty men of one battalion, one hundred of another – the third of his battalions, the 11th, had been virtually wiped out in the centre of Arnhem. Any plans the divisional commander might have had for a move-ment to the east could no longer be put into practice, for there no longer existed a force with anything like the poten-tial required to break the enveloping ring of German armour and infantry. From now on they would be able at the very best only to hold a small perimeter, and hope that 2nd Army would arrive in time to take advantage of their precarious foothold north of the last river barrier between themselves and Berlin.

Gorman called softly for the second time. Bridgman was staring straight ahead, but his mind was obviously elsewhere. O'Neill touched his arm and spoke to him, and Bridgman immediately turned and looked towards the section sergeant. Gorman pulled back his smock sleeve and mimed looking at his watch. The officer looked at his own, grinned suddenly, nodded his head, and turning away he signalled to the other sections to stand down.

Gorman detailed two men as sentries, sent another back to Company HQ to investigate the possibility of heating water for a brew-up, and then, with the detached, automatic movements of the trained soldier, set about cleaning his Sten gun.

He wondered whether he would ever do it again. Barring a miracle, he could see nothing to prevent the Germans from launching an all-out and concentrated attack on a selected area of the perimeter. He knew there was no defence in depth. Once through the outer line, the Germans would find nothing between themselves and the backs of the men facing the opposite direction. The operation as originally intended was finished. Perhaps 21st Army Group no longer had any intention of exploiting their bridgehead, but were pushing on only with the object of rescuing what remained of the division. Gorman looked at the men as they stood in pairs in their slit trenches, one man cleaning his weapon while the other watched the front.

The same pairs drank together, whored together, shared their food and their cigarettes. Became so associated as one entity that section and platoon commanders thought of one as synonymous with the other, posted them together as sentries, and sent them out together as scouts or on a foraging party. To think of one name was to think immediately of the other.

As Gorman unloaded a magazine and rubbed each round with a piece of flannelette before replacing it, he tried to think of individuals who had always stood alone in the company, men whom he did not immediately associate with another man. It had always been Blake and Leyland: now there was only Blake. John Murray and Marsden's Bren gunner, Laverty, were both Belfast men, and when off duty were always together. The difference in their rank had forced Bridgman to make a point of keeping them always in different sections, but their friendship continued although it would probably have been frowned upon in another unit.

He and Ted Armstrong had always been inseparable. They had been called up together and had done their infantry training at the same depot. They had both volunteered and been transferred to the Parachute Regiment at the same time. Together they had come to the Independent Company, and via Africa, Sicily, and Italy they had arrived in Holland, he as a section commander, and Armstrong as his second-in-command. And now Ted was dead. It was hard for Gorman to believe that yesterday morning they had laughed together and shared a cigarette, taking turns at sucking on a crumpled butt, and that now Ted was dead and gone completely from his life. That as he slipped the 9-mm bullets back into the magazine, the body of his friend lay in the empty tower or in an enemy-dug grave somewhere near it, and that they would never laugh again together or share anything any more. If he, Gorman, were killed, they would still be separated by the time that would lie between their dying.

Marsden.

Tom Marsden had no particular friend. In some respects he was similar to Alan Bridgman. He mixed casually with many of the platoon, attaching himself more often than not to Fraser and Hardy, but always with a slight air of defiance and an attitude which implied that he knew they were public school men, but that he did not hold that against them. Bridgman himself was a friend of Gordon Brown, but when Gorman though about it he realized that in fact Bridgman was not all close to Brown, he was simply closer to him than he was to anybody else.

Gorman let his mind wander through the company, identifying men in pairs and threes: the desire for the warmth and affection of friendship was everywhere apparent except in the cases of Bridgman and Marsden. Marsden was single, but Bridgman was married and the father of a son and daughter. Gorman wondered whether the platoon commander had taken to his marriage the same detached attitude which marked him out in the company; whether he looked on his leaves and his marital bed in the same way as he looked on a night out drinking with Brown or some other acquaintance: something pleasurable and to be enjoyed, but in no way more than an interruption in the serious and absorbing business of war.

He looked across to where Bridgman's expressionless face showed, tired and drawn, above the slit trench, and then his eyes drifted to the faint movement in the trees which screened Ramsden's platoon as they lay facing the open ground to the west. He looked down at the road and track junction – at the ditched jeep: On the previous evening, after the platoon's return from the supply drop, they had got comfortably in position, hoping for a respite from the snipers who had challenged their return. Just as quiet had descended, a jeep had come blinding down the track in front of Ramsden's platoon and swung on to the road at the bottom. The snipers opened up; the jeep swerved violently and a heavily built figure jumped out. It scrambled nimbly over the cattle fence and doubled smartly up the fifty-yard gradient to Tim Jordan's headquarters. A pretty active performance for a major-general in his forties. Gorman grinned to himself. General Urquhart had not been immediately recognized, and he had had some fairly abusive language directed at him by various members of the company who considered it out of order for a stranger to attract fire on their positions.

The jeep had been knocked out, and the General's ADC had left it and limped up to join the GOC. Gorman looked at the jeep – lonely, abandoned. Were they all in the same boat?

How forceful was the effort that was being made to relieve them? He shrugged and studied the jeep. Did being a general's jeep make it any different from the others? Was there a jeep heaven, or did they go to the same heaven as men, and serve their masters there? If so, then after this action there would be quite a parade before the Lord God of Hosts. Perhaps General Urquhart would find himself leading a march past the Almighty in that very jeep, for there was no divine right of commanders. They were killed as easily as privates, and Urquhart took more risks than most of his rank. Gorman supposed that the situation had deteriorated to such an extent that Roy Urquhart's most important role had become one of inspiration. By his presence and activity he could strengthen the will of his officers and men to resist: with no reserves there was little else he could do. Gorman wondered why Urquhart was called Roy: he knew that was not his name; he thought it was Ronald. After the division's return from Italy, Urquhart had taken over its command, and as a non-airborne man at first he had been resented. At every level men had been angry that 1st Brigade's commander had not been given command of the division, but Urquhart had gone quietly about his task and had become accepted. He was now Roy Urquhart to everyone

Gorman sighed. He trusted Bridgman, Jordan, the brigadiers, and Urquhart, and even more important, he trusted nearly every man in the Independent Company. He wondered what it would have been like to be in a situation as bad as the one they were in, and be with men and commanders he could not trust.

He reached for his water-bottle and drank a careful mouthful. He wondered at his lack of appetite. They had all landed with one forty-eight-hour ration pack: they had had no other food, and it was now the fifth day.

Blake took his beret off and scratched the back of his head. He had an old scar which itched only when he was tired or hot. Now he was both.

He looked at his watch. Nearly four o'clock. In a few more hours they would have survived another day – they would be sheltered by darkness. He found himself wishing for the comfort of the night. It must come – night must fall – that had been the name of a film. Who had been in it? Ah, yes.

Robert Montgomery. Blake thought it was the best film the actor had ever made. He had been young when he had seen it, and he had found the film exciting but frightening. He remembered one scene of dusk and trees. He looked round him. It might have been this very place, for the same menace hung in the air.

He looked at his men's faces and wondered how much longer they could last without food or water, with little sleep, and with hope which must grow fainter as the hours dragged by. He looked up the track to the north and at the smashed six-pounder in front of him. The previous evening they had been shelled over open sights from a range of a couple of hundred yards. Bridgman had sent down an additional Piat group, with instructions that it was not to give away its position unless it was certain of a kill. The Piat had a range of about one hundred and fifteen yards. The German self-propelled guns had edged their way forward, firing the occasional shell as they came. One had come within range but had remained screened from view. Before Blake could stop him, the gunner, a big German Jew who had spent his early years in Berlin, had got ponderously to his feet and walked almost slowly into the centre of the road, carrying the Piat. He had lain down as if he had all the time in the world, and taking careful aim, he had fired and hit the German SP. Then as the gunner came back to the section position, he had been shot through the stomach. He had put his gun carefully down alongside his number two and with one hand held over his gut he had walked back to company headquarters, muttering over and over again in his comic-opera accent, 'Stuffing German bastards, stuffing German bastards.'

They had heard the clank of the other SPs and tanks as

they retired, uncertain of the range of the weapon which had knocked out one of their number. During the night a six-pounder anti-tank gun and its Polish crew had arrived, the men in hilarious spirits. Even when the situation had been explained to the Polish subaltern, he still treated the occasion as one which lent itself to amusing banter. It was a great game. At first light he would show his English friends how he had knocked out German tanks in Africa.

Despite Bridgman's and Blake's protests, he had insisted on setting up his gun in the middle of the road, its barrel pointing in approximately the right direction. Bridgman and Blake had crouched in the section post listening to the continuous chatter of the Polish crew. When it had become obvious that the anti-tank gunners were not prepared to listen to the warnings of the men who had been on the spot all day, Bridgman had gripped Blake's arm.

'You're too close to them. You'll collect half of whatever's aimed at them. Withdraw your section to what was Gorman's old position, and as soon as it's over get back again as smartly as you can. When they've knocked the gun out, Jerry might follow up with an infantry attack.'

Blake had done as he was ordered, and in the first light he strained his eyes towards the crossroads. Gradually he made out the figures of the Poles grouped round their gun, and heard the murmur of their voices. It was ridiculous. He could not make up his mind whether the Poles were incredibly brave or completely unrealistic. Their position gave them the best field of fire, but the contempt they showed for the Germans was quite unwarranted. The German guns were bigger, and they also had cover from view.

The Germans must have been so surprised that at first

they looked for some trick. The seconds dragged as Blake peeped into the morning light. He could see the trees and bushes to the north which sheltered the German armour, and still they did not fire. He started to hope that they had moved back during the night, but he knew they had not, for he would have heard them. Waiting for the first shot, he felt the same as when, after lighting a safety-fuse, one waited for the explosion. It had to come, but the inability to calculate time accurately prevented one from being quite sure when.

The Germans had fired only twice, and one Pole had staggered into Blake's position as he led his section back. He had a lump of metal in his shoulder and a look of outraged surprise on his face. It should not have gone this way at all. All the German armour should have been knocked out in devastating style. The Pole's pride had been more hurt than his body. The other three Poles lay round their smashed gun. They had shown their contempt for the Germans for the last time.

Now Blake put his beret back on his head and called softly to Tom Marsden.

'I'm going back to see Bridgie. Take over for a bit.'

Marsden nodded a fierce, angry face, and Blake smiled as he crawled back to the cover of the nearest bushes, wondering whether Tom knew what he was angry about. It was doubtful whether he did. Things were not going according to plan. If Tom could have found a definite culprit, he would still have been angry, but it would have been a happier anger, one with a positive direction. As it was, it burned into him, and Blake was a little anxious that in his frustration Marsden might take some unnecessary risk.

He joined Bridgman to the left of Gorman's men.

They exchanged smiles but neither spoke for some minutes. The area in which they had been dug in for days had become familiar, something that belonged to them. It was another billet, in some ways worse than previous ones, but nevertheless their home for the ever-changing present which is part and parcel of a soldier's life. The positions on their sixty-yard front were dug fifteen yards back from the road and, on the rising ground, were seven or eight feet above it; the trees in the grounds behind them were sparse, their branches and twigs broken, and their trunks scarred by the mortar bombs, shells and bullets the Germans had poured into the small area; to their right the road continued past Gordon Brown's positions towards Arnhem. Where the two platoons joined the houses began, and eighty or ninety yards up the road the German tanks which had been caught in the trap on the third day lay like scavenged bones. To the west, the trees were more solid and continuous, like one side of an avenue, and beneath them Ramsden watched the open ground. In front of Blake and Bridgman was the big house and the overgrown gardens. Their unbroken field of fire was no more than twenty-five or thirty yards The close concealment of the cover in front of them was oppressive.

'Why don't they come, sir? One squadron of armour and an infantry battalion, and they would be through us like a knife through butter: and nothing else between them and Div HQ.'

'Christ only knows, Bob. If they had any sense they'd shift the weight of their armour round to the west. The Borders must be bloody well dug in by now, but they're in open country. They're good troops, but it doesn't matter how good they are, no understrength battalion could stop a really determined Panzer attack across that sort of country if it were pushed home. Perhaps they think more landings might be made near the bridge, and they're waiting for that.'

Blake scratched the stubble on his chin, and when he spoke he did so almost apologetically.

'You know, sir, I think they're frightened of us. I think they're hoping that our food, water, and ammunition will run out, and that we shall have to pack in because we'll have nothing left to fight with.'

'You might be right at that, but I shouldn't put too much faith in it. If we were all back in Oosterbeek, I should feel happier. If the whole of our perimeter was in a built-up area, their armour would be of less value to them. They'd have to winkle us out house by house, and they'd have stuffing heavy casualties if they tried it.'

Murray watched the heads of the two men in the command post. Bridgman and Blake. Leyland and Blake. Bridgman and Gorman. Gorman and Blake. He wondered what held them closer to each other than to him. The question was not a new one: he had been over it all before, and had even discussed it with Laverty. It wasn't class. Bridgman had been to a public school, Leyland to a grammar school, Gorman and Blake to neither. It had nothing to do with that, and he could not make himself believe that his being Irish had anything to do with it either. Gorman was junior to him in their rank, but it had been Gorman who had been given the command of the infantry section when Newcombe had been killed in Italy, while he had merely continued with headquarter section. After Leyland's death, Bridgman had made no move to give

Murray the command: he had been content for Marsden to take over, and had Blake's section not had so many casualties as to make it impracticable for it to continue to operate as a sub-unit, Marsden would still have been on his own.

Murray grunted and looked across at McEwan. The big corporal was crouched half-sideways in his slit tench, his legs bunched under him, his hands linked behind his head, and his eyes closed.

Murray didn't like McEwan, but he wasn't quite sure why. The corporal was new to the company, joining it after its return from Italy. This was his first action with them, and so far Murray had found nothing to criticize except a cautious sullenness in the corporal's approach to any job he was given; but caution was not on its own a bad sign. McEwan was tough all right. Murray had seen him take on an American who must have weighed fifteen or sixteen stone. McEwan had been put down four times, but he had won in the end by sheer guts and doggedness. Standing over the exhausted American, his eyebrows gaping open, his lips in shreds, and his face lumpier than usual, McEwan had looked as if nothing less than a Tiger tank would stop him. Despite this, for some reason he could not explain, Murray did not trust the corporal as he trusted other men in the platoon. He felt sure that Bridgman and the other section commanders thought as he did, although none had ever mentioned it.

Murray watched Blake leave Bridgman's slit trench and crawl back to his own. He wondered if perhaps *he* was not trusted by the others in the same way that McEwan was not trusted. He breathed heavily in sudden anger. If it were true, they had no right, no grounds for distrust. He had been with the company a long time, and he had never let them down yet. But in any tricky or particularly dangerous situation it was always one of the other sections which was used or put into the difficult position.

Murray grunted again, his grey, shapeless face expressionless. Time would tell.

McEwan wakened suddenly. For a moment, Murray detected fear in the corporal's startled eyes, then the look was gone. McEwan struggled up and looked over the parapet towards the grounds of the big house. He turned to Murray.

'There's not a bloody thing happened since first light. What the stuffing hell are they waiting for? They know where we are. Why don't they come and get us?'

'Waiting's hard, isn't it, Mac?' Murray's voice was flat and emotionless. 'It's often like this, but you know all about that, don't you? You were with the 51st Highland Div. Wasn't it like this in the desert sometimes? Of course they were farther away, but there must have been times when you weren't actually fighting.'

Murray wasn't very subtle; his sarcasm was as heavy as lead. McEwan stared back at him, his small deep-sunken eyes glinting dangerously under his heavy-boned brows.

'Bollocks!'

The Scot spat into the bottom of the trench, and reached for his water-bottle. Murray smiled without showing his teeth. Suddenly he knew what was wrong with McEwan.

Tim Jordan came back from General Urquhart's order group at eight o'clock that evening. The division was too thin on the ground to continue to hold its present positions. The perimeter was to be contracted. The Independent Company, which had been stuck out on a limb to the northwest since the withdrawal of 4th Brigade, was to move over to the east, to the Arnhem side, to fill the gap which existed between the force being built up under Major Lonsdale immediately north of the Neder Rhine and the remnants of 4th Brigade. The gap had not been of too much importance while elements of the division had been in the centre of the town fighting their way towards the bridge; but now they had been pulled back, and it was what was left of these battalions which went to make up the bulk of the Lonsdale Force in the south. There was an uncomfortably large gap between this new force and the survivors of 4th Brigade.

Two hours after darkness had finally closed down, the company slipped quietly from its positions and pulled back. Bridgman's platoon was the last to leave the area, and he stood with Jordan in the shadow of the trees near the house which had held company headquarters. They talked together in whispers. By Jordan's side stood the Dutchman who owned the house.

He had been a captain of artillery in the Dutch Army, and now that the company was moving out, his only concern was that they were abandoning a good defensive position. He was a tall, thin, silent man, and he had insisted upon accompanying the Independent Company to their new positions. He still had faith in the eventual arrival of 2nd Army. Glancing at the man's shadowed profile, Bridgman felt a strong emotional upsurge, a sense of warmth and kinship with the Dutchman. He personified the resistance of the Dutch people, who had a frightening faith not only in the eventual triumph of the Allied forces, but also in the immediate success of the action being fought on their doorsteps. The Dutch gunner officer was staying with the company until

2nd Army broke through and joined up with the Airborne Forces north of the Rhine.

A subdued commotion in the avenue of trees running south into the divisional area interrupted their conversation, and Jordan moved away to investigate.

Bridgman joined Blake and the bulk of the platoon where they crouched in the shadow of the bushes. The subaltern whispered quickly, 'I'm going to have a look at Marsden and Adams. I shan't be a couple of minutes. Hang on here.'

Blake nodded in the darkness, and watched Bridgman melt into cover as he moved down the bank to the Bren group who had been left to prevent any interference with the company's withdrawal.

Jordan came back and bent over Blake.

'Where's Mr Bridgman?'

'He's checking with the covering party, sir.'

'My idiot of a driver has put a back wheel of the jeep in one of Mr Ramsden's slit trenches. We can't get it out loaded with ammo. We're late now and will have to move off without it. Tell Mr Bridgman to leave one section behind to unload it and lift it out of the trench. They'll have to rejoin us as soon as they finish.'

Blake whispered his acknowledgement of the message, and Jordan moved off to join the remainder of the company where they lay in a long line facing the south, each man's face only inches from the boots of the man in front of him.

Blake and the last section unloaded the jeep, very conscious of the Germans one hundred and fifty yards away from them in the little neck of wood across the open field. Marsden and Adams crouched behind their Bren in a slit trench facing the big house and the gardens which lay between them and the railway embankment. Marsden was angry. Adams was frightened.

Marsden strained his eyes and ears. Peering into the shadows in front of him, his head cocked, he strove to accept and then ignore the sounds made by Blake and his men as they off-loaded the ammunition from the jeep. He could hear faintly the sound of tracked vehicles moving about somewhere beyond where the north-running track turned and disappeared from sight. He thought the tanks were probably withdrawing to laager for the rest of the night. Blake's men were making a bloody lot of noise. Why the hell didn't they take their time? They had all night. It was better to spend longer at the job and get it done than to attract attention and get themselves and the company reserve of ammo blown sky-high. He could feel the faint trembling of Adams's body where it touched his own.

'What's the matter with you? Scared?'

'No, not scared, corporal. Nervous, I think. How long are we going to stay here?'

'It was to be half an hour after the company left. But that was before they ditched the jeep. I shall have to give them longer now. I expect Blake will come down before he goes. We'll see what he has to say.'

They could hear the sound of small-arms fire at many points of the perimeter as both sides patrolled the area between the lines – an area which was getting less and less as the German Army closed its grip on the crippled division.

Marsden's head moved suddenly in the darkness, and his whisper came sharp and clear.

'There. To the right of the gate, in the bushes.'

'What? Where?'

Adams's jerked, whispered questions were an automatic reaction to shield him from what he knew, but did not want to know. He had heard the corporal, and even as his own questions sounded, the answers slipped into place in his brain. He started to move but he was too late. Marsden's shoulder hit him, pushing the young soldier to one side, away from the gun. Adams fell back, half sprawling with one leg tucked under him, his head below the parapet of the trench. Looking up, his mouth open and his breath coming quickly, he saw Marsden take his place behind the Bren, swing its barrel round and then pause for what seemed an age before opening up with a long burst which shattered the silence and made the night alive with reverberating echoes which rolled back on the two men – the ricochets of sound.

Adams's brain worked blindly, spasmodically for a few seconds, and then he was thinking coolly, as he always wanted to think. He was on the wrong side of Marsden to act as his number two. Standing up, he forced his way behind the corporal, squeezing between the NCO's buttocks and the back of the trench. Even as he moved he was undoing his pouch and getting out a magazine to replace the one on the gun.

Marsden was still firing. Adams wanted to look, but was afraid that if he did he would again be found unready when he was wanted. Instead, he stared straight at the centre of the Bren, and when Marsden's hand flew up and removed the empty magazine, Adams was ready with a full one, and the change was effected with the precision of a drill movement on a barrack square. Only then did Adams look down to the road and the bushes beyond. He could make out the forms of two bodies on the grass verge on the far side of the road, but he could not remember whether or not they had been there earlier. It seemed to him that that stretch of the road had held so many bodies during the past two days that it was difficult to remember which they had moved and which they had not. He squinted at the corporal's silhouette. Marsden seemed not to be looking at the spot he had been firing at. Adams tried to follow the corporal's gaze, and found himself looking at a moonlit glade between the house and the bushes; then the open space was alive with running figures and his ears were again filled with sound as Marsden poured burst upon burst after the German patrol. Adams jerked his eyes away from the scene and back to the Bren and was only just in time for the second change. With the third magazine on the gun, Marsden did not fire again, but crouched still and hunched, staring into the night. Adams, too, turned away and looked to the north. He wished his companion had been almost anyone else but Marsden. It was not that Adams disliked the corporal: it was just that there was no give in him, no warmth, no companionship. In the field, in the midst of a danger they all shared, Marsden drew closer to no one.

The sounds from where Blake and the last section were working were faint now, and the engagements of other units seemed very far away. Adams swallowed, and after a quick glance at Marsden, looked away again. As the excitement died out of him, and his body quietened, he felt suddenly very depressed, and tired to the point of exhaustion. He tried to think about when and how it would all end, and found it impossible to imagine a conclusion that carried with it any hint of reality.

His mind drifted to the strange eeriness of the moonlit gardens in front of him. As a boy, he had seen 'A Midsummer Night's Dream', and the scene in front of him reminded him so much of the play that he almost expected the King and Queen of the fairies to appear in the glade to the right of the house. He pulled himself up. Somewhere in front of him were hundreds, perhaps thousands of the German Army, men supported by guns, tanks and aircraft and their foremost objective was his life, and the lives of all the men left in the division.

Blake joined them silently.

'What happened, Tom?'

'Patrol. Fighting patrol, I should think. Too many of them for a recce. They've stuffed off now, but they've left a few behind. Bastards!'

Blake smiled in the darkness. Tom Marsden could put more venom into a single word than anyone else Blake knew.

'We've got the jeep out. We'll hang on with you for another twenty minutes or so, and then we'll all go back together.'

To the men filing behind it, the jeep, barely ticking over, seemed intent on generating a greater volume of sound than if it had been driven at the maximum revolutions of which its engine was capable. They followed its creeping bulk down the length of the avenue of trees. Blake walked in front, feeling with his feet for obstacles, on two or three occasions falling into an abandoned foxhole. At last they reached the road running east into Oosterbeek. Here Blake halted for a few minutes before making a decision. The road itself presented too great a temptation to trigger-happy defenders, and he had no idea which unit might be holding the approaches to this built-up area. He whispered to the driver, the man eased the jeep on to the pavement, and the long crawl continued.

The first firing broke out behind them, and they heard

the shots whistling past them to their right. Blake turned quickly, his intention to order a flat-out run for their own lines, but even as he turned, the defenders in Oosterbeek opened up and returned the fire. They were caught between the Germans and some unit of their own division.

Blake slipped alongside the driving seat of the jeep as the first mortar bombs burst beyond his section, close to where the defenders must be dug in. The driver had stalled the engine. Blake whispered to him not to restart it. He crawled back behind the jeep to order the men into the cover of the front gardens of the houses, but Marsden had anticipated him. He found the corporal lying by an open gateway, and lay down beside him.

Marsden's voice came fierce in the sergeant's ear. 'We'll have to make a run for it. One of us had better go first to let those silly bastards know who we are.'

Blake stayed silent for a moment.

No. We'll get in one of the houses till first light. You can't move down a road with both sides firing at you. You're too restricted. We could make it through the gardens, but that would mean leaving the jeep – and the company's ammo.'

Marsden did not argue, and when the small-arms fire was at its fiercest, and during a lull in the mortaring, the section pushed the jeep backwards into a garage and broke into a house alongside it.

Halfway through a window, Bignall turned and whispered in an affected voice, 'You put the car away, dear. I'll go in and get the drinks.'

CHAPTER FOURTEEN

Bridgman lay in the rubble to one side of the crossroads in Oosterbeek, staring up the road to the west. The CO joined him.

'I'm afraid you can't wait much longer, Alan. If they haven't come through in another five minutes, you'll have to take up your new positions without them. I'll send them on to you as soon as they arrive.'

'If they haven't joined us in five minutes, they won't be coming, sir.'

Jordan said nothing. He knew Bridgman was right. Whatever trouble Blake and his men had run into would either be solved at first light, or it would not be solved at all.

The bulk of the platoon lay out of sight behind the two officers. The night spent within the divisional perimeter had given most of them their first night's rest since they landed. In front of Bridgman was a Spandau, and to his right was a Bren Group which Gorman had joined a few minutes earlier. Jordan knew that Bridgman had been waiting all night for the section to come through, and he knew exactly how the platoon commander was feeling.

Bridgman cocked his head suddenly and listened intently.

Jordan strained his ears and cursed the partial deafness he had concealed from the medics for so long.

'What is it, Alan? What can . . .'

The remainder of Jordan's words were lost in the unheralded roar which broke out to the south of them. To Jordan it seemed as if every calibre of gun in the German Army was firing; interspersing the muzzle blasts of the guns and the crash of the bursting shells he could hear the chatter of German machine-guns, and the slower reply of the Brens as the Border Regiment opened fire.

Jordan had looked instinctively in the direction of the firing, although he knew he would be able to see nothing. Now he looked back at Bridgman. The subaltern hadn't moved except to raise the Spandau to his shoulder. Jordan bent close to him and shouted in his ear.

'What did you hear, Alan?'

'Before that bloody lot started up, I heard an engine out there somewhere. I think it was a jeep. Blake may be warming it up.'

Bridgman kept his eyes staring ahead while he was talking. Following the direction of his gaze, Jordan saw the wide, open road, its surface littered with the debris of war; garden gates hanging drunkenly in the front of window-shattered houses, the stillness contrasting strongly with the noise of the battle being fought to the south of them.

The jeep came out from between two of the houses so fast that it was in the road and turned in the direction of the waiting officers before Jordan grasped that Blake and his men were making their bid to rejoin the company.

The jeep was nearly a hundred yards up the road, and as it accelerated towards them Jordan saw that Blake had loaded

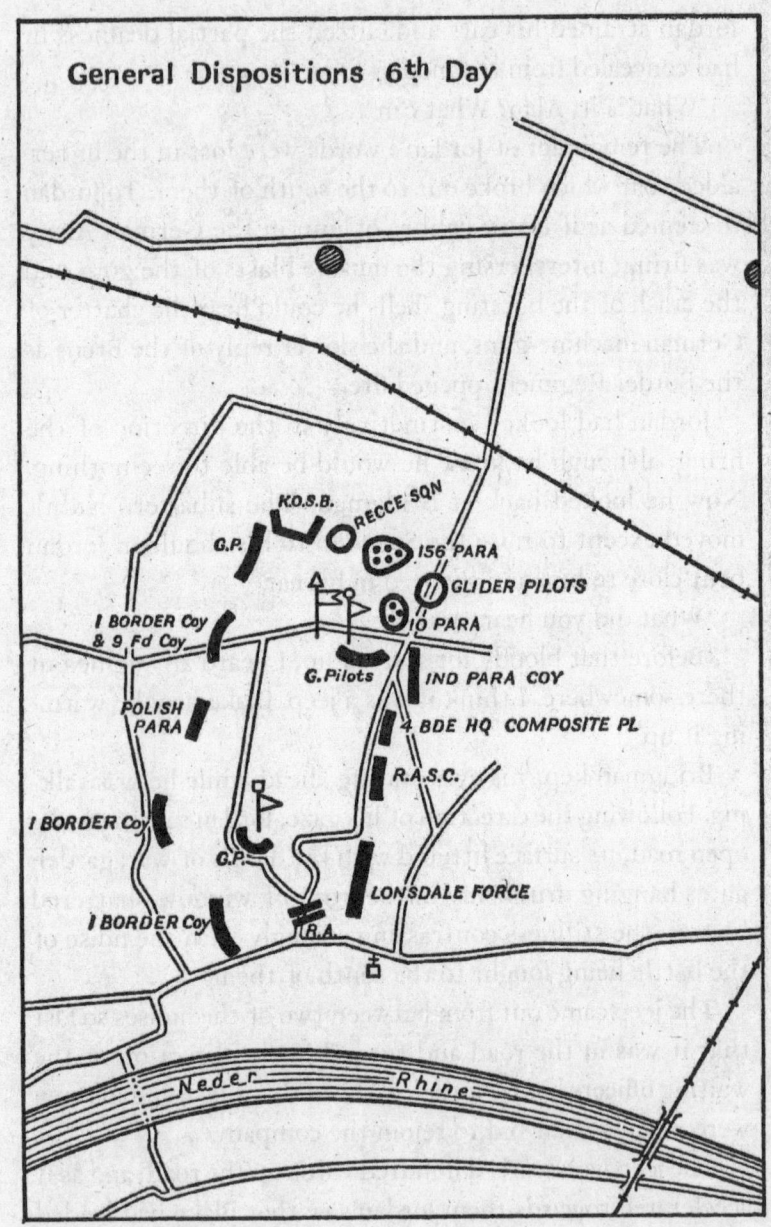

General Dispositions 6th Day

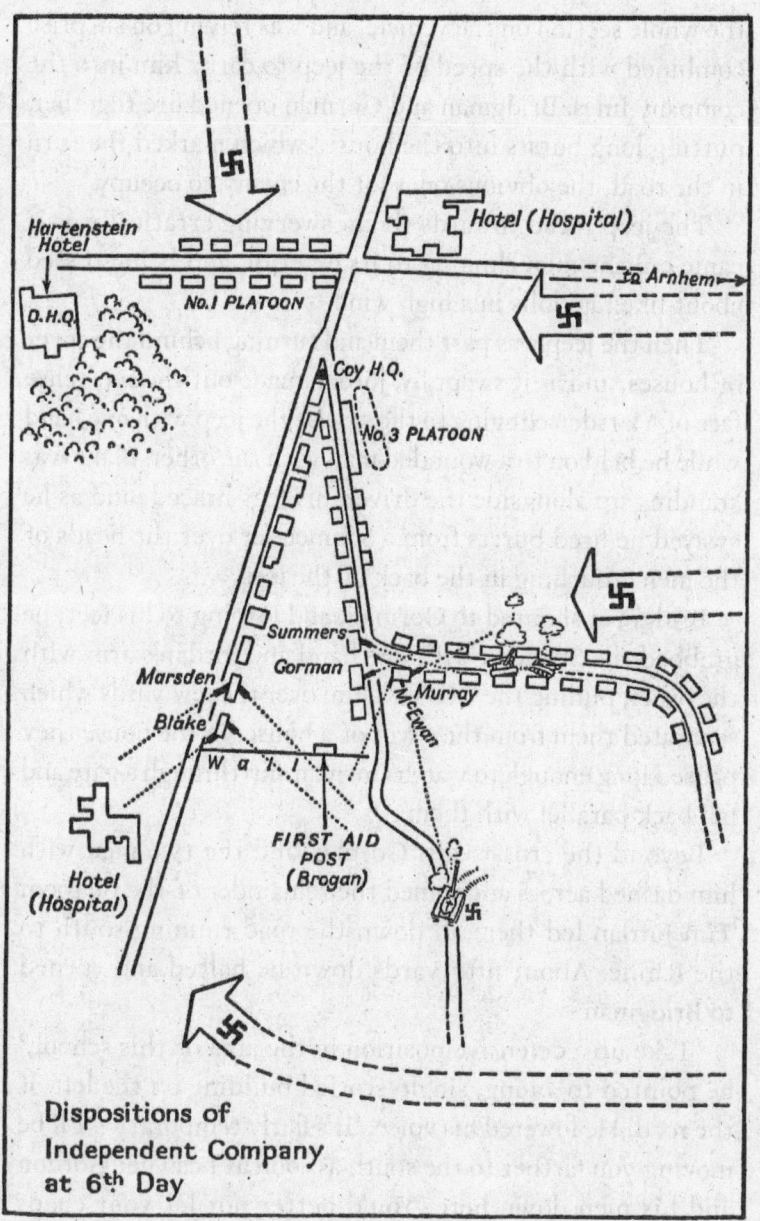

Hartenstein
Hotel

D.H.Q.

Hotel (Hospital)

To Arnhem →

No.1 PLATOON

Coy H.Q.

No.3 PLATOON

Summers

Gorman

Marsden

Murray

Blake

McEwan

W a l l

FIRST AID
POST
(Brogan)

Hotel
(Hospital)

Dispositions of
Independent Company
at 6th Day

the whole section on the vehicle, and was relying on surprise combined with the speed of the jeep to carry him into the company lines. Bridgman and Gorman opened fire together, putting long bursts into the houses which marked the turn in the road, the obvious ones for the enemy to occupy.

The jeep raced towards them, swerving erratically as it came on: the men clinging to its exterior, and being tossed about like rag dolls in a high wind.

Then the jeep was past them and turning behind the cover of houses, and as it swept by, Jordan made out the set, tense face of Marsden clinging to the side of the jeep with one hand while he held on to a wounded man with the other. Blake was standing up alongside the driver, his legs braced, and as he swayed he fired bursts from a Schmeisser over the heads of the men crouching in the back of the jeep.

Bridgman shouted to Gorman, and leaping to his feet, he grabbed the Spandau with one hand and Jordan's arm with the other, pulling the CO with him over the few yards which separated them from the cover of a house. In the house they paused long enough to watch Gorman slip through a gate and fall back parallel with them.

Beyond the crossroads, Gorman and the two men with him dashed across and joined the remainder of the platoon. Tim Jordan led them all down the road running south to the Rhine. About fifty yards down he halted and turned to Bridgman.

'Take up a defensive position in the area of this school,' he pointed to a long, single-storied building on the left of the road. He lowered his voice. 'It's fairly temporary – I'll be moving you farther to the south as soon as I can get Gordon and his men down here. You'd better not let your chaps know they're moving again. They're pretty tired as it is, and they won't make much of defensive positions if they realize they're preparing them for someone else.'

Bridgman nodded. One of the best things about Jordan was the trust he showed in his junior commanders. Too many commanding officers wanted to site every post in the unit, worrying themselves where individual riflemen should be dug in. Jordan stayed long enough to indicate the link with his own headquarters, and to point out the ominous size of the gap between themselves and the scratch forces who held positions between the company and the Lonsdale Force down by the river.

Bridgman got his platoon into the cover of the school, and taking his section commanders with him, he carried out a reconnaissance of the immediate area. He made it as thorough as he could, for he was convinced there would be no further contraction of the perimeter. From now on, units would stand or fall in roughly the positions they were now in.

Bridgman reckoned he had only a few uninterrupted hours at the most. When the Germans in the centre of the town found there was nothing immediately in front of them, they would edge forward, cautiously, probing the area in front of them until they came up against resistance. The last elements of 1st Brigade and of the South Staffs had fallen back during the night and taken up defensive positions under the command of Major Lonsdale in the south. These positions ran northwards from the Rhine, past Oosterbeek church, and finished some three hundred yards short of the school occupied by Bridgman and his platoon. In between, immediately south of the Independent Company, lay a composite platoon from 4th Para Brigade headquarters, and below them a detachment of the RASC. The country in front of these last two detachments was fairly open, but nevertheless they constituted a very weak force to hold a front of such length. The road on which the school lay was one of two secondary roads which came together some sixty yards north of the school. Where they joined, Jordan had his headquarters in a large house. The second of the two roads ran parallel to that held by Alan and his platoon. It ran inside the perimeter, and joined two of the buildings being used by the division as hospitals. Farther to the west, beyond the interior road, lay open ground, then the tennis courts into which had been packed the German prisoners of war, and on the far side of the tennis courts, the Hartenstein Hotel and Divisional Headquarters.

North of the crossroads, Ramsden and his platoon faced east, on roughly the same line as Alan and his men. On the crossroads itself, facing in to the Independent Company headquarters, was the Vreewyk Hotel, the most northerly of the hospitals, and east of it, on the road into Arnhem, was what was left of the 10th Para Battalion, all that stood between the hospital and the Germans.

Alan left one section digging in in the extensive gardens beyond the school, and the other two sections preparing the building itself for siege. He put a screen of riflemen in front of the men digging, and handing over the platoon to Blake, he set out with O'Neill to investigate the gap on his right flank.

Thirty yards south of the school, a secondary road ran east towards Arnhem, but it ran for only a little under a hundred yards before making a sharp turn to the right. This was unguarded, and must become an obvious line of approach for the enemy. Twenty yards beyond the junction formed by the two roads, the one on which the school stood made a slight twist first to the left, and then to the right, but it was sufficient to prevent them from covering the road from their present positions. At this point the interior road was some forty yards to the west, and joined by a brick wall over ten feet high. This formed the base of a triangle, with the house which held Jordan's headquarters at the apex where the two roads joined.

Bridgman and O'Neill walked across the gardens parallel with the wall and looked across the inside road at the positions round General Urquhart's headquarters in the Hartenstein Hotel. Farther to the west the Border Regiment and the 9th RE Field Company faced towards Amsterdam. The perimeter was very narrow.

At mid-morning, Brown arrived with his platoon and took over the school from Alan.

Bridgman gave the details of his reconnaissance to Jordan, and when the CO left to return to his headquarters it had been decided that Bridgman's platoon was to sidestep until his right flank rested on the twist in the road and the wall which cut back above the lower hospital.

Alan gave much thought to the siting of his section posts. He felt a great certainty that these were the final positions. In the positions he now selected, his platoon would fight its last fight: there would be no withdrawal; there was nowhere to withdraw to. They would either hold out here, in this corner of Oosterbeek, or they would be overrun and wiped out.

Except for a short period in the big house, Murray's section had been held in reserve in a counter-attack role for the whole of the action. Alan realized that this could not continue. It was the best-rested section, and of its original twelve members eight still remained: its four casualties had all occurred on the second day, and it had lost only one NCO. Alan was using O'Neill as a runner but the section was seven strong without him. Of Blake's original section, there was only himself, Lance-Corporal Cobbold, Ewing and Bignall. Since midday on the fourth day, Blake had had Marsden's section under command, and this was now reduced to Marsden himself, Hudson, Laverty, McGrath, Adams, and Chambers. The two sections combined numbered only ten out of their original twenty-four, and in addition they had had to bear the brunt of most of the fighting. Gorman had six men, including himself.

Alan put Murray's section in the right-hand corner house on the secondary road running east from the company position, and also in the house immediately above it; the farther house to cover the road approach, the corner house the open ground in front of the composite platoon from 4th Brigade HQ. Gorman's section he put into two houses on the inside of the road on which the school stood. This enabled the section to cover all parts of the approach road up to the point where it turned away to the right. Blake and Marsden's men he put in two much bigger houses on the rear of the two roads. If Murray and Gorman were overrun, there would still be a force between the enemy and divisional headquarters. Dwyer, the wireless operator, he left with Blake at the place where he would theoretically have his own headquarters.

Leaving the men preparing the defences, Bridgman and O'Neill went methodically through the houses in their sector, noting which of them still held Dutch people in their cellars; which contained water in buckets or baths, and which food.

The houses facing east had no cellars, but the ones held by Blake had large ones, and these were packed with Dutch civilians. The Dutch were quiet, resigned, and eager to co-operate. They realized they would be in the way above ground, and that in the circumstances they could render no better service than to keep out of harm's way, and not embarrass the British soldiers by movement about the positions.

At one o'clock in the afternoon, Brown's platoon opened fire, and Alan, who was with Gorman's section, first lit a cigarette, and then looked towards the section commander. Gorman smiled back, his lips turned down and one eyebrow raised quizzically. This was it. Not the end, but the beginning of the end. The hand of the German Army had closed until it was gripping the division on every front. How much force would be required to squeeze the airborne men out of existence they had yet to find out. Bridgman slipped out from Gorman's position and made his way behind the houses until he was at the back of the school on the opposite side of the road. He waited until O'Neill was alongside him, and then they both dashed quickly across the narrow road and climbed through a window to join Brown.

Gorman stood behind the two men at the table in the first-floor bedroom. The table was back in the centre of the room, and behind earth-packed sacks and pillow-cases rested a Piat and a Bren gun, and behind the weapons, Lance-Corporal Summers and Woodley. They looked out on to the eighty yards of open road which ran away from them until it turned sharply to the right. Where it turned, three red-brick Dutch houses stared blankly back at them. Sooner or later, the Germans must occupy those houses: they were probably parallel with them already, opposite Brown and his men.

'Your ears are more important than anything now,' Gorman spoke quietly, his voice impersonal as if he were thinking of other things. 'Keep them pinned back for any sound of armoured movement. To come down this road, they've first to get to that corner.' He nodded his head to the east. 'I should think they'll patrol first. I'm going over to see Murray – to see if we can't fix up some sort of tank trap between us.'

Neither of the men spoke for some minutes after he left them. Each was busy with his own thoughts. Woodley spoke first, but first he glanced surreptitiously at the lance-corporal. Summers was an odd one all right. He should have been an officer. Woodley knew he'd been to OCTU early in the war, but for some reason had not been commissioned. No one knew why, although there had been plenty of conjecture, and a few comic and wild guesses. Generally it had been put down to booze. Summers drank a lot, and it showed in his face. Not in the obvious ways, but his thick, protuberant lower lip hung always slightly open, and his rather prominent eyes remained vacant when other men's lighted up. He was friendly with everybody and nobody. When in billets, he never refused an invitation to join other men for a drink or a party, but he never originated anything. If nobody suggested anything, he simply went out and drank on his own. He was nearly thirty, and therefore older than anyone else in the platoon except Sergeant Nash.

The sudden recollection of the platoon sergeant brought Woodley up with a jerk.

'Wonder what happened to old Jim Nash?' he asked, absently, as if he didn't really expect an answer.

'Bought it, I suppose. Either that or wounded and taken prisoner. What made you suddenly think of Jim?'

'Don't know – just thinking.'

'It doesn't pay to think about the others. The casualties, I mean. When you're hit, you're out of it. You're not only out of it, you're a bloody nuisance to your own people if you haven't been captured. We should all be issued with hemlock, and the moment we're no longer effective we should be expected to take it.'

Summers raised the Bren to his shoulder, squinted through the sights and then lowered the butt on to the blanket-covered table.

'That,' he went on in a quasi-theatrical voice, 'would be rather a *grand* way of dying.'

Woodley looked at the lance-corporal again, sharply. Just one word, and the way in which it had been said, had suddenly opened his eyes. Summers was queer. Woodley blushed as he realized that a man he had known and soldiered with for years was homosexual. He busied himself moving Piat bombs into a handier position. He wondered why he had not guessed it before, and if any of the others had. His mind wandered back over past incidents, seeking some clue he should have seen but missed. In civilian life, Woodley was a musician, and in the course of his work he had encountered hundreds of queers, but he had always known soon after meeting them that they were queer, the majority of them had made no attempt to conceal it. Either Summers was a bloody good actor or he was a non-practising homosexual.

Woodley stood up.

'Shan't be a tick,' he said, 'just going for a leak.'

He left the room without looking at Summers. He felt angry. Not because Summers was queer, not because the NCO had deceived him, but because he had so successfully deceived them all for so long. Woodley felt that it was some-how not right for a man to be so different without other people being aware of it. It took all the certainty and secu-rity out of life. It made you feel that you never knew what you were going to discover next. Christ! Summers might even make advances. Woodley clattered down the stairs, the noise he made an unconscious barrier thrown up between Summers and himself.

As Woodley left the room, Summers half turned and watched him over his shoulder. He winced at the noise the soldier made, guessing the reason that prompted it. He looked at the empty road and shared its loneliness. He resisted the temptation to make a physical demonstration of his misery to himself. He had spent too many hours of his life with shaking shoulders and sob-racked chest, but he conceded a little to his unhappiness: he lowered his head on his crossed wrists and breathed deeply. Since puberty he had lived alone, completely alone, cut off from his fellows not because of his queerness, but because of his refusal to communicate it to others. Fate had decreed that he should be different, he had decided that he should live without the sympathy of understanding. Now that Woodley knew, he could not expect anything from him except an uncomfortable awareness, an unspoken, shared knowledge of Summers's dif-ference, which from now on would make every moment they spent alone together embarrassing to both.

Woodley stood in the garden buttoning his flies. There was now no firing on 3 Platoon's front, but fighting was going on to the north where he believed the Recce Squadron to be, and there was intermittent fire from one of the Border com-panies, and from the area held by the Lonsdale Force.

Woodley fingered the black stubble of his beard. He had a thin face with hollow cheeks, and now it seemed that only skin lay between his dirty finger tips and the curve of his cheekbones. God, he was tired! He screwed up his eyes and stared across at the two big houses held by Blake and thought he saw a movement behind one of the windows. He shrugged and turned back, looking in at the room below their own where Cummings had barricaded himself behind a captured Spandau. They exchanged a few words, and then, leaving the other soldier to his solitary vigil, Woodley climbed up the stairs to rejoin Summers. He paused for a moment outside the bedroom, trying to forgive Summers for something the lance corporal could not help. It was the tiredness, the bone-bloody weariness which was slowly breaking down their resistance. Physical exhaustion had caught Summers off guard, and for one second his façade of normality had slipped. Woodley hoped he had not betrayed his discovery to the other man by his manner. He would try to pretend that he had noticed nothing. He opened the door and went in. Summers was sitting in exactly the same position as he had been when Woodley left him, his left hand grasping the butt of the Bren, his right elbow resting on the table and his hand turned inwards with the knuckles uppermost: his chin resting lightly on the back of his fingers. At once, Woodley thought how odd it was: most men would have turned their hand and rested their chin firmly in the cupped palm. It was going to be difficult to forget.

Gorman found Murray in the farther of the two houses which were his responsibility. McEwan was in the one behind him, the corner house, the southern side of which looked out towards the open ground in front of the 4th Brigade head-quarter platoon. He found a scowling, bad-tempered Murray who muttered and swore as he moved from room to room. Nothing was right. He had no field of fire. To the north he could only see through the narrow gaps between the houses on the opposite side of the road, and he could see only two of the three houses at the road's end. The south was covered by McEwan in the house behind him.

Gorman waited till the Belfast sergeant had finished blowing off steam.

'It looks like a bastard, John, but there's one thing about this sort of position – it's as hard for them to get at you as it is for you to move out if you wanted to. You can get back to us – just, but apart from that you're strictly limited – but of course, you limit them too. How could they get you out unless they brought tanks up to the front door. The houses that block your view prevent them from advancing towards you. The road's covered by my chaps as well as yours, and 3 Platoon neutralizes the backs of the houses on the other side of the road. I reckon your position's pretty good as long as we can stop them getting armour down to you – that's what I really came to see you about. What can we fix up?'

With his problems simplified to this basic one, Murray unwound, and began to speak with authority. Presently Gorman returned to his own section, satisfied that Murray would be all right. He was already getting to work preparing a similar tank trap to the one they had so successfully put into effect on the third day.

Gorman went into the second of his two houses, the one which held only Mocock and Liddon. Both men were behind a Spandau, and as he entered the room they threw him a quick glance and then resumed their watch on their front. Gorman sat down and smoked a cigarette without speaking to either of them. The situation was bad, but even so he thought there was too much tenseness. He sensed it here with Mocock and Liddon, and he had sensed it with Summers and Woodley.

'One of you two had better rest,' he said. 'You can't both sit indefinitely staring out of a window – we might be here for days yet. One of you will have to stay with the gun while the other one rests. I'm going to join Cummings and work turn and turn about with him. You two do the same.'

The two soldiers looked woodenly at him, and then at each other. Liddon, who was behind the gun, jerked his head at his companion, eased his shoulders in the cross-webs of his equipment and resumed his watch. Mocock rolled over and sat with his back against the wall.

'Days! Don't tell me you think we can hold on for days, sarge.' Mocock's flat, Yorkshire vowels turned the negation of a question into something positive. 'Eee, they could come through us any time they liked. Like a dose of salts – couldn't they, sarge?'

Gorman started to deny the possibility, then changed his mind. These men weren't just private soldiers. They were good soldiers, and they were his friends.

'You'd think so, Tom, but they don't. What's true now has been true since 4th Brigade caught their packet and fell back into the divisional area. Why do you think they haven't come through us?'

'I'm stuffed if I know. We were talking about it 'fore you came in. P'raps they think there's more of us than there is. P'raps they're waiting for more guns or tanks or something – though I'd think they'd got more than enough for us little lot without waiting for more.'

Gorman looked at the back of Liddon's fair head. Both men were fair, both Yorkshiremen. Liddon, tall and big-boned, more typically Saxon than Mocock, who was shorter and thicker. Liddon was slower in speech than his friend, and this gave the impression that he was slower-thinking. Gorman knew this wasn't true. He wondered what the big man thought about it, and he asked: 'What do you think, Del'? Do you think they're waiting for reinforcements?'

'No. They're waiting for guts . . . I think 1st and 4th Brigades frightened the daylights out of the bastards . . . they're hoping we'll get too stuffing thirsty, an' too stuffing hungry, an' too stuffing tired to fight any more . . . they're hoping we'll run out of stuffing ammo. I expect they've been hoping we'd walk into the bag like those stuffers did at Singapore and Tobruk.'

Liddon turned and looked at Gorman, and his last words he spat out. 'They're going to drop a bollock, aren't they, sarge?'

'It wasn't the men's fault at Singapore and Tobruk, Del. In both cases the surrender was made at the highest level.'

'Highest level . . . bollocks! No man'd surrender troops who had the guts to go on fighting.'

Gorman laughed and got to his feet. 'You might be right at that, but I'll leave you to sort it out – I'm going to have a look at Cummings.'

He met Bridgman and his runner as soon as he got through the back door, but it was a second or two before he recognized the men with them.

'Hello, Frank. I've got some reinforcements for you.'

Bridgman was grinning. 'I thought I'd take a look in the hospital, and these chaps wouldn't let me leave without them. Bilting wanted to come too, but one of the docs says he's got a fever, so I had to leave him behind.'

Gorman looked beyond Bridgman to where Fraser, Hardy, and Butcher stood, trying to look as if they were there by chance. Butcher's left arm was in a sling, and both Hardy's and Fraser's heads were bandaged.

'Are they all for me?' Gorman raised his eyebrows in inquiry. 'Hardy and Butcher both belong to Blake, don't they?'

'Yes, but you're the thinnest on the ground. I thought I'd give you Fraser, who's one of your chaps anyway, and Hardy as well. With two extra men you should be able to conduct some sort of reliefs. I'll take Butcher back to Blake. He can only use one hand, but we'll be able to find something for him to do.'

Cummings had been on his own for some time so Gorman told him to rest in an upstairs bedroom and put Hardy and Fraser in his place. He outlined the situation of the rest of the company, then left them to return to Murray and find out how far he had progressed with the tank trap.

When he had gone, Fraser said, 'You'll have to man that bloody thing.' He nodded towards the Spandau, 'I'm afraid I never paid much attention when Nash was teaching us how to handle them. If the damned thing jammed, I shouldn't have a clue. Anyway, you were Blake's crack Bren gunner, weren't you?'

Hardy grinned wryly, and sank behind the Spandau, wincing as a movement of his neck started his head throbbing. It was typical of Roy Fraser that he should not know how to operate the German gun. His attitude of 'couldn't care less' was something deeper than a mere pose. Hardy thought he was genuinely not particularly interested in the outcome of the war, or even the particular battle they were fighting at that moment. It was impossible to get his friend to talk seriously on any subject except cricket or tennis, and yet he never shirked a job or sought to avoid anything because it happened to be dangerous. He took everything in his calm, unruffled stride, seeming to affect affectation for the pleasure of infuriating others.

Hardy watched Murray and three of his men carrying armfuls of Hawkins mines up the road and disappear into a garden on the left of it. He thought they were chancing their arm a bit, and he watched the three houses at the end closely.

Fraser slumped down with his back to the wall, beside him. His voice carried its usual trace of condescending banter.

'I'd like to wager that Tom Marsden will be across as soon as he hears that we're back. He won't miss the opportunity of taking the piss out of the wounded heroes, will he? I can almost hear him now – "And the battle of Arnhem was lost on the playing fields of Eton".'

Hardy laughed quietly. He liked Marsden, and he knew Fraser did as well. He also knew that Tom got under Roy's skin in a way that nobody else could. His continual references to gentleman rankers came as near to upsetting Fraser's poise as anything Hardy had seen. Suddenly, without thinking, he asked the question that neither had ever asked the other.

'Tell me, Roy, why didn't you go to OCTU? You must have had the chance.'

He felt Fraser's eyes on him, and turned his head from the window. They looked at each other for a moment, then instead of answering, Fraser asked, 'Why didn't you?' Hardy looked back up the road.

'Because I'm a bastard.'

'We all know that, and a very conscientious bastard too.'

'No – I'm serious. I turned down the chance of going to OCTU because I'm a bastard. I've never met my father – I haven't the faintest idea who he is. It's as simple as that.'

Fraser said nothing for a long minute but sat with his lips pursed; when he did speak the tone of his voice was unchanged. It expressed neither sympathy nor understanding nor surprise.

'I don't see what that has to do with it. I should think you could put what you like on those bloody forms. You don't seriously think they've time to check every application for OCTU, do you?'

'No – but you have to provide a birth certificate.'

'Even so, I can't see that it would have made any difference. With the country at war, I can't see that a War Office Selection Board would be concerned about the legitimacy or otherwise of a candidate's birth.'

'Perhaps not, but the whole thing would have been brought out into the open. Other people would have had to know. I always felt it would be like betraying my mother for a personal advantge. Anyway, there it is – that's why I never went to OCTU. What about you?'

'I didn't go because I didn't want to. There was no particular reason – I just didn't want to.'

Fraser got up and walked to the door.

'I'm going to have a nosey around – see if there's any grub about. If they have a bash, don't be greedy – save some for me.'

And he was gone into the passage leaving Hardy no wiser than before. This didn't worry him much; he hadn't initiated the conversation out of curiosity. He wasn't really curious about Fraser's reasons. He'd wanted an excuse to give his own, and now that he had, he felt a small measure of contentment. It hadn't been so hard as he thought it would be. Perhaps now, if he got back, he'd be able to tell Sybil and, who knows, she might take it as casually as Roy had done.

Hardy saw Murray and his men come out into the road again – Warke, Banham, and Waterson. The way they walked, with their weapons half-raised to their shoulders, would have seemed melodramatic at any other time. They faced up the road towards the houses at the end, and Hardy sensed how their eyes must be probing, searching for any sign of movement.

Murray followed them, paying out a makeshift line made up of curtaining and sheets. There was little hope of concealing their object from the enemy, and it didn't matter just so long as armour was stopped from coming down the road.

A single rifle shot rang out, and Hardy saw Waterson stagger sideways as if he had been pushed suddenly and caught off balance. He heard the Bren in the house above open fire a fraction of a second before his own finger closed around the trigger. Then both sections were pouring fire into the three houses at the end of the road and into the spaces around them.

From the corner of his eye, Hardy saw Waterson continue down the road towards him, his back to the enemy. The other two men had jumped and half started to run back. They both checked themselves and turned to face the direction from which the shot had come. Murray continued to play out the line – and then it was stuck, caught up in something out of sight in the garden.

Murray pulled frantically at it. Failing to free it, he dropped the part he held, and ran back to where it disappeared round a gatepost. Warke and Banham had moved on to the pavement on the right of the road. Banham lay against a garden wall, and Warke knelt behind him. Neither of them had fired, they were leaving covering fire to the sections behind them. Instead they watched for any movement, their weapons held loosely at their shoulders.

Murray reappeared, running fast. He stooped to pick up the line where he had dropped it in the middle of the road, and even as he picked it up he was hit. He sprawled rather than fell, like a soccer player who had over-reached himself in an attempt to get to the ball. Almost at once he was on his feet again, and stumbling in a series of hops across the road. He dropped a three-foot circle of rope over the gatepost, and then passed his cloth line through it. He shouted to Warke and Banham, and the three fell back together, Murray paying out the line as he went.

Hardy saw it all between the spaced bursts he was putting about the houses at the end of the road. He had spotted no movement there, and it was likely the shots had come from the leading scout of a patrol. He ceased firing the moment Murray and his men got out of sight in the farther of the two houses.

He looked at Fraser who had come into the room and now lay alongside him. Within minutes, an hour or two at the most, the Germans would be facing them in force. They would be separate from them by only eighty or so yards of open road.

Without warning, Fraser started to laugh, really to laugh, his shoulders shaking.

'I wonder,' he said, 'I wonder what the Germans would do if they realized that there were only twenty-five men between themselves and our divisional headquarters.'

Hardy looked back out of the window and wondered if the makeshift line would run freely through the rope loop. Whether it would in fact drag the mines across the road when they were needed.

'I found some bottled green peas – I'll go and get them.'

Fraser got up and went out again.

CHAPTER FIFTEEN

Bridgman bent, cupped his hands under Butcher's shin, and hoisted the Cockney through the window.

Blake had most of his men in the back rooms of the house, the ones which faced divisional headquarters to the east, and the lower hospital to the south. He was as worried about the gap below them as Bridgman was.

'They've been mortaring the hell out of Div HQ.' He looked across the open ground towards the tennis courts and the hotel beyond them. 'They must have hit a lot of their own chaps too. The POWs don't stand much chance in there, but they've started to dig in now. How's it going the other way?'

Bridgman looked at the German prisoners huddled behind the wire netting which surrounded the tennis courts. He supposed he should feel sorry for them, but he didn't. If they were unwounded they shouldn't be prisoners. He looked back at Blake's cheerful, smiling face, at his blue eyes, still bright though the whites were veined with red, at his broken nose and pugnacious chin with its harvest stubble of fair hair. He looked to the right of the window where Cobbold and Ewing crouched behind their Bren gun, its muzzle pointing to the left of the hospital, at the gap between it and the trees.

'A German patrol got itself shot up by 3 Platoon. Mr Brown let them come on till they were caught out in open gardens with glass houses behind them. I should think they were cut about a bit.'

They both grinned at the weak joke.

'Well, where do we go from here, sir?'

'I shouldn't think we do, Bob. We just stick it out and hope to Christ 2nd Army extract their stuffing digit. They've had it well and firmly in for six bloody days now.'

'What's the news about 30 Corps, sir? The last I heard was that they were still at Nijmegen. Do you think they stopped to go to the flicks?'

'Nothing'd surprise me, Bob. Nothing.'

'The bridge has gone, hasn't it?'

'Yes, the bridge has gone, and 2nd Battalion with it. I wonder if Johnny Frost is still alive – they did a bloody fine job down there on their own. If 2nd Army had been only two days late, they could still have got over the bridge.'

'What about the Poles? A chap from the Field Hospital told me they'd dropped their Para Brigade, but they can't have landed on the dropping-zone they were meant to come in on. That was just south of the bridge, and it must be alive with stuffing Huns by now.'

'They landed at Driel, immediately below us. They've formed a perimeter on the south bank, so it'll be nice and comfy for 2nd Army when they arrive – if they arrive.'

They both stopped talking and listened.

'That was our chaps – get most of your men to the back – come on, O'Neill.'

Bridgman and O'Neill were out of the room and heading for the rear of the house before the last words were out of the platoon commander's mouth.

Blake left Cobbold and Ewing with the Bren to watch the gap below the hospital. He took Bignall and Adams with him into a back room, and as he shouted to Marsden in the house above him he saw Bridgman and O'Neill sprinting across the last of the forty yards which separated them from the rear of Gorman's section.

Marsden's face appeared from an upstairs window and Blake shouted to him to get his men to where they could cover the gardens. He looked back and saw Bridgman disappear through a back door. The automatic fire was intense, and Blake spotted the muzzle flash from a machine-gun in Murray's position. Gorman's houses blotted out his view of the road where he guessed the trouble to lie.

It was the first time since they had landed that Blake's and Marsden's men had not contributed directly to an action in which the platoon was involved, and this made Blake feel uncomfortable and apprehensive. He couldn't see – he didn't know what was going on. He had to resist the temptation to slip over to Gorman's houses and find out for himself.

'What's happened, sergeant?'

It was Adams who spoke, his voice carrying a slight squeak of bewilderment. Blake looked at him and laughed. Adams was getting better, improving as a soldier every day, but the sergeant found it impossible to imagine the youngster as an adult. He was so open to surprise, ingenuous when confronted by the unexpected.

Blake looked back towards the screening houses. It would be a pity if Adams was killed. It would be a loss to the world of one tiny scrap of naive freshness from its meagre store.

'I don't know, Adams. Jerry's having a bash at one of the other sections. Probably only a patrol – we'll find out soon enough. Just keep your eyes skinned.'

Bignall opened his mouth to speak and then changed his mind. He had been about to say something deflating to Adams but he had stopped in time. He had once seen Blake lose his temper with a man who had taken advantage of another's inexperience to humiliate him, and he decided he didn't want a repeat with himself on the receiving end.

Butcher wandered into the room through the door behind them.

'You blokes don't know how well off you are. Should 'ave been in that stuffin' 'ospital with me. 'Ospital! More like a stuffin' morgue. More stiffs than wrigglers. Me – I was glad to get out uv it. Every time I saw a bloody MO I thought 'e'd come round to polish me orf.'

Butcher paused, and then added, darkly, 'I reckon there's bin a lot uv that th-th-thasia balls goin' on. 'Aven't got time for 'em all, you see – what they do is patch up the ones they think they can save and the bad 'uns, the ones that'll die anyway – they just give 'em an 'elping 'and. Suppose it's the best way reely – long as it's not you that's being 'elped.'

The three soldiers by the window didn't answer, or even turn round. Butcher shrugged his shoulders at their backs.

'I'll make a brew – if I can find any water – if I can find any tea – if I can find a tommy-cooker.'

He got as far as the door and then spoke again, over his shoulder.

''Ere, sarge. D'you think I'll get a medal? Wounded soldier, two fingers missing, fights on wiv 'is comrade. I can almost see the 'eadlines – can't you?'

Blake continued to look out of the window; if you encouraged Butcher he kept on for ever. Butcher went out, grinning to himself. None of them knew how to cope with him, and he loved every minute of their uncertainty.

When he had gone, Adams glanced at Blake.

'Is that right, sergeant? Do they finish them off if they're too bad?'

'No. That's just old soldier's talk. Keep your eyes on the far end of that stable. If they slip past McEwan, they'll come through that way.'

Sometimes they did finish them off, but who knew how often it happened? Although he'd been joking, Butcher was right. There must be occasions when it was the best, the right thing to do. He'd seen men with their stomachs hanging out like gutted rabbits. Not always in pain, but with expressions of shocked incredulity on their faces as they stared with disbelieving eyes at what should have been smooth, unblemished skin. He had seen men who in the first minutes after being wounded were fascinated, hypnotized by the change wrought in their bodies. But the fascination soon went from their eyes, to be replaced by a horrified recognition of the ultimate consequences of what had been done to them. After that came the penultimate look of utter despair.

The firing had stopped some twenty minutes earlier, and Blake waited impatiently for news. The shelling and mortaring of the entire area held by the division had intensified. To some extent it drowned the incessant chatter of small-arms fire which in some place or another was continually being exchanged as German patrols and localized attacks thrust against or probed the airborne men's positions. Every now and again, concentrated automatic fire signalled that a more concerted and determined attack was being made by the enemy, or that covering fire was being given for some necessary friendly movement.

When Bridgman reappeared, he was accompanied by O'Neill and a second man whom Blake could not identify.

Adams said, 'I think it's Wil . . .' His voice died away in a mumble.

Blake looked sharply round.

'Who? What did you say?'

'Nothing. It can't . . . nothing, sergeant.'

Bignall said, 'It's Waterson. It looks as if he's been hit – his arm's in a sling.'

Looking again, Blake, too, recognized the soldier as the small group disappeared into the stable that was being used as a first-aid post.

Adams watched the movement of the men with his eyes, but his mind travelled three days back in time. For one moment, when Blake had asked the question, Adams had been certain that the third soldier was Wilcox, until he remembered that it could not be. His last memory of Wilcox was how, after he had been hit once, he had still clung to the window-frame, striving to claw his way into the room. Adams saw again the mortar bomb bursting behind him, and Tom Marsden looking down at were he lay out of sight in the little front garden. Adams brushed his eyes. Bignall was right. It couldn't be Wilcox.

★

Bridgman and O'Neill joined Blake just as Butcher brought in a jug of tea. They left the Cockney to keep an eye on the other sections, and moved into the room with Cobbold and Ewing to drink it.

Bridgman sent O'Neill for Marsden, and when the corporal arrived the platoon commander put them all in the picture.

'It was only a patrol, and I should think only one of them fired. He was probably the leading scout, and he got as far as the gap between the houses at the angle where the road turns. It was just bloody hard luck that Murray and three of his men were out laying a tank-trap. Five minutes earlier or five minutes later and they might have caught the whole patrol in the middle of the road. Waterson has been hit in the arm – not too badly from what I saw of it – and Murray's been hit in the calf of the leg. He won't leave the section, so Brogan's going over to see him when he's patched Waterson up.'

Bridgman turned to Marsden.

'I've managed to get a couple of your pals out of the hospital above Company HQ. They're with Gorman now.'

Marsden grinned and raised his eyebrows in inquiry.

'Fraser and Hardy?'

Bridgman smiled back.

'Yes, Fraser and Hardy. I don't think they wanted you to know. Any message for them when I see them?' Marsden grinned even more savagely.

'No, not really. Just tell them I know they'll keep a stiff upper lip, and set us all a fine example at the end if there's nothing left to do but die like English gentlemen.'

The six of them laughed at Marsden's barbed words, but Adams's laugh was a little uncertain. To him, Marsden's humour always sounded a little too vicious to be funny. Adams had to remind himself that Fraser, Hardy, and Marsden were friends.

Blake walked to the top of the cellar steps with the last of the tea. A few steps down he found Signaller Dwyer slumped against the wall, his earphones round his neck and his set at receive. He woke him and handed him the mess tin, watching him grow more alert as he drank.

Dwyer put the empty container on a step beside him.

'Afraid I must have dropped off, sergeant. It's bloody hard to stay awake – just sitting.'

'I know. But try to keep your earphones on. If they're just round your neck, anything coming through might be too faint to wake you. Anyway, I'll send Bignall down to relieve you for a couple of hours. He's all right on one of these sets, isn't he?'

'Well, yes. He's better than most of them.'

Blake went back and sent the other man down. Then he climbed the stairs to the top of the house, looking cautiously out of each window in turn. To the east the scenery looked bruised and shattered, as if a giant hand had run its fingers idly through the trees, stripping the leaves and tearing the bark. He could hear sniping from above the crossroads where 1 Platoon faced east into Arnhem, and he wondered how those other men he knew so well were getting on.

He sat on a narrow bed and looked at the sky above the Hartenstein Hotel, trying for the first time since he had landed to rationalize the whole complex situation. At first his mind shied away from the immediate and intuitively convincing conclusions. He sat up on the bed and took deep breaths, disciplining his body as a requisite to the marshalling of his thoughts.

The division, as a division, was finished. No amount of optimism could enable anyone to visualize it being reformed before the war ended. The 1st British Airborne Division was already reduced to small groups of men in houses and holes in the ground, fighting to hold an area twelve hundred yards long by under a thousand wide, in the faint hope that it would form a lodgment for 2nd Army if it succeeded in crossing the Rhine. Blake had no idea as to the effective strength of the division, but he guessed that it had been reduced to somewhere between three and four thousand men. Their own company was already below half strength. 1st Para Brigade, except for the elements under Major Lonsdale, had virtually ceased to exist. 4th Para Brigade was now only about two hundred and fifty strong, one-eighth of its original strength. These two brigades had been the ones constantly in the attack for the first few days after landing. They had not been attacking the line-of-communication troops which Intelligence had assured them would be the only opposition in the early stages, they had been attacking the tanks, guns and infantry of two crack Panzer Divisions under the command of General Bittrich.

Many other units had had more casualties than the Independent Company; the South Staffs had been nearly wiped out, and the KOSBs had taken a severe beating as they withdrew over the railway embankment.

Blake fumbled till he found a bent cigarette. He lit it as though watching the action of someone else – that was just bloody tiredness. He shook his head and looked out of the window again, taking deep, lung-filling drags at his cigarette, and he thought about the company. About old Tim Jordan in Company HQ up by the crossroads. Never far from his wireless set. Never using it unless it became absolutely necessary. Waiting, always waiting for news that one of his platoons was under pressure. Then Blake thought about 1 Platoon. The last runner from company headquarters had told him that Ramsden and his men were holding houses on one side of the street, and the Germans the houses on the other, only thirty or forty feet between them. Movement there must be difficult, if not impossible. As for 3 Platoon, it had suffered the most casualties: it was well below half strength and all its section commanders had been killed or wounded.

Blake found himself thinking methodically about his own platoon, as if he were going through the nominal roll of its remnants. He wondered what Bridgman really thought about it all. It was hard to know with any certainty; one would have to know Bridgman as a man, and to believe that he looked upon you as a man. This was nearly impossible. Bridgman seemed to view everyone primarily as soldiers. His like or dislike of an individual was more than tempered by his opinion of their martial ability.

Frank Gorman was all right. As for Murray and headquarter section, Blake had no doubts about Murray's guts, only his ability. Murray was out to prove something: that he was as good a section commander as the others. This worried Blake, and to some extent he blamed Bridgman for the circumstances which made Murray think it necessary that he had to prove anything. Theoretically, Bridgman had a good case. Headquarter section was for the defence of platoon headquarters, in the role that units of the company had to play, headquarters was more often than not where the Eureka had been set up; the infantry sections would be in position at some distance, and it was headquarter section which formed the last line of defence round the radar equipment. It was logical that Murray's section should normally be kept in reserve, but after the company's pathfinding role had been completed, it no longer made much sense.

Blake thought about the individual survivors. Bignall, the Canadian 'Canteen Romeo' whose successes with girls tended to make him unpopular with some of the other men. Quiet Cobbold, the lance-corporal in charge of Blake's Bren group. A market gardener in civilian life, he had one of the best eyes for ground in the company. Ewing, who had taken Hardy's place on the gun, had been a printer, and it was his trade which was probably responsible for his careful attention to detail. He could always be trusted to do the right thing.

The mental images of his men slid out from Blake's mind, and he found himself thinking about his family. About his father who had taught him his trade as a stonemason, and his mother, younger sister and elder brother. A vivid picture of his home in Worcestershire appeared for a moment in the sky above the Hartenstein Hotel, and so real did it seem that he half rose from the bed to go to it.

He rubbed the back of his neck, gouged at his eyes, and massaged the sides of his head, forcing his ears backwards and forwards till they hurt him. God, he was tired! He stood up. He would go and see Marsden. There was not much they could do except wait, but he would try to work out some constructive fire plan with the corporal. Marsden would either cheer him up or irritate him. Whichever it was, it would wake him up a bit. Bridgman and O'Neill had gone on their rounds again as soon as they had drunk their tea. Blake wondered how Bridgman kept going: he hardly ever rested for more than a few minutes; any section could expect him at any time of the day or night. Blake thought it was a high degree of nervous energy which kept Bridgman on the move. It might not always be the best thing for a platoon commander to be moving about, but it certainly inspired the men with a measure of confidence and a feeling that someone in authority was alive to their difficulties and discomfort, and was prepared to share them. They also knew that the moment trouble hit them, Bridgman would be on his way to join them.

It was nearly dusk when O'Neill joined Blake and Marsden in the most northerly of the two houses.

'Mr Bridgman stays the night with Sergeant Gorman.'

Blake's laugh died as a sigh in his chest. He was too tired to laugh, even at O'Neill's strange phraseology.

'Lance-Corporal Summers has blown up an SP with his Piat. It was a very good shot.' O'Neill paused and ran his tongue pleasurably round his lips. 'All the Germans we killed as they tried to get out. Sgt Murray's tank-trap did not work – he is very angry. A knot in the line caught in the loop: tonight he goes out to put it right with rope. Mr Bridgman has been to the commanding officer. He says the Germans are calling our position the Cauldron. He thinks it is a compliment – I cannot understand why. In the desert there was a "Cauldron" – General Ritchie lost four hundred tanks in it. Was that funny? Was that something to be proud of? I would sooner be the fire round the Cauldron. Sometimes I think the English enjoy losing. Perhaps they think it more sporting to give an advantage to the other side, eh?'

Marsden grunted angrily, but Blake smiled. The German Jew was a very intelligent man, and the sergeant was interested in his views.

'Why do you think it's gone wrong, O'Neill? What do you think caused the cock-up?'

O'Neill pursed his lips. 'I do not wish to offend,' he said.

'You won't offend us. And in any case what the bloody hell does it matter if you do?'

O'Neill shrugged, and his answer came precisely, didactically.

'I think the operation was prepared with great care. The staff work involved to bring the gliders at fifteen-second intervals was magnificent. I think the élan of the two parachute brigades in their attacks was superb and I think the determination of the defence now that there is no hope of the 2nd Army getting across the river is greatly to be admired. I think the planners and commanders gave much thought to the operation. I think they considered every detail except one. It is a pity that they forgot the Germans. Had they remembered them they would have done many things differently. It is better to have a hundred men break their legs falling off roofs in the town than it is to have a thousand killed trying to get there. It would have been better if some planes had been shot down by the flak guns in the town dropping the division near the objective they wished to take – this would have been better than dozens being shot down, and hundreds being hit as they dropped supplies on zones we have never taken because we were too far away in the first place. I think this is an ambitious and daring operation, and that it would have worked if we had landed near the bridge.'

O'Neill paused, and then continued, 'And if the planning

staff had remembered that the Germans would react quickly and angrily to an attempt to cross the great plain to Berlin.'

Blake stood up. What O'Neill said made sense. The operation was sound and logical provided one did not go back and question the first, false premise that only light resistance would be met in the initial stages. The moment that one considered the possibility that a considerable armoured force could be brought to bear in a matter of hours, then the whole operation became nothing more than a desperate gamble. He nodded at O'Neill.

'Well, I'm off to my own house for the night – it'll be dark in half an hour. You'd better join Bridgie now. If you leave it any longer, somebody might make a mistake in bad light and get a bit trigger-happy.' Together they slipped out through the same window and went their separate ways.

CHAPTER SIXTEEN

Gorman crouched alongside Bridgman and peered out into the grey light of the seventh day. Six times they had stood to at night, and this was the sixth morning on which he had seen the sunrise east of Arnhem, coming up out of Germany as a signal for the day's killing to begin.

For the first time for many days there was a complete silence. A hushed silence, as if two opponents had agreed to a short truce while each recovered his wind.

Gorman felt sure their positions would be attacked at some time during the day ahead. He had watched a pattern slowly reveal itself in the German tactics. They were hitting the perimeter continually at platoon, company, and battalion strength, each attack supported by a few tanks and self-propelled guns. They were seeking to reduce and overrun the division's positions individually: blowing them out of one position, burning them out of another, as the day before they had burned the houses over the heads of the battered remnants of the 10th Para Battalion. They kept up a continuous shelling and mortaring of the whole area within the perimeter, making movement of any kind nearly impossible.

Since the contraction of the perimeter on the night of

the fifth day, the Germans had hit every unit in the division except the Independent Company. On their front, the enemy had patrolled and probed at each of the platoons in turn. First at 3 Platoon in the school, and then at his own. Gorman was sure that the lone tank which Summers had knocked out on the previous afternoon had lost its way, and was probably trying to rejoin or join up with some larger force. It had blundered into their positions and been knocked out before the crew had even realized they were in danger.

The Germans had closed right up to 1 Platoon, so that they now held the houses on the opposite side of the road. Gorman felt his breath catch in his throat at the thought of their predicament.

Ramsden's men must be continually keyed up to breaking point. They would have to crawl from room to room on their bellies, never daring to raise their heads above window level except to take a snap-shot or a quick look at the enemy. Gorman guessed, however, they would have several men in the roofs so that they could to some extent dominate the Germans and prevent them from subjecting the men lower down in the houses to a too accurate fire.

Gorman's eyes wandered to the houses held by Murray, and back to the three at the far end of the road. The Germans were in some part of these houses, and they were dug in in the open gardens in front of 3 Platoon. Bridgman had taken a patrol out during the night while Murray had been fixing his tank-trap, and he had been halted or fired at from a number of points, all within seventy or eighty yards of the two platoons.

Gorman sneaked a look at Bridgman's face. It showed as much strain and tiredness as any of the other faces in the platoon. Gorman thought it showed something else as well, something he had noticed in Marsden's and Cassidy's faces. It was hard to define exactly what it was that showed through the tight skin and brightened the dulled, bloodshot eyes. It was not fanaticism, and dedication was too high-flown a word to describe whatever it was that drove them beyond limits which most men would have accepted.

Gorman wondered why, unconsciously, he had most instinctively included Cassidy with Bridgman and Marsden. Cassidy was another of the German Jews. He was a member of Murray's section, and thinking about him now, Gorman realized that he had hardly seen him since the initial landings. He was a man who soldiered on quietly from day to day, barely betraying his general dissatisfaction with the conduct of the war, but every now and again he exploded into quick decisive action which took others by surprise. These actions were more often than not ones which placed him in a position of some danger, but courage alone was not the answer to the question which nagged at Gorman's mind. There were many brave men in the platoon, but their acts of bravery were a kind he could understand more readily than the behaviour of Bridgman, Marsden, and Cassidy.

Gorman's attempt to find the common factor which inspired the three men was interrupted by the sound of armoured vehicles moving somewhere out of sight round the bend in the road above them.

He felt rather than heard the rustle of movement above him and in the house next door. He glanced towards Murray's houses and saw a man signalling to him from a back window.

He was signalling 'armour', and something else that Gorman couldn't make out. He tugged at Bridgman's smock sleeve.

The platoon commander followed the direction of Gorman's hand, staring for what seemed wasted seconds then he was on his feet and heading for the door. He called softly over his shoulder as he went.

'Tanks in the open ground below McEwan. For Christ's sake hold 'em here.'

Gorman caught one more glimpse of Bridgman as he crossed the road and disappeared into the house held by McEwan and his half section.

Two tanks and an SP were turning the corner at the top of the road even as Gorman looked back. No one fired. Gorman tried to make up his mind quickly whether it was best for all guns to hold off, or whether it would have been better for one MG to have worried the armour, keeping them tight-sealed and half-blind. As he wondered, a gun opened up from Murray's house. The leading tank hunkered up behind the knocked-out Mk IV, its gun swinging lazily round to its left. The SP kept on along the still clear left-hand side of the road, its gun pointing straight at Gorman's position. As it drew level with the Mk IV, Summers fired his first bomb. It struck the SP, exploding high up on its thick armoured front. The second bomb hit its left-hand track, and it slewed round in that direction, effectively blocking the road.

The leading tank fired its first shell at Murray's position as Gorman spotted the German infantry spilling out from the gardens round the houses at the end of the road. As he fired at the darting grey figures, he heard all the MGs in the two sections' positions open fire. Both tanks were firing now, and the crippled SP's gun swung back till Gorman thought he was staring down its gaping muzzle. When it fired, he felt the house he was in lift as if it had been jerked off its foundations. He was thrown sideways and finished up in a heap on the floor. He scrambled to his feet and crouched by the open window. Looking out, he saw Murray and Cassidy halfway across the road in front of him. Cassidy was in the lead, and Murray at a limping run close at his heels. Each man carried one of the ugly Gammon bombs in his right hand. They threw themselves behind the cover of the derelict tank which separated them from the newer one behind it. The two tanks and the SP were all firing: Gorman felt the spatter of German small-arms fire against the walls of the house, and then the building was hit by another shell, and he was on the floor for a second time with a great lump of the ceiling on top of him, the taste of blood in his mouth and the sting of plaster in his eyes. He sat up as the house rocked again. He tore the plaster away from his body and rubbed it from his eyes. He crawled back to the window, and saw Cummings sprawled grotesquely over the Spandau, blood seeping from his nostril. He looked dead. Gorman raised his Sten and fired at a patch of grey that showed by a garden wall.

He looked round for further movement. The German infantry had been forced into the cover of the gardens on each side of the road; four of them lay out in the open, two of them moving slightly, and the other two lying very still. He saw Murray fire his Sten under the belly of the Mk IV, and as he fired, another Piat bomb hit the SP on the right of the road. Three of its crew jumped out and started to run back. Gorman put a burst into the back of the one nearest him, and saw the man throw up his arms as the weight of metal hit him between the shoulder blades. A second German was either hit or fell. He turned at once and faced the British positions, squatting on his haunches, his hands raised above his head. The third man, incredibly, ran straight up the road for forty yards and disappeared from sight without being hit.

A movement pulled Gorman's gaze back, and he saw Cassidy leap out from his position beside Murray and hurl his bomb at the tank sheltering behind the wrecked Mk IV. Before it exploded, he was back behind the derelict again.

Gorman waited, not quite sure what he was waiting for. The farther tank had retreated to the end of the road, and now only half of its turret was visible: this and one track, together with the barrel of its gun, showed at the bend in the road. He could see very little of the tank behind the wrecked one, but suddenly it moved, lurching out into the road between the SP and the Mk IV. It crabbed its way round, grinding on a locked track, then it set off away up the road, gathering speed as it went. As it turned at the top another bomb from Summers's Piat hit where its turret joined its body. Two seconds later it was out of sight, the remaining tank backed away, and the threat was over.

Gorman watched the gardens on each side of the road, one half of him listening to the strange new silence that had come down like a blanket over the platoon's positions, the other taking in the firing from the Borders' trenches a thousand yards behind him, and the burst of the mortar bombs exploding behind the Hartenstein Hotel.

Although he had been waiting for it, he was caught unaware by the speed with which the German soldiers burst out from the cover of the houses on the right of the road. But they were not the SS of the fourth day's assault, and the attack died before it began. As the platoon's machine-guns opened fire, the German infantry wilted and made for the gaps on the left of the road. Their rush carried many of them beyond the protection of the houses, and within seconds of their dis-appearance Gorman heard 3 Platoon's guns open up, and he knew the Germans had been caught in the open ground in front of Brown's men. He watched Murray and Cassidy make their way back to the cover of their houses.

Gorman looked at Cummings. He decided he was dead, but he had to make sure. He eased himself away from the window, and started to crawl across to where the other man lay, but before he had completed his first cramped movement the German multiple-mortars opened fire, and the bombs fell on and about the house. They burst in the road where the tanks and the dead men lay; the clatter of fragmented steel beat against brick and tile and tarmac, and the moaning whine of the bombs in the air filled his ears. He stopped and turned back, crouching hunched up behind the breastwork of the window, his head bent and his hands clasped behind the back of his neck. He found himself trying to count the number of explosions, but it was impossible. Thirty-seven or was it forty-seven? The bombs were still falling, faster, it seemed. Bullets sprayed into the wall behind him. He looked back, under his bent arm, and watched the dust falling from the chipped plaster.

This was no good. Anything could be happening outside. He crawled back to the corner of the window and raised his body slowly. He spotted the muzzle-flash of a German gun in one of the houses at the end of the road, and bullets whipped into the room within inches of his head. The firing from the house on his left and from the room below him was continu-ous, and he sensed rather than picked out the exchanges from where Murray's men fought back.

He wanted very much to join Fraser and Hardy, or the two

Yorkshiremen, and he half started for the door, but stopped himself and, changing direction, crawled over to Cummings. Yes, he was dead, and as Gorman struggled to move the soggy weight of his body which imprisoned the Spandau, he remembered the visit Cummings's young wife had made to the Lincolnshire village where the company had been billeted. He had thought the girl attractive and intelligent, and he had resented her too obvious adulation of a man who was after all only a very average member of the unit. Cummings's body fell back against the wall, his mouth opening slowly as if the hinges of his jaw were clogged with dirt. With his hand on the Spandau, Gorman looked into the dead soldier's face, the live eyes and the dead only a few inches apart. He tried to remember what else he knew about Cummings – but there was nothing. A young soldier who now had a widow, and that was all.

He crawled back with the Spandau, feeling a shamed inadequacy at his lack of knowledge of a man he had soldiered with for years.

Cautiously he raised his head and saw that another German tank, a big one, had crept into sight at the bottom of the road. As he looked, it erupted into flames, but the exultation died in him before he could savour it. The tank had not been hit; it was equipped with a flame-thrower, and as Gorman watched, a great tongue of fire licked out and burst like a bomb, spreading round the walls and windows of the empty third house on the right of the street. The flame ran back to the tank, dribbling weakly as it died. Then it belched again, the hot vomit of its blast enveloping the second house, the one which held half of Murray's men.

Gorman fired the Spandau, and firing, he found himself

trembling with a mixture of suppressed rage and despair. He fired into the flame, wondering whether it was possible for his bullets to find a weak point, some part of the armoured miss that was vulnerable.

The flame ran back for a second time. When it burst out it seemed to him that a great ball of fire filled the whole of his vision, blotting out the houses and the sky and everything around him. He felt heat such as he had experienced only once before, when he had stood well back at the opening of a furnace. He felt his breath catch and dry up in his lungs; he was flat on the bedroom floor, his hands clawing at the floorboards, his mouth open and his throat choking.

The heat died away and he raised himself slowly. He snatched a look through the empty window-frame. The tank was going back, was already half out of sight. He listened intently, hearing a cry faintly from the room below him. He stared out, accepting the lack of activity and the stillness as only a temporary reality. He made for the door, crab-like on booted toes and knuckled hands. At the top of the stairs he straightened up, steeling himself for what he was likely to find. First he must be sure who had been in the room below him – they had changed round quite a bit. Summers and Woodley would be in the bedroom of the next house, with Mocock and Liddon resting in its kitchen – at least, they would have been resting until the firing started.

It would have been Roy Fraser and Tony Hardy.

He stopped at the bottom of the stairs, one hand resting on the banisters. He could smell burning paint, and the air in the narrow hall hung dead about him, a devitalized cloak of the intangible, the life-giving oxygen burned out of it.

Moving to the front of the house, he saw the reflection of

flames through the half-open door, and the faint cry he had heard from above became a continuous wailing succession of sobs. He pushed the door back on its hinges and looked in.

The torn-down curtains were burning where they had been flung in one corner of the room, and two armchairs were smouldering, occasional flames darting like spiders across their brocade. The walls were seared, and the paint on the windowsill swelled and popped in soft bubbles. The two men were by the wall on the left.

Gorman stamped the fire out of the curtains, and beat at the armchairs with his smocked sleeve. Then he turned to the bulked, camouflaged bundles by the wall.

As he bent down, the nearer bundle turned, and Gorman found himself looking into the white, unmarked face of Hardy. The dirty bandage round his head showed like a sepoy's khaki turban.

'I was halfway up the stairs when they fired the flame-thrower.' Hardy's voice was high, but steady on a single note of rigid control. He dare not risk an inflection for fear his voice would escape him and race away. 'When I got down, it was over. Look.'

Gorman looked and at first he didn't know what he saw. What he had known of Roy Fraser was gone. Where his fair fastidious face had been was something beyond horror. It was impossible for Gorman to take in and appreciate what had been done to the other man. He simply looked at the smouldering smock, at the shrivelled veil round the neck, and at the hand, twisted and crooked like a chicken's claw, which groped and jerked on the chest.

Gorman heard himself breathing harshly through an open mouth.

'I'll get Brogan.' He halted at the door and asked, 'Are you all right?'

Hardy nodded. Then slowly, letting his glance linger on the window, taking in the sky and the outside air with its less strongly flavoured scent of death, he turned at last to look down at the blacker gap in the blackened face of his friend. He spoke softly.

'Frank's gone for Brogan. He won't be long. Hold on till he gets here, Roy.'

The long, broken succession of sobs had stopped, and out of the lipless cavity came a word repeated over and over again.

'Please . . . please . . . please . . .'

As Hardy remembered his morphia and reached for it, he had to wipe the sweat from his eyes so that he could see.

With his knife he cut through Fraser's smock, tunic, and shirt. He unscrewed the top of the little tube, pierced the seal, and screwed the needle on. And as he made the injection in his friend's upper arm, he realized that no amount of morphia could wipe out Roy's pain, and the plea beat into his head—

'Please . . . please . . . Tony . . . please.'

Gorman and Brogan waited inside the stable behind the angle of the wall. The falling mortar bombs threw the black garden earth high into the air between them and the house where Hardy and Fraser waited. Brogan was ready to risk the short run, but Gorman stopped him. There was no point in risking death for a dead man and he knew no man could survive the burns he had seen on Fraser.

The bombs stopped falling in the garden, and after a

minute or two of silence the sounds of their bursts started again, between Blake's house and divisional headquarters this time. Gorman wondered where they were being fired from. The perimeter was now so tight that the German mortars could be sited anywhere at all – on the Arnhem side where the platoon faced, or on the far side beyond the Border Regiment. Any point within the perimeter was within range of mortar firing from near its limits.

They waited for some moments to make sure that the Germans had genuinely changed targets, and while they waited they heard one short burst from the section post, and then silence. Whoever had fired had either found his target, or it was a false alarm.

When Gorman and Brogan entered the room they found Hardy behind the Spandau.

'Roy's dead,' he said, and turned his face quickly away from them.

Brogan bent over Fraser's body. Hardy was right – he was dead. He looked closer, pulling down the zip on the dead man's smock and opening his shirt. When he stood up, he didn't turn at once, but stood looking down at the dead man. At last he looked round, his eyes flicking over Hardy's averted face until they met Gorman's.

'Hardy's right – he's dead. Shock. If it was me, I'd be glad.'

CHAPTER SEVENTEEN

In the house at the corner of the road, Bridgman stood in the doorway of an upper room and looked at Cassidy's back. The German Jew knelt in the cover of a wall, his eyes fixed on the short stretch of road which was all he could see from his position. In the room behind him, O'Neill faced the open ground to the south, and on his right against the wall McEwan lay sprawled, his dead head resting against the plaster at an odd angle, like a hanged man, and the knuckles of his half-clenched fists resting lightly on the floor, as if he were going to propel himself to his feet at any moment. O'Neill could hear Murray's laboured breathing as he gasped out the last of his life in the far corner near the door.

O'Neill glanced over his shoulder as Bridgman came into the room and bent over Murray, speaking to him quietly, and listening to his broken, whispered reply. He looked back quickly and had time to send a shot whistling after a disappearing grey back as a German soldier ran for the cover of the trees which screened the Hotel Tafelberg, the lower of the three main buildings being used as British hospitals.

'I'm going for Sergeant Blake and his section.' Bridgman's words jerked out, 'I'll send Brogan over — hang on till I get back – I shouldn't think anything'll happen for a bit.'

O'Neill could understand the quick workings of the lieutenant's mind as he considered and rejected a host of possibilities. Half an hour earlier, Murray's section had been eight strong, and the best-rested section in the platoon; now Murray was dying, McEwan was dead, and with the exception of Cassidy and O'Neill, the remainder were dead or wounded.

O'Neill heard Bridgman's footsteps die away as he reached the hall, and heard the faint stir as Cassidy changed position in the room behind him. He looked down at the still smoking hulk of the Panther tank which lay on the road fifty yards in front of him and slightly to his right, and tried to reconstruct the confusion of the short, double action.

When he and Bridgman had arrived in the house in answer to Cassidy's signal, they had found McEwan and Bobrow watching the Panther as it lumbered across the open ground some hundred and fifty to two hundred yards below them. It was firing as it came on, but its gun was directed at the positions to the south, and German infantry was moving in short dashes behind it. They had just had time to take in the situation when intense firing had broken out from Murray's house above them. Bridgman had hesitated for only a moment. Calling to O'Neill and Cassidy to come with him, he had stopped at the door for a second and looked straight back at McEwan.

'If that Panther turns up this way, you stop it. Understand, corporal? You stop it.'

They had left McEwan standing flatfooted in the centre of the room, his mouth half-open and his face scowling.

Crawling through the garden to the house above them, they had caught glimpses of the armour in the road, and as they were about to climb through an open window, Murray had come bundling out on top of them. He had grinned his relief at Bridgman's arrival, and taking Cassidy with him, had dashed to the cover of the knocked-out Mk IV.

When the last tank had retreated to the turn in the road and disappeared, Bridgman, Murray, Cassidy, and himself had turned to McEwan's house to find out what had happened to the Panther. They had found the big corporal and Bobrow pressed back against the wall and peering at where the tank had come to rest fifty yards short of the house. Bridgman had taken one look and turned on McEwan.

'I told you that tank was to be stopped.'

The officer's words had bitten into the hushed stillness of the room, the contemptuous acid of his tone burning into them all, so that even O'Neill had felt ashamed for McEwan.

The Scot had protested loudly, his eyes wide and angry.

'I was waiting for it to get closer, sir.'

Murray had stepped forward so sharply that O'Neill had thought he as going to hit the corporal.

'You yellow bastard! How much closer d'you want the stuffing thing to get? I've tumbled you, Jock. You're all right with your fists – even if you lose, nothing much can happen to you, can it? But this is different, isn't it?'

'That's enough!'

Bridgman's order had brought them all back to reality, and they'd looked out at the Panther. Its gun was traversing slowly, and O'Neill detected a faint movement in the bushes behind it. There was German infantry between themselves and 4th Brigade's headquarter platoon.

Bridgman had made his decision quickly. Leaving Murray, McEwan, and Cassidy in the house, he had taken O'Neill and Bobrow with him. They had barely turned the corner below them when the tank armed with the flame-thrower struck behind them. The hot blast of its final shot passed within twenty yards of where they lay before striking one of the houses held by Gorman. O'Neill sensed Bridgman's momentary indecision, then they were crawling on towards the Panther.

They never reached it. It erupted in a sudden sheet of flame when they were still thirty yards short of it. O'Neill had no idea how it had been knocked out, whether it was by one of the remaining anti-tank guns firing from the Lonsdale Force positions, or whether by men from the brigade head-quarter platoon.

They had stood up to make their dash back too soon, and Bobrow had been hit in the shoulder. As Bridgman and O'Neill had made their way into the burning house, Bobrow had headed for the stable and Brogan.

Now O'Neill let his mind slide quickly over what they had found in the far house. They had only just managed to get the flames under control before moving the still living bodies of Warke and Banham into the hall.

Getting back into the corner house had been difficult with the whole length of the road under observed enemy fire, but they had done it. They had met Cassidy at the top of the stairs, and he had nodded his head at the back bedroom before moving into the room looking out on to the road. Inside they had found Murray and McEwan. O'Neill wondered what had happened. He would have liked to ask Cassidy, but he couldn't do that without leaving his post. Well, it could wait, but it was strange that Bridgman hadn't asked.

★

Marsden, Hudson, and Laverty followed Bridgman across the open gardens. The platoon commander had changed his mind: he was still keeping Blake and a few men in reserve, showing the reluctance of all commanders to commit their entire complement.

Bridgman put them in the lower house with Cassidy, and sent O'Neill to company headquarters for Doc Barber and a stretcher party. Then he slipped across to Gorman, to learn how badly things were going with him. As he and O'Neill entered the back of the house Gorman came to the door of the room he was in and stared blankly at the platoon commander.

'What's the score, Frank?'

'Cummings and Fraser are dead.'

Gorman's voice sounded distant. For the first time in his soldiering he had been shaken out of, not complacency, but an ability to accept with resignation the blows of fate. It was not the death of the two men, or the fact that if the flame-thrower had been directed a few feet higher it would have been he and not Fraser who was lying faceless and dead. It was not the number of casualties suffered by the company or the division. It was as if he had suddenly realized for the first time that their position was hopeless. In ordinary circumstances (if there were any ordinary circumstances in war) anti-tank guns would have been available to deal with the armoured flame-thrower should it return, or they would have fallen back to other houses. But now – now he could see nothing they could do except wait to be burned out house by house. If they fell back and joined Blake, they would be worse off, for armour would be able to advance unseen to within forty yards of them. Uncovered by fire, the derelict tanks would present an obstacle to the enemy for only the few minutes it would take to winch one far enough aside to allow room to pass others through. Only now was Gorman appreciating to the full the isolation of the platoon, an isolation shared by every sub-unit in the division. The knowledge that Major Jordan and the remainder of the company were in position on their left, and that General Urquhart and his headquarters were only a hundred yards behind where they stood, no longer gave him any confidence. Everybody was in the same situation. Support as such was no longer a practicable possibility. In protecting their own flanks, every unit protected the flanks of those on each side of them, but that was as far as it went. Beyond that there was nothing any unit could do to help any other. The platoon was now simply a small group of men armed with rifles, light machines, and a couple of Piats, opposed by anything the Germans might care to throw against them. Gorman shook his head and walked back into the room, and Bridgman followed him.

'There you are, Brogan – I looked for you in the stable. Get across to Murray – he's in a bad way. I've sent for Doc and a stretcher party, but we're going to have a hell of a job getting the wounded out. We may have to wait till it's dark – if they can live that long. We can only just get in and out of the houses ourselves. Cut along and see what you can do for them.'

The medical orderly nodded and turned to go. Bridgman called him back.

'The whole of the short road is under observed fire. There's only one way to get in. Crawl from here till you get to the stable. Work up from there till you get to Murray's house – then make a dash for it. His house will screen you from then on.'

Bridgman nodded towards the road running past the house they were in. 'But there's a bloody sniper somewhere who's got this road covered. I think he's the other side of Mr Brown somewhere – beyond Company HQ, probably in the top hospital. The bastards have captured that, and I suspect they're using it as a vantage point. You'll be all right so long as you move fast across the road. All right?'

Brogan nodded again, dropped a hand to steady his first-aid kit, and then he was gone through the open door. Bridgman looked across the room to where Gorman had got down alongside Hardy who lay behind the Spandau. They both looked bad.

From where he stood flattened against the wall, Bridgman could see the short road more clearly than he had been able to from either of Murray's houses. The wrecked Mk IV and the SP blocked the road effectively, and he knew the burning Panther would stop any armour coming at them from the south. They were boxed in, but the enemy tanks were boxed out. The flame-throwers were going to be the biggest worry.

'What happened here, exactly, Frank?'

Gorman looked over his shoulder, and when he spoke his voice was flat and lifeless.

'After the armour went back they sent another, a big bastard. Either a Tiger or a Royal – I don't know the difference. The flame-thrower was in that. It hit John's houses first, and then this one. If they'd followed it up with infantry, I should think they'd have got through, unless Summers and his chaps could have stopped them. If it takes another bash at us, I reckon we're stuffed. What the bloody hell can we do? What do you fight Tiger tanks and flame-throwers with – your bare hands?'

'We just hang on, Frank. Hang on till 2nd Army get here.'

'Stuff 2nd Army. What about the Poles? Someone said they'd landed south of the river at Driel.'

'That's right. Some of them got over to us last night. Not many, but some.'

Gorman's eyes lit up for a moment, shining with a new hope.

'Any chance of them all getting over? There must be a couple of thousand of them, and they're bloody good troops. I like the Poles – they've got guts.'

When Bridgman didn't reply, Gorman looked back at the still road. He wondered idly what had happened to the German who had put up his hands and tried to surrender. There was no body where he had knelt. He thought about the Poles again. Thought of the perimeter as if it were a drained body, and then thought how it would be if suddenly infused with two thousand fresh and fighting-fit Poles. Perhaps it would alter everything, perhaps they would be able to break the ring of steel which held them in position, waiting for the kill. When Gorman spoke again, Bridgman detected a deep note of bitterness.

'Perhaps it's better if they don't get across. There's enough good troops wasted already. If 2nd Army keep their finger in, it'd just mean two thousand more men lost.' He drew a long, shuddering breath. 'Stuff 2nd Army,' he said, and his shoulders sagged.

Bridgman looked down past the wrecked tanks, wondering what he could say, when he saw two flashes of movement across the few yards' gap between the end house on the left of the road and the left-hand house of those facing him. A burst of fire came from Mocock and Liddon a split second after the last figure disappeared. The distance the Germans had to cover was too short for aimed fire to stop them, but they would have to be stopped. Alan wondered whether Gordon Brown's platoon could help: they might bring an oblique, semi-enfilade fire to bear. He turned back to Gorman.

'2nd Army can't be as bad as they appear to us,' he said. 'There must be reasons we know nothing about that have held them up. At any rate we're in touch with their gunners. They did a good shoot this morning, and broke up an attack on the Border companies.'

Gorman continued to look out of the window.

What d'you really think, sir? The truth. D'you think they'll get across to us – d'you think they'll even try now?'

Staring at the back of Gorman's head, Bridgman wondered what he really did think himself. All he wanted to think about was how first his own platoon, and then the company, would hold the positions for which they were responsible. It had become all-important to him that nothing his unit did should be open to criticism. No matter where any of the faults might lie, he was determined that none should ever be laid at their door.

'No, Frank, I don't think they'll get across. I think they'll be too extended to risk it. But I do think they'll try to get us out. I don't think their reasons will be good ones, or even military ones, but public opinion wouldn't allow them to leave us here. The British will tolerate the occasional sacrifice of a general if a campaign goes wrong through no fault of his – they were prepared to swallow Wavell's dismissal. But they won't swallow troops being abandoned after they've fought well. From a military point of view, of course, it's senseless. If 2nd Army get what's left of us out, we'll play no more part in this war – it'll be over before we're reorganized, and they'll have pretty heavy casualties getting to us. But they'll try because it's all part of the game.'

Bridgman paused and suddenly realized how he would get the Germans out of the houses at the bottom of the road. He immediately felt better. He would make these three houses untenable, if nothing else. But he continued, thoughtfully:

'Our people don't have the right attitude to war when we're winning. They had it all right for a bit after Dunkirk. If the Jerries had tried invasion then, I reckon we'd have pulled every stop out, no trick would have been too dirty. Gas, petrol – we'd have used everything to prevent being beaten. But we don't do enough to win. Once we're on top, we think it's easy, just a question of time. When this lot's over – if any of us get out – I can tell you, almost word for word, what they'll say to us.'

'What will they say to us, sir?'

Gorman turned his head till he was looking back over his shoulder at Bridgman. His face was calm again, the tenseness and despair washed out of it. His grubby face and unshaved beard, his pinched nose and bloodshot eyes could not conceal the eagerness of his curiosity. He really wanted to know what they, the British public and the world, would say about this action being fought in and around Arnhem.

Bridgman didn't reply at once, for one half of his mind was working out the final details of how to clear the Germans from the three houses.

'They'll say,' he said, choosing the predictable clichés, 'they'll say that although the operation was not entire successful, our sacrifice was not in vain. That without our gallant stand other successes would have been impossible. They'll say that this battle will go down in the history books as an example of the indomitable courage of the British soldier in adversity. We shall all be heroes, all those who get back will be fêted, and whether the individual was a hero or a coward, no one will know or care.'

He paused, deciding that he would borrow one of Brown's Piats to help in the house-clearing, and one of his two-inch mortars as well. He went on, his voice rising and falling like that of a trained platform speaker.

'In twenty years' time, the man in the street will never have heard of the battle of Arnhem, or he'll only recall it by an effort of memory. And in fifty years' time the military history books will devote a few lines to it as an unfortunate strategic error, an attempt to shorten the war that didn't come off. That's what we must face now – the bloody operation's a failure.'

Gorman looked at Bridgman again, his face sick and slack. Seeing it, Alan spoke quickly.

'But our platoon hasn't failed, Frank. What we were asked to do, we've done. It would be difficult to see how it could have been done better. We've gone where we were told to go, and we've brought troops, gliders, and supplies when and where we were told to bring them in.' He paused. 'And we haven't lost a position – we've got nothing to be ashamed of. I should think old Tim's proud of the company. Sad at the losses of course, but proud just the same.'

'But from now on, sir? What happens from now on?'

Gorman's face was calm again but wistful like that of a disappointed but well-mannered child.

'We hang on and hope. Hope that 2nd Army does get across to us; hope that something really constructive can be salvaged out of the operation; hope that we're wrong in our criticism; hope that we can continue to hold where we're told to hold till we're ordered to move – forward or back. And in the meantime we kill Germans.'

He looked out of the window, then grinned suddenly down at Gorman.

'And I'm going to kill a few now. At the rate they've been getting across, those houses must be full of the bastards. Keep down and don't initiate anything till I get back. We'll give the swine something to remember.'

He went out.

Gorman heard voices in the hall, and recognized Doc Barber's. He heard Bridgman giving directions about the wounded, and then the voices died away, and he was alone with the silent Hardy and the dead Fraser.

He looked at Hardy, motionless behind the Spandau, only his eyes alive as they searched houses and gardens.

'Christ, but Bridgie's a goer. He never stops. Some officers think when the Jerries leave us alone, then leave them alone – anything for a bit of peace, but Bridgie doesn't think like that, does he?'

'I think he's right.' Hardy's voice was tired, barely above a whisper. But it was firm, and Gorman had the feeling that nothing that could happen to them now would make Hardy break.

'Why d'you think he's right? Why is it a good thing to stir them up?'

'It's not a question of stirring them up just for the sake of stirring them, it's more a matter of never letting them think they've got a firm base to work from. He tries to make them feel more insecure than we are. He wants to impress on their minds that if they tackle us here they're going to be in trouble. If they think they've made a lodgement in those houses, he's going to disillusion them by knocking them out of them. The first move they make, he hits them, and so long as he knows where they are, he hits them even when they don't move. I think he's right. He never lets them get cocky or confident.'

Gorman tried to work out the logic of what Hardy had said.

'But doesn't that just shift trouble elsewhere – perhaps somewhere where the defences are weaker?'

'Of course it does. But if they get the same reaction everywhere round the perimeter, then they waste that much more time probing for a weak spot, and time's the only thing left on our side. The longer we hold out, the better chance we have of being relieved.'

Gorman grunted. Hardy and Bridgman might be right in theory, but he was pretty bloody sure there were some places in the perimeter where men were prepared to lie doggo indefinitely, just so long as they were left alone.

He lay for a long time thinking, his depression pressing down on him like a heavy weight, his body dull and drained. And then, suddenly, for no apparent reason, he felt lighter of heart, freer of spirit, and less tired. And he knew that whatever the eventual outcome, he would not despair again. He no longer cared about 30 Corps or 2nd Army. The Jordans and Bridgmans, the Hardys and Blakes, were worth living up to, no matter what happened at the finish. He smiled. It was ridiculous to feel contentment at such a time and in such circumstances, but he did. He laughed aloud this time, and gripped Hardy's shoulder.

'Hang on, Tony. I shan't be long. I'll just have a look at Summers and Woodley.'

Bridgman and O'Neill crept along behind the houses until they were opposite the school. They sheltered between two gable ends, watching the empty window of a classroom on the other side of the road. The unlocated sniper was somewhere to their left, probably on the other side of Company HQ. They would have to cross the road fast and be sure of a welcome reception.

'Can you whistle?'

'Not very well, sir. I go all right for a bit, then I forget the tune.'

Bridgman's mouth twisted; some part of him was still capable of humour.

'Not that sort of whistling, O'Neill. This sort.' He stuck two fingers in his mouth and blew down on them, silently but emphatically.

O'Neill's face lit up, and he smiled and nodded. Bridgman had never seen the man's face so alive, and he wondered what the German Jew was remembering. Perhaps some game played as a child in the streets of a German town. It wouldn't have been Cowboys and Indians, more likely Jews and Arabs. Bridgman nodded his head at the open window, and mimed a whistle.

O'Neill transferred his rifle to his left hand and put his right hand to his mouth. Alan was surprised at the shrillness of the whistle which rang out – a high, clear musical note, carrying almost the quality of a chord.

The window opposite them remained empty. Bridgman nodded to O'Neill, and the Jew whistled again. After a moment, Alan detected a faint movement in the shadows of the classroom and then a face was cautiously staring out at them. He signalled that they were coming over, and prepared O'Neill by gripping his tense forearm. His voice came low and urgent.

'Now!'

Then they were running flat out across the narrow road. Bridgman felt O'Neill move away from him as they ran, almost imperceptibly moving a pace or two to the right, and he knew instinctively that O'Neill was leaving to him the easy access through the gate. As he burst through it, he saw from the corner of his eye O'Neill taking the low wall like a hurdler, his rifle held straight out in his extended right hand, and his left flung back behind him. Bridgman flattened himself behind a thick buttress of the wall, and waved O'Neill through the window.

Inside, they found Brown and exchanged news. No attack had been put in on 3 Platoon, but during the night the enemy had closed up in the cover of the gardens, and were dug in in some strength right across the platoon front.

Movement in the front classrooms of the school was nearly impossible. The men lay behind their guns, only moving when they were relieved, and then they crawled cautiously to the back of the building where they could sit or stand, and perhaps, if they were lucky, drink tea.

Alan explained the position and made his request quickly. Brown asked no questions, but sat on the bare boards of the floor, his hand curled round the bowl of a long clay pipe he had found in one of the houses.

The mortar group and the Piat gunner were dispatched with O'Neill to rejoin Gorman and await Bridgman's return.

Alan looked at his friend's face. Gordon's eyes, and for some strange reason his moustache, seemed to be the only live things about him. The rest of his face looked like hammered lead or dark-grey putty, and Alan felt that if he pushed his finger into Gordon's cheek, the hole would remain there, the flesh lacking the resilience to spring back. He supposed that he and his men looked much the same, but seeing them all the time he hadn't noticed it.

He stood up and looked about the long room. A row of dead men lay with their heads to the back wall, neatly and tidily. Looking at their faces, Alan realized that he recognised only one of them. He turned to Gordon.

'Who are this lot?'

'Don't know for sure. Some sort of group from brigade, I think. They were here when I took over from you.'

Alan shook his head to clear it. Weariness was beginning to play tricks with his memory. Of course they'd been there, but he hadn't had time for more than a cursory glance at them, noting that one was a senior officer. He'd meant to get them buried, but he'd been moved before he'd got round to it. He grinned at Gordon.

'No wonder you keep that bloody pipe going. Why the hell don't you bury them?'

Gordon scratched the stubble on his chin. 'Been too bloody busy burying our own chaps to worry about strangers, but you're right – I suppose we'd better do something about 'em.'

'Bloody right you had – whew! Can't you smell 'em?'

Gordon stood up and scratched his neck below his ear.

'Don't know that I can really, and none of the chaps have complained. Anyway, where could we bury them now? We can't move out front, and that stuffing sniper has got the back covered. If you see Jordan, ask him to do something about the bugger – he's making life difficult.'

Gordon went through the door into the passage, and Alan slid out from the window and sheltered behind the buttress. He put his head back through the window and called softly to one of Gordon's men. As he started to give the man a message he heard the first mortar bomb land behind him, in the gardens below company headquarters. He waited, his hands tense on the window-frame. The next bomb landed on the roof of a house on the far side of the road. He heard his own voice shouting to the man in the classroom as he thrust himself up through the window-frame again.

'I know where the next bastard's coming!'

And he was right. As his body sailed over the window-sill, his legs high in the air behind him, he heard the bomb land in the road outside, and simultaneously felt a hammer-blow on his left ankle.

He hit the floor, but at once scrambled to his feet. He gripped his ankle with both hands, hard, as if he would press the pain out of it. To keep his balance he had to hop on his right leg, and he was in the middle of this antic as Gordon came in. Brown stopped, his big body filling the doorway. He took the clay pipe from his mouth, slowly, just far enough to be able to speak clearly.

'Have you been hit?'

Alan stopped hopping and lowered his foot gingerly to the floor. The battle, and a week with hardly an hour's sleep, was affecting them all differently, but for some reason he was furiously angry at Gordon's unruffled acceptance of events. When he answered he ground the words out, forcing into them an almost childish sarcasm.

'Of course I haven't, you clown! I'm just filling in time, practising for the Scottish Games, the opening steps of the Highland Fling.'

Brown looked hurt, and as he sat down with his back against the wall Alan regretted his outburst. He took his gaiter off as Gordon sat down beside him. His friend pushed his hands gently away and unlaced the boot. As Gordon eased it off, Alan looked down at his sock, dark and drenched with blood. Gordon pulled the sock off and the blood spurted in a thin jet, splashing Gordon's face and soaking his smock. Gordon pushed his thumb down on the artery, and the bleeding slowed to a trickle. He turned his head and looked at Alan, his face concerned. For a moment Alan felt a great desire to put an arm round Gordon's shoulders and rest his cheek against the black stubble of his friend's beard. Tiredness swept over him in waves, and he shook his head, telling himself that the desire to lie down and sleep was a natural reaction to the shock of his wound.

'Keep your finger here.' Gordon pressed with his thumb. 'I saw a rubber tourniquet in the next room, in a first-aid kit. I'll get it.'

Alan pressed where Gordon had been holding him, and with his other hand felt at the wound. Something sharp moved under his touch. He wriggled it and the blood seeped faster. He turned to one of Gordon's men who leaned against a wall, staring dully down at him.

'Here, see if you can pull this out. It's not in very far – I can move it.'

The man pushed himself away from the wall with his shoulders, a movement which revealed the exhaustion of his body. Far from moving, he didn't want to do anything positive at all. Until Bridgman's voice had pulled him back to the present, his mind had been hanging in a Utopian limbo in which he imagined his body lying on a deep velvet couch, half between sleeping and waking. But he knelt down, the clumsy, uncertain groping of his fingers irritating Bridgman more than the pain of his wound, which had subsided to a gentle throb.

'Never mind. Leave it.' He would get Brogan to remove the bomb-splinter later. 'Give me your pullthrough.'

The soldier looked blankly at Bridgman.

'Your pullthrough, for Christ's sake! Your pullthrough.'

The man reached for his rifle, upending it and opening the butt trap. He took out the rolled pullthrough and handed it to the officer, his face still wearing an uncomprehending frown.

Bridgman snatched it and unwound the cord. He wrapped it quickly round his ankle, using the brass weight as a windlass to tighten the cord. The blood, which had spurted again as he worked, slowed to a pulsing ooze and then stopped. He wrapped his field dressing over the tourniquet to hold it in place, forced his bloody sock over the bottom half of his boot and stood up. He had got to the window when Gordon reappeared in the doorway.

'Sorry, Alan. Can't find that damn gadget anywhere. Someone must have used it.'

Alan smiled back at Gordon's earnest face.

'I've fixed it. It's a good thing I didn't wait for your gadget – I might have bled to death.'

He slid over the window-sill, and with his body flattened against the wall he looked back at Gordon. He winked once, prodigiously, and then he was hobbling swiftly across the street to the gap between the houses behind him.

Gordon watched him disappear, then stood for a long time staring at his friend's discarded boot lying in bloody isolation near the bodies of the dead men.

'Sir!'

The sharp whisper brought Gordon round to see the anxious face of one of his corporals.

'There's a lot of movement. It looks as if an attack might be coming in.'

His platoon's guns opened fire as he followed the corporal through the door.

CHAPTER EIGHTEEN

Mocock and Liddon were waiting for the Piats to fire. The two anti-tank spigot mortars were in the room above them with Summers, Woodley, and the two men from 3 Platoon. Behind them in the gardens were three two-inch mortars and their teams, and with them were the last of the HE mortar bombs.

Bridgman slipped into the room and joined them. He had found a carpet slipper in one of the houses, and it was tied to his left foot with khaki bandaging. The mortar splinter had cut an artery without severing it, and now congealed blood and a tight bandage were sufficient to prevent any serious loss of blood.

'You cover the gap to the left of that house.' He pointed over Liddon's shoulder. 'You won't get time to fire at them after they appear, so you must fire before you see them. Start slow bursts as soon as you see the Piat bombs strike.'

Liddon nodded his fair head and looked sideways at Mocock. The gap was only a few yards wide. He didn't think they'd make a very good killing, but he realized that they represented only one part of the fire plan.

They heard Bridgman make his way up the stairs to the

room above, and then come out on to the landing. He was placing himself where he could get quickly to the back bedroom, the window of which looked down on to the mortar teams in the gardens.

Liddon's finger curled lightly round the trigger. He was thinking about the market garden he and Mocock were going to have after the war. They had added up their gratuities, the two hundred pounds that Tom's uncle had left him in his will, the eighty-seven pounds that he had in the post office, and to this they had added a hypothetical sum which varied each time they discussed it – the sum they thought they might beg or borrow from members of their families. Somehow the figure of a thousand pounds loomed as a necessity in their calculations and every time they debated their future they managed to arrive at this figure, but always in a different way.

Mocock blew his nose between his fingers, wiped them on a rag, and pulled down on his trousers, easing them away from his crutch where they chafed and cut into him. He transferred his gaze from the houses at the top of the road to Del's face. He didn't feel bad lying there alongside his friend, with the Germans only the distance of the short road away from them. They'd be all right – they always were. Like the time when they'd been dropped with eight others in the north of Sicily to blow telegraph posts and railway lines behind the German and Italian troops who were opposing the advance of the American 7th Army. They had been dropped over low hills. He and Del had jumped last, and had landed on the opposite side of a hill to the others. They had never managed to join up, but had wandered about the Sicilian countryside for a fortnight, living off the land, and twice they had shot up parties of German troops. They had been perfectly happy during those two weeks, and Mocock thought he would have been content to spend the whole war in similar circumstances.

They heard Bridgman's shouted order, and Del closed one eye and squinted through the sights. Mocock looked up at the road and waited.

They both saw the first two bombs in the air, heavy and clumsy, the tail-fins rising and falling as if they propelled the bombs in flight. They struck the houses at the end of the road, and as Liddon opened fire Mocock spotted the next two bombs on their way.

After the second strike, Mocock saw the front door of the right-hand house burst open and three Germans tumble out into the garden. One had his hands above his head, the others clutched rifles, but not in the manner of men who were going to use them. They were cut down by fire from Marsden's position before they had time to drop to cover behind the low garden wall.

Mocock heard the mortars fire from behind the house, and he saw one of the bombs fall short and burst in the road just short of the enemy-occupied houses, but the remainder threw up earth immediately behind them. If Bridgman was right in his calculations, the anti-tank bombs would penetrate the outer walls of the houses and drive the Germans out into the gardens behind, where they would be caught in the open by the HE from the two-inch mortars. Mocock saw figures in the gap covered by Liddon and one of them went down before the others were out of sight behind the row of houses on the left of the short road. Immediately after they disappeared, 3 Platoon's guns opened fire, and Mocock knew that some of the enemy escaping from the backs of the houses had moved too far to the north and exposed themselves to Brown's men. It looked as if Bridgman's plan was working.

3 Platoon's Piat and two-inch mortars had been returned to them and both platoon fronts were quiet. A body of Poles who had got over the Rhine on the previous night were to relieve 1 Platoon, and they were to take over the school from 3 Platoon. Brown's men were to take up positions behind the place where a handful of the 10th Para Battalion had been burned out. The reliefs were to be conducted under cover of darkness that night.

After the Germans had been driven from the houses where they had attempted their build-up, Bridgman had joined Marsden in the corner house. The two men were talking quietly in the bedroom which overlooked the open ground to the south. Incessant fire from the Lonsdale Force positions indicated clearly the German intention to cut the division off at its base, and sever its tenuous connection with the Poles below the Rhine.

The bodies of Murray and McEwan now lay side by side – the sergeant had been dead by the time Brogan arrived.

'How did they cop it? Cassidy says he doesn't know, but he sounds a bit cagey to me.'

Marsden asked his question with a kind of brutal defiance, as if he were doing something that wasn't done, but to hell with it.

Bridgman shook his head.

'I don't know. I wasn't here. I should think they caught a burst from down there.' He nodded towards the ground to the east of the captured hospital.

Marsden turned his head to look, and Bridgman studied

his profile. The corporal had shaved that morning. He was probably the only man in the platoon, perhaps in the company, who had. His smock, uniform, and equipment were not at their best, but they looked far cleaner than anyone else's. He was half frowning, but this was habitual, and his eyes were clearer than any Bridgman had seen that day. His rather pale face was set, the jaw-line clearly defined.

'But why should McEwan be facing into the room? He had his back to the window.'

'Christ knows, Tom, and it doesn't matter. Anything might have happened – he might have turned as he fell after being hit, or Murray may have propped him up there before being hit himself.'

Marsden grunted. Unless Cassidy decided to speak, he was never going to know. An unspoken conspiracy of silence was already closing round the incident, an automatic and gentlemanly decision not to discuss an unfortunate affair made by the two men who knew what had occurred. Marsden knew they were not defending the dead men, they were protecting the honour of the company just as they would have protected a woman's honour in another century. The whole thing was absurd – but it didn't matter.

'Is it right that 2nd Army have joined up with the Poles?'

'They have, but not in force. The old man said that an armoured group of some sort had made a dash through Oosterhout and reached Sosabowski, but that the infantry from 43rd Div were still messing around the village. It looks as if they'll get here, but whether or not they'll be able to do anything is another matter.'

'I don't think they should try to get across here. I think we should throw everything we have to the east – towards the bridge. We wouldn't get there, but we'd contain 'em, and 2nd Army could go for the south end – they'd probably make it.'

Bridgman stood up. Marsden's solution might not be the best one, but it had its points. An obvious attempt was now being made to rescue what was left of the division, and this meant that the original objective, the capture of the bridge, was fast being lost sight of. Marsden had overlooked the condition of the three thousand or so men who were all that were left of the division. It was going to be difficult enough to maintain their morale in defence; to launch them into an attack would be an impossibility. There were already many zombies, automatons whose will had been nearly sapped by continual fighting, lack of sleep, and terribly high casualties. It was a full-time job to keep them awake and in a state in which they were prepared to fight desperately to hold on to what they had. To throw them into the assault with negligible support and inadequate ammunition smacked of fantasy. The division was a good one, but it was not made up solely of Tom Marsdens.

I'm off. I'll see you again before dark, unless anything happens in the meanwhile.'

Marsden nodded without looking round. He heard Bridgman go out, pause for a moment for a word with Cassidy in the next room, and then go on down the stairs.

The infiltration of snipers during the last three hours before darkness fell kept the whole platoon constantly on the alert, and by the time they could no longer see clearly they did not know which houses contained Germans and which did not.

Short stretches of road which had been safe, no longer were. The enemy was directing aimed fire at divisional headquarters, and they were sniping into Blake's position from the area of the hospital they had captured between the Independent Company and 4th Brigade's headquarter platoon. Word came through that Brigadier Hackett had been hit badly in the stomach while visiting units of what was left of his command. The Germans tried to break through to the north where Jordan and the men of his headquarters watched the road east into Arnhem, and the big hotel captured by the enemy which now housed airborne wounded and German soldiers. 3 Platoon were getting ready to take up their new position, a position which would make them the meat in a sandwich of German bread. Bridgman prepared to take out a patrol, and on his last rounds before night closed in he arrived at the back door of a house just as Mocock called down the stairs for Brogan. Alan sent O'Neill for the medical orderly, and went up to join the Yorkshireman.

Between them, they carried Liddon's fourteen stone down the stairs and into the kitchen at the back of the house. They screened the window and lit a candle. The bullet had entered Liddon's neck and travelled down into the chest cavity, and the back of his smock was saturated with blood. They got his smock and battledress blouse off, and cut away his shirt and vest.

Bridgman heard Mocock's sudden gasp. He looked down and his own breath caught in his throat. He stared at Liddon's back. A clean bullet wound made no more than a slit in the skin, but whatever this bullet had hit had exaggerated the exit wound so that it looked like a small shell hole. He could see one of Liddon's lungs pulsing in the cavity, and he found himself thinking of the danger of pneumonia.

'Quick! A shell-dressing.'

Mocock fumbled at the tail of his smock, groping for one of the big shell-dressings in the back of his airborne trousers, and as he fumbled he talked to Liddon, his voice broken and despairing when he meant it to be cheerful and reassuring.

''Taint too bad. You'll be all right directly, Del. Soon as we've patched you, we'll get you to the hospital. Brogan's coming. You'll be all right, Del.'

And then Mocock was crying, his mouth wide open and the tears pouring unchecked down his cheeks. His short, heavy body was shaking, and the sobs were tearing their way up from his gut and out through his open mouth. He found one of Liddon's hands and held it in one of his own. He stroked it with his free hand, and then stroked the fair hair at the back of Liddon's neck. Bridgman had to speak to him twice.

'Your other shell-dressing – I've put that one inside. I want one to strap it – to hold it in.'

'I haven't got another one, sir. Haven't you got one?'

Bridgman shook his head and listened for Brogan. He never carried shell-dressings. He used the two pockets at the back of his trousers for grenades, for they might kill several Germans, whereas you could only use a shell-dressing once, and killing some of the enemy was more important than possibly saving one life on your own side. At least, that's what he'd always thought.

'I want a shit.'

Liddon's voice was surprisingly strong, and at the same time casual. He sounded the least concerned of the three of them, but he couldn't see his back.

'You don't want a shit – not now, Del.'

Mocock sounded like an elder brother reproving a younger

one for having a call of nature at an inconvenient time. He sounded almost petulant.

Bridgman said, 'Help me to get him up, and then get something for him to do it in.'

They got Liddon into a squatting position, his hands resting against the wall, and while Bridgman undid his trousers, Mocock searched aimlessly about the kitchen. At last he came towards them, a saucer half held out in his hand.

'Jesus Christ! A saucer!'

Bridgman felt a wave of almost uncontrollable irritation sweep over him, and he had to close his eyes and breathe deeply, his lips clamped together against the explosive words building up in his throat.

'It doesn't matter. Hold him here. We can clean it up afterwards.'

A draught broke through and made the candle gutter as the three crouched together against the kitchen wall. Brogan and O'Neill arrived as Liddon strained in their arms.

CHAPTER NINETEEN

The air hung nearly as thickly as the puffs of smoke which drifted heavily round the edges of the perimeter, marking its limits as clearly as a crayoned line on a map. In shattered buildings and from the holes dug in the gardens of the houses, from the Borders' positions in the fields, and from those of the Glider Pilots under the trees, the division fought on; battalions reduced to tens of men, companies to single figures; platoon positions held by five or six men, section posts manned by pairs, and sometimes by a single soldier. Each man alone, no man an island: all tied together by the thread of the General's command. The despair in their hearts hidden, or at worst partially concealed from each other. The dead blankness of exhaustion masking their faces to a uniform, dirty, grey yellowness.

The Independent Company clung to its houses in Oosterbeek, the approach roads into its positions cluttered with burned-out tanks and half-tracks.

Bridgman walked and crawled his rounds from post to post, fatigue, bitterness, and anger fighting for first place in the turmoil of discontent which sucked at his rationality, urging him constantly to some course of action which would upset the status quo. Death for himself or his men was now something relatively unimportant. What mattered more was the manner in which it would come. He felt a great need to be free, if only for a few minutes, from the encircling grip of the German Army. There were many ways of dying in the field, but falling one by one, the slow harvest of attrition, this was the worst way of all.

Bridgman halted behind the cover of some bushes between Blake's house and the stable where Brogan tended the most recently wounded. He was on his hands and knees, and he sat back till his buttocks rested on his Achilles tendons, drawing his hands in so that his arms hung limply by his sides, the knuckles of his open fists brushing the leaf-mould below the stretched muscles of his thighs. His head sank forward till his chin rested on his chest, and he closed his eyes. The desire for sleep was the most persistent sensation he had ever experienced. He would have sacrificed anything for a few hours' sleep, anything but his pride in the remnants of his command. O'Neill no longer crawled after him. In the last minutes of daylight on the previous evening, just as they were entering the single house still manned by Blake and his men, a German sniper in the roof of the hospital had shot O'Neill. Cleanly, high up on the forehead, killing him so quickly that he had looked in death as calm and dispassionate as he had in life. His dark, saturnine face with its thin lips turned down, his chin raised slightly, a sluggish breeze stirring his fine dark hair, he had lain as if looking at the sky through half-closed lids.

Bridgman shifted, resting one hand on the back of his neck, pulling down on the tired muscles. He shook his head gently from side to side, but the image of the dead German

Jew persisted. He sighed. Who had the greater cause, the O'Neills, or men like himself? If he lived, he would return to his own country: to his wife and son and daughter. If O'Neill had escaped death, he would have returned to what? To nothing but the knowledge that he had helped to rid the world of oppression, to help make it a place where Jews and anyone else might just live free of the fear of subjection and death. Other Jews. Jews other than his own family who were already dead in the camps of Dachau or Belsen, or who had simply disappeared from the face of the earth without their own kin being aware of their going.

He would rest for just a minute more. Then he would go on to Brogan. Perhaps the orderly would have a brew ready. It would be good if Brogan did have tea. It would be wonderful to drink again the tea that Anne made – hot tea from cool hands, one placing the cup and saucer, the other touching his shoulder and drifting up to the hair on his nape. Fondling and enticing till the maleness rose suddenly in him, and reaching out he pulled her to him while the tea in the thin china cup grew cold. To sit with her half-sideways on his knee, his face buried in the soft, cool warmth of her breasts, his free hand stroking the firm beauty of her thighs while they both considered how to anticipate the night.

Between the bush and the garden wall his body sagged slowly until his right shoulder touched the brickwork. In a few minutes he would go on to Brogan. The orderly would have only two men with him, neither very badly wounded. If Brogan thought they would be all right, he would send them back to their sections.

His bereted head touched the wall and his mouth opened, the sudden, drenching saliva of exhaustion running out from his lips and soaking the camouflaged veil he wore round his neck. His will fought the exhaustion without his being aware of it, so that instead of the blank insensibility of sleep, he drifted for a minute-long age, half-conscious.

Brogan stood back in the shadows of the stable which ran at right angles to the wall against which Bridgman had halted. At first he thought his platoon commander had been hit, but watching him slowly keel over towards the wall, the medical orderly realized that Bridgman had been overcome by exhaustion.

Brogan watched the camouflaged smock and the red beret above it, then turned back into the stable, one hand rubbing his auburn hair, the other brushing up the bristles of his thick moustache. He sat down on a broken chair and wondered disjointedly what he ought to do. He coughed, an irritable cough which eased his momentary dissatisfaction with himself. To have to sit and wonder whether or not to bring Bridgman in was absurd. Three, even two days ago he would not have had to give the action a second thought.

Perhaps it was better to leave him, to allow him the rest he would not allow himself; but Brogan knew that that was not the reason which kept him seated in the stable. It was not fear either, he was past fear as he was past every other strong emotion. It was simply that he had not the energy to drag himself out to where the platoon commander crouched against the wall, oblivious to the battle and his responsibilities. If he went and couldn't wake Bridgman, he would have to carry him in. Bridgman was a big man. At the best of times it would have been a difficult job, now it would be impossible.

Brogan stood up and looked at the two men on the make-shift trestle bed. Neither was badly hurt, but anything more than an average effort would start them bleeding again. He went to the door and stared back to where Bridgman lay. He had not moved. Brogan blew his breath out in a great gust, an explosion of sound that was half a sob and half a cry for help. Tears of weakness formed in his eyes, and one trickled down his cheek.

The medical orderly straightened up; he squared his shoulders, theatrically, but the gesture was for his own benefit; there was no other audience to appreciate it. He opened the lower half of the door and made his way along the wall.

As Brogan bent over the officer, Bridgman opened his eyes and stared up at him. Brogan saw impressions flash in the mirror of Bridgman's eyes – bewilderment, apprehension, surprise, and then – understanding.

Neither man spoke, and when Brogan held out his hand Bridgman ignored it. Instead, he pulled himself laboriously to his feet like a man rising under a load. He walked slowly towards the stable, gripping the sling of his Sten gun as if it would support him. Brogan followed half a pace behind.

The German stepped out from a gap beyond the stable, and at first he did not see them. His rifle was slung on his shoulder and he looked very spruce and clean, as if he had slept well the night before and shaved himself that morning. His middle-aged face wore a puzzled look. He was lost.

Bridgman's thoughts stumbled out to his limbs in single uncoordinated words, and his hands hesitated. As his right hand slid up the sling of his Sten, the German saw him for the first time. Still groping at his shoulder, Bridgman was astonished at the speed with which the German moved. The man already had his rifle off his shoulder and the barrel was rising fast.

When the shots came, three in succession, they sounded inside Bridgman's head so that he thought he was feeling them and not hearing them. He got his Sten off his shoulder while he waited for the pain, but the German fell even as he pressed the trigger, and the 9-mm bullets passed above the grey uniform and the outflung arms.

Alan turned to speak to Brogan, and found the medical orderly alongside him, a Canadian .45 automatic thrust out level with his waist and a look of astonished satisfaction on his face.

'That's the first time I've ever fired the bloody thing – I didn't even aim it.'

He turned to Bridgman, his face breaking into a delighted smile which lit up his whole personality and chased the weariness away.

Bridgman grinned back ruefully.

'It's a good thing you didn't – you might have missed. A pistol's like a shotgun, largely a matter of instinct.' He paused, and then went on. 'I'm glad you were here – my reflexes were gone. I was – I was caught flat-footed – I shouldn't have stood a chance.'

They went together into the stable, looked at the two wounded men and spoke to them. The men were not eager, but both were prepared to rejoin their sections, and Brogan and Bridgman stood at the door and watched them as they made their way across the gardens. Brogan broke the silence.

'I suppose I shouldn't have shot that chap. In other units no members of the RAMC carry weapons, we were always told that we were only to fire to protect our own lives. At any rate, I'm glad I did it.'

Bridgman found it strange that in war a soldier should

have doubts about killing. He supposed that Brogan did not really see himself as a soldier.

'I shouldn't worry, Brogan,' he said, 'after he'd shot me, you would have been protecting your own life. You just anticipated events by a few seconds. I'm very pleased you did.'

Bridgman put his hand on the door to open it, and then with no warning at all he was on the ground, his body sprawled in complete unconsciousness.

Brogan climbed through the open window of an empty room in the house held by Blake. The front of the house faced out on to the inside of the perimeter, towards the Hartenstein Hotel where General Urquhart had his headquarters. The left-hand, or southern side of the house, faced the lower hospital captured by the Germans, and their line of communication to it. So far as Brogan knew, Blake and his four men were all that stood between the Germans and divisional headquarters.

Brogan stepped into the passage and found himself within inches of the muzzle of the Schmeisser held by the section sergeant.

Blake let his breath out slowly.

'When I heard you, I felt sure it was another Jerry. The bastards are infiltrating everywhere. I'm not even sure they've not made a strongpoint between company headquarters and us – I forgot to mention it to Bridgie when he was here – I must warn him before he walks into trouble. Christ knows what's happening to us – it was the one thing I meant to tell him when he was here but I'm so stuffing tired I can't even speak properly, let alone think. It's not even funny any more – Bignall took the trouble to go to the back of the house for a piss this morning, and when he got there he forgot to take his cock out. He'd just about emptied his bladder before he realized he was filling his boots and soaking his pants. When I get home – if I get home – I'm going to sleep for a month, and if anyone wakes me I'm going to shoot the bastards.'

Brogan studied Blake's face as he babbled on, the stream of inconsequential, unconnected sentences pouring out from him with barely a breath between them. The sergeant's behaviour was a contradiction of everything Brogan knew of him. At the best of times Blake was not a particularly talkative man. Suddenly Brogan guessed the truth, and he grinned.

'Have you been at the benzedrine?'

Blake stopped in mid-sentence, his mouth open.

'What? Yes, I have. How did you know?'

'They don't only keep you awake. They make you talk. How many did you take?'

'Two. I took one, but half an hour later I felt just as tired as I did before I took it, so I took another. I still feel tired, but it doesn't seem to matter so much now.'

'Well, that's a good thing, because you're the platoon commander. Bridgie passed out over in my aid post. I left him there and came to tell you.'

Blake's face sobered suddenly.

'Has he been hit? How bad is he?'

'No, apart from his ankle he hasn't got a scratch – he just flaked out. He's stuffed like all of us, only more so. I don't suppose he's slept at all since we landed, and if he has it's only been the odd nap. It's a pity he didn't take some benzedrine – I expect he forgot about it.'

Brogan turned towards the empty room behind him.

'I'd better get back to him. There's nothing I can do here, is there?'

'No, there's nothing you can do here. Get back to Bridgie. When I've handed over to Bignall, I'll look in on the other sections and then come to see you. I won't report this to the old man yet – he might send the "I" officer down. We don't want any foreigners in this platoon, and I don't suppose Bridgie'll be out for long.'

Brogan climbed out of the window and made his way back to the stable. The platoon was as well off in Blake's hands as it was possible for it to be with Bridgman out of action. Anyway, his own concern was with casualties – the fit could look after themselves.

CHAPTER TWENTY

As Blake moved in a stumbling run across the open gardens towards the houses held by Gorman, facing west to Arnhem, he was conscious that his thoughts were as uncoordinated as his limbs, and he wondered vaguely whether it was the benzedrine or simply tiredness which made his mind dart from matters of importance to trivialities. The back of his neck felt cold and damp, devoid of feeling, anaesthetized. He felt it must stand out like a bull's-eye on his body, a target for the Germans he was convinced had infiltrated into one of the houses between his own and those held by the remnants of 3 Platoon, who had fallen back into them after being burned out of their new position soon after dawn.

He closed his eyes for a second as he lumbered forward. Tripping on a briar, he opened them again and forced himself to run faster. Sluggish ripples of panic rolled out from the area of his stomach, so tangible that he felt them ease between his clothing and his skin like paper knives opening envelopes. He mumbled as he ran. If they were going to shoot, for Christ's sake let them shoot quickly. He almost wanted them to. To get the whole bloody, useless mess over and done with. He didn't even know what it was about any more, and he was beginning not to care.

He blundered awkwardly through a rickety gate, bruising himself on a post. He was cursing as he went through the back door of a house, and the curses were interspersed with low sobs of exhaustion. The repetitive sounds breaking out of his mouth like bleeps of steam from a valve, and the sudden hurt in his hip became additional fuel heaped on the burning frustration and fatigue which filled him. Then he was face to face with the thin angular calmness that was Gorman, and in the moment of meeting he felt himself become a soldier again. His thoughts slowed and assembled themselves, his breathing eased, his pulse slackened its beat. He was filled with a shame which brought the blood to his cheeks in a sudden rush, and he was thankful for the dirt and beard which hid his weakness from his friend.

They went together to the top of the house, to the stripped bedroom looking out on to the road which ran straight in at right angles to the one on which the house stood. The burned-out Mk IV and the SP blocked the road forty yards away for them. They were safe enough from an armoured attack, but beyond the tanks, where the road turned, the three houses faced them. Every window in them was shattered, and the walls showed holes where shots from Summers's Piat had pierced them.

As Blake explained the situation to Gorman, he looked at the faces of the other two men in the room. Summers and Woodley sat behind a table, well back in the centre of the room, a Piat and an MG 42 side by side in front of them, and their eyes were fixed on the three houses seventy yards away to the east. At any moment during the day, German infantry might erupt from inside or behind the houses and pour down the road towards the section post. Even heavily equipped men could cover seventy yards in twelve or fifteen seconds.

In general, the firing had died down round the perimeter edge, although shells and mortar bombs continued to land inside it. A machine-gun duel was raging to the north, somewhere in the area held by the KOSBs and the Recce Squadron, and to the south, by the river, the Lonsdale Force was heavily engaged. Elsewhere, a rare silence hung over the battlefield. The remnants of the division licked its wounds and waited for what was to follow, and any man who gave serious thought to the outcome knew that one determined attack by the enemy, pushed home with resolution, must break through at any point in the thinly-held perimeter. Only Field-Marshal Model and his commanders knew why the attack did not come, and had not come at any time during the past three days.

The faces of the two men behind the table revealed little to a cursory glance, but as he looked closely at them, Blake became aware of the taut strain underlying the expressionless masks they wore. The stillness of their faces was the result of tight-reined control; they were afraid that if they displayed, even for a moment, the fear and despair in their hearts, or the exhaustion of their bodies, they would never again be able to get it under control. Blake wondered how long it would be before some man in the platoon cracked badly. He had come very near it himself, and at a time when he should have been at his strongest. Usually, added responsibility created its own increased stability.

Gorman pulled at Blake's sleeve, and drew him out into

the passage. He spoke quickly but seriously, licking his lips, pausing frequently, and picking his words with care.

'I don't know what plans the old man has for counter-attacks or except in a general way, but I think it's time for detailed orders to be issued about every bloody post we have. It's obvious what the Germans are up to. They're confident. Absolutely cocksure 2nd Army aren't going to get over to us in force. That's why they haven't bothered to launch an expensive attack. They're going to shell us, and bomb us, and mortar us out of existence. They're going to keep on doing what they did to 3 Platoon this morning on the other side of the hospital. They'll fetch tanks up close during the night, and then shell and burn the houses over our heads. They're going and to annihilate us in detail.

'We've got to know in advance exactly where to give ground and exactly where to hold. Where we counter-attack – and with what, and where we let a position go and seal it off, and we've got to know in advance what we seal it off with.'

While Gorman spoke, Blake watched his face. The skinny sergeant was in deadly earnest. He had thought a lot about what he was saying: it was something which had absorbed him for hours. His whole approach to the tactical situation had become theoretical, and he stabbed with a thin finger as he made each point.

'As I see it, when they come, they'll come straight up this road – they've been sticking to roads all the time. They'll come at me and they'll come at Marsden. With us out of the way, there's just your chaps between them and Div HQ. How many men have you got?'

'Four.' Blake spoke abruptly. Gorman, alone with a few men in his section post, had succumbed to the disease common to isolation. He could see nothing beyond his own immediate surroundings. For him the battle of Arnhem had become centred round their platoon and his own section in particular.

'If we go, 3 Platoon will have to launch an immediate counter-attack to re-take our positions. It's the only way to keep a body of troops between the Germans and the backs of the men on the other side of the perimeter. If it's only Marsden's position that goes, you could move your chaps up to my right and seal them off. What do you think?'

Blake looked down at his hands before replying. When he looked up again he showed none of the concern he felt about Gorman's waning judgement.

'You may have a point, Frank. If I have to go to the old man before Bridgman gets back on his feet, I'll put it to him. In the meanwhile, you hang on here. Let one of these chaps sleep, and one in the next house. You've got a chap downstairs with a Bren, haven't you?'

'Yes, Hardy.'

'Well, you take turns with him. I don't know about you, but I'm just about on my bloody uppers. Somehow we've got to get all the rest we can.'

Blake left from the back of the house and moved to his left. As he passed a tumbledown shed in the garden, he heard the whine of a mortar bomb, and dropped where he was. The bomb landed behind him, towards company headquarters, and was followed by another, much nearer this time. Blake scrambled on his hands and knees into the shed and lay down behind the door. He peered through a crack and saw the great spouts of black earth which were flung up in the gardens as the bombs exploded. It looked as if they were in for a sustained mortar-stonk. He looked quickly round the shed. Mortar bombs explode on impact, and provided he had some sort of cover he was not in much danger, but the roof was a bit too flimsy to be relied on. He pulled a trestle and some loose planks towards him and erected a makeshift cover for his back and head. He watched and listened for a few minutes. The bombs were falling much more frequently, and it seemed certain the company positions were in for a battering, but with most of the men in the houses they were not likely to have casualties except where fragments found their way through open windows. The mortaring would make movement pretty hazardous and that was all. The sergeant wondered how much this kind of mortaring was intended as psychological warfare: the enemy must know that nearly all the company posts were in houses. It might, of course, be the prelude to an attack: on the other hand it might simply be half an hour's hate intended to subdue the spirit of the defenders.

A bomb landed on the roof of the house behind where Blake lay and he heard the clatter of broken tiles on the top of the shed. His stomach turned over sluggishly, and he screwed his eyes tightly together, cursing himself softly. Only a short time ago he would have ignored the near hit: perhaps it would not even have registered on a mind occupied with more important things.

He took out a filthy handkerchief and wiped his face and the back of his neck. Then with determined concentration he set to work on his hands, paying particular attention to the wet webskin between his fingers. It was important that these parts were dry and clean, and for a few seconds he became completely lost in what he was doing, staring with fixed interest at the little balls of dirt which formed and rolled away under the gentle rubbing of his handkerchief. When he had finished, he put the handkerchief back in his smock pocket. The rest of his hands, black with grime, seemed unimportant. They were dry. It was the cloying, unclean wet of his sweat that must be eradicated.

He thought about Gorman and his two houses, and his grandiose schemes for counter-attacks. If Gorman's and Marsden's posts were overrun, 3 Platoon would be concentrated in the backs of the houses they held, and would face the Germans across the forty yards of gardens. The perimeter, on a front of fifty yards, would have been contracted by the same forty yards which separated the two platoons. Counter-attacks in such circumstances were as practicable as attempting a battalion objective with a section. There was only one thing for the division to do, for the two and a half thousand men who remained out of the ten thousand who had landed, and that was to hang grimly on to every house and every slit trench they held, sealing off every loss as it occurred. There would be no counter-attacks. No matter how good their calibre, handfuls of exhausted, battered men, with no artillery support and only occasional glimpses of friendly aircraft, could not attack fresh troops who were supported by 88-mm guns and tanks.

The mortaring showed no sign of easing up. If he waited for it to lift he might be stuck in the shed for hours. He was commanding the platoon – he ought to do something about it. He eased the door back and settled the Schmeisser on his shoulder. He waited for a lull, and when it came he sprang to his feet and darted out of the shed. He was behind the cover of Marsden's house when a bullet fired from the area of the upper hospital whined yards behind him. He hurtled across the road and struck the door with his fist.

There was a faint movement at a window to one side of him, a pause of a few seconds and then the door opened and he found himself looking at Bridgman.

He stepped quickly inside the little hallway and started to speak, but Bridgman cut him short.

'Where have you come from now?'

'I've just left Gorman's section . . . well, about ten or fifteen minutes ago. I got caught in the open by that mortar stonk. I had to take cover.'

'Have you been near company headquarters?'

'No, not yet. I was going up there after I'd seen Marsden.'

Bridgman turned and started to make his way up the stairs, talking over his shoulder as he went. Blake followed him. 'Come and have a look at this. I think the old man's in trouble. It's hard to pick out his positions in the smoke, but there are houses burning at the crossroads.'

They reached the top of the house and climbed a makeshift ladder into the attic. Bridgman guided Blake across the rafters to a hole in the tiled roof, and the sergeant looked out to the north.

The whole area round the company headquarter's position was a mass of billowing smoke, and at first Blake thought that all their houses were on fire, but as he watched, the heavy wind from the northeast dropped and the smoke retreated. Now he could see flames rising above the rooftops, a half circle of fire. As he strained his eyes, the wind blew again, and the smoke blotted out the positions. He stepped back from the hole in the roof.

'It looks like the houses on the other side of the crossroads. What do you think, sir, is there anything we can do?'

Bridgman took the position Blake had left and looked out.

He could go and find out for himself; he could get back to the wireless set; or he could send someone else. He felt so tired that it didn't seem to matter what he did. Benzedrine was overrated, or else it took some time to work. Brogan had pressed it on him when he had insisted on leaving the aid post, but it didn't seem to have had any effect. Without speaking, he moved back and made his way down the ladder with Blake behind him.

They went into one of the bedrooms and found Marsden bandaging Laverty's upper arm. The corporal looked up as they came through the door, the movement of his head quick and decisive.

'They sniped Paddy, and then got knocked out by their own tank. It's a proper cock-up down this road but I think it helps us more than it does them.'

Marsden grinned viciously, and moved from Laverty till he was flattened against the wall, looking down the road. Bridgman closed up behind him and peered over his shoulder. Two houses, thirty yards down the opposite side of the road were burning.

'What happened?'

'Jerry got into those houses. I don't know when – we didn't see them. Paddy spotted movement about half an hour ago. He was waiting for a decent shot at them when a tank came up, and he must have showed himself to the bastards in those houses. They fired at him and hit him in the arm. The tank crew must have spotted their movement and thought it was us. They put four phosphorus shells into them and then stuffed off. Cassidy got two of them as they came out.'

Bridgman sat down on the bed, and only just stopped himself from burying his head in his hands. Marsden was watching him from the window, and Blake from the door. Cassidy had not moved from where he crouched behind a breastwork of furniture and mattresses. Looking at the German Jew's face, Bridgman's mind slid away from the immediate problems.

For some reason he could not explain, Cassidy had always annoyed him, made him feel in some way uncomfortable. Marsden had the same effect on him, although to a lesser extent. Both were good soldiers, but whereas Marsden betrayed his critical irritation at what he considered was anything less than the maximum effort, Cassidy never revealed what he was thinking, but time and again acted on his own initiative in ways which showed that he had his own ideas about the conduct of war, and that these ideas were not the same as those of the majority. Cassidy was almost too good to be true – the perfect private soldier; and at the back of Bridgman's mind lurked the suspicion that Cassidy would also have made the perfect platoon commander.

Bridgman shook himself to his feet. He would go to headquarters himself, if for no other reason than that he would fall asleep if he remained in one place.

CHAPTER TWENTY-ONE

Adams frowned as he watched Bridgman make his way behind Gorman's houses and up towards company headquarters. The platoon commander's movements were erratic and hard to reconcile with what Adams knew of the safe areas and the danger zones. He would amble along for a few yards, double sharply for a few paces, and then fall back into a leisurely walk; his chin sunk on his breastbone, and then thrown up with his head moving alertly; his Sten gun hanging limply from his hand, and then in sudden readiness across his body.

Twenty yards short of the bushes and shrub which lay to the south of the headquarters, Bridgman stopped. He stood as a man might who was looking out to sea from a cliff top, his mind far out over the waters. Adams saw him sway slightly, shake his head, and then drop to the ground. He crawled laboriously into the cover of the bushes.

As Bridgman disappeared, Adams felt the muscle round his throat contract. He became as frightened, although in a different way, as he had been on the first day of the landing. He was watching the first sign of disintegration in an idol; the flaking at the edges of a man he had thought indestructible.

If Bridgman went, Adams could believe anything: that they would never get out, that the war could be lost, that he would never see his home again.

The first shell bursts from the artillery barrage broke the train of Adams's thoughts, and he snapped alert, the skin tightening on his scalp and his eyes opening in apprehension. The barrage built up, reaching a new high pitch which surpassed anything Adams had experienced before. The company area and the ground between it and divisional headquarters were the targets, and the shells crashed into the gardens and houses without pause, till all sound became one unbroken roar.

He saw a chimney stack and part of the roof of one of Gorman's houses disintegrate like a child's toy struck by a heavy hand. A shell burst in front of the stable where Brogan had his aid post, and when the smoke cleared Adams could see the half door hanging drunkenly on one hinge. Another burst in the gardens midway between Adams and Gorman's position, only twenty yards from where he knelt behind the window breastwork. Without actually losing contact with the floor, he felt himself lifted by the blast, and as he sank back he relaxed completely so that the whole of his body and head were protected by the brickwork.

Now that he could no longer see, the noise seemed to increase and close in on him, as if sound itself were a weapon of the enemy: a weapon to beat him senseless and incapable of action.

He lay down at full length on his stomach and cupped his hands over his ears. He could feel his thighs and calves trembling, and for minutes he lost touch with the world about him as he fought to control his muscles. And when at last they stilled, he found his arms and shoulders shaking in their turn. Their movement stopped instantly when the house he was in was hit twice in rapid succession. The close crash of brickwork and the tearing of timber high up in the third storey was more real, but strangely less frightening than the enveloping roar outside.

Adams forced himself across the room to the door, trying frantically to remember if any of the section were above the ground floor. He moved on his hands and knees, and because he dragged his rifle in his right hand he had to stop and think how to open the door, staring at the knob for some seconds before reaching up awkwardly with his left hand and turning it. He crawled out into the hallway, and nearly bumped his steel helmet against Bignall's as he crawled from the room opposite. Bignall rested one hand on Adams's shoulder, and putting his mouth close to his ear he shouted.

'Get down the cellar, but stay near the top of the steps. Here, take this with you. If you feel me pulling on it, get out as quick as you can and join me in there.' Bignall jerked his head at the room he had just left. 'I shan't pull unless they attack – I've sent the others down already.'

Bignall gave Adams a rough push towards the cellar head and crawled back into the room he had left. Adams looked down at the cloth in his hand, and his eyes followed the strips of curtaining till they became a tablecloth and disappeared round the upright of the door. He crawled to the top of the cellar. It was dark, but a faint glow showed somewhere below in the darkness. He turned and felt at the stairs with his feet, easing his body slowly down the steps. He felt sodden and heavy, like a sack of wet wheat, and his flesh registered nothing when it made contact with the sharp edges where treads and risers met. Only the bones in his hips and elbows told him that the weight descending was a body and his own.

Marsden opened the door and Hardy slid into the hall. As the corporal closed the door again, Hardy leaned back until his shoulders rested against the wall behind him. He was breathing asthmatically, his breath whistling out between his open lips. He had come fifty yards through the barrage, and he was exhausted to the point of collapse.

'What is it?'

Marsden's voice was sharp, impatient.

'Gorman sent me over – the Germans are in the next house.'

Hardy stopped talking and breathed quickly, the urgency of his lungs making faint rasping sounds at the back of his throat. His eyes seemed to tumble and drift in his head, signalling the incoherence of his mind. He took two deep breaths and shook himself; his eyes stopped their wayward drift, and when he continued his voice was controlled.

'The next house to you – not us. Mocock saw them at a window and hit one. They didn't come up the road. They must have worked their way through the gardens on the south side. You're in trouble – what are you going to do?'

Marsden stared at Hardy for a moment without seeing him. He was visualizing the layout of the two houses. They were a semi-detached pair, and the one the Germans were in was the one hit by the flame-thrower the day before. He had vacated it because he had insufficient men to hold both. Now the enemy were nine inches of brickwork away from him. His only hope lay in the possibility that the Germans did not know that British troops were in the house next to them. They had been fired at from Gorman's position, and it was just possible they were preoccupied with the danger from that direction.

He bent down to unlace his boots, at the same time raising a hand to his lips. When he spoke, his voice was a hoarse whisper.

'I'm going to mousehole 'em – if they don't mousehole us first. Bridgman's gone to headquarters – you'd better tell Blake what's happening – he's just gone back to his section about ten minutes ago. If they don't know we're here, we've got a good chance. They won't see you if you go straight back – this house will screen you. I don't see how they could have seen you get here either . . . They may have just spotted you as you went across to the stable, but that doesn't matter. Have you got any plastic?'

Hardy rested the muzzle of his rifle against the wall, and saw Marsden grimace at the scratching sound it made. He slipped his haversack off his shoulders and unbuckled the straps, reached inside and took out two pounds of the plastic explosive they used to fill the stockingette of the Gammon bombs. He passed it to Marsden. He would be glad to be out of this. He hesitated for a moment, then whispered to the corporal.

'Not much point in telling Blake – there's nothing he can do. I'll stay and give you a hand.'

He took his gaiters off and started to unlace his boots. With his head bent he could not see Marsden's face, but he could guess at its expression as the corporal's whispered words reached down to him.

'I knew it. All you public school blokes are the same – all bloody heroes. It's funny too – because you all want to live – you all want to go back to your tennis and your cricket. If I was like you and Roy . . .' He stumbled for a moment, remembering Fraser's death. '. . . I'd be at the bottom of the deepest cellar. I wouldn't care how I finished the war – just so long as it was in one piece.'

Hardy stood up, grinning. It was the first time he'd heard Marsden on the defensive. It made him feel better.

'Come on.' Marsden jerked his head irritably and headed for the stairs, Hardy following him. 'We'll flush 'em out from the top – Laverty's not too bad – I'll stick him at a window on the south side with a Bren. Gorman's got the road covered. They'd hear us getting into the attic, so we'll go through the bedroom walls.'

Signalman Dwyer's head jerked up, and he slid the earphones over his ears and listened. The old man was calling Ramsden, reassuring him about the headquarter position. They signed off, and Dwyer combed back through his hair with his fingers, pushing the headpiece off so that it hung round his neck.

In the half-light of the cellar, he felt choked, restricted. He loosened the camouflage veil round his neck, and then reached down and unclipped the tail of his smock. He felt no better. He ran the zip of his smock down as far as it would go, and opened the front of his shirt; undid his fly buttons and pulled his pants away from his crutch. The air touching parts of his flesh which had been covered for so long made him feel a little easier, and he put a hand inside his shirt, pulling the clothing away from his armpits and rubbing at the wet hairs. He eased his testicles away from his thighs, experiencing a mild pleasure as the cooler air struck between his legs. The faint stirring on the steps below him, where Chambers and

McGrath rested, came to him like country sounds heard from a distance, and the pressure of one of Adams's boots on his right shoulder became light and of no consequence – like the hand of his girl touching him lightly.

He had lain like this on his last leave, disordered and unbuttoned behind the haystack where he had made love to Molly on the day before he had returned to the company. They had lain there all the afternoon and half the evening. It had been the first time they had had each other, and although he would never have admitted it to any of his friends, it had been his first time with any woman except the whore in the brothel in Algiers. The only thing that had worried him since was the doubt that it was her first time with a man. She had seemed so sure in her movements compared with his uncertain awkwardness.

He was glad he had had her. His first – he wondered if she was to be his last.

Woodley scratched his beard with one hand and beat a silent tattoo on the blanket-covered table with the other. He tried to keep his eyes on the three houses which Gorman had insisted he and Summers treat as the primary danger, but every now and again he threw a quick glance at the house next to Marsden which had been occupied by the Germans.

From where he was he could see the back door through which Hardy had disappeared fifteen minutes earlier. He wondered vaguely why he had not come back.

The fire in one of the two burning houses had gone out, but the other was blazing fiercely. The wind was not strong, but it was steady and carried sparks and writhing tongues of flame towards a third, as yet untouched, house. There was a house alight between 1 Platoon and company headquarters, and beyond the HQ flames and smoke were so thick that it was easy to believe that all the northern part of Oosterbeek was on fire. The earlier fires in Arnhem proper must have been got under control by the Germans, for he could see nothing of them now but occasional gusts of heavy smoke from still smouldering ruins.

'Now I know how Nero must have felt. It's inspiring, you know – in a way. You're a musician, aren't you, Woodley? Do you feel any inclination to play?'

Woodley took his gaze from the three houses which were beginning to dance and change shape as he watched them, and turned his head till he was looking at Summers's profile. His head turned very slowly, each jerked inch of movement requiring a separate effort. When he spoke, his words came thickly, reluctantly, as if they were loath to leave the security of his mouth. His tongue felt woollen and strange, barely alive, and as foreign to his mouth as a sick, furry animal that had crept in for shelter.

'I don't care if I never play again – just so long as I get out of this alive and intact – and that gets less likely every bloody hour.'

Summers continued to watch the houses, but he pursed his lips in a deliberate, consciously judicious way.

'You surprise me. I should have thought the artist in you would have lifted you above such mundane thoughts as survival at any cost, but of course you don't believe in survival at any cost, do you?'

'No . . . yes. Yes, I do. What does dying in the right way matter when you're dead?'

'Not at all, *when* you're dead, but I think the moment of

dying matters very much. Death is . . . death is the ultimate object of life, isn't it? One might almost say that it is the orgasm of living.'

'Now you're talking balls. An orgasm is pleasurable, something which in life we try to attain and repeat over and over again. Death is the end of all pleasure. The end of music and dancing, of eating and sleeping – the end of love and orgasms. You're talking cock!' Woodley's voice had risen in a sudden, hysterical anger, and the thickness of his tongue and mouth made his voice almost a squeak. 'I want to go back to the music and the dancing, and the eating and the sleeping. I want to go back and make love to beautiful girls. I want to have physical orgasms – not mental ones at the point of death, but I suppose you . . .' Woodley saw the skin tighten on Summers's cheek, and he changed what he was going to say in a stumbled rush of words, '. . . I suppose you think those sort of ambitions too commonplace. They're not elegant enough for you.'

Summers threw Woodley a surprised look, then looked back at the houses.

'Why are you here, then? I don't mean in the Army – you had no choice about that. But why the Parachute Regiment? Why the Independent Company? Why are you at Arnhem? All the acts which brought you here were voluntary ones. Did you choose the Parachute Regiment because you thought it held the greatest chance of survival, the greatest chance of returning to your wining and dining, to your music and your orgasms? Now, who's talking balls?'

'I'm here for the same reason that most of us are here – because I was bored to death in the unit I was in, and I was ready to do almost anything to get out of it. Now twist that into something.'

'And this was the only way to break the monotony? You can't ask me to accept that — it's too bloody specious and you know it.'

Woodley turned his head back till he was looking out again through the empty frame of the window at the sombre picture of the dead road, the crippled tanks, and the burning houses. His brain worked sluggishly as he tried to unearth the real reason, the first impulse which had sparked off the chain of events, whose end lay here in the smashed and burning houses of Oosterbeek. He noticed idly that the third house was now well alight, and that the first house, which had appeared to have burned out, was blazing fiercely again.

In a way, Summers was right. It hadn't just been boredom, but his crawling mind refused to close with the problem. It was too big, too far away, and he didn't want to know.

A series of muffled explosions, so close together as to sound like a racked cough, came from the direction of Marsden's corner house, and Woodley's eyes went from the far end of the road to its nearest corner.

Smoke and dust hung as a dissolving screen in the heavy air outside the windows of the semi-detached pair of houses which Marsden's men and the Germans shared. As it cleared, Woodley saw the door of the farther house open and two grey-clad figures burst out through it into the garden. He started to swing the MG 42 round but before his head had dropped to the sights the door in the nearer house opened and Marsden was crouched just clear of the porch, firing bursts from his Sten at the two Germans. A movement at an upstairs window drew Woodley's eyes up, and he saw Hardy firing at something out of his sight in the garden. Almost at the same instant, Cassidy's face appeared at a bedroom window in the second house, the one the Germans had occupied. Woodley could hear a Bren firing from the other side of the buildings, and he guessed that some of the enemy were trying to break clear to the south.

Marsden slipped into the second house, and Woodley waited for the next move, his body tense and his face slack. The seconds ticked slowly away and he felt his eyes begin to close. The muscles in his neck ached with the effort of holding his head up behind the sights. He guessed that Marsden and his men had blown their way into the upstairs bedrooms, and then while a couple of them followed up with grenades, the others had waited for surviving Germans to break out. He heard a 36 grenade burst: there was a pause and then a burst of Sten fire, and as the sound of the grenade reached him, Woodley saw the tiles lift on the roof of the second house. They were clearing the attics.

He heard a single shot and then minutes of silence. A rifle with a veil tied tightly round the muzzle was stuck out from a lower window. It was waved twice quickly, and then withdrawn. The house was clear of Germans.

Woodley swung the machine-gun back on to the three houses at the bottom of the road. He glanced at Summers, who smiled back crookedly.

'Well', he asked, 'what's the real reason for you being here?'

Woodley felt anger begin to rise in him, and then it was gone again. He shook his head wearily.

'I don't know. I really don't know. Whatever the reason was it was a bad one. I wish to Christ I'd never heard of the bloody regiment. I suppose you know why I'm here – why we're all here?'

Summers continued to smile but he looked back down

the road, his eyes raised above the houses so that they took in only the white cumulus clouds which drifted above the smoke of Arnhem.

'I can't *know*,' he said quietly, his voice almost diffident, 'but I think I've a pretty good idea. A few – the youngest and those who have never grown up – they're in this because of the promise of excitement, the chance of glory which they saw as an abstract thing. But most are in for a very different reason. Nearly every one who deliberately puts himself in the way of danger is driven to some degree by the death wish, they . . .'

'Bollocks if you think I've any wish to die, you can think again.'

'I don't think you have – now, at this precise moment. I think that with people like you – and I think most of the people who have the death wish are people like yourself – the seeking of death is a subconscious thing. And what's more important, something which can be worked out, destroyed by experience. For you, the discomfort, the sordidness, the sheer bloody misery of this preparation for death has driven out the desire for it. Even for your subconscious, it no longer has any attractions. It's not death which defeats your subconscious purpose, but the hard labour of dying. You're not dedicated enough.'

Woodley did not answer. Without moving his head or his body, he had gone to sleep.

Bridgman faced Blake in the faint light shed by the lamp which the Dutch civilians had kept burning in the far end of the cellar.

'I want you to take over tonight, Bob – I'm going to sleep

here – I'm going to sleep all night. I reckon that tomorrow will be the last day – one way or the other it will finish then. And I want to be fit for it. Get Gorman to relieve you so that you get some rest, but don't wake me up unless it's the real thing. I'm sorry to do this, but I've misjudged my own physical ability pretty badly – I've overdriven till I've stuffed myself. Taking only an hour or two won't do me much good.'

Blake nodded. Bridgman was right: in his present condition he was a greater liability than an asset to the platoon. All his reactions would be slow and his judgement bound to be faulty.

'Very well. I'll make one last round, and then I'll stay by the set unless something happens.' Blake hesitated for a minute, then asked, almost as a matter of form, 'Anything to tell 'em, sir? Any news of 2nd Army?'

'They're trying again tonight, but if they slip only a few hundred over to us it'll do no good. They'll have to make crossings of at least brigade strength if they're going to do anything worthwhile.'

'How's the CO and company headquarters?'

'The Germans have closed right up to them – they're facing each other from the opposite sides of the street. The old man's cheerful enough, but it's pretty serious. If they take headquarters, Mr Brown's platoon and this section will be cut off by directed fire from 1 Platoon, Gorman and Marsden. There's nothing we can do, Bob, except leave it to the old man and trust to luck.'

Blake said goodnight and climbed up the cellar stairs.

Bridgman moved over to a space at the far end of the cellar, and sat down with his back against the brickwork. He looked at the nine Dutch men, women, and children who lay or sat along the wall to his right. For three days they had barely moved, except to relieve themselves, or eat the little food they had. The only water they had drunk had been fetched for them by members of the section in the house above their heads. There had been very little of that, and Blake said there was no more to be had. The last static tank had been drained: there was not a drop of water left in the company area.

They were good people, Bridgman thought, as he looked at their huddled figures. They hadn't whined once, and when they had to ask for something, they did so quietly. If their request was refused, they accepted the refusal without complaint.

He stretched out at full length and pulled the collar of his smock up till it half covered his face. He relaxed his body, letting his breath out in a long sigh that seemed to last for minutes, and his body became suddenly heavy as if a great weight were pressing down on it.

In one sector the Germans had granted a truce so that the wounded could be handed over to them. Tim Jordan had said that at one time there had been fifteen hundred wounded men packed into three buildings. It couldn't go on – tomorrow would decide.

CHAPTER TWENTY-TWO

Mocock was thinking about Liddon, already a prisoner of war, perhaps already dead. They had got him to the aid post a few minutes before the temporary truce granted by the Germans for the handing over of the wounded. Mocock wondered when he would see Liddon again – if he would ever see him again.

Alone in the shattered room, he looked out at the grey beginning of the ninth day. The early light and the fires in the burning houses distorted the scene in front of him, a scene which had changed only in detail during the three days the platoon had been in its present positions. Mocock had not slept at all during the night; the slight sounds made by the Germans as they worked their way up the road, moving from one unoccupied house to the next, had been enough to prevent him from even dozing. He had no idea how close the nearest Germans were to him but he suspected that they were in many of the houses in the short street, perhaps even in that on the other side of the road to his left.

With Liddon gone, the battle held no further interest for Mocock.

A slight movement in one of the gardens attracted his

attention. He turned his head slowly and watched the place dispassionately. A small bush shook – he glimpsed a German helmet – a figure showed – withdrew – reappeared and began stealthily to slide over the low dividing wall. When the German was nearly over, Mocock shot him; wondering how the man could be such a fool as to think he could move undetected within twenty-five yards of his enemy, and at the early hour when all troops stood to.

The German jerked slightly and stopped his forward shift. He remained where he was on the wall, his stomach resting on it, his head and shoulders towards Mocock, his hips and legs out of sight.

Mocock opened and closed the breech of his rifle, laid it down and shifted back behind the light machine-gun. He watched the body for some minutes. It must have been a good shot to kill the German instantly. The range was very short, but the drifting half-light made accurate shooting difficult. Perhaps he had not killed the German after all, perhaps he was only wounded and lying doggo. Perhaps he had missed him altogether.

Some of Mocock's lack of interest evaporated, and he watched the body more closely. Had it moved, or was it set-tling as the blood cooled? The grey serge had moved, but so had the bush behind it. Perhaps the wind had stirred both. But it might have been the German's legs moving the bush.

Mocock moved again, and picking up his rifle he fired another carefully aimed shot. This time he aimed at the back of the German's neck where the short hairs showed above the hanging helmet. Mocock had time to see the body twitch like a flea-bitten dog before the German machine-gun opened up through a window in the house opposite him – fifteen yards away.

Mocock crouched on the floor behind the table. He had thrown himself off the chair and on to the ground in the second his ears had heard the first sound, and his eyes caught the muzzle flash of the gun. It was impossible to believe that they missed him. He heard a bullet strike metal, and as he pulled the LMG down with him he felt it jump in his hand. Slightly to his left, the enemy would be firing at an angle across his front. The German gunner put one more burst into the room and Mocock saw and heard the plaster as it dropped from the wall. He heard Summers's and Woodley's gun open fire from the house above him, and he started to crawl to the door. He would have to look for another room.

He felt the pain in his bicep before he had moved more than a few feet. He let go the carrying handle of his gun, and slipped his left hand through the front of his open smock. His inquiring fingers slid between his shirt and his white Saxon skin. Up, over the point of his shoulder, and slowly down the outside of his upper arm. He felt the blood, not much, but sufficient to wet the skin and guide his fingertips to the small slit which gave under their pressure. It wasn't too bad – it had missed the bone. He'd be all right – not like Del with half his back missing.

He crawled through the door, dragging his gun with him. Outside, he headed for the stairs, his ears straining as he tried to locate the direction from which a sudden, new firing had broken out.

Blake and Bridgman were watching a small gap in the trees just to the east of the captured hospital. For two hours, since first light, German infantry had been making their way in pairs through to the big hotel where more of the wounded

lay. They had had all night to get as many men as they wanted
into the building under cover of darkness, and yet they had
chosen to do it in daylight. The watching men could not
understand the reason for the Germans' action. They had
posted Adams in the roof where he had a clear view of the
gap, and he had knocked out a number of the enemy, and yet
they still came on. Every fifteen minutes or so another pair
would appear for a few seconds as they dashed across the
open space. Adams would fire a single shot aimed through
his telescopic sights, and then Ewing would put a burst from
his Bren into the bushes ahead of where the running men
had disappeared. Usually there was only one – Adams was
a good shot.

Blake pulled at Bridgman's arm and pointed to where a
German and a British soldier had appeared side by side in
the hotel grounds. The British soldier held up a piece of
white sheeting on which a bright red cross had been roughly
marked. The platoon commander and the sergeant watched
the two soldiers. They had turned to each other and appeared
to be arguing. The smock-clad figure of the airborne man
seemed the more authoritative. He cut the other off with a
gesture of his hand, and turning back he waved at someone
out of sight in the hotel grounds.

A British jeep jerked out from a cluster of small buildings
and made its way on to the road. Bridgman looked through
his binoculars. An airborne major was driving, and alongside him sat a German soldier, the butt of his rifle resting
on the deck of the vehicle. Behind them, two blanket-
covered stretcher cases lay side by side. The jeep reached the
road and turned to the north, towards the watching men. It
halted in full view of them, and Bridgman wondered how

many other eyes were fixed on the stationary jeep. Another movement attracted his attention, and he swung his glasses to the right. A ragged file of figures came into view, limping and supporting each other as they stumbled along. They were evacuating the walking wounded, but this was no organized truce. British and German MOs were acting on their own initiative.

As the line of men reached it, the jeep started to move slowly up the road with the two soldiers, the British and the German, walking ahead of it, the red cross held between them.

The last of the line reached the road, and a German ambulance followed it, bringing up the rear.

Bridgman watched the jeep crawl past the house he was in. He recognized the major as an MO from one of the Field Ambulances. He was unshaven and his face was drawn, but he did not look as tense and apprehensive as the German soldier by his side. Alan studied the halting line of men, here and there picking out a face he knew, and then the last of them was past and only the German ambulance had still to come.

It had dropped back and halted some little way from the end of the shuffling line, unable to move at the slow pace of the wounded men. Now it moved forward again, this time in jerks as if learner-driven. Outside the window from which the two men watched, it stopped again as if to allow the broken-gapped file to get farther ahead.

So suddenly that Bridgman and Blake were taken completely by surprise, armed Germans leaped from the back of the ambulance on to the road surface. They bunched badly for a moment, and then moved forward, towards the watching men. Bridgman swung his Sten up without moving his feet, and he felt Blake move slightly away from him, to give them both more room. In the instant his finger closed round the trigger, and before the sounds of his own shots reached him, a burst from Ewing's Bren registered in Bridgman's ears.

It was all over so quickly that it was difficult to believe that for a few seconds the road had seemed to be filled with the enemy. Three of them lay where they had fallen, bunched together in death, each man touching another. Two had thrown themselves into a ditch on the other side of the road, one of them with a convulsive jerk which might have been the desperation of his bid for safety, or perhaps the impact of lead in his back. One German stood in the open gate to the garden. He stood weaponless, his rifle thrown down. His left hand rested on his helmet, and in his right he clutched a dirty white handkerchief which he shook nervously rather than waved at the British soldiers.

He stepped warily towards the window, his eyes frightened and near despair. Blake felt Bridgman move, and turning his head quickly he saw that the platoon commander had raised his Sten to his shoulder and was taking deliberate aim at the man five yards away from him and unarmed. Blake moved instinctively, without thought. He grabbed Bridgman by the shoulder and pushed him, hard.

Bridgman staggered under the thrust of the sergeant's hand, and his head swung round, his face expressing an anger Blake had never seen on it before. Before he could speak, the German was at the window, climbing in, his mouth open and uttering the plaintive whines of a puppy which uses its very helplessness as a weapon against aggression.

Blake watched the rage go from Bridgman's face, not

suddenly as an impulsive emotion comes and passes, but slowly, a bit at a time, the result of a conscious effort to control.

'Take him to headquarters – perhaps they've enough men to spare to guard prisoners.'

Blake gestured with his Sten towards the door, and the German moved quickly. As he followed the prisoner, Blake looked back. Bridgman had taken a grenade from his pouch and had drawn the pin. He was looking towards the ditch on the far side of the road.

Marsden crawled through one of the holes he had blown through the dividing wall which separated the semi-detached houses. He sat on the dirty, boot-stained coverlet of the bed and opened the linen bandoliers he had brought with him. He stacked the five-round clips of .303, and thought about how he would distribute them. In another bedroom, Laverty watched the open ground to the south. His arm wound had stiffened up, his preoccupation with the nagging pain and discomfort of it making him less of an asset than he should have been. Marsden decided to replace him on the Bren with Cassidy.

As Cassidy heard Marsden's instructions, he watched the house on the other side of the road. In the rooms round the corner, out of his sight, Germans were facing Gorman and his men, only the width of the road between them. Sooner or later they would discover that Marsden's section was only twenty yards from them on their flank. His present position held out more interesting possibilities than the one Laverty occupied, but that in itself was not a good arguing point. He would have to go.

He heard Marsden move behind him towards the door, heard the corporal's boots hesitate, and then his voice again.

'You were here when John Murray and McEwan bought it. What happened?'

Cassidy wondered why Marsden wanted to know. They were dead – what did it matter? But perhaps they would all be dead soon, and if they were, his telling wouldn't matter either.

'McEwan shot John.'

He could feel Marsden's eyes on the back of his head, and he wished he had denied knowledge of the incident. He could have said that he was in another room, and that it was all over when he got to them.

Marsden stood at the door, his body tensed in anticipation.

'I guessed that, but how? And who shot McEwan?'

'How? That's easy. But why? Who knows why – I don't. I don't suppose they knew either. They were so different – perhaps that's why.'

Cassidy was looking at the houses on the other side of the road, but he was seeing the two NCOs faces as they had stood only a few paces apart, all their hatred for each other pouring out from them. From quiet, taciturn John Murray, in a stream of violent uninterrupted abuse, and from McEwan, rage and fear which had burned and glowed to white heat as he heard the façade of his courage torn to shreds.

'But what *happened*?' Marsden's voice was sharp, insistent.

'There was always bad blood between them – but you know that. It started in the Ram Hotel in Newark.'

'Yes, I know. They were out drinking together, and McEwan started looking for trouble – wanted to start a fight with some REME chaps or something, and expected John to back him up. When he wouldn't, McEwan called him a coward – but that's old hat. Why should it be finished now? What sparked it all off?'

Cassidy made a sound, half sigh, half cynical chuckle.

'There's always a final act – a last straw, but who knows what has gone before? I suppose Bridgman can be blamed for some of it.'

'Bridgman?'

'It's difficult to put your finger on it, but somehow he never gave any of the dicey jobs to John. He didn't doubt his guts, of course – nobody did except McEwan – I suppose he just didn't think John was as good as the others, and John couldn't understand why. I suppose he brooded, and in the end all his discontent was directed against the only man who had ever doubted him aloud. John had to prove that he was as good as any of them, and not only that, he had to prove something else. He reckoned that when the cards were on the table McEwan would be the one who was yellow, and of course he was right. McEwan was all right in any scrap that wasn't final. He could take punishment even a bad beating, but the idea that he could be killed knocked all the guts out of him.'

Silence grew in the room. At last Cassidy looked round. Marsden was standing in the door, nodding as he took in what he'd heard. Then his head snapped up, and he looked at Cassidy.

'Right! Thanks for the trailer. Now let's have the main feature. What happened?'

Cassidy turned back to the street, and the story came from him like a dull recitation of something burned into his brain forever.

'Bridgman went to stop the Panther that McEwan should have stopped – John had started to bawl McEwan out before Bridgman went, and after he'd gone he kept it up. He baited him. He just went on baiting him. He was trying to force McEwan to admit that he had no guts. John meant it to shut McEwan's mouth for good. He was going to make McEwan so conscious of his own cowardice that he'd never be critical of anyone else – but he misjudged. Either McEwan had a bit more guts than John thought he had, or a bit less. He just stood there looking at John – it seemed to go on for ever. John called him everything he could lay his tongue to. You could see McEwan's face keep changing. You could see him begin to believe that what John was saying was true, and his eyes would shift about, looking at anything but John. Then he wouldn't believe it. For a second or two he'd convince himself that John was wrong, and when that happened he'd glare at him, and you could almost see him steeling himself to do something. But each time, John's words just beat him down. That is, each time except the last. When he did move it was so fast that I didn't see his Sten come up. One second McEwan was standing there taking everything John said, the next, John was going down. Christ, he moved quickly!'

Marsden was looking at the back of Cassidy's head, but his imagination was picturing the scene. He could see the whole thing, all except the end.

'But McEwan – who shot McEwan? Not John. He could never have done it. He had a burst in his chest.'

This time Cassidy's head came right round, and smiling quietly he looked at Marsden.

'John was a good section commander. Not all that intelligent – but sound. I liked him. We're in a bad way at the moment — bloody bad. I suppose the text books would say that every man, every round helps, but I don't think McEwan had anything to give us. Even now I think we're better off without him — don't you?'

For a moment Marsden stared at Cassidy, his lips tightening in a grin that held no humour.

Cassidy raised an eyebrow. 'Hadn't you better go and get Laverty?' he asked.

Marsden nodded slowly, and without a word went out to tell the Belfast gunner that he was to be separated from his Bren. It was only when he got to the other door and stood looking at Laverty's back that he realized that Murray and Laverty, the two friends, were in the same room — Murray stretched out dead against the wall, and his townsman crouching wounded and in pain at the window.

Adams lowered his rifle and watched the German soldier. The man had dropped his rifle, and the hand which had held it was extended in front of his stomach. As his knees buckled slowly, the hand moved hesitantly backwards and forwards, drawn to his wound and yet afraid to confirm it. He broke the fall of his body with his left hand. He squatted back on his heels, his head rolling on his neck, and his face turning blindly about as if seeking the origin of his hurt. He started to get up, his arms beating feebly at the air like a fledgling bird's, but changed his mind or was unable to manage it. He sank back, both hands coming together across his stomach. He threw one appealing glance up through the trees at the sky, and then his head dropped forward on his chest. He remained for a long time kneeling, his hands folded devoutly, as if in prayer.

Adams watched him till he fell over on to his side, his legs straightening, and one arm coming up to cover his face.

There was a movement in the trees and two figures emerged, a German and a British. They carried a stretcher between them, and laying it down they lifted the wounded man on to it. Before picking it up, the British medical orderly stood to one side of it, facing Adams. His body concealing the movement from his companion, he gave the thumbs-up sign, then turned quickly away and lifted his end of the stretcher.

Adams watched the three men disappearing into the trees towards the hospital. The pattern formed earlier was repeating itself. Each man he had shot had been removed almost at once, leaving no evidence to warn those who followed. Adams wondered who the British medical orderly was, and if he would ever meet him.

Gorman had started to cough as he moved out from the back of the lower of his two houses, and within seconds of the first explosion of air from his chest he was hanging on to a fence, retching like a sick dog. He retched and coughed till the sweat ran down his face and the bile out from his open mouth.

The last cough died in his throat, and the last trickle of bile cupped itself behind his lower lip, forming a pool as bitter as defeat.

He turned his lip down and spat. He took a hand from the fence and wiped his face, feeling his legs tremble under him as he straightened them.

He found the gate, and braced himself for the short dash to the upper house. His legs gave him the last of their strength, propelling him forward through the gate. They got him one pace into the open before giving up, leaving him sprawling and splay-legged like a new-born colt. He balanced awkwardly, fighting to stay on his feet, one arm making swimming motions in the air, his mouth opening and closing, biting at the air as if he sought to draw himself along by his teeth.

Every nerve in his body became alive with apprehension, and his muscles contracted, an instinctive armouring of his body against the strike of the bullets which must come from the house on the other side of the road.

He felt strength flowing back into his legs as the fear of death recharged them. He knew he would never make the cover of the upper house in time, and the thought of going back to the cover behind him didn't occur to him. He threw himself sideways and down behind the low garden wall, and as he crushed the flowers under his body he heard the bullets from the German machine-gun passing above where he clung like a limpet to the earth below him and the brickwork against him. He heard one of their own guns reply, and lifted his head slowly, raising his face an inch or two from the earth into which it had been pressed. He rolled his eyes up under his brows till he could see the comparative safety of the house beyond, where Summers and Woodley were fighting back at the Germans opposite them. Twelve feet to cover. He tried to work out his chances calmly. How long it would take the enemy gunner to swing back on to him if he leaped to his feet and made the dash – *if* he had the strength to make the dash.

He saw the German stick grenade from the corner of his eye, tumbling stick over canister through the air. He followed its flight for what seemed an eternity, his eyes wide and his mouth open. It dropped behind a hunk of brickwork which had been blown down from the chimney stack, and as it disappeared from sight he knew he had a chance. He buried his face again and waited for the explosion. It came with the whistle and dirt of brickwork; a tremor of the earth, and an uplift of his heart as he realized that the brickwork had saved him from the metal death in the canister.

As he raised his head again, the second grenade landed in the soft soil six feet away from him.

It was strange to stare with fascinated eyes at the instrument of his own destruction: the smooth round cylinder – so different from their own egg-shaped grenades – and the plain wooden stick. But that wasn't the way to die – not the way he was capable of dying. To make one desperate effort and run for the cover of the house would be a last fight for life – but a losing one, for he would never make it even if he had twice the time left.

He heaved himself up in the second of his decision. He turned his back on the grenade, his head and shoulders above the wall, and he was firing at the Germans in the house when the grenade burst. Their returning bullets struck the front of his head and neck as the shrapnel from the grenade buried itself in his shoulders and loins.

Bridgman was giving his orders for a breakout to the river, and to the boats 2nd Army had brought up. He looked at the three men who commanded what was left of his sections. Blake, the only sergeant out of five, Marsden the only corporal out of four, and Summers, one of the three surviving lance-corporals. In the bad light of the cellar their faces were barely recognizable. He could trace no expression on the beard-stubbled faces, but from his intimate knowledge of the men he knew what he might have seen in a better light.

Blake's face would not have changed. His hollowed cheeks and bloodshot eyes were the result of nine days of fighting and sleeplessness; there would be no reaction from him to the news of the division's withdrawal except an acceptance of new orders to be carried out. Marsden would look angrier than usual. He made no allowances – for him this was the final act of inefficiency and incompetence. He would have found it difficult to specify at whose door the failure of the operation could be laid, but he would be satisfied that *they* had stuffed the show up somewhere. Summers would be looking weary, cynical, and detached.

'. . . and remember that absolute quiet is essential. Every man must wrap his boots in cloth. It's raining now, and the clouds are low. This'll help us, but it'll be hard to keep contact. Make sure that every man undoes the tail of his smock so that the man behind can hang on to it. Bofors from 2nd Army are firing star shells to give us the general direction – if we're split up, keep between them – they'll be fired to east and west of us. We'll form up at the back of Mr Brown's position twenty minutes from now, and remember – not a sound. If they guess we're breaking out they'll be after us.'

In the darkness Bridgman overshot his position at the company rendezvous, and only when he came up against Tim Jordan did he realize that his platoon was at the head of the column instead of in the middle. Jordan decided quickly, and whispered:

'It's not worth changing, Alan. Stay where you are, and I'll get 3 Platoon to close the gap between themselves and 1 Platoon.'

The CO moved back into the darkness, and Alan lay down at the head of his handful of men.

Waiting, Alan wondered whether Jordan was right to leave the order of march as it was. Phil Ramsden with 1 Platoon was bound to have been briefed as to the best and safest route to the river, while Alan himself had only the vaguest notion of the dispositions on the other side of the perimeter.

Jordan came out of the darkness and knelt by Alan's side. Behind him, Alan could pick out two or three shadowy, crouching forms. The CO's whispered words came quickly but with no trace of urgency.

'We'll move in one minute. Pass the word back now. The sergeant-major will act as a link between you and me.'

He moved away before Alan could answer him, before he had fully appreciated the significance of the CO's words: Jordan himself was leading his company out.

They passed to the north of the Hartenstein Hotel, which had housed divisional headquarters, listening to the crump of shells as they landed in the positions they had vacated only twenty minutes earlier. They turned south on a track between the almost leafless trees, the soft, drizzling rain soaking and reviving their deadened flesh. The lightly wounded marched with their platoons, and somewhere to the rear Doc Barber and the RAMC orderlies shepherded and helped those too badly hit to be sure of getting out unassisted. In the dark sky, they could pick out the guiding star shells fired by the 2nd Army guns, and they could hear the sharp exchange of fire which came from the southwest where the Poles and a battalion from the 43rd Infantry Division fought to hold the Germans back from the river crossing.

The sergeant-major moved from the CO and his small order group back to where Alan headed the column. His voice came low and clear through the rain.

'The country's getting closer — I think you'd better close up, sir.'

Alan spoke over his shoulder and lengthened his pace till he could make out the blurred group of figures ahead of him. As he did so, he saw beyond them the silhouette of a house against the sky, and in the same instant he heard the challenge from the cover of the garden on his left.

'Halt wer da?'

Alan felt the sergeant-major's hand close on his forearm, but even as he felt it he was reaching down for the German stick-grenade stuck into the gaiter on his boot.

As he pulled it clear, a German Spandau opened fire from a window in the house in front of them, the bright flash of its muzzle blast illuminating the falling figures of Jordan and his small group.

Alan dropped to the wet earth. He unscrewed the base of the stick, pulled the cord, and rising on one knee he threw the grenade into the garden on his left from where the challenge had come. As he flung himself back on the ground he sensed the sergeant-major dart to the right of the track and into the cover of the trees. The Spandau fired again, a succession of long bursts which cut the air inches above the heads of Alan and the men behind him.

Flattened against the earth Alan eased his Sten forward, but before he could raise its barrel the sergeant-major opened fire from the right of the track, and Alan saw the flash of the German gun alter as it was switched over to the newer threat.

Blake was alongside him now, firing his captured Schmeisser at the windows of the house. Alan called to the section behind him for grenades, and it was Scruffy Butcher who crawled up with them.

When they had cleared the house, they regrouped in the cover of the trees and Bridgman counted heads. Apart from the sergeant-major, he and Blake and the remnants of his section, and in addition, Marsden, Cassidy, Woodley, and Summers.

He sent Cassidy back along the track to see if he could contact the remainder of the column, and turning to the sergeant-major lying by his side spoke quickly.

'They're nearly across the perimeter. This must be as far to the west as they've penetrated from the hospital. There can be only a narrow gap between us and the Border positions.'

The sergeant-major grunted. 'The Jerries'll be back. They're using the nights to infiltrate, and this house is bang on the escape route from the north.'

Cassidy rejoined them, dropping on the far side of Bridgman.

'I couldn't find them, sir. Only Slattery from 1 Platoon, and he's dead. He must have copped an unlucky one from the house. I should think Captain Rutherford has taken the company farther round to the west.'

Bridgman thought quickly. Cassidy would be right. The orders were to get down to and across the Rhine. Rutherford, Jordan's second in command, would see his first duty as getting the bulk of the company to the river. He turned again to the sergeant-major.

'We'll take our own line. We'll go through the trees here. If we go any farther over, we'll attract fire from whoever's holding the west flank.'

The ground was boggy under the trees, and the rain made it worse. As he made his way cautiously forward, Bridgman thought of the cleared house they had left behind them, and wondered how long it would remain empty.

He thought of Jordan too. Before leaving the area of the house they had turned over the bodies of the small order group, but the CO's had not been among them.

Bridgman and his party groped their way through the sprawled figures on the mud flats leading down to the river's edge. They found the tail-end of the company waiting to embark. Gordon Brown was the last man.

Adams listened to the two officers' voices as they spoke quietly together. The Germans were mortaring the mud flats heavily, and he could hear only snatches of their conversation between the almost continuous burst of bombs and the sudden cries of the newly wounded.

'. . . Jordan made it . . . bullet snicked the bridge of his nose and temporarily blinded him . . . rolled into a ditch . . . got out on his own . . . your platoon's embarked . . . last of the company.'

Then Bridgman's voice, '. . . house cleared . . . right across escape route . . . bastards'll be back . . . be stopped.'

Adams shook the arm of the man next to him, and heard Summers whisper, 'What is it?'

'Nothing . . . I just wondered who it was . . . what's going to happen now?'

He couldn't make much of Summers's reply. He seemed to be reciting – something about a bridge and Horace or Horatius.

There was a sudden lull in the mortaring. A figure crawled out of the night and touched Adams's arm. He heard Blake's voice in his ear. 'Who's that?'

'Adams, sergeant.'

'Where's Mr Brown?'

'There, I think,' Adams said. Before Blake could move, the figure above where he lay turned round, and as the officer's head came close to their own, Adams could see one end of Brown's moustache silhouetted against the sky. He felt another form move up beside him, so that four heads were almost joined, their bodies stretching out like the limbs of a star-fish.

'It's Blake, isn't it?'

'Yes, sir. Mr Bridgman asked me to find you.'

'Yes . . . where is he?'

'He's gone back, sir.'

'Gone back! Gone back where?'

'To the house – he told me to find you and say would you see the rest of his platoon over.'

Gordon Brown started to swear, a long stream of curses directed at nothing in particular, and then breaking off, '. . . was he alone?'

'No, sir. He took Marsden and Cassidy with him. I offered to go with him although I didn't want to – but he said no – he just wanted Marsden and Cassidy. He said,' Blake stumbled his words as if not understanding their meaning, 'he said I was a soldier, and should get the men out and do a soldier's work – what do you think he meant, sir?'

Adams waited for the officer's reply, hardly breathing in his bewilderment.

'I don't know, sergeant.' Brown's voice was quiet, and sad with the sadness of loss. 'I should have thought that he was the soldier, and a very dedicated soldier, but . . . but I just don't know what he meant.'

The fourth head spoke, and Adams realized that it belonged to Summers.

'So he knows. I didn't think he was that intelligent.'

'What do you mean, corporal?' Brown's voice was sharp.

'I'm not knocking him, sir. He's dedicated all right . . . I just didn't think he knew what he was dedicated to. But he must have done – he chose the right Herminius and Lartius. His dedication isn't to soldiering, and nor is theirs. They *are* good soldiers, but that's incidental. Their dedication is to death. I think they – he – realized that this might be the last opportunity in the war to find it legitimately.'

There was a long pause, and Adams heard the chug of a boat's engine, and then Lt Brown's voice.

'You seem to know a lot about it, corporal. Do you suffer from the same disease?'

'Of course, sir. But in not quite such a virulent form. There are other and more temporary ways to escape from life when it becomes unbearable. Drink is one of them.'

The bow of the boat thudded into the bank, and they all stood up. Adams tried not to be too eager, but he was grateful when Blake pushed him forward into the boat.

ARNHEM
by Al Murray

The Battle of Arnhem is one of the best-known stories in British military history: a daring but thwarted attempt to secure a vital bridgehead across the Rhine in order to end the war before Christmas. It is always written about, with the benefit of unerring 20/20 hindsight, as being doomed to fail, but the men who fought there, men of military legend, didn't know that that was to be their fate.

By focusing on the events of one day as they happened through the eyes of the British participants, and without bringing any knowledge of what would happen tomorrow to bear, Al Murray offers a very different perspective to a familiar narrative. Some things went right and a great many more went wrong, but recounting them in this way allows the reader to understand for the first time how certain decisions were taken in the moment and how opportunities were squandered.

Tuesday, 19 September 1944 was that terrible day which became known as Black Tuesday. From just after 1200 hours, while plans were being made to seize the initiative and optimism reigned, to the following midnight, when Arnhem was burning and the Allied fortunes looked very different, a mere twenty-four hours changed the course of the war.

Al Murray has always been obsessed by Arnhem, and in *Arnhem: Black Tuesday*, brings all of his knowledge, interpretation and enthusiasm to bear to tell the story of one of history's great heroic failures differently for the first time.

CASSINO '44

by James Holland

There is no such thing as an easy victory in war, but after triumph in Tunisia, the sweeping success of the Sicilian invasion and with the Italian surrender, the Allies were confident that they would be in Rome before Christmas 1943.

And yet it didn't happen. Hitler ordered his forces to dig in and fight for every metre, thus setting the stage for one of the grimmest and most attritional campaigns of the Second World War.

By the start of 1944, the Allies found themselves coming up against the Gustav Line: a formidable barrier of wire, minefields, bunkers and booby traps woven into a giant chain of mountains and river valleys that stretched the width of Italy. At its strongest point perched the Abbey of Monte Cassino.

It would take five long, bitter winter months and the onset of summer before the Allies could finally bludgeon their way north and capture Rome. By then, more than 75,000 troops and civilians had been killed and the historic abbey and entire towns and villages had been laid waste.

Following a rich cast of characters from both sides – from front-line infantry to aircrew, from clerks to battlefield commanders, and from politicians to civilians caught up in the middle of the maelstrom – James Holland has drawn widely on diaries, letters and contemporary sources to write the definitive account of this brutal battle. The result is a compelling and often heartbreaking narrative, told in the moment, as the events played out, and from the perspective of those who lived, fought and died there.

THE SAVAGE STORM
by James Holland

With the invasion of France the following year
taking shape, and hot on the heels of victory
in Sicily, the Allies crossed into Southern
Italy in September 1943. They expected to
drive the Axis forces north and be in Rome by
Christmas. But even after Italy's surrender the
German forces resisted fiercely, and the swift,
hoped-for victory descended into one of the
most brutal and protracted battles of the war.

Though shipping and materiel were already
being safeguarded for the D-Day landings, there were still high
expectations of the progress of the invading armies, but those very
shortages were to slow the advance – with tragic consequences. As the
weather closed in, the critical weeks leading up to Monte Cassino would
inflict a heavy price for every bloody, hard-fought mile the Allied troops
gained.

Chronicling those dark, dramatic months in unflinching and insightful
detail, *The Savage Storm* is unlike any campaign history yet written.
James Holland has always recounted the Second World War at ground
level, but this new epic brings the story vividly to life like never before.

Weaving together a wealth of letters, diaries and other incredible
eyewitness documents, Holland traces the battles as they were fought –
across plains, over mountains, through shattered villages and cities,
in intense heat and, towards the end, frigid cold and relentless rain –
putting readers at the heart of the action to create an entirely fresh and
revealing telling of this most pivotal phase of the war.

**'This excellent book reinforces Holland's reputation
as the busiest and most popular military historian of
the Second World War working today'** *Spectator*